About the author

Victor Headley was born in the parish of St Anne's
Jamaica. As a teenager, he moved to Kingston
beore leaving Jamaica for Britain in the nineteen
eighties. He toured as a musician in a Reggae band
for several years before publishing the runaway
best-selling Yardie trilogy. These books established
Victor Headley as the most powerful thriller writer
of his generation and one of the most successful
Black British novelists of all time.

Victor now lives in the Congo.

D1422349

Also by Victor Headley

YARDIE
YUSH!
EXCESS

Off Duty

Victor Headley

NEW ENGLISH LIBRARY
Hodder & Stoughton

Copyright © 2001 by Victor Headley

First published in paperback in Great Britain in 2002
by Hodder and Stoughton
A division of Hodder Headline

The right of Victor Headley to be identified as the
Author of the Work has been asserted by him in accordance
with the Copyright, Designs and Patents Act 1988.

A New English Library paperback

2 4 6 8 10 9 7 5 3 1

A CIP catalogue record for this title
is available from the British Library.

ISBN 0 340 77024 4

Printed and bound in Great Britain by
Mackays of Chatham plc, Chatham, Kent

Hodder and Stoughton
A division of Hodder Headline
338 Euston Road
London NW1 3BH

This story is in memory of Beverley Green and Humphrey Reid. 'May your souls abide under the shadow of the Almighty.'

Many thanks and respect to all the people
who have supported me from the start, to
those whose lives have inspired me and to those
whose love has protected and nurtured me.

'May the words of my mouth and the meditation
of my heart be acceptable in thy sight,
oh Jah, my strength and my redeemer.'

CONTENTS

PROLOGUE

For Real!

London, England, June 1995

'Nobody move!'

I glimpse Rico adjusting his bow tie at the last second. Behind us, three rows of fine, groomed guests are fixing their best expression on their faces. I have a thought for Superintendent Wilkins; the call inviting me to the wedding came through at the headquarters and it was Wilkins who passed it on.

To my right, Rico's sister, Mimi, whispers: 'Smile then!'

I smile, turning from Mimi to her mother, Miss Ruby. I think I can read pride in her expression, but also something beneath it, in shadows.

CLICK CLICK

That's that; the official wedding picture. Rico's white suit will look fine. He's always favoured white clothes, so it was a safe bet that was what he would wear on his wedding day. I can't help reminiscing about another wedding, in Spanish Town ten years ago. Rico was bridegroom to my sister then. Lucy was in white too, that sunny day.

'Take another one!' someone shouts.

'Yeah ... Take one more.'

Rico waves to the photographer.

Those who had started moving go back to their positions

on the steps of the town hall. I cross my hands in front of me, then my eyes switch back to the camera; the photographer is just about to press the button. I feel myself straightening up; I don't know why but I've never liked having my picture taken.

And then, as we all wait for the CLICK, the weirdest thing happens: Rico drops down ...

Most of the guests on the upper steps don't realize right away what is happening. It's just that one moment Rico is standing up in front of them and the next he's crashing through the second row relatives, collapsing on a couple of Nicola's cousins. I'm one of the first to notice the small red stain on the left side of his chest, dark against the white silk. Then Nicola sees it too. I hear her scream ...

Kingston, Jamaica, Spanish Town Road, September 17, 1983 8.45 p.m.

The two boys sharing an ice-cream cake in front of the cinema couldn't have been over eleven years of age. From the passenger seat I saw one of them, the one facing the street, stop as he was about to push a handful of the sweet into his mouth. He said something and the other one, skinny in an oversized Adidas tracksuit top, turned to look at the car. I lost sight of them as we turned right into West Avenue but you could tell from their reactions that the boys knew who we were. In these areas, survival skills are learned before you can even walk; I knew that from experience. We picked up speed right away, Rico handling the steering wheel with such dexterity, you would have thought he was born with one arm. He was right-handed but shot with his left, and very accurately too. I never quite figured that one ... In the back, I heard Tips snigger.

'See dem start run, sah!'

Rico didn't answer. An unlit cigarillo stuck in the left corner of his mouth, he was doing forty miles an hour down the avenue and everybody, young and old, was diving for cover. The group of youths Tips was referring to had been gambling around a makeshift table on the right side of the road, just in front of a yard. We were only about a hundred yards away and by now, most had spotted the speeding car and made a run for it. Through the blur, I could make out tense faces watching us like they'd seen the Grim Reaper himself. I saw two of the boys dart inside the yard and towards the back, where they would jump the fence onto the derelict site at the back. Rico still hadn't slowed down. Three youths were sprinting down the road. One of them, tall with a flat cap, swiftly crossed to the left side and took the wall of a house just like a hurdle-racer.

'Tips, check the spot! We going after him.'

The tyres cried out as Rico slammed his foot on the brakes, swung the steering wheel all the way leftwards. The big Datsun hardly stopped at all. Tips didn't expect it to, anyway. He had been on Rico's team for three years and knew the play. His back door was already open. M16 in his right hand, he sprang out of the back seat like a tiger in flight, all 170lb of him in motion. I had time to hear him shout:

'Police! Don't move or I shoot ouno bloodclaat!'

Then we were off, speeding down the road like maniacs, Rico driving one handed with that blank look on his face. His big .45 was already out, stuck between the edge of the seat and the side of the automatic gear compartment.

'I know weh him ah go, dat lickle fucker.'

Rico's tone was almost amused. I can't say I ever saw him angry, not really angry. He'd get annoyed now and then but nothing more. All the same, he'd squeeze a couple of shots into someone's skin without a frown. I dug my feet into the floor as we skidded into a left turn. Rico pushed at full speed for another hundred yard then hitched a very sharp left into a dark recess you could only spot if you knew it. Another right turn and we were at one end of a dirt track with overhanging trees on both sides. The fugitive was counting on the car being too big for the narrow lane and sure enough, it seemed to me as if a motorbike would just about be able to find its space through there. Rico stopped the car, revved the engine and turned to me.

'I don't feel seh him armed . . . but watch it still.'

With that, he pulled out his revolver, stuck it out of the window, his eyes scanning the darkness ahead through the windshield.

'You don't t'ink seh him run to the road,' I asked.

Rico had a little smile, still watching in front of him, not even looking at me.

'No man; dat is what him want we to t'ink . . . but him still in deh, I feel him.'

I had learned over the last eighteen months that when Detective Inspector Rico Glenford 'felt' something, he was usually right. I had come to trust him and that meant putting my life on the line. It was one of those things you got used to. So I got out of the car. I knew what I had to do. My clip was already engaged. Eyes peeled, I started moving ahead, gun at the ready, listening to the night sounds around me. No matter how long you do these kind of exercises, I guess you always feel tense. It is that tension that keeps you alive. Old-timers on the force had told me this, that the day you relax is the day you die. Keeping low, my senses tingling, I stopped; I thought I could feel the man's presence for a fraction of a second, like Rico . . .

The beams from the Datsun carried to about seventy yards; after that it was back to darkness. I reached that zone, progressed a little slower towards the end of the lane until I got to the road. A little group of people had gathered, mostly men but also a few nosy women. Maybe the fugitive's girlfriend was amongst them. They fell silent as I faced them and I didn't bother look at them too long. The fact that they were there confirmed what Rico had known from the start; the youth was still in the lane, somewhere. Now the real work started.

I turned back and slowly, methodically, I checked every

opening onto the lane, peered cautiously behind every pile of half-burnt refuse, inspected bushy recesses on the other side of broken-down fences. I knew the fugitive wouldn't take the risk of getting back out onto the avenue; Tips would have been only too happy to claim him. A light film of sweat coated my back, though not enough to wet my string vest under the shirt. My head was light, all senses on alert. I wasn't really worried about the darkness; in fact, I can see in the night better than a lot of people. As I was coming back onto the lane from an overgrown yard I heard Rico's voice.

'You better come out Rusty, I don't have time to play tonight.'

Rusty, wherever he was, must have been feeling the pressure. I only knew of him by reputation. He was a close associate of the man we really wanted. Rusty and Brinks, as the other one was known, had been recently released from Gun Court. The charge of murder didn't stick in front of the judge. Malicious rumours had it that the judge had been leaned on by someone with an interest in keeping Brinks running his area as before. Because many established area dons had been either killed or run out in the big shake-up after the elections, the areas were now run by former soldiers. Brinks was just about twenty years of age but I had seen his sheet; he had all the required qualities for the job. Most of these new top men were more inclined to violence, and gunplay especially, than the men they had replaced. Today, Brinks had shot dead his opposite number in nearby Denham Town, giving us a second chance to take him down. He was ours, or he would be as soon as Rusty stopped playing hide-and-seek.

I turned around slowly, the brighter zone behind me, listening to Rico at the top of the lane.

'Come out, Rusty man; ah nuh yuh me want, so nuh badda fret.'

Rico's voice was mellow, like he was talking to a good friend of his. All the same, he knew that to suggest a bad boy could be afraid was an insult that would wound Rusty's pride. I turned back, looked towards Rico. He hadn't moved, still standing behind the open car door, his left arm hanging over it. I was stepping away from the thick shrubs bordering the old wall on the left side when a whole tree collapsed and dropped right on top of my skull. At least, that was what it felt like. I realized I was hitting the ground. The first thought was for my gun: I didn't let go of it. In the couple of seconds it took me to raise my head, I clearly heard:

'Carly, stay down!'

Then my eardrums went underground to escape the big boom. Later, I could have sworn to feeling the whizz of the slug close above my head, much too close. Someone twenty yards away from me screamed. I got up slowly, having first assured myself that Rico was really through. He was walking up, taking his time. He got up to me while I was still checking my bones. My left shoulder hurt rather badly but my head was okay.

'Wha'ppen, sah?'

I didn't answer Rico. When I got to Rusty, he was writhing on the ground in the middle of the dirt lane. At the other end, a sizeable crowd was now huddled, keeping to a reasonable distance. Rico stood over the bleeding man.

'You shoulda come out when I tell yuh to; ouno too damm fool.'

He sounded almost like he was sorry for shooting off the back of Rusty's leg. I went back for the car and we slung Rusty in the open boot. Rico wasn't going to let him blood out the patrol car backseat, no way. At least a hundred pairs of eyes watched our every move, but nobody said anything too loud. I guess they felt sorry for Rusty but only a fool would have dared passed a comment either way until Detective Rico Glenford had left the scene. We got back inside the car and drove off, right around the way we had come, to pick up Tips. As always in these circumstances, the whole area was upside down. Tips had half a dozen youths spread-eagled in the middle of the avenue. As we arrived, he was busy crunching the fingers of a stocky man with a head of short locks into the concrete with his heavy army boot.

'Talk or I broke your hand; whe Brinks deh? Eh?!'

The man shouted out: 'I begging you, officer; me nuh know . . . I swear.'

Rico got out of the car after me. He shook his head, the cigarillo still in his mouth, still unlit.

'Tips man, yuh nuh hear seh the man, ah swear! Let him go, is alright.'

Tips relented, lost interest in his victim as he noticed the open boot and walked down to check it out. Rico ordered the young men to get up off the road. He took a silver lighter out of his slacks pocket, lit up his cigarillo.

'I want ouno do me a favour,' he said while studiously puffing on the long and slender brown roll. 'The first one ah ouno see Brinks, tell him; him shoulda stay ina Gun Court.'

The last piece of sentence was dropped with a long squint towards the group of silent and tense youths. Tips was already seated in the back of the car; he only liked action, the 'long talk' never was his forte. We left the area to a troubled night. Somewhere in the throng of sullen faces glaring at us from both sides of the road as we drove out, was the next in line to become top man. Business had to go on.

Down at Jubilee Hospital, they tried to deal with Rusty's leg. In a sense, he was real lucky; the heavy bullet had just grazed his right calf, taking away a piece of his flesh, but the bone was untouched. Rusty told us all he knew, gently prodded on by an impatient Tips. The area man shot dead by Brinks was, unfortunately, a cousin of Tips's wife. It's a small world, as they say.

We dropped Tips home in Papine then drove back down leisurely. Cruising down Hope Road, the window rolled down, I could feel the release that always comes after the action. The nervous tension of all the muscles was gone and the night wind brushing my face helped relax me. Rico seemed to be absorbed in the tune from the car radio.

'Tell me something,' I started without turning to look at him. 'You know I did hear that shot pass my head earlier on?'

There was a pause as both of us were looking through the windscreen, then I heard Rico laugh.

'I know seh is something you 'ave on yuh mind.'

I turned his way.

'Dat was a chance yuh take, sah.'

'A chance? No man, not'ing to do with chance.'

I waited a few seconds. I was pretty steady under fire and Rico knew I was. I almost didn't feel like insisting, he sounded so sure of himself.

'A night shot, at fifty yards . . .?'

Rico turned to look at me, his eyes narrow as always but with a hint of a smile on his mouth.

'I hit dat boy right where I aim.'

'What if I moved?' I insisted.

Rico waited until after the road junction.

'Then I might have missed him,' he said simply, light in tone. He could see I didn't quite feel good about it.

'Look man; in this job, we have to trust each other, you know.'

He added: 'When it comes the other way round next time, if you feel you can hit, do it. From you tell me to freeze, I trust you.'

It didn't really reassure me that much at the time, even if I knew he meant it. Later on, I would find out exactly how far he trusted me. When he stopped the car to let me out, he asked: 'Yuh settle in alright?'

I had recently moved into a new house with a new girl. I couldn't be sure which he was referring to.

'Yeah, it alright.'

Rico smiled, that one-sided, mocking smile he kept for the very few people he was close to. I got out of the car. The juke-box of the bar down the road was pumping out bassy sounds.

'Tell Lucy I will see her tomorrow,' I told Rico before pushing open my gate.

'Alright!'

The car was already reversing out.

The next morning we picked up the trail, working on Rusty's shaky information. We knew Brinks wouldn't go down just like that. He was a killer, not an occasional one but a real, certified one who had only been let back out on the street through circumstances. He must have figured that Rusty would talk, because he had started moving from the spot he was holed up in and we finally caught up with him near Riverton. There was Rico, Tips, an officer named Brown and me. Brinks knew one thing; Rico wasn't coming to arrest him, not this time. He had no place to run so his only option was to go down fighting, preferably taking one or two of us along.

Around one o'clock that night we went down with two cars, blocked both exits from the house he was said to sleep in. We didn't know for sure whether he was alone in there. As it turned out, there were three men sleeping in that house that night. One of them was the owner, a middle-aged man with a whingy voice who had nothing to do with the play. He was arrested then released later. His nephew was a local man who had become notorious during the elections. He had recently returned from overseas. He pulled out a gun from beside his bed and let out two rounds into Brown's vest. He died in that bed.

Our man Brinks probably wasn't asleep. He had time

to make a run for it through the window and bolted across the yard at the back, scaled the wooden fence only to find himself in the glare of Rico's car beams. Brinks threw himself on the ground in the dirt and fired two shots straight at the car. One of them hit the windscreen but there was no one there. I was standing near a big tree, covering all the back area. Rico appeared twenty yards to the left of Brinks, as he was getting up to run. Rico called him, he turned and fired at the same time, real fast. But Rico was faster. One shot, full in the chest, ended Brinks's short reign. One case closed, or two rather; we found out later that the other gunman was already wanted in connection with a robbery the previous month on the North Coast.

For that week, the body count for all the squads read: Arrests; 18, dead; 5.

Being a policeman in Jamaica in the early '80s was no joke. I don't know what it was like before that; I was just another one of the ghetto youths on the other side of the fence.

It was Rico who took me into the Force. Rico who met and married my sister. Rico who left her, left the police and finally left Jamaica.

Now I was looking at him on the steps of a register office in London, looking at him and knowing he was dead.

CHAPTER ONE

Old Times

Nobody in my family ever was a policeman, I'm almost sure of it.

I'm the first one. I remember back at school we were once asked what it was we would like to become later. We were only young, around five maybe. I was one of the first few got asked and when I said 'a teacher', everybody laughed. But I really wanted to be a teacher, it seemed so ... respectable, so powerful. It didn't quite turn out that way, but I still got the respect and the power ...

Things really started to get harder around 1975, I think. That was the year our mother died, the last day of January. She'd been kinda sick for some time, years. She couldn't work too hard, got short of breath and tired easily, but all the same she kept going to her job as a housekeeper in Mona Heights, day in, day out. After she died, Lucy and me stayed in the house but Auntie Pauline looked after us, Lucy was still at school, me too, most of the time anyway ... Although we could take care of the running of the house, Lucy was only thirteen and had to be supervised. Auntie Pauline, our mother's first cousin, lived a few streets away and was always home with us anyway. She said I was not yet a man at fifteen, so I'd better be good. But she was a nice person really and she did a lot to get us through that bad time.

The same year, our father who had been living mostly in America for years but who still supplied financial help, had an accident at the pressing plant where he worked and got laid off. Quickly, he stopped writing, didn't send help any more, probably couldn't afford to. Once he wrote and told us he was coming back home, but we never saw him again. A friend of his wrote in 1978 to let us know he was in hospital and really sick. There was nothing me or Lucy could do; five days later, a telegram announced his passing. Life went on. A hard life where you had to scheme every day just to get enough to feed yourself. The late seventies was when you'd hear a lot of people saying how the country was going to blow up if things didn't get better soon. Unemployment was at the highest; the price of the goods in the shops didn't fit at all with what the average sufferer in our part of town could afford.

By the time I got to turn sixteen, things did get a little better for us. I had started doing small jobs for the bigger men who ran the area and they seemed to trust me. It means a lot for a boy to have someone, a big man, treat him with respect It makes him feel like he's graduating, being taken in. In the scheme of things in the tough areas of Western Kingston, you had to grow into it, pay your dues and, most importantly, know how to keep your mouth shut. Discretion was always essential in the view of the big men I grew up under. That was okay with me because I've never been a very talkative person anyway.

All my early years, since I could walk, I think, I had only cared for two things: football and bicycles. I got to be a pretty good footballer, but my real talent, what I loved above all, was riding a bicycle. People could hardly see me without my bike. The very first one I got from my uncle Clifford who lived in Denham Town. He brought home this red bike one night when I was around five or six. And that was the single greatest thing anyone had ever given me. I kept it up, turned into the best rider of my area by the time I was eleven. I've always felt that my thin and long frame suits bicycle riding perfectly. At that time bicycle artists, youths with no nerves at all, skilled, precise and swift, often made their mark as 'snatchers' ... Anyway, the big men knew my name. So I began to be allowed to hang around them, listening keenly to learn and become what they were. Obviously, that affected my attendance rate at school.

Even before mother died, I had started to get into problems with her because she said I liked to 'sleep ah street' too much. Truth is, everything was happening around the local sound system, all the important things a boy my age had to learn in order to get rank. And the sounds played at night, so I'd do anything to escape her vigilance. It was easy enough to do, she was already so weakened by her sickness. Though I had never been a really hard child to control, I think, there were times when I must have seemed real stubborn to our mother. And she in her younger days, never hesitated to get onto my hide when I got too bright. I remember a time when, aged thirteen, the magnetic attraction of the night sessions made me forget myself and I got home around four-thirty, tipsy off a stout I had drunk. The woman caught me getting in, noisy as I was, grabbed the thick and supple tree branch she kept handy and proceeded to hit me all over the living room. I recall the impact of the blow being dulled by the effect of the liquor in my head and her own failing strength.

'Yuh just dark and long and maaga, just like him!' she'd cussed, swinging into me with the branch. That was the last beating I ever got. I know she wanted my best. She wanted to keep me in school. She tried.

Anyway, I got to start attending the sessions in and around the area from that time. After mother died, I felt it was down to me now to strive to feed us two, so I needed to get myself more into the action. By then I had got too big for Auntie Pauline to control and when I started to bring home the odd five-dollar note to show from my time hanging out with the rankins, there was nothing much she could say. That was the point where my ambition to become a teacher got sunk. But then, if I was a teacher today, I'd probably be unemployed.

Back in those days, my role model was Jingles. Named Hopeton Ezekiel Morrison he was the youngest boy of a family of five. His last sister, Martha, was in my grade at school. Tall and big-boned like the rest of them, she was a good student but very quiet and reserved. Me and her never got to talk that much. The Morrison family seemed to have been prominent in our part of town for a long time. Their grandfather owned a shop/rum bar, their father added a mechanic repair shop to that and somehow everyone in the area had dealings with the Morrisons. The oldest boy, Isaac, got a break to go to work in the US in the early seventies. He came back after a few years, having married and obtained his papers. He didn't stay long but I learned subsequently that he was still working closely with his brothers.

Nat, the second one, had set up a big ganja trading operation, farming, distribution, export and this made the family even stronger. Jah Nat, or Natty as he was often called, was tall and dreadlocked. An intense, civil but serious individual, he was a trained mechanic, operating his father's garage while at the same time keeping his own, more lucrative, business rolling. He ruled over our area with a mix of discipline and benevolence that kept us all in check. As far as I could understand at the time, Natty made sure no one went hungry and that the area was secure from outside attack. He was a protector. That's why it was such a shock when he was arrested one morning, coming into town from Westmoreland, and locked up on a ganja charge. The police said they had found several pounds of prime sensimillia in his car and although we thought he would get help from the big men we sometimes saw come down to visit him, the judge gave him a three-year sentence. It was only later that I got to understand the real reason behind this. It was then left to Jingles to take over.

Jingles was different to Nat. Although he lived as a Rasta, he was more of a street man. Whereas Nat loved to spend his time in the hills with the farmers, checking on his crops and grounding with the brethren, Jingles was more into the area runnings, very popular, very good at making connections. It was this that got the attention of the party men who controlled the destiny of our impoverished area of Western Kingston. They were into him because he was, apparently, more flexible than his older brother, more inclined to play the game, their game. All in all, Jingles got as much from them as they got from him. I know now that he had foreseen the change that was about to happen in the relationship between the politicians and ghetto people. He had no illusion about where the partisan politics was getting us and who were the only ones to benefit from it. The number of funerals for victims of political violence had started to make many people realise there was nothing to be gained from the slaughter. Jingles was one of them. I think his understanding of the relation between poverty and power got too dangerous for those who thought they were manipulating him . . .

People loved Jingles and he always had a little time to hear their problems. It was Jingles who arranged for our mother to find another job that kept us fed and clothed after she lost the first one. Though times were hard, we all got by with a little help from the Morrisons and their rule over all of us was a benevolent one. This much I remember well.

CHAPTER TWO

Politricks

West Kingston; September 21, 1979 9.15 p.m.

'Shocka, turn down the music!'

'This ah commando mission ... I need some sounds to vibe up.'

'Me say turn down the bloodclaat music, man!' Bernie growled.

'Cha ...' Reluctantly, Shocka obeyed.

'Right, I want everybody to keep cool. I don't want no rash moves, see? ... Skidder, don't lose the truck.'

I was doing sixty, keeping a car between us and the target on Marcus Garvey Drive.

'I have it. Just tell me when.' I answered, eyes set on the Toyota pick-up ahead of us.

Seated in the back, Bernie was scanning the traffic through the windscreen, waiting for the right spot. For the third time, he repeated the instructions.

'Right, don't forget: we block the truck, Shocka and Ritz jump out and stick up the two man dem, run dem away, then ouno jump in. Ritz drive, we follow ouno behind, a'right?'

'Yeah, man ... we got it.' Ritz and Shocka sounded sure.

I knew my job, I was confident I would do it perfectly but why did I feel that tingling at the back of my head? There was just about enough traffic on the road to allow us to operate without looking too conspicuous. At that hour of the night, if we stuck to the timing, hijacking the truck wouldn't take more than three minutes. It would just be a 'change of crew' in fact ...

'Skidder, yuh see the board up deh?'

Some big advertising poster a couple of hundred yards ahead.

'I see it.'

'Alright, I want yuh to block the truck right under there.'

I had my orders.

'Ouno hol' on tight,' I said. I could see enough space in front of the pick-up. Signalling, I gassed up the Mazda and overtook the car in front. Pedal still down, I started to level with my target, glimpsed the profile of the men in the cabin. There was total silence in the car. Next to me, Shocka had his feet flat on the floor, left hand already against the dashboard. I caught the glint of metal in his right. Once the car had just about passed the truck, I started to edge inwards, forcing it to first slow down, then pull towards the side of the road. The horn blew twice. I pressed my own twice also, to confuse the driver some more.

'Ready!' I shouted.

One sharp twist of the wheel and I squeezed the truck to the side, unconcerned about the little jerk I felt as its bumper hit the back of our car. Nobody had said anything about not scratching the car.

With a screeching of brakes, the truck stopped, the Mazda at almost forty-five degrees across it. Right away, I saw Shocka jump out, gun already pointing at the window of the truck, while Ritz was doing the same from the back.

'Hands up! Put your focking hands out the window, now!' I heard Shocka's gravelly voice bark.

I had the engine running, ready to move out again. The truck had stalled; probably the driver wasn't that good at his job. I saw both him and his passenger jump out of the truck, hands reaching high for the stars above. Overdoing it, as he always did, Shocka had his gun stuck against the driver's forehead. He finally let him run away, followed by his partner. Both men took off as if they had Satan in track shoes at their heels.

Ritz was already in the cabin, trying to start up the truck. When I heard the first gunshot, I thought it was the sound of the engine spitting, but then there was the second explosion, the dull crack of the impact against the body of the Mazda. Then I saw the bright beams of a car speeding up towards us, on the wrong side of the road.

'Ritz! Move it, man!' Bernie shouted from the back.

Two more impacts, one directly through my windscreen, where Shocka had been a few minutes earlier.

'It don't start!' I heard Ritz call back.

'Wha' de bomboclaat?!' Bernie growled. 'Ritz! Ouno come, we movin' out!'

I was keeping my head down. Right in front, I could make out three silhouettes running from the car that was now stopped in the middle of the road, twenty yards away from us. They had left the full beams on so that it was hard for us to really see what was going on. My brain was busy calculating how to get us out. Cars had stopped in front and behind, drivers scattering in the darkness to get out of the way.

I heard several gunshots, some coming from the back of the truck. I couldn't see Shocka so I guessed that was him shooting back. Only three guns had been issued for the mission. The windscreen went down with a crash: they were trying to hit the driver!

In the car, Bernie had his gun in hand, trying to see a target to hit. Ritz was firing, covering the space between the Mazda and the truck. Then I heard him shout: 'Shocka got shot! Bernie!'

Bernie shouted back: 'Come back in, Ritz, get in the car. I cover yuh!'

I saw Bernie kick open his door and stand up by the

car, shooting. Ritz was shooting too; he was almost at the passenger door.

'Get in, we goin'!' I called out to him.

Then there was the blaring of a horn, loud and continuous over the gunshots, coming from the back. I saw a car trying to make its way to where we were, but several vehicles were blocking the way.

'Bernie, it's a set-up. Let's go!' I called out.

Bernie had seen the new danger. He was already turning to get back inside the car when he dropped to the floor and cried out.

'My leg!'

I couldn't hear Ritz's gun and couldn't see him any more. 'Ritz!' I called again. No answer. Quickly I peered through the missing windscreen. Ritz had almost made it back to the car, but a bullet had cut short his escape. My mind went numb and I don't know why but I suddenly didn't care to make it out alive. Ritz was a man I had always respected and to see him eyes wide open in the dirt iced my blood. I opened up my door, dived down and grabbed the gun Ritz had dropped. Cowering behind the Mazda, I started firing towards the vehicle arriving from the back. I squeezed out two shots, then the magazine clicked empty.

'Skidder! Skidder, we going! Come on! Skidder!?'

Bernie had got back inside the car. I rushed back in, threw the gun on the passenger seat and grabbed the wheel. Shots were still peppering the Mazda. The road was blocked ahead by the first car. The other one had managed to make a way through and was just getting to us now. There was maybe one way out and it would depend on how fast I was . . .

The engine was still running. Keeping my head real low, I gassed up and slipped into reverse.

'Bernie, lie down!' I shouted.

It was not conscious, the way I reacted, just reflexes taking over. The gas pedal down all the way, I lifted my left foot off the clutch suddenly. The Mazda lurched backwards in a roar, rushing into the incoming car. There was an resounding crash of metal and the shooting from the back stopped. Without delay, I put the car into first and steered all the way left. Fire was still coming our way but it didn't matter to me any more. I wasn't gonna die without trying, that was the only thought on my mind, and the cold anger in the pit of my stomach was like raw acid.

Zing zing.

Two more bullets hit the inside of the car. I had no time to look behind to see how Bernie was doing but then I heard his gun bark three times, the shots ringing close behind me. He was trying to clear us a way. The way the car spun, skidded and then bit the tarmac, I had made a ninety-degree turn and climbed over the dividing verge to the other side of the road before I knew it. The panic was such on both lanes that it was the haphazard stopping of the vehicles that saved us. The two cars in pursuit were still trying to push a way out of the scramble when I put down my foot and left them standing. Once I managed to slip into East Avenue, we were almost home free. I knew the ghetto streets as well as anyone in West Kingston. When I finally parked the Mazda in a safe place, there was very little rubber left around the left back wheel.

Three days later came the reckoning for that night. It was the evening of Jingles' engagement party. His fiancée was my sister.

A group of girls in freshly imported US denim suits were gathered around Lucy, commenting on the quality – and the cost – of her engagement ring. I was leaning against the bamboo back fence, sipping on my Heineken with no apparent interest in such trivial conversations. The looping bass line had me nodding at mid-tempo, my eyes set on the domino game being disputed a little further away by the outdoor kitchen. A red sun was making up its mind to set above the roofs, smoke from the fish grill at the far end of the yard tinting it to my eyes. I gulped another mouthful from my imported brew before easing off the fence, headed for the gate.

At the front of the bar, Saturday afternoon was even busier than usual. An engagement party was a good occasion to gather around. Spread over the front of the bar/shop, smoking and drinking, all the crew was there. Scotty, Pocker, John Dread, Berris, Lookman, Lloydie, Ratty, all Jingles' lieutenants, young men in their twenties who were directly involved in the running of the area, first in line for the action when needed. Six months earlier, half-a-dozen more would have been present but were gone now, because of untimely demise or jail sentences. Jingles himself was perched atop the veranda wall of the family house, a little way from everyone else, pulling on a ganja spliff. I thought his eyes stopped on me for a fraction of a second from beyond the wafting smoke. I finished my beer.

Right now, the Don seemed absorbed in a meditation and no one was too eager to interrupt it, but he looked up, as we all did, when the white Toyota appeared from the left side of the street, coming our way. It wasn't in alarm though: all access to the area was monitored twenty-four hours a day, the roads dug up in a zig-zag pattern to prevent the type of high-speed drive-by shootings that were becoming the norm in the state of open warfare that prevailed between neighbourhoods.

No, the vehicle that stopped in front of the house was known, expected even. From Jingles' closed expression, I guessed he wasn't too enthusiastic about the appointment. The man that extracted himself from the back seat was well known, notorious even. A policeman named Parson, he was a large man who moved with the grace of a Sumo wrestler, his huge arms stuck out of his beige short-sleeved shirt. But he wasn't the important one; that man was sitting in the front of the car. Parson didn't greet anyone, just scanned the surroundings with a look of deep suspicion before opening the passenger door for his boss. This was a politician named Mr T. and he was never seen without his personal bodyguard. The two men could not have been more different. Parson was a man of very few words, a giant shadow who never smiled. In contrast the MP smiled easily, behind his aviator shades.

'Jingles, how you doin', man?'

Mr T. walked up to where Jingles was still sat, on the wall. The MP was of average height with a gently bulging stomach under his imported shirt.

'Alright, sah,' Jingles answered soberly.

No one else had moved, but all eyes were set on the two men. The driver of the car, a slim, dark man known as Albert, had switched off the engine and sat at the wheel, the radio on.

'I heard the news ... Congratulations.' Mr T. sounded genuine enough.

Jingles' eyebrows hardly moved in acknowledgement. Presenting his wishes wasn't the goal of Mr T.'s visit

'We need to talk,' he said, without missing a beat.

Jingles tossed away his ganja stub and slid down from the wall. His mane of locks neatly tucked under a dark blue beret, his thin, sparsely-bearded face made him resemble an ascetic preacher more than a garrison town don. From the corner where he had been cooling out, Lookman moved towards his boss. Parson gave him a blank stare, out of habit I supposed. Normally, Lookman and Bertie, the two 'captains' as it were, would attend such meetings between Jingles and Mr T. But Bertie had been on the run since the night of the hijacking and today's home call was precisely about that disastrous operation. The atmosphere wasn't warm, to say the least. Jingles was about to lead the little group inside the house.

'Come.'

That's all he said before going through the gate, and he was looking my way. He didn't even stop to check the order had been received.

That single word was like my graduation certificate. I had

started as a youth, being taken in to become one of the soldiers for the area. I had only been on the outside, doing small jobs for Jingles, picking up what I could, in the hope that some day I might be found ready for bigger things. That is usually the way things work for a youth coming up in the ghetto order of things. Three months earlier, after Bionic, Jingles' appointed driver, had got shot and wounded in an ambush, I had been picked to drive him on a move to Red Hills. Scotty was there too. On the way back, we ran into a vanload of youths from Arnett Gardens and I have never been able to explain how but I got us three and the car safely back to the area, under fire. That was how I became the new driver.

Lookman threw me a glance that was less than friendly but I ignored him. I never quite took to him, and he didn't show much kindness towards me. But he was over me in the order of things and that was that. So I followed after Lookman, Parson's giant bulk closing the march.

Through the half-open window, the sounds of the evening filtered through from the yard while in the rather small but tastily furnished living room an ominous silence reigned. Mr T. had the settee, while Parson had perched on a bar stool just his size, to the right of his charge, inexpressive as a big eagle. I was the furthest from the visitor, sitting straight in a straight chair, with Jingles to my left. He was grave-looking, hands crossed in his armchair. Lookman in his yellow and white tracksuit sat between Jingles and the MP.

'Your move on Wednesday night made a big impression . . . but not exactly what we expected.'

That was not a good start from Mr T. He wasn't really smiling as he said that. Jingles seemed unwilling to even answer him. Mr T.'s tone wasn't quite cold yet but it was getting there . . .

'That was a very sensitive operation. You were supposed to give the job to intelligent people.' He paused and shook his head. 'What the hell happen, sah?'

The MP's drawl, when it came out, told of years spent studying in the States, on the East Coast probably. Jingles was in a sombre mood; he didn't seem to like the way Mr T. questioned him. But he calmly looked the man straight in the eyes.

'It was a set up.'

'A set up?!' Mr T sounded like he'd never heard of the term before. His eyebrows rose above the the tinted shades.

'De man dem did know seh we was coming. No other way, trust me.'

Mr T. kept a couple of seconds of displeasure floating through the room.

'I gave you a very strategic mission to carry out for the party, vital to our plan of action, and you turn it into a shootout! . . .'

The exasperated tone showed that Mr T. had most certainly been asked questions about his handling of the 'strategic mission' by his peers at the party headquarters. Jingles didn't have much love for the elegant man facing him, I could feel it. He explained, expressionless: 'We did work exactly according to plan. But by the time we blocked the pickup, two more cars come up. That's when the shooting started.' Jingles paused, before he dropped his voice: 'Them was expecting us, me ah tell yuh dis!'

Mr T. wasn't pleased. He said quietly, 'Your boys shoot two police officers, one dead already and the other one might not make it. There's gonna be hell to pay.'

Parson's face confirmed that statement.

Over the years I knew Jingles, I had rarely seen him as silent and contemplative as in the last three days. He took time to look at the visiting MP then at his bodyguard. Eyes not really seeing him, he spelled it quietly to Mr T.

'Tell me something, sah; you give me instructions to intercept an arms shipment . . . Nobody else supposed to know about the move, seen? . . . Even my soldiers didn't know what the mission was about . . . and when them get there, them find two carloads of plain-clothes police open fire. Dem never even know seh ah police. What you expect them to do?'

'The police said they responded to a shooting incident . . .' Mr T. pointed out soberly.

Jingles shook his head. 'And I tell yuh seh nobody fired a shot until dem start.' Jingles turned to me. 'My youth here was driving one of the cars. Carly, tell the man what happened'

The straight gaze of the stocky, well-shaved man switched to me from behind his shades. I fixed him, same way.

'We block the pickup, two of our man come out and stick up the driver and the passenger, tell them to get out. It's then that the other car them reach the spot and right away shots start lick . . .' I paused, took a breath.

'The first man by the truck get shot first, the other at the front get shot dead when the second car come. The man dem keep firing as I try drive out. My man at the back get shot ina the leg. We get 'way still . . . Dem never give we a chance, sah.'

Mr T. looked at me in silence for a couple of seconds, solemn as a high court judge. Then he asked: 'Who shot the two officers?'

I shook my head slowly. I could feel Jingles' eyes on me.

'The only two man with guns from my car got shot first. I couldn't see what happened at the back.'

The man nodded, leaned back in the settee, thinking.

'Bad business,' he said. 'Very bad.'

I could see Lookman's eyes, cold and narrow.

'I lost two men down there,' Jingles stated coldly.

Mr T. didn't offer any condolences. He grieved only for the lost opportunity; the political impact of the revelation would have nicely rubbed off on him. But it had all gone sour, although nothing too bad would come off of it. The rest was just not his concern. He sighed heavily.

'This was our only chance to expose the government in arms dealing. Dem import weapons all the while, but this time my information was tight. With something like that in the press, everybody would have made them responsible for all the violence. We could have proved them was planning a coup to set up a Communist dictatorship. The election was ours, you understand that?' He sounded like a weary teacher.

Jingles understood that. He said: 'Your information never said police was involved.'

Parson's expression had turned even darker. Wearily, Mr T. rubbed one hand over his close-cropped silvery hair. Someone was doing some 'freelancing' on both sides; that was for damm certain. He would have to deal with this one later, no doubt ...

'Anyway, the first thing now is to deal with this police-killing problem. Them not going to stop persecuting us until dem get somebody for it, you know that.'

You would have believed the MP was personally at risk, the way he sounded. We had suffered a major raid the day after the shooting and another couple of men had been taken away.

'So what you expect me to do?' Jingle asked, his eyes deep into the politician's own.

Dusk was settling outside the window. The aroma of jerk chicken was drifting into the room.

'A policeman has been killed. You know the rules, Jingles.'

'Yeah, I know the rules. What about the families of my two dead soldiers ...? What about dem, sah?'

Like any good politician, Mr T. knew how to use silences and body language. He blew out some air between his lips; his expression was almost sorrowful.

'You understand I can't get any funds for that kind of things, especially in these circumstances ... but I will try to work something out.' That was a generous intention, then he added: '... as soon as this police business is sorted out.'

You don't get any colder than that.

Lookman hadn't said a word but his eyes were on Jingles, intense. He understood, just like Jingles did, what the politician was asking. And he also knew very well that Jingles was expected to do it. I watched Jingles as he said, bland-voiced:

'Look sah, things getting heavy down here, I have to tell yuh. No money nah run and the youths dem getting nervous.' Jingles sat up to point out to the MP how bad the situation really was. 'So far, I keeping things under control but my boys dem have families to feed and cyan feed them. Dem start screw when I take back the guns dem after dem do a job. The other side have guns more than we, it look like, so nobody likes to be without, you see wha me ah deal with? Right now, too much man get dead and my people dem ask for guns. Dem vex.'

This was a realistic analysis of the situation. The atmosphere in the area was tense. It was getting worse by the week. Death came fast and plenty and everybody got touched

'I know that, Jingles, I know . . .' Motion of the hands from Mr T., a concerned nodding of the head. 'Look, all we want is to get rid of these Communists, that's the cause of all the problems in this country. Once we get to win the elections, you'll see that the economy will pick up. There'll be jobs for everybody, Tell your people to be patient, wait a few months till voting time.'

'Yeah . . . I'll tell them.' Jingles said.

You could see he knew more than anyone that this type of argument didn't work any more with the hungry youths, risking their necks in the shanty towns' political battlefield. The mood out there was severe, the day-to-day survival drastic. Mr T. got up. The devoted Parson had preceded him; he hadn't made a sound since getting out of the car.

'I really have a lot to do, I can't even stay to celebrate with you . . . I hope you won't feel no way, Jingles?'

Real smooth . . .

'Cool.' Jingles was laconic.

We were all up, left the room in a file and emerged in the cool night air. A lively, bumpy bass line greeted us first. The festive atmosphere around the bar contrasted with the mood just now in the living room. Behind me, Lookman was saying something in Jingles' ear. Parson was already at the car door, waiting for his boss to get in. I inhaled deeply, realized I didn't feel good inside. Just one of these feelings I sometimes get. I watched Jingles get to the car door and stand there talking with Mr T. for a moment. Or rather, Mr T. was talking and Jingles' eyes were still. Mr T. made a move with his hand, like to wave him goodbye before he got into the passenger seat and the car took off. I remember thinking about Bernie out there on the run . . .

I always trace the turn my life took back to that day, Lucy's engagement day. Everything I did subsequently, good or bad, was the direct consequence of what was said and left unsaid, at that meeting. Jingles moved out that night, just went away for three whole days, leaving Lookman and Scotty in charge of things. Lookman reported the results of the meeting to the half-dozen men directly concerned one way or another. In any case it was clear what was asked here; everyone knew the score when it came to police. That was a death sentence, summary, you know . . .

For hours the first day, we sat in the back of Scotty's yard, spinning and turning the problem every which way but couldn't work it out. The facts were these: two supposedly plain-clothed policemen had got shot, one of them killed and whatever it took, someone was going to pay for it. Whether these guys were on police business or working as 'protection' on their own time had nothing to do with it. They had taken away five youths the following day and no one had seen any of them since, not even the mothers who had gone to beg at the police station. The MP had messed up, now he was scared and came to demand a human sacrifice. Either we gave them the right one, dead or alive, or they would take one or two of the others; it was as simple as that. Some pretty rough men were there, brooding men who had taken their share of the vicious warfare between neighbourhoods that politics and poverty had trapped them into. All of us had seen death at close quarters and learned to live with it, day in and day out. But no one here thought it was in any way right to give away one of our own, just because someone up there had miscalculated in their paranoid little schemes. Whether it was Bernie who had done it, or not.

The second day, there was news of a shooting between police and some men from Nannyville on the previous night. Later in the afternoon, Bootlegger, a youth from Rema who had family in our area, arrived with a story about a man being shot in an hospital ward when he was supposedly under police guard. Bootlegger pointed out that the man had first been shot for no worse reason than being caught smoking a ganja spliff in his own yard. He wasn't even wanted and no one knew who had shot him in the hospital. The atmosphere was getting tenser everywhere. Every day that brought us closer to voting time brought us deeper into mindless violence. At the end of the third day, Jingles appeared. It was hard to tell with him but he didn't seem as upset as when he'd left. He simply said he'd seen Bernie and that he wasn't too badly wounded. He would make it. That was all but I guess all of us always knew Jingles would never have given the order to 'tag' Bernie. Then the alternative options started being discussed ...

Later that night, I came home from the Sleng Teng bar at the end of our lane to find Lucy and Jingles sitting in the dark on the veranda cane chair our mother had got made by a visiting craftsman years before. I would have left them but Jingles had me sit down, offered me one of the beers he'd brought over. Lucy soon left us. Jingles didn't say much for fifteen minutes. I didn't ask him where he had been to, he didn't say, but he asked me what the men had thought about the situation. I told him no one found it right to give in to the demand; we all thought the mess-up had been none of our doing and that we had paid for that with two lives already.

'What going to happen to the youths them take 'way?'

'Not'ing, but them will keep them inside for a little while.'

'And Bernie?' I asked again

Jingles took a sip from his beer.

'Bernie ha fe travel ...' he said soberly, then he turned to look at me full through the semi-darkness of the veranda, 'This is between me and yuh, seen?'

I nodded gravely, appreciating the esteem I was being shown.

'Seen.'

Jingles stretched in the chair, then belched to ease off his chest.

'A lot of t'ings going to change, Carly ...' he said wearily, 't'ings changing already. It's not going to be like this any more.'

I didn't interrupt him.

'Yuh see how a man who don't even live in the area can come and tell yuh seh "do this, do that," and we do it? That ah go done, trust me.'

He had to be right.

'Look pon this thing yah, sah: we take all the risks, we get shot, and we do the killings, and for what?'

He was talking to himself as much as to me, I realized but I knew something important was coming out here. Jingles shook his head.

'Yuh know something, my youth? I done 'nuff t'ings in my life I'd have love to change right now, but I know this; is not man whe wicked, it's the system.'

Jingles had a hollow laugh and for a moment I wondered if he'd taken that much beer to get giggly, but he turned to me.

'Hey Carly, yuh ever hear seh one MP shoot another one from the other party?'

It sounded so unlikely that I too had to smile at the thought.

'Well,' Jingles said, 'look how we so mad fe kill another man just because him live 'cross the borderline, eeh!'

I knew what he was talking about.

'Dem t'ings deh fe done,' Jingles shook his dreadlocked head. 'Them man deh want the same thing we want: food, clothes and shelter.' He paused again.

'And yuh know why dem want we dead too? Because dem big man tell them seh is we stop them from getting it.'

'Makes no sense,' I said. It didn't.

'No sense at all,' Jingles said. 'And most youths now start realize it. He stopped, then straightened up in the chair, leaned a bit towards me.

'Make me ask yuh something; yuh know seh man and man from both sides sit down and talk, big area man, like me . . .'

I could see what he meant but had never really considered that, given the deadly nature of inter-area wars at street level.

'True yuh nuh know!' Jingles sat back, thoughtful.

'So we going to have a peace treaty again?'

The elation and goodwill of the first one the previous year had been shortlived.

'Peace . . . peace is not for now, you know, Carly,' Jingles sighed. 'Peace don't suit everybody,' he added cryptically.

There followed a couple of minute when he just sipped some beer. Me too, while the street night sounds around us died down gradually.

'But the politics done with, trust me . . . Is money ah go run 'tings now. The youths dem coming up, youths like yuh, ouno not going to need the politicians dem no more. Is a different time ah come up, a different set ah youths.'

I meditated on that, since Jingles didn't say anything else for a long time. He was right: times were changing, and the youths too! I finished my beer, feeling the need to rest, to lay down and forget, for a few hours at least, what I was and where I was. Then, after he had swallowed the last mouthful of beer from his can, Jingles asked me quietly, just above the crissing of the night beetles: 'Suppose I give the order to deal with Bernie . . . how much ah dem man deh woulda do it?'

I can't say I hadn't thought about that in the last three days but Jingles' timing threw me off. A hell of a question to answer. An order from the top man, the area 'notch', to a soldier is a very serious thing. Discipline, at that time anyway, was essential and to disobey an order or trespass one of the unwritten laws of the ghetto wasn't taken lightly. Killing a policeman threatened to bring down indiscriminate retaliation by the police, something a don would be held responsible for by his people. To prevent this, he had to execute the sentence on the guilty man and 'deliver' the body to the police. Simple enough.

'I don't really know . . .' I answered truthfully.

Jingles was looking in my eyes, I felt it.

'What about yuh; yuh'd have done it, Carly?' he asked again.

Jingles was right: change was coming. The last few months leading to the 1980 elections saw a savage escalation of violence that cost hundreds of lives. Street battles were fought between opposite neighbourhoods, but also between police and either side. As always, many innocents paid the price, as well as actual participants in the killing. Hardly a day passed without funerals. Adding to the political killings were those due to robberies. As always in such situations, many took advantage of the general mayhem to go on the rampage, robbing and looting. At the same time, lots of guns started to come into the area. Now almost everybody could have a weapon. The shock troops on the front line had sophisticated guns: M16, Uzi, that kind of thing. No one knew where all this was leading. Richer people left the island in a hurry, even those locked up in one of the more secure areas of town. But in Western Kingston, no one went anywhere; we just kept getting up every day to the siege-like situation, looking out, watching and waiting for things to happen.

And they were happening. Raids from the other side, from the police and the army; petrol bombings, ambushes, kidnapping and killing were all daily occurrences and we had to learn to live with it. As it is said, 'watch and pray', and that's all we could do. For me, it was a school, an education, the benefit of which only manifested itself years later. I think what I saw during that period shaped my perception of people and how far they can go, given the right motivation (or the wrong one). By the time the place caught fire, I was totally integrated in the 'live' forces of the area.

Jingles seemed to depend on me for more important functions, I was becoming his 'right hand' and although I was aware that not everyone might appreciate it, I did my best to prove worthy of the confidence put in me. I had already been doing some runs with him to the countryside from time to time, whenever his ganja business required his attention. I knew most of the men he worked with, learned the ins-and-outs of the trade. It got me extra earnings too; I soon had enough money for a Honda bike I couldn't really venture too far with it but it was mine all the same, and it got me respect. I was coming of age, with all the edge of living dangerously and surviving it.

The month before the voting was due to take place, Jingles, Lookman and two soldiers, Willie Skates and Googles, went on an important mission one morning to pick up something outside town. What exactly took place on the way back, we didn't find out until later, but they were ambushed and their car raked with automatic fire. Only Lookman survived to spend the following year in Gun Court for a gun he said wasn't his. Two days later, in the midst of that madness, Lucy had her baby.

CHAPTER THREE

Against All Odds

The very first memory I have of Lucy is that of a really tiny, wrinkled little thing screaming out. I wasn't too fond of her at first, mostly because she was getting all the attention and I had lost my spot. Funny how love starts. My resenting the arrival of this 'intruder' didn't last long; pretty soon I was spending more and more time watching that little wiggling baby grow up day by day, and she seemed as interested in me as I was in her. When Lucy started walking, I was the proudest boy on the block, convinced that I had played a major part in getting her to take her first steps. Our mother was so sick when she had Lucy, I learned later that she almost died. Mathilda, my older sister, took charge of the house while our mother was in and out of hospital for some months after the birth. Mathilda also took care of Lucy, like a real mother, at twelve years of age. Mathilda was from a different father. For a long time, our mother wasn't sure whether she could have any more children. After her first husband left her and young Mathilda, she eventually met our father and in the course of time had me, then Lucy two years later. She survived that, got back well for a couple of years then sick again. They said she suffered from 'sugar': diabetes.

Mathilda was something else, for real. She was tall for her age, long in the bone, like me and Lucy. But whereas we stayed slim, Mathilda was bulky. I mean bulky, not fat or just big.

Imagine a sixteen-year-old girl from the countryside, fit, tall and muscley; that's Mathilda at twelve. Needless to say, she didn't make many enemies in the neighbourhood! As long as Mathilda was around, no boy would take set on me for anything; my big sister didn't play. When I was twelve, before our mother died, Mathilda had finally given in to the advances of some American guy she had met while he was visiting. After two years of courtship, she got married and left us to follow him to Texas where she still lives happily.

Lucy and I grew up real close because it was just us two, sharing the good times and bad times of childhood. I never really understood why our parents drifted apart, and I guess it happens to a lot of people, so I took it as a fact of life to just cope with. Sometimes I think about my father, and I understand now he did what he thought he had to do. Lucy wrote to him and they kept it up for a few years, I think, although she stopped talking about the letters as she got older.

Up to age fifteen, Lucy was just another raggedy ghetto girl, very skinny, very faastie, afraid of nothing, who'd much rather ride a bicycle around the block and play draughts than hang around with the other teenage area girls. She had two good friends and she had me, although I was not there to be with most of the time. Then, within a short year, she changed. I was the last to notice obviously, but then I started to see some of the boys hanging around the house, outside, talking to her whenever they got a chance, less so when they knew I was home. I never had to watch out for that before. Now Lucy was getting shape, filling in, looking attractive. Even her face turned pretty, the face of a young woman. Sixteen-year-old Lucy had become one of the prettiest things in the area, although most guys were being respectful in front of me. I didn't have a reputation as a 'bad boy' like many others, yet it was known that I never failed to stand up for my rights and that my calm outlook should not be mistaken for weakness. Anyway, as long as nobody disrespected her, there was nothing to worry about. Lucy was straight-talking and could defend herself.

Nevertheless I was the last one to know and not a little amazed when, one fine morning, no less than the don himself, Jingles, appeared at the gate of our house and asked to talk to me. Having done nothing reprehensible I assumed it was about some important mission. Still, for Jingles himself to come calling, it had to be serious! To my great surprise, the man sat with me on the veranda and told me how much he liked Lucy and that they had been talking for a while. The reason he had come, he said, was that he didn't want me to get it wrong and he preferred to tell me himself rather than I found out from someone else. He also said that Lucy had told him he would have to talk it over with me. I was surprised but didn't let it show. I felt honoured, first that Jingles had come and showed me respect in that way, and then that my sister would give me so much consideration. Both ways, my status was sure to be on the rise in the neighbourhood. I sat there, reflecting, thinking about it for a moment. I recalled Lucy had conveniently left the house early to go and visit Aunt Pauline. Jingles was a big man by then, in his early thirties, had at least four children I knew about, two by a very noisy area woman with a mouth like a butter pan, named Hortense. But he seemed sincere, assured me that he would look after Lucy well and make sure she continued studying. What could I say? I told him I was honoured he had come to inform me and that if Lucy was happy, that was okay with me. After Jingles had left, I remember feeling like a man who had just been offered a wage increase. Without being opportunistic, I realized this unexpected development was very good for me. Later that day, I talked it over with Lucy. She said she wouldn't be with Jingles if I objected to it for some reason. I liked Jingles, fortunately. I couldn't see how I would have dealt with this if I didn't!

Anyway, they got together and I watched Lucy blossom into a happy young woman. And I was the don's brother-in-law . . .

I was against Lucy bringing Aisha to the funerals. For some reason I thought that these type of events were not something young children should attend. Especially since, in that case, the baby was only days old and I couldn't see what good it did her to be at her father's graveside. But Lucy was determined to bring her child to say goodbye to the daddy she would never know.

Dying was an everyday thing in the area I grew up in, especially during those years of political turmoil and I saw a lot of funerals. Some of these funerals were for family members, some for friends or neighbours, but I have never seen anything like Jingles' sending off. Though he was still a young man – Jingles died seven days short of his thirty-fourth birthday – the man who had been our area leader was well known and had done good to a lot of people. He also came from a very large and united clan, strong-headed men and women and many came from various parts of the island to bid him farewell.

The sun was out, that Friday. The Morrisons' home was full of people. The yard and the surroundings had been occupied by throngs of friends and neighbours, most of whom had been there ever since the first day of the wake. It had been a traditional wake, conducted in the old style, with food, drinks, songs and stories like they did it in the countryside. The last night had been an emotional affair and many a testimony ended up in tears. Big men, many who had seen death at close quarters for years, and dealt it too, unashamedly wiped tears from their battle-scarred faces as Jingles' deeds were remembered by his comrades and peers.

This had been a painful week. The day before, we had buried Willie Skates and Googles, the two soldiers who had died in the ambush with Jingles. They had their funerals together, on the same day, because the two men had not only been friends and comrades in-arms but were also cousins, related through their mothers' side. It was hard to bear, the grief being double, and also because that family had lost no less than five people in that year alone!

Finally, shortly before eleven, Jingles' coffin was lifted from the platform where it had laid for the night and put onto an open truck. It had been the wish of the Morrison family that their son should take a last ride through the town he had loved, so that everyone could say their goodbyes. Many top men from other areas, of the same political allegiance as ours, were there with their crews, hard men used to burying friends and loved ones.

But the thing that marked Jingles' funeral the most was that word had come from the other side that the day would be respected as a day of peace, the peace he had done so much to promote. It was known by now that Jingles' death was not the doing of the 'enemy', but had occurred as a result of some police operation which the police commissioner had been at a loss to justify and which he promised to investigate seriously. Some people were talking about a 'contract' executed by renegade police officers. Area leaders from over the political divide, who all knew the departed, had imposed a curfew to their troops for twenty-four hours, in memory of him. This showed real respect, and although none of them came to the funeral (they weren't really expected to; the goodwill wouldn't extend to that in our still volatile environment), the wreaths they sent through third parties were placed alongside those from family members and friends. In a way, Jingles achieved even more through his death than he had in life.

The family had refused a police escort for the procession, whether because of the unexplained circumstances of the death or simply because the curfew guaranteed us security for the funerals. Lucy was in the second car, surrounded by the mother and aunts of the departed, Aisha cradled in her arms. Throughout the wake nights, I was impressed by her courage and composure. She was still a very young woman and the ordeal of giving birth to her child only days after she had been robbed of her husband was something horribly heavy to endure. But she stood firm, although I could read the disarray in her veiled eyes. I knew the real pain would hit her later, when the emptiness settled in her still tender heart.

So the procession left our area, cars, buses, trucks and even bikes following slowly, scores of people lining our route all the way to the cemetery. All Jingles' close lieutenants, middle-ranking and other soldiers were there, dressed up for the occasion to pay their last respects to their don. All except Lookman, still awaiting sentence in Gun Court. Today we passed at slow speed alongside roads we would usually avoid altogether or drive by at speed. It felt strange after all these years to break old survival habits!

At the burial ground, as we all stood around the hole freshly dug in the dark earth, listening to the parson's words of peaceful rest and reward somewhere beyond, I recall being filled with a great weariness. I had been sad during the days that followed his death, angry even, but now all that was left was the feeling that nothing mattered any more. Jingles had been the father I had not really known and lost too early, the older brother I had never had. He was the only man who had helped me to make sense of the madness we all lived within, and his advice and example had forged my way of thinking. He had instilled me with a sense of values in a world where it was easier to have none. Now he was gone and I found myself wondering whether it was any use trying to follow his good words, since his wisdom had not prevented his early death. That's what I felt on that sad and sunny day.

I had seen them trailing the procession when we had left the area. They knew everyone knew who they were but then they kept their distance and so no one paid them any mind. Jingles had died at the hand of the police, or rather of some police elements but no one was sure yet what or who was hiding behind them. And so the fact that a lone unmarked police vehicle should follow the procession was not enough to provoke. There were only two men in the car. The driver was a tall, dark detective known to almost everyone. Horace Brown was tough but fair, as ghetto police officers go. He sometimes gave you a break if the offence wasn't to do with guns. The man he was driving wasn't known to me, nor to the soldiers I asked, but he was obviously higher ranking than Brown. They parked some way off the burying ground and stayed in the car, so it was hard to make him out. Some of our people said he was an American cop who was on a mission in Jamaica. Some said he was a judge, or a criminal lawyer. In any case, they stayed until everyone was gone, just watching the whole proceeding through their tinted windscreen.

That night, we all sat around Morrison's bar and sipped on beer and rum, as we were meant to do. I could almost feel Jingles' shadow floating amongst us. There was no real sadness though. The grief of death had been for the first few days but now that the body of the departed had been laid to rest, it had made way for a feeling of togetherness, as if the passing of the man had brought us closer and done away with futile quarrels and divisions. The one thing I could read in all of Jingles' soldiers was uncertainty. We all knew an era had passed. None of us could tell what the next one would be like.

CHAPTER FOUR

Ghost Chasing

The worst part of death is who misses you, they say ... What do you do once you have buried your friend, son, husband? What do the loved ones left behind say to each other that makes sense? What do you tell yourself that can help you to get back up from the well of pain you're sinking in, and go on living? We sat around the living room, in our funeral clothes, searching for anodyne words, for anything that would break the shroud of silence. Now that the crying was all over, I had to start my mission.

The word 'mission' kept coming up to my mind, for that's what it was. I had spent the last few nights going over old times, the years spent working under and then with Rico, all that I had learned from him. This was the man who had turned my life around. Most probably I had him to thank for being alive today. More than that, he was my friend, the only real one I ever had. Back there in the London cemetery we had just left, inside that pretty wooden box, there lay a part of me, a chunk of my heart and the rest of it needed the light of truth to go on beating. Until I found out the reason why Rico was gone, I wouldn't be able to feel any more. Already I was aware of the tightness in the pit of my stomach, and I knew it wouldn't go until the day Rico's death was explained. That was my life's mission.

The police had been with us from the first day, uniforms

searching the scene, interviewing all those present on the town hall steps that morning, inspectors at the house, questions, snooping around to find clues. Two of them came in plain clothes the following day. They were very polite with Nicola, seeing her fragile state of mind. I was interviewed next.

The detective inspector, in charge, McCallum he said his name was, tall and rotund with a pronounced bald patch, asked me what relation I was to the dead man.

'I'm the best man,' I told him.

He seemed to find it particularly interesting that I had come from Jamaica especially for the wedding. He asked me what I did back home for a living, I said I was doing security work. I wasn't sure why at the time, but I didn't feel like telling him what my real job was. All the same, he was too perplexed by the killing and didn't ask to see my passport, which was just as well!

The younger man was also tall, with a head of red hair. While his boss was busy in the other room, he said: 'We see quite a few murders around here, but this one's kind of ... special, if I may say so, sir.'

'Did you find the shell?' I asked, realizing I might sound too knowledgeable, but the Englishman simply shook his head.

'Nothing. All we have is the one bullet.'

I didn't ask anything else, but I already knew it was a sniper's rifle shot that hit Rico, most likely equipped with a 'scope. Everything pointed to a contract killing. And the police knew that too.

'Did you ever get anything on my friend? I mean, did his name ever come to your attention?' I felt funny asking that about Rico.

'You mean, was he connected to the local crime scene?' The red-haired policeman shook his head. 'Not that I know, sir.'

I could see the policemen couldn't make sense of it all. They had nothing on Rico, he wasn't in the country illegally and he had no contact with the local criminal elements they were only too familiar with.

'Well, we must pursue our investigation. Once again, you have our deepest sympathy, madam.' The inspector said as he got up. 'We will be in touch, should anything come up. His English sounded almost literary, his accent clipped and rolling. 'Come along Mitchell.'

The redhead, he didn't look over twenty-three years of age, followed him out. Watching the two white men leave, I wondered whether the legendary tenacity and competence of the British police would solve this mystery. Maybe another black man dead didn't mean that much to them, just another murder case in their day's work. But for me, that particular murder was too close to my heart to rely on strangers. I was going to find out who and what had taken Rico's life, if it was the last thing I'd do.

The second day after the funeral, I was just sitting in the kitchen, watching a sunbeam on the table, like a bright finger on a white board, turning things over in my mind, when Miss Ruby walked in. She had been staying upstairs with Nicola, keeping watch on her. Miss Ruby was a professional nurse, she knew all about these things.

'Good morning, son.'

'Good morning, madda.'

She switched the electric kettle on and came to sit down across from me. For a while she said nothing, just sat there, not really looking at me, her eyes set on the sunlit garden through the bay window. I was fiddling with a pen, a blank page of notebook on the table in front of me.

'Yuh writing a letter?' she asked, getting up to answer the 'click' of the kettle. I watched her pick up a mug and prepare her tea.

'No . . . it just help me to t'ink.'

'Yuh want some tea?'

'No, t'ank yuh, I'm alright.'

'Yuh have breakfast already?' Miss turned to look at me.

'I not really hungry, yuh know madda.'

She came back to sit down with her steaming mug.

'Yuh mus' try and eat, son . . .'

I watched her stir up her tea, slowly, with application. I waited, listening to the intermittent roaring of vehicles as they passed the house. Miss Ruby never seemed to grow old, or so it looked to me. She didn't look much different from the first day Rico brought me to her, a good ten years earlier. Ever since that day, she had been like a mother to me, better even; she had been a friend, a confidante, someone I could always bring my troubles to and her advice had always been unfailingly right. This morning though, I couldn't help but feel strange before her composure. There was an elderly woman who had seen her only son being shot down right in front of her eyes, on his wedding day, yet in the week since then, she had shown more strength facing this horror than even a grown man like me. I almost would have felt better had she broken down and needed my support; her weakness might have made me stronger. But that wasn't the Miss Ruby I knew.

'Nicola is not well. The doctor coming to see her.' She took a sip of the hot tea, then added. 'I t'ink she might lose the baby.'

Our eyes locked for a few seconds, she didn't flinch. I rubbed my aching head, feeling myself sinking deeper in the horror. Miss Ruby took another sip, her hand steady around the mug, as if she had just announced that the day might be rainy. How much pain can one person take before their very soul gives up and dies inside?

'I can't make sense out of all this, madda, it's like a nightmare,' I said.

'I can't either, me son, but somehow, this is God's will, and there is nothing me or yuh can understand about it.'

I inhaled deeply, let the air out slowly through my mouth, letting her words sink in.

'You know,' she said, putting her mug back down on the table. 'When Rico started as a policeman back home, I didn't like it but that is what he wanted to do.' She paused, reflecting on those long gone days. 'He told me that was his job, so all I could do was pray every day that he would come home at night. After a while, I just accepted the risks, like he did.' Miss Ruby smiled, looked straight at me. 'He used to say that the bullet to kill him wasn't made yet.' She paused and for a while her face looked real peaceful. 'Rico was always lucky.'

'That is what I can't deal with, madda. Him survive plenty t'ings, him coulda get killed 'nuff times back then, and 'nuff police used to lose dem life on the job. But nobody could get to him.' I shook my head. 'For him to get killed now, as a civilian, and especially ina England!' I paused, bitterness increasing as I stressed the sad irony of the drama. 'Somet'ing wrong here, madda, me ah tell yuh . . . somet'ing wrong . . . and I must find out what it is.'

Miss Ruby drank her tea in silence, eyes down into her mug, but I knew she was deep in thoughts of her own.

'I want to ask you. I know Rico always kept business and family separate,' I said. 'But . . . do you have an idea, is there anything you noticed . . . recently, anything he might have said?'

For a while, I couldn't tell whether Miss Ruby had even heard my question, or if she just wanted to ignore it. She sat still, her hands clasped around the now almost-empty mug on the Formica table top, the lines around her eyes and mouth deeply etched into her dark skin.

'Yuh know how him was, Carly; him never talk about work or any of him business to me.' She dipped her lip in the tea, slowly, like older folks do, taking their time in every little everyday act. Her fingers remained clasped around the mug as she put it back down on the table, her eyes lowered, as if she was concentrating on its flower design. The murmur of the radio from the living room drifted through the silent space between us for a few seconds.

'Rico gone,' she said. 'God only knows why, and not'ing can ever bring him back.' Miss Ruby lifted her gaze to me. 'Whoever responsible for this could hurt you too, Carly. Yuh is all I have left, yuh must try and go on with your life, do your best. I think Rico would have wanted yuh to leave t'ings as they are.'

Our eyes were locked for a short moment. I understood what her feelings were, what she was afraid of, and I guess it made sense. Surely this was the voice of wisdom. But for a man, a certain kind of man, honour, duty, prevails on wisdom. For an obligation is just this: if you don't feel it, you don't have it. And I felt it. But I couldn't tell Miss Ruby this.

Nicola kept to her bed for the next couple of days. The doctor came and checked her out, said the baby was still alive, but she was weak and needed rest. I found her in the living room one afternoon, staring blankly at the TV screen. I could tell she wasn't following the game show. I sat with her, gently got her talking. I didn't know her, not really. We had just spent a little time together when Rico and her had met back home the last summer. Right now, I could see she was still too numb with pain and shock to concentrate on finding answers to my questions.

'He was so popular with everybody. He had a youth football team organized in the area, was working with locals on setting up a social club. It just opened two weeks ago. A lot of the kids around here looked up to him and he always had time to listen to their problems. Even the local policemen said he was doing a great job. Everybody loved him.' Then she started to cry again.

'What about friends, Nicola, did he have any friends, who was he moving with?'

'He never brought anyone home, except his cousin, Brenda. She came for dinner once, but she lives down south.' I tried to figure out who Nicola was referring to, but it didn't ring any bell.

'Nobody called here for him, never?!'

Nicola shrugged, wiping her eyes with the kerchief she kept tight in her hand. 'Only people he worked with, from the cab office or the security firm.'

I knew Rico had no friends as such back home. Acquaintances, yes; people he helped out or who did small jobs for him, relatives who called on him for help once in a while, but in truth he was a man who didn't let anyone get too close to him. You couldn't tell from the way he dealt with people, but he was the kind of person for whom trust was a dangerous concept. With him, trust was a matter of percentage. He'd trust a person up to a point, and was always ready for the eventual letdown or betrayal. No, in fact, when I really got to know him, I realized that betrayal was something Rico always expected and was ready for. And so he would never give anyone the chance to hurt him. That was the way he was and that's why he didn't look for friends and was quite happy to keep none. Except me.

'I know you're tired, Nicola, I know you feel sick, but I need to ask you certain things, so try and remember something, anything strange or unusual in the weeks before it happened. Did Rico say anything you didn't understand, did he act different ... did he seem upset or nervous?' Unless Rico had changed drastically from what he was before, I knew the answer would be 'No'. There was a man who could have a gun barrel against his forehead and still drop a joke, deadpan. Colder than Rico, you'd have to have steel nerves.

'No, I can't say I noticed anything.' Nicola shook her head. 'Except,' she started to think, 'I think he was looking for someone, the Friday before. He took me shopping, he called the cab office a few times.'

'What did he say?'

'He asked Loretta, the controller, for someone.'

'Who?'

'Loretta, she works there in the daytime.'

'No, I mean, who did he ask for?'

She shrugged.' I don't know. He just asked if someone had called in, he didn't mention no name.'

Just like Rico, I thought, never let anything slip.

I wasn't sure where to start. I didn't know the town, what Rico was into, who he was dealing with. I just had to retrace his steps, think the way I knew he would be thinking. But then two years is a long time, and London a totally different environment from Kingston.

Since I had arrived in London the day before the wedding, we had little time to talk. Nicola and him were into last-minute details, busy making sure all would turn out right. I could tell Rico wanted Nicola to be happy, telling her to stop stressing, that everything was taken care of, but Nicola seemed to be the worrying type anyway, more than the average woman planning her wedding. She'd keep asking him about the church, the dinner, the cake, all those little details that can ruin a wedding. The fact that she was pregnant made her even more tense. Rico smiled and tried to reassure her that all was under control. We spent the evening at home, finding a little time to talk after Nicola had finally gone to bed. I can't say I noticed anything strange or unusual about him. I had not seen him for two years but nothing seemed that much different about him.

I felt sure that, even if Rico had kept whatever serious problem he had from his wife and his mother, I was the one person in the world he would have told about it. Especially something that might be a question of life and death! I couldn't accept that Rico wouldn't have known he was in danger. This was a man who had spent the greater part of his life on the battlefields of downtown Kingston, had lived with and dealt death on a daily basis. Surprise simply doesn't exist for a man like that, for he's always ready for the unexpected. If he had known a shadow was over him, as he must necessarily have, why wouldn't he tell me about it? That just didn't make sense.

I let the matter go. No use stressing Nicola any further with painful reminiscing. I asked her whether there was anything she needed, anything I could do for her, but she simply shook her head. I felt like she wasn't really seeing me, like her empty eyes looked right through me. It made me feel bad just watching her, knowing the hell she was going through, her happiness having turned to horror in an instant.

CHAPTER FIVE

Off-Duty Enquiries

What does an ex-special police unit leader do when he retires and emigrates? Community work? I wasn't sure. At any rate, my first move wasn't to the local social club ...

The Alley Cat, Friday evening, warm and breezy. Beenie Man blaring out of the speakers onto the pavement where bunches of black youths were milling around, darting in and out of cars, some modelling on powerful Japanese bikes with pretty girls at the back. Home from home ...

I managed to slip through a gap to the busy bar and shouted out to get me a Budweiser. Fortunately the stocky brown girl back there could read lips, a useful skill in her position. I went back outside, leaned back against the wall of the pub and observed the plays. You didn't need to be a highly-trained narcotics agent to realise some dealing was going down. Two fairly fit girls in printed mini-dresses gave me the eye as they passed me to enter the pub but I kept a straight face. The descending night was cool, the music pumped right through me and the beer tasted good. But a couple miles away, Rico's cold body was boxed up and buried. That image kept my stomach knit up inside.

An hour and two Budweisers later, I had politely declined the offers from three 'vendors', made idle chat with a couple of drinkers and quietly ignored the inviting smiles of several sexy girls. I was wondering whether Rico ever even visited places like these, the way Nicola had described her late husband's lifestyle. And I could hardly walk around with his picture asking questions. After all, everybody knew about the previous week's fatal shooting by now.

There I was, a policeman without a badge on a strange turf, out to find the man who had smoked his best friend. A friend who had nothing but friends, from what his widow was telling me. But then, a wife is always the last one to know, and Rico would have kept her in the dark no matter what he was doing. He was good at that.

I noticed her because she was different. From ten yards away she was walking through the clusters of people gathered around the pub, looking straight in my face, or so it seemed to me anyway. Leaning back with my Bud in my hand, I kept watching her move my way, though I was sure she wasn't coming to me. Amongst dozens of girls in tight, revealing outfits, complicated hairdos and catchy make-up, girls who had gone out of their way to be noticed and desirable, she stood out. Yet her dark hair was simply tied up in a ponytail, and she wore nothing more than a baseball shirt and jeans. As she passed by a group of three ragga-looking youths standing a little way from me, three pair of hungry eyes followed her and stopped where she finally stopped. She stood there for a few seconds, said nothing. So I waited, still unsure what to expect.

'Hi!' she said.

'How you doin'?' I replied.

My mind was searching for a reference. I would have had to lose all the brain cells in my head to forget someone that pretty. Her accent was British, her voice pleasantly mellow. She was studying me, her large eyes staring into mine.

'You're new in town.' She asked, but it didn't really sound like a question.

'You could say that.'

'You're Jamaican, ain't you?' There was curiosity, and a little caginess in her voice.

I smiled, shook my head slowly. 'I try to pass as a Chinese, but it doesn't work.'

She laughed and two small dimples appeared in her lower cheeks. Her skin had the tone of honey, warm and smooth.

'I'm Joy,' she said.

'Joy,' I repeated. 'That's nice.'

'Not really,' she said, 'but that's what my mother named me.'

I smiled. Somehow I felt close to this beautiful stranger, a weird sense of déjà vu or whatever people call that. Playfully, I asked: 'You want to guess what my name is?'

She pouted a little, thinking. 'Hmm, Leroy? ... No? Winston? ... Everton?'

I was shaking my head, letting her go through the traditional Jamaican first name register. 'Carlton?'

I must have squinted. It was a rather common Jamaican name but still ... Joy waited, then a sly grin appeared across her face.

'Sorry, I cheated.'

'Eeh? How that?'

Joy waited a little, enjoying my puzzled expression, then 'I saw you at the wedding,' she said simply.

She wasn't smiling now, neither was I. We were eye to eye, completely oblivious to the music and movement around us. The mention of the wedding had cooled down the vibe for me.

'I didn't see you,' I said.

'I know, I was at the register office ...'

I nodded. I was going to ask, but she explained, 'I'm a friend of the bride.' A quiet pause, then she asked, 'How is she?'

'Not too well but she'll make it. The doctor was afraid she'd lose the baby but it looks like she's gonna be ok.'

'I guess that's one good thing. It must be really horrible for her.'

'True,' I said.

Somehow, it made me feel even closer to that woman I didn't know, the fact that we shared that painful experience. I had all but forgotten about the half-full beer can in my hand.

'Would you like a drink?' I asked.

'Ok, a Coke please.'

I left her and went to get her drink, using my height to call the barmaid's attention over the heads of the two rows of people crowding the bar.

'You come here often?' I asked Joy when we were both leaning against the wall.

'I don't go out that much. I came for a drink with a friend from work, before the crowd got here.'

We watched as an older man staggered out of the pub, cursing someone or something, trying to find his balance and the right direction, the one he was supposed to follow to get home. After a few yards towards us, he must have realized he wasn't going the right way, so he turned around, carefully, then shuffled along towards the opposite corner, still muttering to himself.

'Under his waters . . .' I heard the girl say.

'So, where you from?' I asked. It wasn't hard to tell she had grown up in London, but I was asking about her origins.

'I grew up here, but I was born in the West Indies.' Not in Jamaica, that meant.

'Really?'

'I don't sound like it, do I?' she smiled.

'No.'

'My parents brought me here from Guyana when I was five. I went to school here. I've lived in this area ever since.'

That sounded interesting. Music, beer, a pretty girl but my police instinct was still awake.

'You must know everybody 'round here, then,' I said, taking a sip of my beet.

'I know a lot of people, but I don't mix much.' She must have interpreted my eyebrow move as a doubting gesture, with

56

me meeting her amongst a pub crowd. 'Like I said: I don't go out that much. But once in a while, I need to relax.'

I nodded in agreement.

'We don't have this kind of weather very often in England,' she added.

'I come at the right time. I said, joking. Then I remembered the wedding, the reason I was here. I think Joy remembered it too because she fell silent for a moment before asking, 'What about you? You're married?'

'I was.'

'Ah!' she said, like she understood, but I could see she wanted me to expand on that.

'We tried but it didn't work out. And you? What's your status?' I asked.

The young woman smiled.

'My status?' She repeated the word. Her eyes looked away for a moment before she said, 'Well, I am ...' she searched for the right terms '... single by circumstances.'

'Oh.' I didn't feel like asking for any details. We talked about this and that for a while, cooling out as more and more people arrived, spread alongside the pavement with their drinks, enjoying the early evening. The night had fallen by now, warm, spiced with calls, horns blowing from the arriving vehicles, the sounds from the pub system blending in and around, swathing the scene. I was in no hurry to get back to the house where Rico's shadow hung over everything. And I felt I had best get a feel of the town, of this area, which had been Rico's stomping ground, his new home from home.

I caught sight of a droptop Saab turning into the busy road, parking across the way, opposite the Kentucky take-out shop next to the pub. It drew my attention first because it was a very beautiful car, red and black with chrome trimmings and a booming sound system that almost drowned the sounds from inside the pub. At the back, all tight dresses, showy hairstyles and jewellery, three fairly pretty girls were throned like catwalk models on a spree. Giggling, they got out onto the pavement, aware of the looks from many in the crowd, making a spectacle of it, visibly enjoying the attention.

The front-seat passenger, a squarely-built man with a broad brown face and an open tracksuit top over a vest and a heavy gold chain, had let the girls out. He was also enjoying the stares, looking like a rich heir with no worries other than finding an enjoyable and novel way to spend out some of his fortune. The man said a few words to the driver before leading his cargo of expensive-looking girls across the road and inside the pub.

I couldn't quite make out the driver's face underneath his baseball cap. He was leaning back in his seat, taking in the loud beat of a session cassette. Dark-skinned, slimmer-built than his friend, wearing a buttoned-up white shirt, he seemed uninterested in all the action going around him. I heard Joy ask: 'You know him?'

'Who?' I turned to look at her.

'That man, I thought you knew him, the way you're staring.'

I smiled. 'He probably looks like someone I used to know back home.' There was no question that the man was Jamaican, It was easy to tell.

'Maybe it's him,' she insisted. 'He's only been here a year or so.'

'Yeah?' I stole another glance at the driver, relaxing in his fat leather interior. There was something familiar about him, but then again, a man can look like another.

'He used to be in Canada, they call him Roddy.'

'Wha', he's a friend of yours?' I asked.

Joy shook her head. 'No, he ain't. But his friend, Boogga, the one who was with the girls, he used to go out with my cousin.'

'Yeah?'

'That was a couple years back ... he's a bad man.'

'Gangster?' I asked.

Joy shook her head. 'No, but he likes to beat up women.' She added: 'He's a pimp.'

I looked at the girl. 'It's a hard job.'

'That's not funny!' she said

'What about this one, Roddy. Is he a pimp too?'

Joy made a face. 'I don't think pimping can buy a car like this one.'

I didn't think so neither. Through the cover of the crowd, I kept glancing at the driver. I never forget a face or a physique, which is a serious plus when you happen to be a policeman. I couldn't help feeling I knew the man from somewhere, but couldn't quite place him. The name was nothing to go by; most men from back home, especially notorious ones, adopted another moniker once they got abroad.

Soon, Boogga came back to the car without the girls. As he got inside, him and Roddy had a short conversation, then they left. I turned as they passed, just in case. If I knew him, chances were Roddy knew me too and I preferred to keep one on him, you never knew ...

I spent another half-hour talking to Joy. She was enjoyable to be with, sounded knowledgeable on a lot of topics. I felt like she was in no hurry to leave, probably she found me interesting, or maybe she was just lonely. After a while, there seemed to be more space around us as people moved out in little groups.

Joy explained: 'They all going to Bluebird.'

'Bluebird?'

'It's a sound that plays early sessions in Stokie on Fridays. Everybody goes there after leaving here.'

'You goin'?' I asked.

Joy shook her head. 'No, I had a hard week. I'll go home and watch some TV before going to bed.'

'You live far from here?'

'Not really. In Wood Green. You know where it is?'

I said: 'No, but I'll find out.' Our eyes locked for a few seconds. She looked so serious all of a sudden.

'I won't give you my home number, but if you want to call me at work, that's ok.'

'Alright.'

Out of the small purse she carried, she gave me a card with her work and mobile phone numbers on it. I promised I'd call.

'How you getting home?' Joy asked.

'I'll get a taxi, but I need to walk a little first.'

'Don't get lost,' she said.

'I got your number,' I replied.

There was that look in her eyes again.

Back at the house, Miss Ruby was asleep in front of the TV. I woke her up and she went to bed. I got myself a snack and watched the end of a movie before getting some rest.

The next morning, I started checking some documents. I had got from Nicola the last few statements of their joint bank account. She didn't mind giving them to me. In fact, Nicola didn't mind anything, she looked so weak and tired. The statements didn't show anything unusual, only the income from the security firm, Nicola's salary from her nursery-care job paid in monthly, and the cash withdrawal and cheques to cover the expenses, mortgage loan repayment, etc. I made a note of the amounts paid in, just in case. I asked her for the phone bills, home and Rico's mobile, but she said she didn't know where he kept those. I eventually found them later when I spent some time going through Rico's desk drawers. There again, I didn't find anything that could have put me on track, like official letters, bills, receipts, contracts, etc.

The home phone bill was remarkably regular in that most of the numbers called were identified by Nicola as Nicola's sister's, her workplace, her dentist, the cab office, the security firm office, and a few others which didn't reveal anything odd.

Rico's mobile phone bill listed calls to pretty much the same numbers as those from the home one. It was amazing and expected at the same time. You couldn't get anyone more security conscious than Rico. As they say: once a policeman, always a policeman. Whatever Rico might have been involved in, he sure couldn't get caught through his phone calls! Yet, there was one call, placed the very morning of the wedding, only a couple of hours before the fatal photo shoot. The number had been left on the cell phone memory and didn't figure anywhere else. From what Nicola said, the code placed it in West London. I copied it and placed it in my wallet, for later use.

Amongst the pile of papers, I also found half a dozen Western Union and Jamaica National money transfer tickets, featuring amounts of up to a few thousand pounds. Most were addressed to Lucy or to Mimi, Rico's sister. I spent a little time meditating on this, since the income I had checked on the bank statements didn't seem to match that kind of expense. I would have to talk to Mimi later. The first thing to my mind was that that money wasn't from the same source of revenue. Here at least I had something to go on. But then, not everyone feels they should be totally truthful with their tax returns. I now needed to try and find out what kind of money was really coming from Rico's businesses.

Stuck between two bells, one for a cloth wholesaler and one for a shipping agent, the metal plate read RUFFNECK SECURITY. The three-storey building with aged brickwork squeezed between a pub and a kebab shop in a busy corner of Whitechapel. The early afternoon was mellow, with lots of people milling around the colourful market stalls. Once I had pressed the buzzer, and answered the query from a feminine voice, there was a couple of seconds silence until the door clicked open. The stairs, beside being narrow, creaked at every other step under my Clarks, up to the second floor. A bulky black youth with a half-mohican hairstyle and a Snoopy T-shirt stood on the landing. He mumbled 'cool' and passed me on his way down, the old wood groaning under his weight.

RUFFNECK SECURITY 'Please ring the bell,' it said on the door. I did and it unlocked from inside. The office was rather small, with a couch and two tall potted plants alongside the wooden desk and metal file cabinet. The back wall had framed pictures of various groups and individuals, members of the security team, photographed with entertainers. I didn't pick out Rico's face in any of the shots. The man was either picture-shy or modest.

'Good afternoon,' I said.

'Hi, please have a seat.'

Two dark eyes were scanning my face from behind the desk, a light-brown face framed by sleek black hair, clipped at the back. The features were clearly defined, pure, delicate and oriental. She wasn't smiling, just staring. So I stared back.

'My name is Carlton.' I said.

'I know,' I heard the woman reply. That must have made me look surprised, and it brought out her smile. 'I have been expecting you.'

'That's good!' I nodded.

The phone rang and the woman spoke a few words to whoever was on the line, very professional, her perfect English diction belying her foreign appearance. She was watching me while talking, and I was watching her too. I put her around twenty-three to twenty-five years of age. She put down the phone.

'Rico told you I was coming,' I said.

She took a little time before answering, I thought I saw something like a flicker of pain or distress in her eyes.

'He said you were to be his best man.'

'I was.' I could see she felt bad about Rico's death, but she didn't know how to talk about it to me.

'My name is Zafirah, with an "h",' she offered.

'It's a nice name,' I told her. 'I've never heard it before.'

'It's Arabic.'

I smiled. 'Nice. Are you an Arab?'

'I'm Bengali,' she said, then added, 'but I was born here.'

There was a little silence. I sensed she wanted to say something, didn't quite know how to start.

'You were Rico's best friend.' That wasn't really a question. I still found it strange to speak of Rico in the past tense.

'We worked together, back home. Yes, he was my best friend.' I could feel that she shared the pain that I felt.

'You come to ask me about the business?'

'Well, Zafirah.' I waited to see if she'd correct my pronunciation, but she didn't. 'There's a lot of questions I have in my mind, and I've got no answers so far.'

Her deep eyes shifted to the large plant to my left, then came back to focus on me.

'You're going to find out who did it.' Zafirah's statement, for it was a statement, took me a little by surprise.

'I intend to, yes,' I said, very coldly I realized.

'I know you will.' She was looking right into my eyes. 'Rico said you were very good at your job.'

What exactly did this young woman know about my 'job'? What did Rico tell her and how much of it was the truth?

'Tell me, how long did you know him?'

Zafirah pressed something on the computer keyboard in front of her.

'He offered me this job when this firm opened, almost two years ago.'

'Hmm, and where did you meet him?'

'Where?' Zafirah asked, 'Or how?'

I smiled.

'You really are a police officer,' she nodded. 'Well, believe it or not, the first time I met Rico he saved my life.'

I was just looking at her, waiting.

'No, I mean, really! It was just like a movie.'

'Yeah?' I raised my eyebrows. Her voice had picked up a note of excitement new to me.

'I'm telling you. Look: I'd been to a night class in Stamford Hill, I was living in Tottenham at the time.' She paused briefly. 'It was winter, one of those freezing nights. Okay, so I'm trying to get home, and there's these young guys, black guys, you know, just out of a pub. As I passed them, one of them called out to me but I just kept on going.

'So I walked on and these guys started following me. At first I thought they might just be going down the same road to the bus stop. They were talking loud and laughing, but I didn't really worry. Then, as I turned down to get towards the bus stop, they got closer behind me and started calling after me. I walked faster, so did they. Eventually I stopped because one of them had overtaken me. I was surrounded, you know?'

I nodded, interested.

'So, here I am, back against the wall, and these four guys, big enough guys, started telling me I was "dissing" them,' she stressed the term, 'that I thought I was too nice to talk to them.'

Zafirah, like she was going back to that moment, stopped and breathed out.

'I could see they had been drinking. At least two of them were quite menacing, very loud in the street. I told them to leave me alone, but they laughed and called me names, so I cursed them, I said they were cowards. There wasn't much people passing by, so I was getting kinda . . .'

'Scared?' I offered.

'No, not really scared, but I remember thinking I couldn't possibly fight them, so I was looking to run, if possible.'

I could relate to that, but she sounded brave.

'So, one of the guys came closer, grabbed me by the jacket. I kicked him in the leg.'

'Really?' I must have looked like I didn't believe her.

'I did, I wasn't going to go down without a fight!'

That impressed me. 'So, what did the guy do?'

'He cried out. I had winter boots on, and I was very angry by then, so I guess his shin felt it.'

'Didn't he hit you back?'

'Oh yeah, he did. He backhanded me, but the slap wasn't so bad, because I had started moving out of the way. I tried to run out, but one of them caught me by the waist and started to lift me up. I realized then I was going to get hurt.'

'And?'

'And ...' She was enjoying the suspense I could see the glimmer deep in her eyes.

'What happened?'

'What happened?' she repeated. 'Well, what happened was I was kicking and screaming, trying to get back down but that guy was strong, so he was holding me up. All of a sudden, I heard this voice saying ...' Zafirah changed her accent to sound like the voice. '"Put her down!" The guys heard it too, because everything stopped. I managed to wrestle out of this guy's bear hug. I saw this car, parked up, and there was a man standing there, just looking at the guys.'

'So, what happened next?'

Zafirah shrugged.

'Well, I moved towards the man, I just went right up to the car. He told me, very quietly, to get in, and I did.'

'And what did the guys do?'

'The tallest one, I remember he was the most drunk of the four, big guy, he said to the man ... to Rico, "What the fuck you want?"'

'Yeah?' I was interested by that answer.

'He said something else, very rude. Then he started moving towards the car. Rico was standing by the bonnet, very calm. I was sitting in the passenger seat, the music was still playing and the engine running.'

I mentally sketched out the scene. Classic set-up. I waited.

'Rico said something like: "It's best you go home and

find your own woman, friend; this one doesn't look like she wants you!"

'I was still a bit shaky but it sounded funny how he called the guy "friend".'

'And what did the guy do?' That was the part I had been waiting for.

Zafirah shook her head, a little smile on her lips.

'He cursed Rico, real bad words. Rico didn't move, he didn't answer. So the guy stepped up to the pavement, running like he was going to dive on Rico. I was a little worried. Rico didn't look that big to me, and the other guy looked really mean!

'The guy was swinging a punch at Rico, who still wasn't moving. Then, I see his right hand lift up from the side and I watch the big guy stop. He stopped moving for a second, then he just dropped down on the bonnet of the car, and that was it, he didn't move again.'

'Cold?' I nodded slowly, appreciative.

'Cold, I'm telling you. And then, his friend was just behind him now, with something in his hand. I couldn't see what it was, but I remember thinking it wasn't a gun because he wasn't pointing it. He was coming down fast, but Rico had seen him, so as he raised his hand, Rico stepped to the side and hit the man on the arm or the shoulder, I think. I heard the man scream, then he stopped because Rico had thumped him in the chest, with his tool, whatever it was. And that was it.'

'That was it?'

'Oh yeah,' Zafirah smiled 'The other two guys were still on the pavement. I don't think they wanted to get involved with the argument, not after the way their friends had been dropped! Rico didn't even look at them. He just walked to the car door and got in. The first guy was still spread across the bonnet, unconcious, so Rico just reversed the car a little, slowly, to get him off. The guy dropped to the floor and the car passed by and then we left. He drove me safely home. And he offered me the job.'

It seemed incredible to her, even now, you could tell. Zafirah was right: it was just like a movie! The phone rang; after a short conversation, she put it down and said, 'I need your advice.'

'My advice? On what?'

'Well, I am not quite sure what to do; I'm running a business but I haven't got a boss any more. Should I close down or keep running it, and if I do, who's going to get the jobs?'

I understood what she wanted to know. 'How does this work?' I asked.

'How? We provide security personnel to promoters, agents, mainly show business people. We cover public events, indoor or open air, as well as close protection for entertainers if required. We guarantee a professional service at the best rates.' Zafirah sounded like a TV advert.

'Is business good?' I enquired.

'We've never lost a customer. We're a reputable company, registered with the authorities. People always come back to us for more work. All our employees are screened and properly trained, definitely no "cowboys".'

'Who trains them?'

'Rico ...' There was a little silence, then Zafirah asked: 'Who's going to take care of business now?'

'So, tell me something: you know how to run things, right?'

She shrugged. 'I know how to deal with the administration, the day-to-day affairs. But it was Rico who went out and got the jobs. He knew a lot of people.'

I reflected, listening to her, that I would need to know these people she was referring to. Selling security services could lead to problems, especially dealing with show business characters, who can be volatile individuals, to say the least. Was it from this side the enemy came? From where she stood, Zafirah couldn't be aware of any troubles Rico might have come up against.

'Did Rico ever bring anybody here, people he did business with?'

'Not really. Once or twice he passed through with friends of his, but he usually left them in the car.'

'None of them ever come up here?'

'Only one time,' Zafirah conceded, after searching in her mind. 'He brought this man up to make a call to Jamaica. They didn't stay long.'

'Was he Jamaican?'

She nodded.

'Did he introduce the man to you?'

'He mentioned his name but I can't recall what it was.'

'Do you remember what he looked like?'

'Medium height, slim, dark-skinned, Indian-looking. I remember him because he was fresh.'

'Fresh?' Zafirah was using the term as we used it back home. I guess she was drifting towards Yard culture unawares.

'Yeah, he kept staring at me, so I asked him why.' Zafirah was digging up her memory. 'He said we would make a wicked "oriental" mix, me and him, because we had the same bloodline.'

I smiled. 'What did you say to that?'

Zafirah's eyes twinkled. 'I told him he was probably right, and if he could convince my father and four brothers he was a true Muslim, then we could arrange for the wedding.'

I laughed at her nerve. I was starting to appreciate the mentality of this little woman. But who could this man be and what was his relation to Rico?

'Did you hear what he was talking about on the phone?'

She shook her head. 'I don't listen to private conversations.'

'Yes, I understand, but you might have overheard something.'

'He didn't talk for long, and his accent was a little too strong for me. I think he was talking to a woman, something about money he was sending. I heard him mention a camp, Park something, he seemed to be sending the woman to see an officer, some colonel, I'm not too sure.'

'Well, you overheard quite a lot,' I teased Zafirah.

So, Rico let a friend of his use the phone to inform a woman he was sending money. He wanted to contact an officer. Maybe he was himself a soldier. That didn't amount to much. Another phone call came through, some employee of the firm.

'I'm going to let you work,' I said to Zafirah.

'When are you coming by again?'

I shrugged. 'In a couple of days time. I need to check a few things, look for leads.'

'So you want me to keep operating here?'

'As long as you get bookings, might as well do it. I will check around, try to contact some people to get jobs in, okay?'

Zafirah was looking at me curiously.

'What?'

She smiled. 'You're just like Rico said you was.'

I smiled at her. 'I guess it's a compliment.' Zafirah nodded. 'Yes, it is. Call me tomorrow.'

I said I would and left. Spinning in my head the few elements I had learnt, I spent a little time strolling through the area before jumping on a bus full of returning school children.

'He's on his way in. Have a seat.' Her name was Loretta, she was large and brown and sullen-looking as any minicab office controller might be.

I had had a brief conversation with Tips on the day of the wedding. Tips was a sergeant in the Jamaican Constabulary Force when I first started. Broad-shouldered and jovial most of the time, he was talkative and open; at least that's how he came across. He had got drafted to the special crime squad on the recommendation of an influential officer who happened to be his father-in-law. That was what I heard at the time. His reputation was that of a fearless and somewhat brutal man, doing his job with enthusiasm. As far as I recalled, Rico and him were never that close, more because of personalities than rank differences, I guess.

England had been good to Tips if weight was any way to judge a man's prosperity. We were roughly the same height but there had to be around eighty pounds weight difference between us now. As I watched Tips from the cab office window, getting out of a beige Ford it brought to my mind images of the same man springing out of a Jeep in his dark blue fatigues. Now he was wearing jeans and a yellow ganzee that hugged his stomach.

'Wha'ppen Carly?'

'Alright. I come check yuh. Yuh busy?'

Tips shrugged. 'Busy enough, but me ah de boss. I can always free up meself. Come, make we take a walk.'

I followed the man down the stairs to the street. The day was bright if not really warm, with shoppers and workers on lunch-break, school kids and loiterers, all milling around the junction area. A police van, white and orange striped, was parked on the other side of the road, checking on the driver, the young and black driver, of a new-looking Audi. Tips took me through a back street to a little cafeteria half-full with people. We sat either side of one of the square, plastic-covered tables at the back. The smell of fried food permeated the cafe. A waitress wasn't long in coming.

'Hi Bernie, how's it going today?'

Short and blonde, eyes that spoke of late nights and daily worries, she had her pen and notebook at the ready. The accent was thick and rapid, to me anyway.

'Fay, this is my friend Carlton from back home.'

The woman smiled at me. 'Hi Carlton, you're on holiday or you've come to join Bernie here?'

'Just on vacation, you know.'

'That's nice,' she said 'What will it be today, Bernie?' She seemed to like his name.

'Gimme the usual.'

'What about you, love?'

'I'm not really hungry.' I said. Fay seemed disappointed. 'I'll have a cup of coffee.'

'Right. Coming up.' The waitress left us. Breakfast had been some hours ago but something about the place told me to avoid its cuisine.

'Looks like you settle down alright,' I said.

'It wasn't easy at first, especially getting used to the climate. When the cold hit me the first year, I well wanted fe fly back to JA, trust me.'

'T'ings got heavy in the Force after you left, you must a hear 'bout it.'

Tips nodded but he didn't comment.

'Nobody ever find out who shot Barley . . .'

Tips licked his lips, glanced around the noisy restaurant room. Barley, his former partner in the Crime Squad, had been found shot through the back of the head inside the house of a known drug smuggler early one afternoon. Everyone knew it was Tips who tracked down the man and executed him the very next day. Nothing would have come of it a couple of years earlier but the incident was investigated by the newly established Internal Affairs. There were disturbing details, like Tips' partner having been killed from behind at close range, traces indicating his body being placed inside the house after the killing. Then there was the drugsman's body showing knife wounds, and his wrists with rope marks, all of which reflected badly on Tips' version of events. There were rumours that a sizeable stash of cocaine seized by Barley had disappeared. In any case, after the affair, Tips' behaviour worsened and his already violent temper turned into a compulsion to kill suspects without discrimination. Nobody wanted to work with him any more. Eventually, he resigned. Some people said he was a marked man and leaving the island was his only way out.

'I left all that behind, Carly. The past is dead and I'm alive. I never look back.'

I could feel there were no 'good old days' to reminisce about.

'So, Carly, what you gwan do now?' Tips asked, lighting up a cigarette.

'I want to do some shopping. What's the best place for that?'

Tips seemed a bit surprised; maybe he was expecting something else.

'I will take you around, man. Don't worry 'bout that.'

His food arrived so he concentrated on that for a moment, bantering with Fay like they probably did every day. I was glad I hadn't risked ordering but apparently Tips relished traditional British food. I watched him swallow a mouthful.

'I went to Rico's office yesterday,' I said. 'I want to try and find out if he had problems with some people he was working with. What do you know about that?'

'Boy, I don't really know about that side, you know. All I know is him was providing security people for most big entertainers when them tour over here.'

'You don't hear nothing from that side?'

'No ... This is England you know, Carly, t'ings different here. Rico get 'nuff contract for show and t'ings, maybe some other firm get jealous.'

I asked: 'What about woman? You t'ink him coulda mess with the wrong woman and some guy get jealous?'

'I don't know, him never tell me. Yet again, a man don't tell him friends dem everyt'ing.'

'Something is wrong here, Tips, something wrong.' I shook my head.

Tips put down his fork. He could see I wanted answers and he couldn't give them to me.

'Look, Carly, when Rico first come up, I was just starting the minicab office, so I give him a car and him work for a while.'

Tips wiped his mouth with a napkin, crushed it in his large hand and dropped it onto his empty plate. 'I try help him out.'

A pause, as Fay came by and picked up the bank-note Tips had put on the tab.

'After a while, him start move around and set up the security business. Him do a big summer show with Bungee and some other big promoters, him cover the Luciano tour. I know him supply the security details when the Monster crew come over. So, the man was mixing with big-timers, and since everybody know him from back home, dem rather use him than some local set dem don't know about. That's all I can tell you. I don't really mix with certain crowds, you know that.' Tips licked his lips, shook his head.

'It hurt me, Carly man, fe real. Hurt me to know seh the man leave Jamaica to get 'way from problems and come here to make life, and things end up like that.'

'We must find the guys who killed him Tips, me and you.'

Tips threw me a strangely unsteady glance. 'I left the police business behind, Carly, trust me.'

'You still think like a police, and you always will, I know that.'

Tips said nothing. His back strained the plastic chair back, his eyes surfing somewhere in the room behind me.

'Look, Tips,' I said, thinking of something. 'Maybe you prefer to keep on the side, I don't know how t'ings run here. I can deal with the digging up myself, just try and help me, tell me where to dig, okay?'

Tips sighed. 'T'ings different over here, man, I must tell you this. Back home, you is a police and you can do it your way. But over here, you a civilian, right? You can't go around stirring up things too much, you see what I mean?'

I didn't answer. That was precisely what I intended to do: stir up things. But I needed a direction, a lead, someone or something to put me on the right track. I sat back and told

Tips: 'I see Marsha once in a while, you know. She still 'round Patrick City, I think.'

Nothing moved on Tips's face. 'Yeah . . .'

That wasn't even a question. Visibly, Tips didn't wish to talk about the long-suffering wife he had left behind. 'Wilkins still there?'

I nodded. 'Still there.'

Knowing the relations between Superintendent Wilkins and Tips, I knew it wasn't an enquiry about his old boss's health.

'Tell me something; you never miss it?'

Tips looked at me like he didn't know what I was talking about.

'The Force, man; you never miss the work, the people them?'

He took a few seconds to say, 'I miss back home, yes.' His big frame started straightening up in the chair. 'But I don't miss working for nothing, risking my life for some foolish pay cheque at the end of the month. No, that I don't miss.' He paused, squinted. 'But as soon as I get enough to set up my own t'ing, I'm going back, back to my village and live easy, trust me, Carly.' Tips got up, stretched and yawned. 'Come man, I take you to the stores. We ha fe bush you up!'

The same message again, for the third day running. I put down the receiver and sat back. There must be a reason why Rico had called that particular number on the morning of his wedding. It was a home number, not a cell phone one. A woman's voice was on the answerphone but what was the nature of Rico's call: personal or business? If the woman was Rico's woman, from near or far, it would explain why the number didn't figure on the cell phone listing or the house phone billing? But then why call her from his cell phone on the day of his wedding? What was so urgent that made Rico transgress his own security measures?

I had been thinking about all that for a few days now but

I couldn't get any answers. My instinct, any policeman's best friend, kept coming back to it and so I now needed to find out who she was. Did Rico get through to the person or did he leave the number recorded to call it back later? I folded the piece of paper and put it in my wallet. I needed to find the address for this number . . .

A slight drizzle had hovered over the town all morning. I had been trying to find an excuse to go out but I was desperately thin on leads in my investigation. I could feel something out there that would answer my questions but I was getting tired of turning the few scraps of information I had over in my head. I was alone in the house; Nicola was down by her sister, Miss Ruby had taken a trip to the market.

The previous evening, I had spent hours trying to get hold of Tips but in vain. He wasn't working, from what Loretta told me, and I just couldn't get through to his cell phone. Since he had promised me he would dig around for me, I felt especially frustrated. Tips was the only contact I had, the only one I felt would care about the mystery of Rico's death. Yet I couldn't help thinking he wasn't eager enough, not as much as I was. Maybe he had guessed there were some very serious people behind this and he wanted to avoid getting targeted. But Tips had always been a tough man, known to be fearless, so I couldn't imagine anything that would stop him from finding his friend's killers. Yet people do change; maybe that's what happened to Tips. For me, danger in this mission meant nothing. Someone had killed Rico, not face to face like a soldier but from afar with a rifle, like a coward. As long as I was alive, I was going to be looking for him.

CHAPTER SIX

Town & Gully Runnings

Jamaica, January 1981

Aisha wasn't quite walking yet but she spent a lot of time standing up on her tiny legs, holding on to chairs and people's legs. She was a precocious child; you could see the intelligence in those dark eyes of hers, the way she fixed anyone coming to the house that she hadn't seen before. Apart from her mother, Auntie Pauline, Miss Simone (Jingles' mother) and me, couldn't no one hold her; she'd scream loud enough to deafen the intrepid who would try that.

The morning was a little grey, two women were passing by the veranda, arguing loudly about some domestic quarrel the previous night which had got out of hand and had the whole street involved.

'Yuh see if ah me, I'da chop him up!' one of them said with a mean tone.

Standing up in my lap, Aisha stared at the man standing at the gate. I wasn't much happier to see him than she was. Pushy was one of my area men; he had never done me no wrong but I got this 'feel' for people and somehow I had never taken to him. He was around my age, brown and flat-faced with shifty eyes and slouching shoulders.

'Wha'ppen sah?' I asked curtly.

'Lookman wan' see yuh,' Pushy said. He was Lookman's errand boy. I could see he expected me to follow him right there and then but I had planned to spend the morning working on my bike and didn't feel too pleased with the unexpected call.

'Tell him I soon come,' I told Pushy.

He waited a few seconds, like he was going to say something else, then he turned and left. Aisha watched him until he moved out of sight. That child had a way of staring that was beyond her years. I played with her for a while, tickling her tiny ribs, just to hear her laugh. I really enjoyed spending time with Aisha, and she was cool with me, never giving me any trouble or making noise like some babies do. I really didn't feel like moving out of the house, especially to go and see what it was Lookman wanted.

Since taking over the running of the area shortly after his release from Gun Court Lookman had been nothing but bad news. Apart from the half-dozen men directly attached to him, body and soul, no one felt too good about him being the new man in charge. No one said so, but the hold he had on people wasn't out of love but out of fear. The man was bad, in all senses of the term, even for the times we were living in. Lookman was one of those men who seemed to derive pleasure from others' pain. He was a cruel man in a cruel environment, thriving on it. Even though the post-election mood was one of peace and conciliation, officially anyway, the undercurrent of score settling was never too far beneath the surface. In the battle-scarred areas of Western Kingston, the rampage of the eradication squads had everyone edgy. Very few guns had been handed to the police to comply with the amnesty and the wicked methods of the squads created a climate of fear. Most of the main gang leaders had flown out to safer places in the States, Canada and England, especially those from the losing party. Former lieutenants like Lookman had been let out of jail and were now the new dons. Though most were young men who had started to relish the trappings of the political games and declared themselves committed to peace in the ghetto, many lacked the wisdom and aura of respect of the former leaders. Consequently, they ruled through strict discipline which was, more often than not, a very subjective thing.

And the balance of power had shifted too. The MP, Mr T., was still coming to the area like before. Him and Lookman seemed to get on well. But something in the relationship between the politicians and the area leaders had changed, all over Kingston. The influx of guns on the streets had brought about a sense of independence in the up and coming youths that wasn't there when weapons were under the strict control of the bigger men. Now, almost everyone had a piece hidden somewhere, within easy reach. But added to that, and part and parcel of the new situation, was the emerging drug trafficking. The ganja trade, which had helped alleviate the mental and financial pressure of the sufferers, was being gradually abandoned for the much more lucrative cocaine business. Though it must have been happening for a few years, confined to the 'higher circles', the drug trade was now taking over the poorer areas like a tidal wave, with its few success stories and many casualties.

I took up Aisha and carried her to Lucy in the back yard where she had set up a small sewing shop under the zinc shed. That girl could turn any little cloth piece she found into a something! She showed me a half-finished christening dress she was making for a friend's child, another project for a big money woman she had met. Lucy was making a little with her skill and felt good about it. That and her child was her world, plus me of course. And they were mine. I left, stopped at Uncle Bap's shop and got a peanut punch, answered a couple of greeting over the couple of streets I took to get to Rammy's bar. Everything happened around Rammy's bar these days . . .

The last table in the back room, in the far right corner, was where Lookman held court. Echoes from the radio in the bar were fuzzing through. I had passed two checks already in the form of little groups of soldiers casually hanging out in front of the bar and on the terrace itself. Peace didn't mean carelessness.

I saw Lookman, busy finishing a large dish of soup. The five men squatting in various corners of the old board room were not having breakfast. I sauntered towards the table, the way it was to be done for someone asked for by his boss but not running. I kinda nodded to Baz and Moneymove (or Move as he was more commonly known). From a chair to the left I could feel Pushy's curious gaze.

'Wha'ppen Carly?' Lookman interrupted his feast for a brief moment.

I said: 'Cool Lookman, wha ha gwan?'

He left off looking at me, dug up another spoonful. 'Ouno wait fe me round the bar. Me and Carly ha fe talk private.'

Even the three men dropping cards on a long bench near the entrance heard and got up to leave the room. I knew what it was going to be about and didn't like it, but I sat in one of the chairs across from the hungry man, a few feet from the table. Lookman swallowed a little round dumpling, chewed with application, his jaws swinging sideways in the action. With an eleven o'clock breakfast like this oxtail soup, he wasn't worried about lunch!

'The people them from last week want' see yuh again,' he said. Lookman wasn't the most subtle of men; he was very direct most of the time, except when he needed to work his way around someone that he had no grip on. I didn't feel too hot for a replay of the previous week's move but it was good money, although I assumed Lookman kept the biggest part for himself. He was looking at me, knowing how I felt about it.

'I don't know, yuh know.' I'm not a very talkative man, Lookman knew that. He could see the idea bothered me, but I had the right profile and he trusted me to fulfil that mission safely.

'Watcha man,' he told me after extracting a piece of bone from his mouth, sucked clean. 'Is money we ah deal with, right?! From we can deal with them people and make good corn, then ah so we gwan do it, yuh understand?'

I understood, but that was also one of the things I've always truly hated in Lookman: the way he asked you this question, making it sound like an insult, like he thought you must be dumb or something. So I said: 'I understand . . .'

The move was risky, which didn't worry me usually, but I felt bad about what I was doing, which never works if you are a soldier following an order. Drugs was a serious offence back then already.

'Alright.' Lookman said, getting hold of his dish. That meant he considered the matter done and expected me to make the move just the same way. He was holding the bowl with two hands, now, drinking down the thick soup.

'Is something else I wan' ask you, Carly.'

The dish was down on the table, empty. Lookman took his time to pull out his ratchet, selected a match from the box lying on the far corner of the table. When he had a decent toothpick, he got to work, methodically. With a sizeable gold chain glittering over his green and black ganzee, the man was observing me in a way that told me he probably was thinking of the best way to tell me something. For someone like him, rather rash, to take that time; it had to be something I wasn't going to like. Yet Lookman took me by surprise here.

'I gwan ask yuh something, but maybe yuh already hear 'bout it . . .'

I said nothing. My eyes locked Lookman's own for a while. He waited until all his top teeth were done. Then it came out: 'Certain people tell me t'ings 'bout your sister, yuh know.'

It wasn't at all anything I had expected. 'T'ings like wha'?' I asked coldly. Now, any fool knows you must always be careful how you mention a man's mother, sister or wife. Sister maybe more than wife even; it's the same blood after all . . .

'Maybe it's just rumours, dat is why I prefer ask yuh first.' Leaning back in his chair, Lookman wanted to sound fair but I couldn't help feeling he liked what he was doing just now.

I said: 'Den ask me nuh!'

'Yuh know anyt'ing 'bout your sister getting friendly with a police?' It was as unexpected as a stone hitting me but I didn't reel back. A few weighty seconds ticked by.

'Who tell yuh this?' I asked calmly.

Lookman shrugged, dug the space between his bottom front teeth. 'Just people, yuh know how not'ing never stay secret.'

I could hear two things in what Lookman had just said: he wanted to protect his informer, and he believed what he had been told. I inhaled deeply.

'I don't love dem kind ah talk, yuh know, sah.'

'Yuh t'ink me love to hear dem t'ings deh, star?!' It wasn't sympathy, more like disguised sarcasm. Since I kept silence while taking in the impact of the allegation, he added: 'Maybe ah rumour still . . .'

I didn't like the tone of that, didn't like the casual expression on Lookman's face. The implications of such an accusation were serious. I said with a blank voice: 'Anybody spread dem kind ah rumour better know whe dem ah do.'

Lookman had finished picking his teeth clean, he dropped his elbows on the table.

'Yuh know seh me ah fe check it out still, right?'

I hadn't moved. We sat across the table, gaze to gaze. This was the don, but this was the accusation and it didn't matter right there and then who was what. I could have sworn I read a brief twinkle of pleasure in Lookman's eyes. I asked very quietly, taking my time: 'So, tell me somet'ing, sah . . .'

My stare slid over to the market scene painting on the white wall of Rammy's back room, then back on spot.

'. . . Somebody calling my sister a informer, ah dat?'

I felt my body tense and cold with anger, my head light.

I'll never know whether Lookman would have answered, I was the one to break the silence that followed my question.

'. . . Because I ready fe answer dem any time.'

I got up. Lookman's eyes were narrow on me. I heard him say deeply:

'Watcha now; yuh betta cool down, y'hear?'

I don't often lose my cool, but I was aware my voice had risen up one level. I stood where I was. Lookman was a bigger man than me, and as my 'don', someone who could sentence me right there and then. But that meant nothing to me in the circumstances. I looked straight at the man, told him without a hint of expressed threat:

'One t'ing with me, y'know sah: when it comes to my family, I take it serious.' I paused but kept the eye contact. 'So anybody try disrespect dem ha fe deal wid me.' I had said what I wanted to, and it didn't matter what Lookman felt about it. I saw him push out his mouth like he was thinking about something, or holding back from saying something.

'We deal wid this later,' was what came out. The voice was almost dismissive of the matter, yet I could read on Lookman's face he hadn't liked my challenging him. I turned and walked out, left the bar the way I had come, without looking in no one's face. I could feel eyes on my back though, all the way out onto the avenue.

The roasted black breadfruit was still too hot to peel, so Prim lay it aside and got back to stirring the rundown on the stove. Sitting on the house steps, I sipped some more of the bush tea she'd boiled for me. I watched her moving around effortlessly, her dark blue cotton dress shaping her young and full body. It wasn't hard to let go of the bad thoughts that bugged my mind and drift into a lighter mood. Prim always had that effect on me, her mere presence instantly chasing away any worries and negative vibes I might had. It was just a bit harder this morning; I couldn't quite dismiss the bitter taste left by my 'conversation' with Lookman. I hadn't explained anything to Prim yet but she knew me well enough. I had marched into her yard half an hour before, after stopping at home and she had seen right away I wasn't feeling good. She didn't ask anything though, just sat me down, got me a hot drink and continued sorting out lunch. Her mother was away visiting a sick relative in the country so Prim had to take care of her two younger siblings and her father. From over the common wall, a woman voice called out: 'Beg yuh lickle oil, Miss Prim; me run out.'

Prim went to deal with her neighbour, Mrs Beckett, a short, brown and very nosy woman whom everyone called 'red bucket' but only behind her back, for she had a very bad temper and two very big sons. I finished the tea, leaned back against the doorframe. It had been raining heavy earlier that morning but now the heat was coming up. The initial cold fury I had felt had subsided but I didn't feel any better. I couldn't help the words running over and over in my mind, insistent, insulting, but I knew myself well enough to keep calm and stay in control of my reaction. That was something you learn very early when you grow up where I grew up, else you don't last too long. So I had come to see Prim, because she always knew how to help me make sense of things in times of troubles.

She finished cooking the lunch, served it, watched me eat like she always did. Prim was eighteen but her ways made you feel she was older than that. I had heard her family say on several occasions that she had the look and the attitudes of her grandmother on her father side. That's why they had nicknamed her 'Prim', like her. Louise was her first name, but I preferred the other one.

'So, who upset yuh now?'

I had finished my plate. Prim had cleared up everything and washed and dried the dishes. She was sitting beside me on the concrete steps. She had waited until then to enquire because she knew, on an empty stomach problems often seem worse than they really are. I kissed my teeth, went to the standpipe at the back to rinse my mouth. Once I sat back with the glass of Kool Aid she'd prepared for me, I briefly summed up the situation to Prim. As always, she listened quietly, not reacting in any way. Prim was someone you could tell the most unexpected news to

84

and she would just look straight at you with those dreamy eyes of hers, and not utter a word until you finished. Then she'd asked what she needed to. Wise beyond her years.

'Yuh talk to Lucy?' Prim asked after she was sure she had heard all I had to say. Lucy and Prim were the same age, had even been in the same class for two years in primary. Though they weren't best friends, they got on alright and Prim would come to the house to visit me quite often.

'I just come from there.'

'Whe she say?'

I took down some of the Kool Aid.

'She say Lookman try put argument to her 'nuff times and she brush him off, dat's why him start turn against her.'

Prim said nothing for a while, then finally: 'Dat man wicked.'

'Him better know who him ah try diss, yuh see me?' I said sombrely.

The way I felt about that business, knowing now the real reason behind that malicious rumour, I could have done something drastic and my face must have mirrored my state of mind because I heard Prim say: 'Nuh badda go an' do him not'ing, y'know Carly. Just hol' it down, your time will come.' She knew I wasn't a violent person but certain things could get me real cold-hearted. This was one of those things.

'But yuh nuh understand how this t'ing go. From people start believe seh Lucy ah informer, somebody will hurt her. Lookman don't have to do her not'ing; him just set her up.' We kept quiet for a while, the early afternoon sun hopped in and out of the small white clouds still spotting the blue sky. Somewhere in the distance, three long bursts of a siren wailed.

'Everybody loves Lucy, man. Him cyan deal wid her dem way deh.' Prim said with conviction. Then she added, a little lower: 'But it's true seh ah long time him ah look her still.' I turned from my inner meditation to my girlfriend.

'How yuh know dat?'

Prim shrugged. 'Ah long time him ah watch her, but him ha fe cool after she get with Jingles.'

And I had never even had a clue! Now I could understand the man's motivation. It was very much in the nature of Lookman to take revenge on Lucy for spurning him, and quite clever too was the way he was going about it. Yet he had not taken into account what I might do. Or had he? Strangely enough, the next thing Prim said sent me even further into introspection. It was almost like she had read my mind.

'It's not just Lucy him going for, yuh know, Carly.'

Though it hadn't come to me right away, upset as I was about my sister, I was starting to link up the whole connection. Prim was doing the thinking for me. She was looking into my eyes.

'Lookman never liked the way Jingles take yuh up as fe him "right hand", yuh must know that. T'rough yuh ah yout' to him, yuh shouldn't get pon dem level deh. So when Jingles take up Lucy, dat vex him even more.'

I didn't answer anything. It all made sense. As far as I remember, although she made a point of not asking me about my business, Prim had always warned me about trusting Lookman.

'Well, it looking like the right time come,' I said. I had made up my mind that if Lookman was planning to take me out, he would have to pay the price. Yet I guessed he wouldn't come up and face me himself. Though I had many friends, there would always be someone to do the dirty work for him. After all, he was the don.

'Yuh cyan take him on, Carly. Too much people deh 'round him.' Prim's face showed concern. She knew I wasn't a fool to go and act out of blind anger but then again I wasn't afraid, for sure. It would be better for me to take the initiative, I thought. I didn't like the idea of waiting for the hit. I wasn't going to sit here and let it happen.

'I have to move Lucy and Aisha out.' I said, working out

things in my mind at the same time. I had already switched to the war mode.

'No man, this is your spot. Anyhow yuh do that, is like she do somet'ing.' Prim put her hand on my arm, shook me gently so that I turned to face her. Prim's youngest brother passed by on his way to his lunch, I hardly noticed him.

'Lookman cyan touch yuh just so,' Prim pointed out calmly. ''Nuff people rate yuh round yah.'

I looked at her. I knew she was afraid deep down. In these times, you might be in your yard talking today and in your grave silent tomorrow, as they say. It was as simple and as frequent as that. The way Lookman had me set up, what was I supposed to do? Prim wanted to keep me alive, I knew that, so I had to listen. She might be a woman but she was braver and smarter than many men I have known. She told me: 'Just go and talk to Barky first.'

I had to admit it was sound advice. Lookman might have worked his way up to the position he now held and he acted like he was in charge, but even he had to consult with Barky before taking major decisions. The old man had been a tough area leader in the fifties, had known the fathers of all of us and seen us grow up in the neighbourhood. Though he was over sixty now and afflicted by failing eyesight, Barky was still very sharp and nothing escaped him. He was one of the survivors, one of the few who could still talk about the old days, before politics took over and split the ghettos in two. Prim was right; I had to talk to Barky.

Barky and I went to see Lookman. We were us three in the old fenced garden at the front of Miss Daisy's place. I say garden because it was, a cramped little 'bush' place on a few square yards of 'Town'. Pear tree, banana, guinnep, Miss Daisy even had a custard apple tree in there. She was getting too old to tend to everything herself, though. You had to go through the lush yard to get to the small fowl yard at the back of the house. Lookman liked to retreat there with only a few men with him. Miss Daisy was his 'step grandmother-in-law', as he called her ... He didn't want to show open disrespect to Barky, you could see that, but Lookman was basically telling him that this was 'his ground' now and him alone 'run t'ings'. I told him up front that I would not disrespect a man like him but anyone trying to slander my sister would have to deal with me. I had talked to her and I 'responsed' for her.

Barky didn't want to talk too long with Lookman, I could see that too. It was known that the new man on the block was not his 'flavour' because he didn't like either the gratuitous brutality or the new preoccupation with narcotics of the youth he had seen grow up since babies. Lookman called him father, like all of us did, but never came to him for advice. Baz and Kickers, two close 'associates' of Lookman's, had eased out to the fence to let us sit and talk it out but it was obvious they remained within earshot. I had no secrets anyway.

I made sure I repeated what I'd heard from Prim, as an unspecified rumour so as not to be confrontational, and pointed out that my sister was a young mother who should be left alone. Lookman was a good talker but I caught the fleeting cold look in his eyes. Barky said that we were then all agreed that it was a misunderstanding and that Lookman was a man who knew better than to listen to malicious gossip. I said I kept no grudge, that it was my duty to stand up for my family. Lookman didn't insist, said it was certainly a mistake and that it was also his duty to keep things clean in the area. The way he said 'clean', I didn't like it. There was something in his tone. Anyway, Barky and I left Miss Daisy's place and went back to his yard. He told me not to worry too much. Now that the various sides to the story had been aired, Lookman would have to ease off to avoid the build-up of bad feelings a side-taking amongst his 'flock' would provoke. There had to be more pressing business to attend to.

Barky had me sitting down in his modestly furnished but clean living room, on his old red cloth-covered spring divan until after sunset that day, relating to me the way things used to be in the heyday of the western side of Kingston, before the times of my own father. Barky could tell a story though! That man would have you hanging to his words, craving for the details of the crazy tales he had in his grizzled venerable head. No matter what you had waiting out there, there was no way you'd leave until the outcome, whether you were young, middle-aged or old. I've seen the roughest of the hardbitten men of our times laugh like little schoolboys at some of the coarsest of Barky's larger-than-life stories. You need laughter somewhere in your life, especially when darkness grips your insides and you feel like doing the worst. Barky knew that, and I laughed with him that evening, relived with him some of the wild hours of his life.

Then I went home where Lucy and Aisha had sunk into sleep on the little couch. Aunt Pauline had covered them up, then dozed off on the veranda chair. She insisted on making me something for supper. I ate, took time to sit on the veranda after, mulling things over. That's how I deal with things. I turn them over and over in my head, look in every crevice and corner, lift every stone, just to make sure I'm not overlooking anything, being careless. I locked up and went to brush my teeth, got ready for bed. In the morning, I still had to deal with my bike.

A week later, I rose early and by six I was riding down the highway heading for Westmoreland. I had called Wilton, my associate down there, the previous evening and he told me he was ready for business. Wilton was Jingles' cousin, who farmed the crops of sensimillia he'd export. I had got to know him well through the runs I had done with Jingles, taking care of his ganja enterprise. When he died, I had kept things going with Wilton. I didn't have all the contacts needed to handle the export side of the trade yet but the little network I had organised to supply various outlets in Town kept money coming in for me and the family.

The tension between me and Lookman had gone no further. He treated me no different than before, although that meant absolutely nothing with someone like him. Everyone knew he was a two-faced, slippery somebody, who would smile at you while plotting your demise. But then I wasn't naive either so I kept up my guards and tried to make the best of a bad situation. I did the drug run for him downtown, got him his money and he paid me what he thought was right. I didn't argue about the amount; I just wanted to avoid depending on that sort of income and anyway, I had my own runnings. Lookman knew I had picked up some of Jingles' ganja trade. He knew where it was at but Wilton had never liked him or trusted him, so that side was closed to him. Anyway, like many up and coming rankin's, his sole interest was the blooming cocaine trafficking and the quick multiple returns it brought.

I got to Grange Hill just before eight thirty, having made one stop on the way to drop off a little money to an elderly aunt in Old Harbour. Wilton's wife told me he had left for the farm around six, so I followed a youth called Maximouse up the dirt trail leading to the plantations. The sun was warm already, the twenty minute walk had me breaking a little sweat. We reached the little bamboo cabin where Wilton's workers took turns to sleep, two by two, to guard the young plants against pirates and thieves. A dreadlocked youngster I knew as David was busy boiling some cornmeal over the fire, a small stick of herb blocked in the corner of his mouth. Maximouse led the way through the six-feet-tall herb tree clogging the patch of land around the cabin until we arrived at a small clearing lined up with smaller, greener plants. Wilton was checking his prime crop personally, handling the spindly-looking trees one by one, plucking a leaf here and there. He motioned me to come over, handed me a small bulging bud he had just carefully plucked from one of the peppermint-like scented stems.

'Look 'pon de red bits dem!'

Though top-grade herb is farmed in many parishes of the island, somehow you could hardly get better than the strand that grows on Westmoreland's rich dirt. Wilton was more a scientist than a simple farmer, having been raised by his ganja-farmer father who had taught him all he knew about the intricacies of producing the most potent female herb prized by 'gourmet' smokers all over. On those regular visits, I had got to learn much more about choosing the right herb. The funny thing is that I don't smoke myself. I tried, like most youths do, but it's not really the thing for me. I'm not really a 'good' drinker either! On the two occasions I really followed friends and got drunk, I ended up in terrible fights. Anyway, I always used to go up and choose my bags, then I'd sent back a team of youths, to bring it into town through various 'safe' channels. Despite the roadblocks, the herb always got into town, even when things were real hot. The few times where the tightness of the clampdown on the city actually made herb hard to find, I think there were even more casualties than usual. Right now, the vibe was calm and I expected my merchandise to hit the stores by the following week.

So I followed Wilton along the rows of sweet-smelling sensimillia, until he was satisfied all was well with his babies. The main January crop was already bagged up. This one was a second, smaller batch which Wilton would mostly keep for himself and his neighbours. For a herbman like Wilton, business and pleasure were two different and separate things! He gave a few instructions to the two men clearing another patch of ground a little higher up, then we trodded back up towards the cabin. Wilton was a short, muscular youth in his early twenties, well-known and well-liked in his countryside. His mother and Jingles' mother were sisters. One had moved to Town on marrying, the other one had stayed in the country. They looked quite alike. When you saw one, you'd see the other. Even Wilton had many traits from Jingles, I could tell. We used to get on real well. I sat down with him, Maximouse, David and Wilton to deal with the porridge. Or rather, the porridge dealt with me, dropped in my stomach, sweet and heavy, sent me to sleep later on in Wilton's house!

Wilton already had my herb cleaned and pressed, tight and compact under a truckjack, in bags for me. We had agreed on the deal, fair both ways as usual. Once we got back down, Wilton asked me whether I wanted to come with him to a show where his brother Billy was singing. I had met Billy before; a calm, intense, serious-looking youth. Once you got to know him and he got to know you, Billy was a very nice person, very honest and a good friend to have. Him and Wilton had less than a year's age difference, they were brothers and brethren, all the way. I had planned to get back to Town that evening but I thought about the suggestion. Wilton explained it was a local promoter, another ganja trader, who had set up the event. The bill featured a few guest celebrities, plus local artists. Dubbed the 'Roots United Festival', the show sounded promising, so I said I'd come along and leave the next morning. We spent the rest of the day sipping juice, eating ital food and exchanging points on the state of the island. The country areas had suffered much less partisan violence than Kingston. Even in the larger towns, things had been contained. But every youth gathered around me that afternoon knew of the place I lived in. Though they tended not to trust a 'townman' that much, due to the dishonest behaviour of some, Jingles' introduction was all I had needed and over the years I'd known them they were all good to me.

Around five thirty, before sunset, Wilton parked his Lada in front of Billy's gate. The two had the same father and had grown up in the same village. Their two mothers never actually 'socialized', from what Wilton explained to me, but Billy's mother loved Wilton dearly. Billy wasn't even home right now. His mother, after grabbing and holding Wilton in her sizeable arms for a hug, said he had gone to the barber's around four and she hadn't seen him since. Wilton laughed and said that, no matter how long Billy spent in the barber saloon, his hairstyle would never be as pretty as his own. Billy's mother made a playful grab for Wilton's short locks under the beret he wore. Billy showed up around six thirty, found us eating cake and drinking soursop juice near the little outdoor kitchen at the back. He didn't have much of a haircut, nothing that would take two hours to do anyway. He greeted me warmly, said he was glad I was coming along to the show, that he was going to get ready and 'soon come'. We left the house after eight.

Wilton only knew one way to drive: fast. I was something of an expert driver in Town, but the speed at which he sent the Lada around some of the bends above the deep drops of the hilly country, in the darkness, had me wondering whether the half-smoked stick of weed in his mouth hadn't impaired his judgement. But Billy seemed calm, so I got used to it. Billy had explained to me that the show we were going to was organized by a friend of his who had insisted he, Billy, should make a guest appearance. He said he wasn't into the 'fame business', he only sang for the love of music and the upliftment of people. Strictly culture, he said. Dressed in a silky light blue shirt and grey pants, Billy looked every bit a successful performing artist. His grey felt hat, a present from a friend back from the US, sat on the rear window shelf. Right now, he was busy relating with brio an encounter with a policewoman earlier in the week which had Wilton laughing hard.

Once we had crossed the border into St Elizabeth, it didn't take us too long before we entered Braes River, where the show was happening. The lines of cars, customized vans and big bikes showed the promoter had done a great job. I identified quite a few vehicles which had made the trip from Kingston. We found a space a few hundred yards away from the gate. A booming bass line drew the crowd towards the fenced-up area like a magnet. All around the gate, corn, fried fish and jerk chicken vendors heckled and stirred up the atmosphere with their colourful jibes to each other in good-humoured competition.

'It's a big show!' I said, impressed, as we walked towards the lit-up area around the entrance.

'Yeah man, 'nuff artists deh pon the bill,' Billy confirmed. He was looking left and right as he leisurely walked on, the felt hat pulled studiedly over the left side of his head. Dressed as an artist, he walked like one, unhurriedly, making sure people noticed him as he passed, his face a mask of satisfied indifference. After all, he was a guest and those who didn't yet know this soon would. He answered, with a slight nod the greetings of a young man astride a motorbike. Wilton was busy screening the noisy crowd for pretty girls, true to himself. There were many to admire, it must be said, all glittering in their sequinned dresses, colourful leggings, large earrings and elaborate hairdos.

Once we reached the gate, Billy took one brief look at the line of ordinary fee-paying revellers and decided this was not for him. Wilton and I followed as he stepped past a dozen people and came to a stop right in front of a rather tall and lean man with a holster-style leather pouch around his shoulder. Clean-shaven with slanted, alert eyes, the gateman picked up the banknotes handed to him by a bearded man in a green shirt and pushed them inside the pouch. Swiftly, he then tore a small paper ticket from a pad on the table in front of him and gave it to the man, who stepped inside without a word. On the other side of the purposely narrow entrance, two other men stood casually, talking and smoking cigarettes, apparently unconcerned by the whole thing but anyone observing them long enough would have noticed that nothing happening in a radius of fifty yards around the gate escaped their attention. A keener look around the empty beer crates behind them would have spotted the canvas travel bag neatly concealed there. This might be a country dance but this was Jamaica, the land where the unexpected is always at hand. Next in the line was a group of three young women, but before money could change hands, the thin gateman stopped to throw a hard look at the man with the hat standing in front of him. Because he couldn't make out the face and because that meant the man wasn't ranked in the clans of entertainers and top men whom he all knew, the gateman's tone was less than cordial when he asked: 'Wha'ppen, sah?'

Billy was a nice person, not especially aggressive by Jamaican standards, but he had never liked disrespect and that tone of voice and stare were far from friendly. The group of girls plus the others in line behind them were all looking at him now, especially so because he had passed them over and was not being let in with the acknowledgement due to a celebrity. The two men on guard were also watching, although their conversation hadn't stopped.

'Ah me, man: Billy Bee.' Billy said, his voice expressing some surprise at not being recognized but not angry.

The gateman's eyes drifted to Wilton and I, then right back to that 'Billy Bee' he didn't know and had apparently never heard of.

'Look now, star. Ouno haffe get back ina de line, seen?' Whether it was the indifference of his tone of voice, the way he switched his attention back to the next in line or the collective 'ouno', which denied any distinction to him specifically, but something about the gateman's attitude had just got Billy stirred up inside. Added to that was the little guffaw from one of the young women behind. Billy switched stance before letting out.

'Listen man,' he dropped coldly. 'I man due fe appear pon stage tonight as a special guest, and I don't like the way yuh a handle me, y'hear. Better yuh check with de boss before yuh get me vex in yah, seen?'

Spoken loud enough over the ambient noise, together with a blank stare from beneath the rim of his hat, the remark cooled the temperature down a few degrees. I saw the tall gateman's face harden, his lanky frame straighten up some more. Visibly, he was a little touchy. The two men a few yards away on the other side hadn't moved but their eyes scanned our three faces for a sign, something which they might recognize. I thought one of them stopped on me a little too long ...

'Seh wha?' the gateman spat, his tone very unfriendly this time.

Billy wasn't moved by his threatening attitude. The guy had 'dissed' him, the way he saw it, and he wasn't about to give ground. That was Billy; you could have stuck the barrel of a shotgun against his temple, if he felt he was being wronged he was going to speak out, and that was that. Behind him, Wilton was already edgy. I watched in silence, alert. I didn't think it wise to intervene, but didn't wish the argument to go too far. No one in the waiting line was making any comments.

'Skippy, hol' on!' The voice of one of the two guards prevented the exchange from going any further. I guessed that the man who had spoken had some kind of authority over the gateman who just stopped short but kept staring, hostile. Impassive in his oversize printed T-shirt, the man produced a two-way radio, out of thin air it seemed, and proceeded to get in contact with someone somewhere. After a short exchange, which we couldn't hear from where we stood, he looked at Billy.

'Is alright, yuh can go in,' he said calmly.

Skippy didn't like that at all. How could that be, and he didn't know him as no celebrity? He tried to get one over all the same.

'Fe him friend dem mus pay the rate,' he growled, his eyes hard us.

'Cool Skippy man, low dem.' The man with the radio insisted without raising his voice. The scornful glance Billy dashed Skippy's way as he passed him was something to see. Wilton and I followed him, stepping confidently. I was relieved that the confrontation didn't go any further; I was only here to enjoy myself, after all. Once inside, we soon forgot the unpleasant incident and settled down in a corner not too far from the stage, where much comings and goings were taking place. Speakers, amplifiers and instruments stood at the ready, technicians and helpers were busy making last-minute checks. A Heineken in hand, I relaxed, taking in the crowd around me, absorbing the pumping of the bass, my ears tingling with the calls of the men and the laughs of the girls. It felt great to be there.

We were mingling amongst a small group of Billy's friends,

exchanging remarks, sharing jokes. A few of the women around us deserved special mentions for their beauty and I wasn't insensitive to them. Yet, unlike Wilton, who as an inveterate 'hunter' had already made a move on a short girl in a clingy dress, I kept cool. My style was less 'up front', more subtle, working on the eye-contact type of thing. Besides, in a situation like this one, it would be unwise to make a move without first checking the intended target wasn't someone's woman. You learn not to make that kind of mistake. From where we stood to the right of the stage, the area seemed to be mostly taken over by artists and their crews. I recognized one or two unmistakable faces, artists of some fame from Town, a few others originally country-based, all looking relaxed. No one was fussing and that is the way it should be in Jamaica. Everyone is a star and a star is just the boy next door who knows only too well that his strength is his background, his roots, be they a country hamlet or a ghetto lane.

I watched Wilton pulling on a large cone of odorous ganja, the smoke cloud from his spliff drifting upwards to join the larger one that covered the entire arena. Though I was probably one of the few men not indulging in the herb, just passive inhaling had me feeling like I had consumed an ounce of the stuff all by myself.

'Watch dem now!' Billy called my attention to a group of three steppers warming up the crowd with their wild antics on stage. When they had done their number, the MC, a pudgy man with a moustache and a bright red silk suit, bounced onto the stage, seemingly unable to stand still for a second, pacing up and down, shouting, deejaying, singing and talking in his microphone all at once. He got an impatient response from the audience, assured them that the artists they were shouting for were about to 'blow up' the place tonight. Behind him, the musicians had walked on the stage and started getting ready, rim shots from the drummer punctuating the MC's cleverly incoherent speech.

'Lo-o-o-o-rd ... have mercy!' The MC's shout introduced the beginning of a popular rhythm by the band. He jumped on the spot twice, twirled like a dervish, spread his arms like a crucified figure and almost collapsed right in the middle of the stage. The drummer interrupted the track and then restarted it right away. Thousands of voices rose in pleasure. I literally felt the thrill through my body. Beside me, Wilton shouted like he'd been stung by a wasp.

'Are you ready?' the MC asked loudly, as if he could have any doubt about the state of the crowd.

Wilton said something in my ear but I hardly heard that. I guessed it had something to do with the brown-skinned girl he was holding on to. Billy's head was bobbing in time with the drop of the bass. All around them, no one was keeping still, the way the vibrations had taken over bodies and minds. All the faces radiated undiluted pleasure. Even the hardest men in the crowd, some of whom you could tell were original roughnecks, looked like Sunday morning church faithful in rapture. Looking back, this was one of the nicest shows I ever have been to, because it felt so warm and together, so brotherly.

Half a dozen artists 'blew up' the stage, then I noticed Billy starting his progression through the crowd towards the right side of the stage. Wilton didn't move from where he was. I cooled off right by him, watched Billy's head, the back of his felt hat disappear around the back of the stage.

'Him don't even look nervous; dat good!' Wilton said in my ear.

'Why, him usually get stage fright?'

Wilton took a draw from his spliff before answering. 'Tonight is the first time him ah go pon stage.'

The MC came back on, looking more and more disorderly, and started jibing and joking. He got everybody excited, because the show was so nice and everyone so in tune, it just couldn't be interrupted too long. After a last joke, the MC asked:

'Ouno ever hear a bee sing yet?'

They must have thought it was yet another joke. Someone shouted 'Riddim!'

'Well, tonight ouno gwan hear it, 'The MC paused, glanced back towards the side of the stage.

'Jamaica. I bring now on stage, live and direct ... the new singing sensation ... exclusive ... the man called ...'

He paused for effects while various calls erupted from the impatient crowd.

'Please welcome ... Billy Beeeeeeeee!!!!!!!!'

The drummer slapped the hi-hat then let out a powerful roll. The bass rumbled, fat and deep, kicking the rhythm alive. On stage walked Billy, looking good. I looked at Wilton, who nodded and grinned; his girl seemed happy too. The MC shouted the name one last time, lest anyone forget, greeted the artist warmly then bounced off the stage. There stood Billy, mike in his right hand, gazing at the faces. The band was pumping hard, waiting for the man to get into his first song. I was waiting for Billy to start, like hundred of others. The popular Shank-I-Check rhythm already had the bodies moving but instead of getting down to it like he was supposed to do, and let the music take care of things, Billy called out:

'Hol' it! Cease Iyah!'

Obediently, the band cut out. There was a pause, a few seconds of relative silence.

'Yes, crowd ah people, greetings in Jah name!'

'Gwan wid de rhythm, man!' A voice shouted from the opposite side from where we were standing but Billy seemed determined to talk first. He took a few steps towards the left of the stage, swaying in a way I hoped was studiously calculated and not due to any of the herb or beer he had taken earlier on.

'Big respeck to each and everyone, seen! Big respeck to my breddrin Beres who set up de show.'

'Done wid de talkin! Let off!!' a rough voice called out a few yards in front of me. Wilton pulled on his spliff, watching his brother's first public appearance, admiring the way he handled himself. I was wondering why he didn't just cut out the speech and start singing.

'Hear me now;' Billy said in the mike 'I wan ouno know she ah de first time Billy Bee ah perform pon stage, seen?' This, I couldn't help thinking, had to be a mistake. One look at Wilton's face confirmed that impression. The crowd was growing impatient and Billy should have sensed it. Even the musicians seemed to be wondering what the hell the artist was waiting on to get going.

'Go ina it nuh man!' A woman shouted behind us.

'I man love ouno, fe real.' Billy assured his audience, peering into the faces below him. That was really a nice thing to say but the audience was hot, ready to go and wanted action not words. It was like stopping right in the middle of some steaming hot lovemaking, when your woman is moaning loudly to keep going, to declare your undying, eternal love to her in a long, beautifully-worded speech. Great, but just not the right time.

Billy finally turned to the band and called: 'Yes. Gimme de riddim, Iyah.' I breathed with relief, told myself everything was going to be alright after all. The drummer rolled in and the rest of the band joined in, like they had been waiting to do for a while. Billy made a two-steps skanking move, nodded in time to the drop of the bass, raised the microphone to his mouth.

To be frank, in all the years I had listened to songs and singers, I had never heard anything quite like those first notes that came out of Billy's throat and flew out of the stacks of speakers into the night air. There and then I realised why the artist had called himself Billy Bee.

'Yee-e-e-e-e-e,' Billy shrieked in a high-pitched, sustained note. He nodded twice, waiting for the kick of the bass drum then came again:

'Yee-ee-ee-ee-ee,'

A longer harmony this time, flying high above the rhythm line. Hat thrown back, his left hand pointing to the dark sky above, Billy was finally living his dream. Yet not everyone shared that dream, it seemed to me, from what I could read on the faces around me. I looked at Wilton and for the first time that night saw puzzlement in my friend's eyes.

'Yee-ee-ee-ee-eee.' Billy's voice came again, insistent.

The bee was now in full flight, so to speak, sending out what sounded like a mating call. My unease increased when a couple of whistles erupted from the audience. Then I heard distinctly coming from just behind me, maybe even from one of the 'friends' who had been around Billy a little while earlier: 'G'way wid dat bloodclaat!'

Billy was too deeply involved in his 'singing' to notice such little signs of impatience of his public. Not so much dancing as bouncing on the spot, hopping left and right in between 'yee-ee's', he felt it, you could tell. To be fair, it wasn't a bad song when he got to eventually sing some words. Anyway, after a few more long minutes, he got to the end of his first number. Billy even got applause it must be said, fair if not warm. Up to this point, things could still have gone alright. Unfortunately, Billy felt too happy to really adapt himself to the tastes of the audience. A lack of stage experience probably also played a great part in what happened next.

Some crowds are easier to please than others. That night's wasn't too rough by Jamaican standards. All an artist with a minimum of talent had to do was build on the atmosphere, follow on from where the performers before him had got the audience. I knew that too well, I could have told my friend. But I was much too far away from the man I could see smiling on the big lit-up stage. I heard Billy declare:

'Right now, Billy Bee gwan give ouno a special style, seen?'

'Run de ridim, man!'

'Music!'

Calls were coming from the crowd for the show to go on, for it was music these people wanted, nothing else.

'Acapella style,' Billy told them with a confident grin.

'Oh no!' I thought to myself.

'Come off, man!' Someone shouted, rather unkindly.

Billy turned briefly to the band to signal to them he had no need of their services. Then he straightened his hat on his head, got a little closer to the edge of the stage and leaned over the mike in a concentrated pose.

'Jonathan . . . he was a gun man,' he started. Billy swayed on the spot.

'Jonathan, he had blood on his hands . . .' Billy punctuated this verse with a strident 'yee-ee-e', stamped his right foot down.

I heard a woman laugh somewhere on my left.

'Blood money! He was eating blood money.' Another foot-stomping.

That was when some of the most vocal elements in the crowd lost their patience.

'Come off, man! Wha happen to yuh?'

Other things were shouted. I caught the word 'eeediot' amongst other rather nasty comments. Billy hadn't stopped singing yet. The bandsmen looked increasingly frustrated. Wilton told me, 'Him better stop that!'

That was exactly my opinion. It was only after a few more insults that Billy realized things weren't going too well. He stopped and peered around at the crowd. That particular song didn't seem to fit the public, he seemed to be reflecting. He looked truly perplexed that his lyrics weren't appreciated, how some people were so ignorant. Above all, he didn't like the insults he had just heard aimed at him, that had nothing to do with music. That was personal, he was sure of it.

'G'way wid dem foolishness!' a voice growled right at the front of the stage.

Billy's final mistake was to focus on someone in particular, something which all artists know they must never do, no matter how badly a show might go. This applies especially to Jamaican audiences, critical at the best of times. 'Cho,' the frustrated singer let out as he stood up by the edge of the stage, dejected, 'Yuh nuh know 'bout music, man.'

The seconds that followed that statement convinced me that all was lost and, had I been next to Billy, I would have swiftly led him off the stage. But Billy was alone out there, alone with his courage and his bitterness at having his first ever public appearance spoiled by some unappreciating uncouth 'guy'. Suddenly, unannounced, a pop bottle came crashing at Billy's feet. Right then, I saw the bass player, who stood right behind Billy, unplug his instrument and step quietly towards the back. But Billy didn't get wise to this. Instead, he got angry.

'Hey, I don't want a man come disrespect me tonight, seen?'

Spoken like a true bad boy! Roughneck style was the last thing Billy should have tried to play on that particular audience. Suddenly the mood wasn't for peace and brotherhood any more. I saw Wilton frown, and immediately after heard the crash of a beer can landing against the bass drum. The third projectile hit Billy's left leg. By then, all the musicians had reached the back of the stage. It wasn't their quarrel after all and they might even have lived through similar experiences before. Bravely, the MC stepped on the stage and tried to intervene.

'Please, is love we ah deal wid.' It was all he had time to say before a few more bottles and cans hit the stage and made him run off. Against all common sense, Billy the Bee was still up on the stage, trying to dodge the shower of bottles. He had stepped back but he should have realized by now that it was his presence alone which angered the audience. It took a straight hit to the chest to convince him he should move, fast, if he wished to see another day. But before that, he added insult to injury by shouting in the mike.

'Ah wha de raasclaat? Ouno crazy???'

I saw a man prop himself up onto the stage, followed by another one. I also had time to see Billy's hat dropping off his head as the aspiring singing star made an undignified and rapid exit through the back of the stage.

'We got to help him!' I shouted to Wilton above the chaotic noise. Wilton looked at me like I was insane.

'Yuh wan' get yuh head bust too?'

On the stage, the MC managed to get things to calm down after a few minutes. With great skill and humour he restored some sort of order and eventually brought back the musicians and introduced a new artist, well-known and liked, who got the show rolling again. Like everything else in Jamaica, the incident passed away and half an hour later you couldn't have known a man had almost been lynched on stage.

I felt kind of worried about Billy. At least half a dozen men had taken off after him and by now he might well be lying in the bush beyond the back fence with his throat cut. But Wilton seemed calm enough. I had to insist to convince him that he should leave his girl and come looking for Billy, not wait till the end of the show. Billy was nowhere around the back of the fence. We got back to the car but he wasn't there neither. Wilton and I started driving back the way we came, slowly, looking both sides of the road into the darkness.

'Yuh t'ink dem catch 'im?' I asked.

'Fear give man wings.' Wilton shrugged confidently.

We passed a small wooden shack with a faded Coca-Cola sign barely lit up, crossed over a small stone bridge. Wilton stopped the car.

'Him must be round here,' he said, looking around outside. He got out of the car, leaving the engine and the lights on. I followed him. The night was alive with the sounds of crickets, the gentle rush of water from the small river down below. We walked either side, in the brightness of the beams, searching. There was no sign of the Bee.

'Billy! Yaow, Billy!' Wilton called out.

I was looking around, almost jumped when a noise came out to my right and a silhouette emerged from the bush. It was a shadow of his former magnificent self that got in the back of the car. Billy's clothes were all mudded up, he was limping and the expression on his face couldn't be described. He was silent for a while and neither of us said anything to him. Then I heard him ask Wilton in a surprisingly steady voice:

'Yuh pick up me hat?'

CHAPTER SEVEN

The Showdown

That Westmoreland trip. I still wonder sometimes what would have happened if I had timed my moves differently, and if Billy's 'yee-ee's' had not kept me outside Town that night.

Getting down from West in the early morning hours, six o'clock, was nice enough. The breeze slapped me playfully, riding out along the still clear road, and I stopped once to relieve my bladder. As soon as I hit the outskirts, the vibes got tight.

Just outside Spanish Town, I got flagged down by a jeep with three uniformed police who looked at me suspiciously. They asked me all kinds of questions, searched the small parcel of yellow yam, plantains and limes I carried on the back of the bike. One of them searched my pockets, my waist. They said youths from my area had robbed a business in Spanish Town the previous evening and I looked like one of them. They made as if they wanted to shake me up, but I told them I had been visiting relatives and was going back to look for my sister and children. They checked the bike, hinting I probably had stolen it. 'Whe yuh get money fe buy bike?!' One of them kept looking at me from behind his cap visor, like he wanted me in. Finally, they let me go, as I wasn't much action for the start of the day.

The traffic was a little more dense on the way to Three Miles. I spotted him about the same time as he did me. It was

Kickers, sat astride his bike, against the stall of a coconut and mango vendor. I eased off the gas and got out of the traffic, circled to where he was. He didn't move from where he was perched, his eyes watched me stop from behind the black mounted sunglasses. Kickers always was a stylist. A bearded man was talking with the Rasta fruit-seller.

'Wha'ppen?'

I was searching for a sign that his presence here early morning had something to do with me. It had.

'Me ah wait for yuh from time, man.' Kickers said soberly. He didn't so much as move his head when he talked.

'Wha'ppen?' I asked again, more concerned now.

Kickers said just three sentences.

'Hear wha': Lookman beat up yuh sistah last night. Yuh bettah watch out fe him. I come fe warn yuh.'

Words alone can kill a person, I am convinced of it. They can make a person's heart stop. It took me seconds of pain to ask.

'Weh Lucy deh?'

'Down ah the hospital.'

Another sentence, digging deeper into my guts.

'Weh Lookman deh?'

I saw Kickers shake his head.

'Nobody nuh see him from last night.'

A woman in a yellow headscarf was negotiating a mango at the stall. The traffic behind us was steady in the rising early sun.

I don't know what it was I felt, but it was very, very cold. I never forgot it. I hadn't come off the bike; only the engine had been off. I kicked it alive. Some things I couldn't tell from Kickers' voice, but I had to speak.

'Thanks, y'hear, Kickers.'

Slim, even slight in build, with sticking out ears and a quiet disposition, Kickers was of my 'promotion'. We sparred at dances in the early days, played many football games on the same side. Right now, he had become one of Lookman's three main soldiers. He was down with the trade he ran, taking care of Lookman's business interests: his most 'trusted', if that meant anything. Kickers had gone up to that level because he was a ruthless youth, fearless and downright wicked when it came to war. Me and him never had a bad vibe in all these years.

'Hear wha',' Kickers called out over the engine. 'Him nah go come alone. Yuh know how it go.'

I stopped to look through his glasses, following his lead. What was I going to do, concretely? My mind stopped on one particular spot two streets away from mine. Kickers was there before me.

'That gone.' He told me simply. Then I heard him say: 'Yuh know the burn-out shell out ah de back ah Guttu shop?'

My eyes were in his, there.

'Left back wheel, dig.' That was all Kickers said, and that morning, he gave me a chance to stand up. He gave me odds to make it. I'd say I owed him a life right there. I never forgot that. I couldn't put it in words, so I just nodded slowly. Then I turned the bike around and left him sitting right there. But he knew what I meant.

What went on in my mind that morning, riding down with a veil before my eyes? All I can truthfully say is that my only calculation was death and how to apply it to my enemy. Though my heart was on seeing Lucy, I had enough flair to reject that option. The way I figured it now, and Kickers had confirmed that, my physical elimination was Lookman's aim, nothing less. I would not be fool enough to think I'd even make it to Lucy's hospital bed. Lookman had made his plan long ago apparently, and I had been blind to it. I was to go because I wasn't in his plans, I had been Jingles' soldier, and he had failed to win Lucy from him, even now that he was gone.

I avoided the obvious route to where I was heading, knowing full well that I was expected. The trouble was, I didn't know just how Lookman had tied up my 'hit'. At the same time, was it safer to ride through the main road to avoid an ambush in one of the back roads? After hitting the spot Kickers had given me, I would have to be smart and get it done quickly. I realize now I didn't really think it through properly. I didn't even know where Lookman was right now, unless he just sat at Rammy's and waited for me to arrive ... How could I be about to go after a rankin in full daylight with a single gun, knowing I was likely to face half a dozen heavily-tooled-up men! That's how crazy I felt. I was the rabbit going after the hunter and his dogs.

I hid the bike a little way off, made it through the lanes to Guttu's old car repair workshop. I got what I was looking for, where Kickers had said it would be. The old rum drinker wasn't there, and his two apprentices getting greasy around an engine knew me and didn't pay too much attention. Now the real mission was on. I felt a little more ready to face whatever might come but then, I had the awareness of what would happen if I got stopped by a patrol with a piece in my waist. It didn't really matter to me what happened after, or whether there would be an after for me. I just wanted to get to Lookman.

'I might be going down ... but I ain't going down alone!' That was all I knew as I turned off the corner of Maxfield Avenue. I didn't feel anything wrong, didn't notice anybody paying special attention to me. I passed the movie house, slowed down to avoid a handcart. The sun was higher up in the limpid sky above me, the heat was coming along now. Inside, I was cold.

They say you musn't hate your enemy, because hatred affects your judgement. For me, it must have been the eyesight which went first, else I wouldn't have missed it. On a mission, I was like an eagle — nothing escaped me — but that morning, my thirst for revenge messed me up. By the time I spotted the overtaking vehicle, it was already at my back wheel.

In a few mad seconds, I locked in on what was happening. I swerved right to avoid the bumper of the van, gassed up to slip through the breach between the car in front and the pavement. I made it, overtook one car on the inside, twisted the gas handle to slip past a second. I had to shift into the right turn I could see just ahead.

I was twenty yards away from that escape route when the first bullet hit me. Actually I didn't know what it was, didn't think about bullets, funnily enough. Some kind of cramp, a stunning shock, gripped the left side of my back. I don't think I heard the explosion until after the blow. I didn't let go of my right grip though, didn't crash. I kept going. I remember cutting across, away from the road. A startled woman dropped to the ground just a few yards ahead of me. I heard some screams above the noise of engines. The basket of yams and fruits at the back of my bike flew off as my front wheel hit a big stone. When the bike jumped again, I thought of it as another stone. Some kind of iron hammer hit me in the back, lower than the first time, and I lost my breath. I crashed badly, felt a shock to my forehead.

My mother always said my skull was tough like rock stone. I must have passed out but only for a few seconds, because I came to lying on my belly, with a feeling like I didn't have a body any more. I had been shot once before but only in the arm and that wasn't anything much. I could hear voices. I opened my eyes and the first thing I spotted through a blur was the white van's tyre about twenty yards away. They had turned the corner. I didn't move, wasn't sure I could. Two legs dropped in to my field of vision, out of the van, started towards where I was. They were going to make sure I was dead: the hit must have been well paid. God only knows why I didn't just accept the fate I had been handed, just lay there and let it happen. Probably it was this cold anger still alive within me, even in that second state. I had told myself I wasn't going down alone. I couldn't see the face of the man coming to finish me off, but I knew it wasn't Lookman somehow. I felt bad about that. Something thick was blocking my right eye but the left was clear, and I could feel a bulge sticking into my stomach: the gun was still there. I saw the legs maybe five yards distant, still coming my way.

I must have been fast for a wounded man, though I couldn't tell before I started if I would be able to move at all. My left arm was spread out, useless I felt, but the right was cocked up under me from the fall. I clenched my fist, the fingers worked. All in one I did it: moved my wrist inwards and grabbed the butt of the revolver, in an almighty effort rolled onto my unhurt right side and pressed the trigger hard. The arm wasn't extended and that is probably what took the hitman by surprise. I shot from the ground, he didn't see it coming. Twice I pressed, almost without aiming. Each shot felt torn out of my body, so much pain could I now feel in my left side. I glimpsed the face of the man, the black gun in his hand. He dropped, probably just as he was about to squeeze the trigger because I got a shot from him. It felt like a punch as all air left my chest. I went out.

Two days later I came back. The doctors told me later that the chances I'd survive the coma I had fallen into were not great. I had lost a lot of blood. One of my lungs was punctured. But I made it.

Waking up I soon noticed I was under police guard 'round the clock. Lucy was at my bedside and she later told me it had been for my own protection. Lucy. I almost went back into the coma when I saw her. Kickers had never explained what Lookman had done to my sister. Lucy said later that he accused her of 'showing off' in front of him as she passed Rammy's on her way home from Auntie Pauline's. Half-drunk and high, Lookman developed an argument with Lucy. Though she knew how to ignore such a provocation, certain things said you can't ignore. So when she talked back to him and shamed him in front of his friends, he came rambling and stupidly hit her in the face. Lucy wasn't weak, although slim, and before Lookman could see Lucy getting up from the blow, she had flung a piece of stone right in his face. In the ensuing action, several men tried to intervene but not fast enough to stop Lookman slicing Lucy's face. As scars go, the ratchet could have made more damage but it showed, and for a woman that's cruel. But she survived that, and you could see the only thing that mattered to her was my own survival. She thanked God and all his saints when I surfaced on that hospital bed, I recalled that later.

I made a quick recovery, the doctors seemed pleased I pulled through and after two weeks, I walked out of the hospital well enough: my left arm was in a cast and the right handcuffed to a large police constable. They sat me down in an office in Half-Way-Tree police station, in front of a desk piled with papers. The kind constable who manacled me to the back of the chair by my 'good' right arm came back after a few minutes and placed the gun I had used on the day on top of some file in the middle of the desk. Then he went out and left me there waiting.

I waited for what seemed like an hour at least. Apart from a couch against the back wall and a metal filing cabinet under the window, the desk was the only furniture. Through the open door, for a good forty minutes, I watched uniformed and plain clothes police pass by, listened to bits of conversation. I wasn't really worried about my fate, it was the uncertainty I didn't like. Just as I was getting fed up with waiting, a short and plump woman constable in uniform stopped and looked at me, asked me if I wanted a drink. I was surprised. That was a first! I said I would. Maybe she had mercy on me because my arm was in a sling; anyway she brought me a Coke and disappeared. From time to time I could catch the crackling of radio communication in the office next door. There was a lot going on, apparently. Then, when I was starting to think I would spend the day like that, a man came in and stopped by the desk. He just looked at me for a few seconds, without a word. Medium height, round-faced with a dark brown complexion and a low haircut, he wore a light green suit, white shirt with no tie. I couldn't rightly say I knew his face but there was something familiar about him. He was clean-shaven but for a short, well-groomed moustache. His eyes fixed me, brown and hard but without animosity.

'Lewis!' he called, not too loud, but right away, the big constable who had shackled me earlier came in.

'Take off the cuffs,' the man in the suit told him, which he did before going out again.

'I'm Detective Inspector Glenford,' the man told me.

It didn't ring a bell with me, but I said, 'Good morning, sah.' Might as well be polite, as courtesy could play in my favour. I expected him to sit at the desk and start asking me questions but he quickly browsed through some of the papers scattered there, took a pen out of his inside jacket pocket, made a few scribbles on some of the sheets then left without a word. I didn't even think of running out of the station. I had checked the layout coming in and it was clear I wouldn't make it to the entrance. I felt a little better without the handcuffs, and more dignified too. The painting on the wall behind the desk showed a solitary silhouette atop a misty mountain top with reddish clouds behind. I spent a few more minutes checking it out. There was a kind of sadness in there, to me anyway.

I heard his voice giving instructions to someone before the detective came back in the office. He pushed the door closed and sat at the desk this time. For a couple of minutes, he was making notes in a pad he'd taken out of one of the desk drawers, scribbling finely line after line, stopping once in a while to search his brain it seemed. Eventually, he leaned back in the comfortable leather armchair, tapping his pen against his chin. I could see he was looking my way but not really seeing me, considering some other problem. He nodded to himself, then asked me directly: 'Your name?'

'Carlton Nash.'

'Hmm.' He made a sound as though he was reflecting on the sound of my name. I had been 'interviewed' by police before, so I expected more questions, in the usual rough mode but this man didn't seem in a hurry. I watched him cock his head slightly towards the door, picking up on the crackling phrases over the radio.

'You're on a murder charge, right?'

Thrown off balance, I took it in. It was a question that just begged a 'yes' on my part, but it wasn't the way I saw it.

'I just get out of the hospital today. I don't get charge with not'ing yet, sah.'

That little rectification made the detective smile. 'Yes, not yet.'

I knew, all the time I lay in the hospital, I would have to face the police sooner or later. It would have been easier to die on that street corner in a way, but my only regret was not being charged for Lookman's murder. Detective Glenford picked up his pad and started leafing through it, methodically. Twice he looked up at me, his face expressing nothing much. I didn't really like the way he stared. My arm was itchy bad!

'Tell me, where did you get the gun from?' He wasn't looking at me, he was asking it like any other question, matter-of-factly.

I repeated the same thing I had given to the first policeman who came to the hospital to interrogate me.

'I found it.'

That made the detective look up from his pad. He sounded jokey.

'You people are really lucky, you know. I have never found a gun yet in my life, and I'm a policeman!'

It seemed to amuse him, genuinely. It didn't amuse me somehow. I was starting to wonder why he didn't behave like the other policemen I had come across.

'Tell me, Carlton. This gun, you found it before or after the elections?' he asked. He was waiting for an answer from me, knowing I knew it was a trick question. If I said before, he'd ask why I hadn't given it in at the amnesty. If after, why did I keep it? I had his eyes into mine. There was no joke in them.

'I found it that same day,' I said simply. There was no

cockiness in my tone, the policeman didn't take it bad. He even nodded, still checking something in the handwritten notes on the page in front of him.

'OK.' He put the pad down on the desk. 'Let me see if I get the story right.' His back against the chair, the man adjusted his shirt collar before telling me: 'Your don cut up your sister, you find a gun and go out to shoot him.' He paused, but not to await any confirmation on my part. 'Then, on the way to revenge, you get ambushed by two gunmen, probably hired by your don. They shoot you down, but you manage to kill at least one before collapsing badly wounded.'

The dyamm man makin' it sound like a newspaper article! I was thinking. All the same, fancy talk or not, that was the living truth. 'That is exactly what happened, sah. God knows!'

'Look, let's leave God out of this,' the detective said. Then: 'So now your don is still alive. You too but you have a murder charge to face. Tell me, Carlton: who's the winner?'

I didn't answer to that, but he must have read the anger in my stare. There was a long silence between us, a few bursts of cracking on the radio next door. Detective Glenford sighed heavily, leaned forward from his vantage spot. His elbows perched on the edge of the desk, he said, 'You think I'm your enemy, don't you?'

It didn't seem to matter to him that I kept not answering most of his questions.

'And you think the next man across the border is your enemy too, right?'

I kept quiet. Quietly he asked me: 'So, how many men you killed before that?'

No policeman had ever asked me such a question. But this one was serious; he was real relaxed about it, like someone discussing a bet at the tracks or something.

'Carlton, I'm going to ask you one question and I'd just like you to answer me truthfully.'

He paused, while across the desk, his inscrutable eyes

weighed me out. What kind of a policeman was this one, with his games?

'Have you ever killed a man?' he asked, very serious.

I looked at him blankly but he went on.

'Tell me if you have ever taken a man's life while you looked into his eyes, at close quarters, I mean ... Have you?'

The face of the man leaning comfortably in the leather chair was intense but calm, his tone almost detached. He gave me half a minute during which I realized I would never answer that question. He knew.

'It takes nothing to do it with this, though!' He pointed casually to the grey muzzle on the table near the ashtray.

'OK, Carlton,' he said after looking away to the window, open on the rumours of the town, the still free and their daily runnings.

'You don't know me, but I know you.' That didn't sound like good news, but he went on. 'Oh, not just you, but almost every street man across the areas. I have a lot of information.'

From the corridor came two knocks and the door was pushed half open. Detective Glenford made a little beckoning sign with his left hand and a sturdy uniformed policeman stepped to the desk. He only threw me a brief glance but it was one of those that let you remember that when a policeman has seen you once, it's for ever. He whispered something close to his 'boss', waited for a reaction. All this time, since the knocks, Detective Glenford had been observing me with that indefinable meditative look he had and it was starting to annoy me. He glanced briefly at the big policeman and nodded twice. The other one moved out swiftly.

'So, Carlton Nash, Carlton Nash.' Detective Glenford squinted, like the name had to bring up something from his memory. It did. 'Yes, Carlton Nash, aka Skid, or Skidder, ... born ... '59 ... no, '60, involved in sectarian violence between areas since quitting secondary school aged fifteen, became driver to ex-area leader Jingles, then his right-hand man. Operates a small-scale ganja operation, distribution mostly. Parents both dead. Lives with his sister and niece. Doesn't smoke. Five arrests, no convictions.'

Spelt out non-committal in that impersonal tone, this could have been the eight o'clock news but it wasn't. It was me, my life. And how the hell did he get to know me so well? I have always been pretty straight-faced but I must have shown some surprise that morning.

'Information, Carlton, information is power.' He smiled, not really a happy smile, but a smile. I knew he would soon get serious. 'This is my job here. I want you to understand this. The thinking is this; you must know your enemy well if you want to defeat him. That's why my job is to know everything I can about you, all of you.'

He got up and went to peep through the window, came back having satisfied his curiosity. He sat and played with the key-ring he hadn't let go of since coming in.

'I was born and bred in Kingston,' he started. 'Papine, left the island at fifteen to follow high school in the States, California. Only came back to spend summer holidays. I started studying to become an attorney and became a policeman instead. Life's funny, eh?

'You know why I decided to come back home, Carlton?'

He was looking at me but I had nothing to say about that.

'I came back here to see if what I have learned could help, because I don't want to see what happened in the States happen here.'

That sounded serious. I was starting to feel edgy about all this talk. *Let's get done with this*, I was thinking, *send me to court for murder and done!*

But I was to learn Detective Rico Glenford was never a man to rush. I must have looked bored. I heard him ask: 'You know what else I know about you, Carlton?' He had gone back to lean against the chair.

'You are not involved with drugs ... am I right, sah?'

'It's true.' I answered simply, impressed in a way.

Then the detective dropped: 'You know why Jingles died?'

I would have to have been a very cold, very dead-inside man for my face not to show something. The man knew he had got through to me now.

'Jingles died because he didn't want to play ball. Because he didn't like the drug business, and he didn't want his people to be dealing with it.' The detective let it sink in before adding: 'Him refusing to get Bernie killed was just an excuse. They were gonna kill him anyway ...'

There was a hard stare between me and Detective Glenford. Right now, he wasn't no policeman to me any more, he was talking about my family.

'Come on, Carlton. Who had the most to gain from Jingles' death?'

That kind of meditation was getting painful to prolong.

'You're mad, right? I'm gonna tell you something even stronger. Jingles was dead the day he started to have peace talks with the other side.'

There was a silence.

'Certain people didn't want to hear about another peace treaty, that's not good for their business. And Jingles had already done a lot for the first one, he was a big man.' Thinking about Jingles had never been a pleasant thing to do any day of the year since he had gone. Next, I heard Detective Glenford ask me, very normally: 'You want to know who set up Jingles?'

I kept alternating between looking at him and the calendar behind him. Who the hell was this man anyway? My eyes went to the policeman's own, waiting. But he was a player, a man who loved to toy with feelings, other people's feelings.

'Tell me something, Carlton,' he squinted at me. 'You was driving on that arms shipment job, wasn't you?'

I didn't expect that. He pushed on as I stared blankly. 'I'm pretty sure it was you. Anyway, the reason I ask: you ever find out who gave away the play?' No one ever had, as far as I knew. So what was he talking about? Then it got worse.

'We'll get back to that later,' he said, switching scene. 'Tell me if you remember; on the night Jingles died, who was driving him on the mission?'

I knew that, but I wasn't prepared to discuss it with him, whatever he knew already. He said. 'Lookman was driving, wasn't he?'

'It wasn't Lookman.' I said simply, like I cared to prove him wrong for once, him and his know-it-all attitude.

Detective Glenford's face expressed surprise. 'It wasn't him?' He frowned, like caught out. 'You sure?'

I wasn't revealing anything he didn't know, I felt, so I said: 'The driver died.'

There was a reflective silence, then the man said, 'Hm hm.' shaking his head slowly. He gave it fifteen seconds of suspense before declaring calmly, 'I wasn't on the scene, but I reached it just after they had taken the bodies away and I can tell you this; there was blood on all the seats, except the driver's.' He waited for the implications to rise up in my mind, then he laid it all out. 'Lookman was driving Jingles that night. He switched with the other guy, I forget his name, at some point. That way he was making sure the ambush would work.'

The man had shaken me right there. What was he saying? Then he threw me down, thumped me inside.

A pause, two still eyes on me. 'The contract was given to some dirty cops, working with the blessing of certain influential men. That's why you couldn't drive that night. You got lucky on a job once before. If you got lucky again, you might have saved Jingles.'

I was retracing and criss-crossing the allegations this man was handing me against what I knew as facts. He must have followed my inner reasoning, for Detective Glenford said casually, 'The police had no reason to want Jingles dead: on the contrary, you follow me? . . .' I saw him shaking his head with what looked like sadness, or maybe frustration.

'You want to know why I'm telling you all this, instead of giving you up to my colleagues along the corridor?'

He waited, seeing I was still turning what he'd just told me around in my head.

'I'm telling you that you and all the others putting your lives on the line out there don't know what the hell is going on.'

I said nothing.

'It's not about area, or party any more; all this is done with.' He paused. 'It's about drugs and guns, lots of guns . . .'

I didn't take the stare personally. The man in the suit asked, 'You know how many police officers got shot and killed on duty last year, Carlton?'

I didn't.

'Thirty-two.' He waited for it to impress my conscience. 'So the police must change too, and that is where I come in. My job is to organize the "counter-attack", as I call it.'

If he was trying to scare me, he'd wear himself out, but he explained patiently.

'The mission I've been given is to form a unit independent from the politics, totally clean . . . like the Untouchables. You've seen the movie?'

I had. I nodded, wondering what I was doing talking cinema with that policeman now!

'I'm gonna organize a strike force that's gonna cut down the trade in Jamaica before it even spreads.'

From what I had seen happening on the street, it was going to take a lot of work, but I said nothing, and he went on: 'I have been back over a year now, things are moving fast and I'm almost ready to start operating. With intelligence backup, I've got good men, real tough and dedicated fighters.'

That man sounded serious about his work. That surely meant more pressure out there for the guilty and the innocent alike. Then, as I thought on darker days to come, Detective Glenford said, very straight-faced: 'Look, I've got an idea. I'd like you to work for me.'

I thought I had heard wrong at first, but he was waiting for my reaction to his 'idea'. I let him have it up front.

'Yuh better send me straight to Gun Court, sah. I'm not no informer.'

Detective Glenford shook his head 'That's not what I'm talking about.' He gave me one of those long drilling stares of his, then switched to another side, as usual with him.

'Tell me something, Carlton.' He paused to watch me with what looked like a glint of amused anticipation. 'Suppose I let you out.' I must have seemed interested.

'Suppose I let you go free . . .'

I knew he wouldn't do it, but I had nothing to lose supposing, just to go along with him.

'. . . Drop everything. I let you back out on the street. What are you going to do?'

I thought about it for a full minute. The policeman waited. I would have liked to answer him something positive but I just couldn't. He knew.

'You've got three options, basically.'

He spelt them out.

'You leave the island and try your luck in another country. It might work.'

I waited for the other two.

'You go back to your area, shoot it out with Lookman and, if you stay lucky, you could become the new don.'

I kept my eyes on his.

'But for how long? . . .'

He raised his eyebrows, waited before continuing, but I had nothing I cared to say.

'Or, you're really unlucky and some guy from the other side sees you somewhere and gets himself a name and a lump sum for your life.'

My face reflected my perplexity. Detective Glenford flashed the wicked semi-grin of a flattering crooked car salesman.

'You're a big man now, you've got a rep,' he said, then added with mock respect, 'You're the man who took down the great Pitpat.'

What the hell was he talking about now? From his satisfied grin, I think my face provided Detective Glenford with his favourite moment of our conversation.

'Oh yeah, you've been away from the street, and we kept it out of the *Gleaner*.' I heard him say it: 'You took down Pitpat, Carlton. You're a rankin' now. Congratulations.'

I know I have rarely been as shocked by any news in my life as I was that morning. I had had no more than a flashing glance at the face of my 'executioner' that morning, stunned and weakened by the first two bullets in my body. Detective Glenford shook his head wisely.

'I feel like I know your mind, Carlton. You're not a runner. Listen carefully now, I won't make you the offer twice. You have two choices here.'

I was still reeling inside from the implications of what he'd just told me, but Detective Glenford was merciless now.

'You can decide to change your life, join my team and really start anew. I can straighten everything for you.'

An insignificant flick of the two hands outwards.

'Or you can take your chances with my friends down the corridor, and maybe, when you get out, you'll become a big shot down there. Maybe not.'

He sat there watching me take it all in, his deep eyes letting me know he was serious, no games involved. Detective Glenford was leaning back from the desk and its pile of papers.

'It's your play, Carlton.' He said. 'You get up and walk down, or you take your chance with me.'

CHAPTER EIGHT

Trading War Stories

I have never believed in luck. Whatever tight spots I got out of, however close the escape, I never thought of myself as lucky. Rather, I always saw that as a sign that my number wasn't up yet. What happened to me after the shooting, I see as something 'pre-set', some choice I was given to make. I got it right and moved away from the no-win situation I was in. At the time, I wasn't thinking like that though. I spent a whole week in the lockdown before I took the deal I was offered. Detective Glenford told me I had survived the three shots for a purpose. He said I had kind of died and come back. I was like 'born again' ... that's what he said ...

The first day I wore uniform in public was the week of Bob Marley's funeral. We toured the areas in a jeep; me at the wheel, Detective Glenford in front, and a veteran sergeant called Braddock in the back. This was a special day, in more ways than one. As far as I can remember this was one of the rare days when there were no killings in Kingston.

Most days were full of violent incidents, whether crimes, quarrels, domestic fights, 'accidents'. Also the regular police raids in the garrison towns, in search of weapons, added considerably to the already tense post-election atmosphere. There was a feeling amongst people from the losing party that the actions of the Force were somewhat one-sided, although I can say from experience that the other side suffered their share of pressure too. The motto was 'get the guns', which translates easily to 'get the gunmen'. To be caught with a gun in Jamaica at that time was bad news. In Kingston, it was death. The irony of it, and I found that out fast, was that more and more guns were coming in. Money from the trade was being used to bring in the hardware needed to run the trade. The old order had broken down. The youths on the street were no longer held in check by powerful dons and except in a very few areas, the deadly race to become the top dog was open. In this cheerful atmosphere, I now represented the law.

The first few months on the Force were the most perplexing I had ever lived through. I needed to redefine myself and everything else from a new perspective. The fact that I had walked away free from a murder charge (I found out later that it was never even filed; no one in the Force seemed to worry too much about Pitpat passing), that alone was weird. It made me realize how strong Detective Glenford's position already was at that time. I learned later that he'd been given a free hand by his superior officer, Superintendent Wilkins, to set up his unit. Now this one I knew from reputation. That man had a huge aura around him, a name that was feared, and respected, which is not the same thing. Wilkins was a hard man but a fair one. I personally knew of half a dozen youths who owed him their lives. (At that time, like now I guess, it made a big difference for a ghetto youth which policeman's hand he fell into.) Wilkins had gone up through the ranks, survived two elections as a garrison town officer, and the murkiest of political intrigues to become the youngest Detective Superintendent in the Jamaican Constabulary Force. Even before being sent on training in the US, he was already known as a tough man yet Wilkins was someone with a deep understanding of the root cause of crime and violence. Coming from a poor family, raised on the deadly Southside streets, Wilkins had first-hand experience of what it was like to grow up in a deprived and hopeless environment.

He was a hard man in a hard job and in Rico Glenford he had found the perfect instrument to implement his policies.

'Law enforcement ...' Detective Glenford said one hot afternoon towards the end of my training, '... is not about catching criminals and locking them up.' He had just put me and a dozen other recruits through two hours of hard work, practising 'urban zone control' techniques, as he called them. We were all easing off in the headquarters bar, sipping on ice-cold drinks.

'If you think like that, you're missing the point.'

We were all listening keenly to the boss. He had worked as hard as anyone else, constantly directing us, correcting our moves, coaching us step by step, until he thought what we were learning had become automatic reactions.

'You see, never think it's a "we and them" situation. It's not.' Glenford paused and looked around him. 'The man you are hunting is just like you and me, no different. Simply, he is reacting to a situation in a way that he has learned. He's a gangster only because he has adopted a different set of values than you, the policeman; that's all.'

After a sip from his can, he added with a little smile: 'I think you all know what I mean.'

I knew at least four of us on the team knew exactly what he meant.

'Law enforcement, successful law enforcement, is about knowing the people you're after, knowing them well, their reactions, their way of thinking, their feelings or lack of feelings. Then you can be one step ahead, be pro-active.'

'Pro-active' was one of those terms that Detective Glenford liked to use. To him, it meant not waiting for the crime to happen, but acting ahead of it. Even triggering it at times, although that was a concept not everybody on the Force agreed with. And that was where the 'use and control of informants' policy really set in.

I always heard a lot of people say that there are no facts

in Jamaica. Though I was never naive, I realized after my first months on the Force that most of what I had grown up believing in was a lie. Like most youths of my generation, I stood up for a cause, defending values which I learned from my elders were right, and fighting against 'the other side'. I saw many people around me die, and this made me even more convinced that we were right and 'they' were wrong. I believed all those on my side to be as determined as I was and prided myself on belonging to the 'right' camp.

What I learned later is that we were all pawns, cheap and expendable, to the hands pulling our strings. There had never been any sides. After the elections, youths from across the borders started to get together and associate to do business, just like the big men had been doing all along. Nobody was dumb enough to kill or die for colours anymore. The new game was money-making and nothing else. Life got even more violent, if anything, but at least you knew what was at stake.

'How you think Scotty died?' Rico Glenford asked me one morning as I was driving him alongside Marcus Garvey Drive to a call.

'Some guys shot him over a woman at a dance in Clarendon.'

Rico Glenford glanced at me from behind his shades and shook his head with that little amused smile he flashed once in a while when he had you quizzed.

'Right, but the girl was a bait and the two guys were paid by Lookman.'

I didn't answer. The whole picture was just about shaping up in my head. Lookman had set up Jingles, then set up Scotty until he could be the don. And on top of all this, I found Lookman was on the police payroll! There was one little detail I needed to know.

'So, is when Lookman started to work for the police, before or after Jingles died?'

There was silence in the car for a while. Detective Glenford knew by now I wasn't stupid. From the answer to that question

I could deduce whether Lookman alone had planned Jingles' demise or whether it had all been a police set-up.

'It's not as simple as that, Carly.' Rico Glenford said with a sigh. 'Jingles really upset the politicians when he started having peace talks with the other side. Lookman was easier for them to control, y'understand?' I didn't answer anything. Inside my head, Mr T.'s slimy smile flashed past.

Somewhere on the east side of town, someone had picked this warm morning to rob someone else of something and we found four bodies on arrival on the scene. It was almost routine. I spent my days driving in and out of violent scenes, more than before even but there wasn't much reaching me any more, I realized.

By temperament, I have always liked to be good, if not the best, at whatever I do. Like the Bible says: 'Whatsoever you do, do it with all your might,' and that's the way I see it. I did it for football, for driving, and I did it in my new 'occupation'. For one, if I was going to be a policeman, I didn't want to remain in a low position, not for long anyway. So I started studying how to get ranks. The luck I had was being close to Detective Glenford, Rico as he asked me to address him in private. That man had flair, live instinct for people and situations. He had picked me and three other ex-'gangsters' to be in his unit, four out of almost fifty cases he had studied in the course of a year. The rest were all policemen already serving or ex-soldiers he had picked himself. I never quite got out of him why he did this, what criteria made him decide we wouldn't turn on him or let him down at some point. But none of us four did . . .

For two years, I just drove the 'boss' wherever and whenever he needed to go. He had me tested under pressure, and got to trust my reflexes after a while. I learned a lot just listening to him directing operation, watching him evaluate information, taking instant decisions. In all the years I served under his command,

I have never known Rico Glenford to make a bad assessment of a situation. Only once he almost slipped, and it was the last. I came under fire with him quite few times, but never saw him lose his cool or his concentration. And all the men on the squad had the same respect for him, and him for them. We were a tight team with a tough coach.

Looking back, it was around Easter 1990 when evidence of deep corruption in the Force emerged. It was becoming widely known, and embarrassing to the Commissioner. For some time an atmosphere of suspicion, and in some cases open antagonism, existed between units. Even between certain individuals. There was no comradeship vibe anymore. We all knew someone whose integrity was questionable and questioned. Every day it was business as usual, with the added fact that you never knew for sure who might be shooting at you any more. Though the problem within the squad was not as widespread as in other stations throughout Town, we still had a few 'wet' individuals who operated undisturbed.

Rico was pushing for a crackdown and I remember closed door meetings around that period, getting very animated. Wilkins seemed reluctant to take the measures which Rico, and a few other officers, were pushing for. Not that Wilkins was ever suspected by any of us to be a part of the 'problem'! Not ever, and the future proved he was a good man. But for some reason, he was holding back on dealing with the problem emerging in his units.

CHAPTER NINE

The Way We Were

'You have to rise over this, me son. Sometimes people are not meant to stay together. The most important thing is what we learn from each other.'

Under the thatched roof of the outside kitchen I was munching on a piece of hard dough bread. I had not eaten breakfast yet and the bread felt sweet to my hungry stomach. Two fowls were busy chasing each other for the crumbs I had dropped on the ground. Miss Ruby insisted I should sit with her and proceeded to dispense me some of her wisdom while cooking. It was Sunday, rain had poured down all morning and the sun was still hesitating to come out. For the past week, I had been trying to hide the problems I was facing. No one else could have noticed it, but Miss Ruby knew me well enough not to be fooled. She had felt the turmoil in me, the way a mother knows a child's troubles. Ever since the day Rico had brought me home to her, Miss Ruby had cared for me, above considerations of bloodlines and made me feel like the second son she never had.

No matter what I was telling myself, I knew the breakdown with Merleene was affecting me more than I wanted to admit it. Hurt feelings are one thing, an aspect which most men have to deal with at some point when the relationship on which they have based their future begins to strain at the seams. But what I was losing was deeper, more vital to my balance, and affecting the way I related to life. For me, being who I was, a wife and children represented stability. It was an outlet for the sensitivity which men who grow up where I did learn very early to suppress.

Apart from Lucy, there had been no real family to connect to since our mother died. In the life I lived, where death was a constant presence and immunity to emotions an essential requirement of the job, someone who cared whether you came home or not, some little arms to hug you when you came through the door made all the difference. With my daughters I could forget about the shadow of dead eyes and stench of spilled blood which were my daily reality. I fed on their affection, quenched my thirst for purity with their innocence. These two little women were my reasons for feeling alive. And to think they wouldn't be there at night, for me to kiss their sleeping eyes . . .

As for Merleene, for all the allowances I tried to make for her difficult character, the split came at a time when the pressure from the job had worn down my reserve. I knew when we started I was marrying a woman used to easy life and pretty things. Her father warned me about this and although I really thought the love we had for each other would help us overcome all, ultimately we failed.

I wasn't without blame. No matter how much I tried to leave my troubles outside the front door, the pressures of the job, the unsocial hours and the relative hardship took their toll on Merleene. We both tried to cope but in the end there were more reasons to split than there were to keep going. If only we could have seen it the way it was, instead of hanging on, splitting, then running back to each other after a month. We kept trying to cope but emotions can turn on you and when that happens, then you start hurting the other one just because you're hurting. It made no sense, telling ourselves that we were not just staying together for the sake of the children.

As I sat watching Miss Ruby preparing her salt fish, I could feel weariness creeping up on me. It was not some new sensation but something which had been there all along, for years, and which now resurfaced to overtake me and my wounded soul.

'It happens to a lot of people, there is never no guarantee when it comes to love between man and woman.' With expert dexterity, Miss Ruby chopped her onions onto a board, poured them out into the waiting hot oil. 'It happened to me and Rico's father. He was a good man, I don't have a bad word to say about him.' The woman wiped her hands on a kitchen cloth, turned to look at me from behind her glasses.

'He was a man like any other, not any worst. Even though he was seeing other women, he never neglected us. We had our arguments, like any couple, but I believe we loved each other.' Miss Ruby paused. I had never heard her speak about Rico's father. Rico himself only told me one day we were talking that his father had died in the States years ago, when he was still in school. Then he switched to some other topic.

'I still believe he would have come back, if he had lived long enough.' Then she got back to her cooking.

I said: 'I will get used to it, madda, it'll take a little time, but I will.'

'I know you will, son, 'cause you have the strength, and the Lord knows the heart of his children, everyone of them. These things happen for a purpose.'

'True.'

'Look pon Rico and your sister; dem really love each other but the two ah dem have strong characters. Dem break up today, make up tomorrow and break up again. That is the way dem is. Some people can live like this all dem lives, and some have to let it go some day. That is just life.'

That was one problem I couldn't talk about. I knew Lucy could be very ignorant, I had told Rico as much at the beginning. To be truthful, I had never thought they would last a month, so when Lucy announced that they were going out, shortly after I had joined the Force, I simply shrugged and said that was their business, nothing to do with me. It couldn't be a bad thing that they got together. I knew my sister well enough to realize a man like Rico might bring her the stability and discipline she needed. Bringing up Aisha was something Lucy could do on her own, but she needed to have mental support for herself, have someone other than me she could rely on and respect. Because our father was missing for most of her childhood, Lucy had grown into a tough, resourceful young woman. That's what helped her to survive the streets. She could make it alone as a mother, but she now needed to be a wife, and Rico seemed to be the right man for the job. As they say, it seemed like a good idea at the time.

'The job we do can be really difficult for a woman to cope with though!' I said.

'Hmm, but it's what ouno choose to do, and if it's the way ouno make a living then, it's up to the woman to deal with it.'

That was true. And looking around, I knew not many of the men I worked with lived happy and fulfilling family lives!

Rico arrived around 1 p.m. He had taken a trip to the countryside to check on the building site he had started a few month before. I had been there once with him, a good drive through the hills of Trelawney to get to the piece of land he had got from relatives on his father's side, and where he had started to put up a house. 'Piece of land' might be the wrong description for a spread of fertile fields of several acres comprising a river and several orchards. Rico told me he was planning on retiring there to raise crops and grow livestock. The house was well on the way, due to be finished early the following year.

We ate together with Miss Ruby then both of us sat in the backyard with a couple of beers. It felt good to relax on a breezy Sunday afternoon like this, in private. This was better than going and have a drink in the appointed bar uptown that all off-duty police had made their home. Rico's radio was by his side, switched on low, just in case. We talked about this and that. I needed to forget about my marital problems, or at least get an objective angle on it, and a few beers might just help me to achieve that.

'There's a shakedown on the way,' Rico said, opening up his second Heineken.

I waited for the follow-up, knowing he must have had new info.

'The boss isn't playing. He's going to make waves.'

Since his appointment, the Commissioner of Police had promised a 'dusting up' of the Force and things were now about to happen, seriously drastic things . . .

'Any names?'

Rico shrugged. 'Not yet, but a lot of people are getting nervous, from what I hear. He's making a lot of enemies already.'

It was obvious from the comments circulating around that the man wasn't loved by all. 'Some people have a lot to hide, and a lot to lose,' I said.

Rico nodded, took a sip from his beer. 'Things getting rotten, somebody got to do something.'

'If police making deals with the criminals, it makes no sense risking your life out there.'

These were bad times for the JCF. Increasingly, we were coming across evidence that the people we were going after benefited from help, information and even outright cover from police officers. On one or two occasions, it was obvious that the people we were raiding had been tipped in advance. Because we were a special intervention unit, theoretically under an independent command, that meant that someone from the inside, from our ranks, or at least having access to info on our operations, had leaked news to outsiders. Wilkins was well aware of this, and although many of his old promotion comrades resented the investigations conducted by the Commissioner, he remained supportive.

During all the years of political cross-border fighting, the local police officers were doing a hard job that couldn't but involve their personal loyalties. The area they lived in determined their affiliations; there was no such thing as being neutral. The politician could help with housing, appointments and promotion. How far this influenced the police in their daily duties varied, and the higher the rank, the more it mattered whether an individual was partial or not. This was always the way politics had interacted with law enforcement in Jamaica. But now it was all about money, big money. Business had taken over. Knowing the right people and doing the right kind of favours could make a huge difference to a poorly-paid policeman. The little area youths they had been keeping in check for years were becoming seriously prosperous men, the new power players on the block. Thus, even officers who had up to now kept their integrity were finding it difficult to resist the lure of the spare cash dangled in front of them by the new 'community operators'. There was no way to explain the affluence of some of our colleagues without linking it with this phenomenon.

'You hear about Buggy?'

'No, wha' happen to him?'

'He ran out of luck,' Rico said cryptically.

Buggy had been causing us problems for over a year. Only nineteen years of age, and a former 'colleague' from my area, he had been credited with at least seven murders in and around Kingston, all drugs-related. Having managed to get himself connected to relatives of his in the States, the youth had started bringing in cocaine and moving it around, making himself a lot of cash in the process. From what we could work out, he had been running a string of couriers and his regular supply of high-grade powder had made him a big name on the local crime scene. Buggy used to be a quiet, almost shy, kid at school, the youngest of four brothers and a brilliant footballer. At one point, there were talks of him being called to the national team. Two of his brothers had been killed during the 1980 elections and the other one was rotting in Gun Court. Somewhere, Buggy had picked up bad ways and the next thing I knew, his picture was pinned on the wall of our operation room.

On a few occasions, we had been close to getting to him, but he seemed to have the uncanny ability to disappear just before we got there. Rumour had it that he also benefited from some 'cover' from a police officer, but nothing was ever proved. The last I had heard of him, he had made it out to Canada. That was three months ago.

'Him come back?'

'Yeah,' Rico said. 'Got deported from Canada last week, shot dead yesterday, trying to escape, from what I heard.'

The way Rico said it, I felt he didn't believe the story. Maybe someone didn't want Buggy to get to court.

We spent the whole afternoon cooling out in the backyard, talking about friends, family, other places, anything to get us away from the job, I think. Neither of us was much into drinking, but now and then, like today, we felt like just sitting and lining up half a dozen beers. Maybe hoping to forget for a while the life we lived, for a few hours. But then we would wake up and there was another mission lined up, another street, another crime, another day of living on the edge, weeks after weeks, months after months.

It was late September, warm and breezy on Constant Spring Road. The previous evening, the celebration for Lucy's birthday had lasted until three in the morning, and sure enough the champagne had left its shadow on my brain. It took a hot fish soup, first thing in the morning at the headquarters mess, to clear up my head. It turned into a fairly routine day, two arrests for murder and a drugs-house raid,

I was planning for a quiet evening at home with a video of the latest Schwarzenegger, borrowed from a friend now waiting in my glove compartment. Babsy had called me earlier on, but I told her, nicely, that I needed time off and I'd call her later. We'd been going out for a couple of months and so far I was enjoying her company. But I kept it easy. After the hard time and bitterness that led to my divorce from Merleene, I needed some time before starting anything serious.

The work scene was intense; hold-ups, gang-related shootings, drugs robberies. Every day had its catalogue of interventions from our squad which ended, more often than not, with body counts. The amount and sophistication of weapons on the street was such that we had been issued with modern equipment imported from the States, just to keep up with the other side. In most cases, the men we went after tended to be ready to shoot it out with us. That was why we were usually called out for any gun-related incident, the local police being unwilling to lose more of their people trying to arrest better-armed and highly-motivated gangsters.

Hand in hand with guns went hard drugs, cocaine now being widely available and getting cheaper all the time. These provided untold amounts of cash with which the youths purchased more guns. The transit in personnel to and from the nearby United States had undoubtedly influenced the propensity to crime and the inclination of these young men to use violence. The official line was that crime had in fact been 'imported' by elements returning from the US after time spent with the Jamaican gangs operating there. The number of deportees we had to monitor supported this thesis, although this alone didn't suffice to explain the situation on the streets of Kingston. The decrease in living standards was also part of the equation.

A tough job, where the only way to relax in the evening was to detach yourself from what you had lived through during the day. Some of my colleagues behaved as if dealing with violent deaths on a day-to-day basis didn't affect them, and I guess a few had become immune to it. Yet any man with a soul becomes weary of the sight of corpses and the smell of blood. But it was my job, not one to get rich from but I believed someone had to do it. Some people had to defend the population of our island against the encroachment of the deadly narcotics world.

I was less than half a mile from home when the crackling

of the radio pulled me out of my thoughts. I turned down the volume of the muisc, picked up the set to answer my call.

'09 – 09 – Unit 1 calling – do you copy?' Rico's voice sounded urgent through the crackling.

'09 speaking, Chief.'

'Carly, where are you?'

'About five minutes away from home.'

'We have a problem, meet me in Spanish Town, the lane behind Matty's bar.'

I knew the place, a noisy drinking den. 'I'm on my way. Should I call for back-up?'

'No, come alone.'

I spun around and gassed the Toyota back down the avenue, wondering what it was Rico was dealing with. For an armed response, he would have requested back-up. Rico was brave but never careless or foolhardy. Maybe it was personal, maybe he needed something done discreetly, as it sometimes happened. I blew my horn to clear the road in front and broke a third speed towards the meeting point.

I found Rico's jeep at the entrance to the dark alley behind the bar, road lights on. Another vehicle, a white van with sliding door, was parked alongside a zinc fence. There were a few people around, overspill from the bar but you could see they were keeping well away from the parked van. Though I wore casual clothes, my arrival was observed in silence. Any speculations on the situation from the onlookers was expressed quietly, from a distance. A man was at the wheel, Rico in the passenger seat. When he saw me approaching, he motioned towards the side door, so I opened it and got in. In the semi-darkness, I could make out orange crates piled up at the back, Heineken boxes and a couple of plastic drums behind the front seats.

'Carly, look who I found, by chance.'

The man in the driving seat looked less than happy about this 'chance' encounter. He was small in stature, with a head of bushy hair and a goatee beard. His eyes seemed still and blank when I searched them. I rarely forget a face; names on the other hand are a little harder for me to recall at times. This man knew me too, I was sure of it, the way he averted his gaze after the first contact.

'I was on my way to meet a friend,' Rico explained, 'when I noticed this van parked by the bar, badly parked in fact. When I checked it out, it had a puncture but when I saw who was changing the tyre, I had to stop and offer my help.' Rico turned to the silent man. 'You should be happy I came along, Fitz, you could have got robbed. This is a bad area!'

It sounded like genuine concern for an old friend from Rico. For an old friend it was; I now could place that face. A few months before, we were on a routine patrol of the docks when we were called to a warehouse where a burglary had taken place. We got there to find a dazed watchman, tied up like a pig and bleeding like one from a deep gash in his forehead. The man was Fitz. He told us that he was jumped by two men; that was all he could remember. He had been working there for three weeks and when we checked had no criminal records. The owner of the warehouse lost a few thousand dollars' worth of clothes, we left the case with the local police.

'Alright, Fitz?' I asked kindly, not wanting to blame him unfairly for my ruined evening.

'Alright, officer,' he said. From his tone of voice, you could tell he was in trouble.

'Fitz is doing a favour fe him cousin, Carly. He's taking this van to Town.'

'You still working down at the docks, Fitz?' I asked.

'No officer, I get laid off.' Fitz's voice was weak, strained.

'So now you run errands for your cousin, right? Look.' Rico took a note out of his shirt pocket, passed it to me; a new-looking US hundred-dollar bill. 'Fitz's cousin pays him in currency.'

I looked at Fitz, who seemed uneasy and was trying to avoid my eyes. His were white and large, shifting from Rico to me to the poorly lit alleyway outside.

'Night-time delivery is more money. Fitz is doing overtime.' There was a dose of humour in Rico's remark but it didn't get through to Fitz, the way his thin face seemed frozen up.

Rico said, matter-of-factly, 'Carly, beg you pass me couple oranges from the crate over there.'

I went down into the van and opened one of the top crates.

'No man, gimme some from the crate underneath; them more ripe down there!'

I moved the top crate and lifted the cover to pick up some fruits inside. Under the first layer of oranges I could feel paper, thick brown wrapping paper. Probing further, I closed my fingers around a cloth-wrapped bundle, brought it out.

'Come bring it here, Carly.'

I handed Rico the bundle but he said: 'It don't look like orange in deh though! Open it up, make we see.'

It sure wasn't oranges. Two new-looking, dark and smooth automatic handguns, Glocks. I held one in each hand, looked at Fitz. He wasn't happy, Fitz.

'What you think, sah?'

I shrugged. 'I don't know. Maybe oranges don't bring in enough money; maybe Fitz's cousin branch out into another business,' I said.

'Fitz never know anything about it, you know. You can't even trust family nowadays.' Rico sounded sad at the way Fitz's cousin had dealt with him.

'How much your cousin pay you fe this favour, Fitz?'

Fitz swallowed and told us. 'Three hundred dollars.'

'US?' Rico asked.

'No, sah.'

Rico shook his head. 'You know how much money you have in this van, Fitz?'

The unfortunate man didn't answer.

'Oh yeah, you don't know, I forgot ...' Rico dropped

wickedly. 'Well, massah, from what I checked, with the shotguns down here, it's about fifteen thousand US you carrying.'

'Shotguns as well?' I raised a quizzical eyebrow.

'Yeah man, look under there!'

I lifted the Heineken boxes and found half a dozen gleaming pump-action shotguns wrapped in bundles of old clothes.

'Streetsweepers, that's what they call them back in the States. Clean everything within fifty yards. Someone going out to hunt big game it looks like, eh Fitz?' Rico said.

Not a word either way from the sweating driver.

'So, which part you was taking all this, man?' I asked Fitz. I didn't get an answer, and there is nothing more frustrating for a policeman to ask a question and not get an answer. Especially so when you would prefer to be somewhere else than with the man who refuses to answer.

'Fitz', I said, 'better you talk now, 'cause if we carry you down to Central, dem man deh will handle you rough ... Wha yuh ah say?'

You could almost hear Fitz's brain ticking in the silence of the night. I knew what he was thinking too.

'So, where we going?' Fitz was visibly nervous, even in the darkness. With only the faint glow of a solitary street lamp, I could see beads of sweat on his narrow forehead.

'Officer, I beg you, arrest me, take me to the station.' The voice was pleading, deep and shaky.

'Fitz man, ah de first time I hear anybody beg fe get arrest. What happen to yuh?' Rico said, pleasantly. But Fitz wasn't joking, he really wanted to be taken away.

'I ... I can't go.'

'I'm getting impatient, Fitz, I'll give you one more chance. Where we going?' Rico's tone was just that little bit colder. He hardly ever lost his composure. In fact I never saw him get angry with a suspect, but you had to know when not to try his patience. Now it was getting late and the find was a serious one. Fitz must have realized he was deep in trouble.

'I suppose to bring the van to Heavensdale,' he said, real quietly.

Rico and I exchanged a quick glance. The guns were not going directly to one of the garrison towns of West Kingston. Heavensdale was a nice area, residential. Usually, we only ever got as far as the men handling the missions for the big guys, and they knew better than to reveal their connections. But someone had got unlucky tonight, and this was an unexpected break for us.

'Where in Heavensdale, Fitz?' Fitz muttered an address. I knew what was going on in his mind.

Rico nodded. 'Okay, start the engine.'

Fitz swallowed hard, wiped his face with one shaky hand. 'I beg you, sah, take me to the station.'

'Take you to the station?' Rico said 'I can't understand you, Fitz. You know what will happen to you when I show dem man deh what you carrying?'

'If I go with you, dem will kill me.' There was real terror in the man's voice.

'Who is dem?'

No answer.

'Alright Fitz, I gwan tell you the truth. I don't want you, you're not big enough for me. I'm trying to give you a break so you don't have to spend a few years in GP. If all goes well, I'll let you go.' Rico paused. 'But if you don't start this van now, I'm giving you up to my man dem down at Central and you'll get charged with the rest of your friends dem, okay?'

'Fitz,' I said, 'you're gwan be late for your delivery.'

'He's right, you know. You better make haste.' Rico motioned to the driver. 'Start the engine.' It was a hard decision for Fitz, not much of a choice. He looked at both of us in turn then switched on the ignition. The van shook and started up.

'Carly, sit with him, I'll follow. And Fitz . . .' Rico looked into the man's face before jumping out of the van '. . . don't make no wrong moves and everything will be alright.'

I stepped out and followed Rico to the jeep. 'We got onto something here, Carly, I'm not sure yet what it is, but this is not the usual ghetto supply run.' I looked back. The miserable figure staring at us from behind the van's windscreen was hardly the type of soldier we would expect to find on an arms run.

'Which man downtown is going to send this one on a mission like that? Alone, one hundred US in his pocket and a small arsenal?! Somebody is trying a t'ing.'

'You want we check it out?'

Rico nodded. 'Yeah, the area we going to is off limits. I want to know who the hell is bringing in guns down there and what for.'

'We've got to meet Fitz's cousin,' I said.

Rico took a cigarillo out of his top pocket, placed it at the left corner of his mouth.

'Hmm, it's going to be a surprise. Get your presents ready.' He climbed aboard the jeep and kicked on the big engine. I went back to the van and the sweating Fitz. We drove off first, Rico following behind. My car was left at the bar until later.

I told Fitz to drive carefully and went to the back. Digging a little, I found some cartridges for the shotguns in one of the crates, 12 gauge, big bore. I loaded one up, didn't arm the pump just yet. Back in the seat, I placed the mean-looking instrument between my legs. I had my automatic on my hip, ever ready. I knew Rico's jeep had enough equipment inside to handle a small assault. Fitz had eyed the shotgun and looked even more nervous now. I didn't really feel much like talking and neither did the little driver. Somewhere in a nicer part of town, someone was waiting for him. Rico and I weren't invited; we would have to gatecrash the party.

Set at the end of a steep rise, the mansion looked large and pretty. Big halogen lamps spaced throughout the surrounding garden bathed the grounds and house in a sea of brightness.

The concrete driveway beyond the locked metal gates ended in a parking bay to the left. From my hiding place, behind the passenger seat, I could see a town car and a four-wheel drive Landcruiser.

Fitz had to play his part well to get us inside the grounds. Any nervousness could wreck the surprise. Rico had left his jeep a couple of streets down the hill and followed the van on foot, an SLR strapped on his back. He was using the blind side as a cover against any peering eyes from the house. Fitz was stressed, it was plain to see, even though I had reassured him that, once inside, all would go well as long as he got out of the way. The barrel of the shotgun behind him did little to steady his nerves. He twitched as I armed the pump.

There was no guard but the intercom at the gate crackled as we stopped. Then a man's voice came out, impatient.

'Wh'appen, Fitz? Yuh late!'

Someone was watching from the house apparently. I crouched low inside the darkness, very still. The eye of a camera pointed down from the top of the left-hand concrete gate pillar. I had a thought for Rico, knowing he would spot the camera and find a way to avoid it.

'Cool. I catch a puncture ina Spanish Town.'

Fitz's voice sounded fleety but it must have seemed convincing enough through the line, because there was a buzzing sound and the tall gates started opening. Fitz drove up, parked right in front of the main door, just like I told him to do. He climbed out. Bursts of loud music came through from the house. On the porch, a man appeared, tall and skinny-looking in a white string vest.

Peeping from my hiding spot, I couldn't quite make out the face underneath the baseball cap yet the voice rang a bell. Something stuck out of his belt, dark against the vest. Since we didn't know how many people could be awaiting the van, we knew we would have to play it by ear, seizing the moment. All my senses alive, the familiar pinch pulling at my stomach pit and one finger around the shotgun trigger, I waited behind the sliding door.

'We t'ink seh you get hol'up somewhere, man. Everyt'ing cool?'

I couldn't see them because the exchange was happening right on the other side of the door. But I was getting the bad feeling that Fitz was going to flinch. Whether he would try to give us up discreetly or his nervousness show through, I knew inside my guts something would go wrong. The plan was for him to open the sliding door, so that I could surprise the man. After this, we could make our way inside and catch the rest of them unawares. Five, ten seconds and no sign of any moves on the door from Fitz.

'Yeah man, but that dyam wheel gimme some trouble. First I couldn't find no spanner, then the bolt dem was rusty.'

What the hell was he talking about the wheel for, instead of opening the door? Surely we could expect more people to come out of the house any time, and that would make the play even more difficult. I licked my lips and waited, hesitating to grab the inside handle myself and burst out on the man. I hoped Rico would have found himself a vantage point to cover the entrance.

'Maxi was getting nervous, man. Open up, make me check ev'rything deh.

I tensed up, backed up to the side of the door. I could feel the metal against my back, the barrel of the shotgun lined up with my shoulder, pointing upwards. The door handle clicked and the panel started sliding back. The baseball hat appeared into view. I couldn't see Fitz. One quick step and the gleaming barrel end came into contact with the slim man's neck.

'Police. Keep still!' I told him firmly but quietly.

The man froze, only his eyes slid sideways to make me out. I heard him say: 'You dead Fitz.' Pretty calm, he was.

I stepped down carefully, scanning the surroundings rapidly, my shotgun directly against the man's throat. Fitz just stood to my left, eyes wide and arms hanging down. I pulled the gun out of my prisoner's waist, slipped it into mine.

'I want a straight answer, bway. How many friends in deh?' I asked. My eyes met those of the man I was sticking up, I had the feeling he knew me from somewhere.

'Two,' I heard him say. Still no sign of Rico, but I knew his ways. He was waiting in the shadows to see who else would come out before revealing himself. That set me up as bait, but then there were only two of us.

Was it the creaking of the window opening or the metallic sound of a gun being armed that I heard first? In any case, something at the back of my head tingled and I dived to my left just as bullets came peppering the side of the van, around where my head had been. Someone up there was monitoring the guests! I hit the ground, rolled over and crawled under the vehicle, coming out on the other side. Another burst of automatic fire came down; I had moved towards the front of the van already. I could make out a silhouette at the first floor window. Coming out, my shotgun levelled towards the shadow up there, I squeezed the trigger. The upstairs window blew up. Two separate barks boomed out behind me, aimed at the same window.

I moved forward, eyes searching for any movements. The slim man disappeared inside the house. Fitz was lying still on the ground before the open van door. A running silhouette emerged from the shadows, heading straight for the open front door. Sparkles from the SLR muzzle as slugs peppered the front of the house. Rico was moving in, both weapons blazing.

'Take the back!' I heard him call out.

I sprinted around the house, rearming as I moved. After one quick glance around the corner, I pushed on towards the back of the house. I arrived just as a pair of sliding doors opened on a man in a boiler suit. He saw me a fraction of second after I did and that made the difference between his life and mine. By the time the muzzle of his machine gun levelled on my chest, less than twenty yards away, I caught him full in the side of the body. I watched him fly backwards, saw the glass shatter as he hit the bay window and crashed right through it. A burst of his weapon lost itself somewhere in the night air. From inside the house, I heard the barking of a big .45. Running on, I leapt over his spread out corpse with its missing rib cage and passed through a large kitchen. Plates of food waited on the table. Automatic gunfire burst upstairs: question and answer. The second voice sounded like an AK47; our hosts had some heavy equipment. I took the stairs, my shotgun pointing up. Two shrill screams rang out, out of place amidst the firefight.

'Carly?'

'Yeah.'

'Get them girls out of here.'

I saw two bare legs, then two more, before the terrified girls appeared on the second flight of stairs. Their eyes met mine, I motioned them down. The brown one, short with dyed blonde hair, had little on save for a brassiere and a short skirt. She was frozen scared, her arms holding her head, crying already. Her darker friend, in shorts and skimpy top, seemed braver. She took the other one resolutely by the hand and dragged her down the steps past me.

'Stay down there!' I told them, then climbed up to join Rico.

One short burst, then the answer from the AK longer, furious. Still careful, watching the doors in case someone was hiding in one of the rooms on the first floor, I progressed to the far corner. Rico's SLR lay at his feet. He was reloading his .45, crouched in a low stance, his cigarillo pinched in his jaw.

He shouted: 'Police! Throw your gun out, come out with your hands up!'

A long burst of automatic fire raked the wall opposite, chipping away the plaster.

'One man inside there with an AK,' Rico said, motioning

with his head towards the door next to him. 'Go around through the next room, see if you can draw him.'

Playing the bait again, I moved back to the last door, walked in carefully, even though I knew Rico had cleared all the rooms he had passed on the landing. The bedroom was vast, well-furnished and empty. I went to the window and opened it. I could see the gate, the grounds and a water fountain far to the right by the boundary wall. Looking down, there wasn't much to get a foothold on. Back inside, another angry series of rapid shots, followed by the sound of two single explosions.

A small bathroom occupied the right-hand corner of the bedroom I was in, just a shower, a sink and a toilet bowl, expensive tiles on the walls, thick rug on the floor. We were wrecking a rich man's house. A door led to the adjoining room. I tried it, found it locked but right away, it drew fire, slugs boring through the wooden panel. I had already retreated behind the shower wall, out of the way.

'I found a connecting door inside here,' I shouted out to Rico. I knew that would cause the man holed up inside to get even more nervous. Sure enough, another volley of shots rang out, tearing more holes through the door. Rico's gun barked again, twice. Not to be left out, I edged forward, pointed my barrel towards the panel and squeezed. A loud 'bang' some smoke, then a large hole in the middle of the door. I rearmed the pump. Something moved inside and Rico called out.

'Give it up, man; we don't want to kill you.'

Silence.

'Your friend dem can't help you again. Be smart, throw your weapon and come out.'

Still no answer and no shots from inside the room. Maybe the man's ammunition were out. Or it could be a trap to draw one of us in to get shot.

'Right: ten seconds, then you done,' Rico announced. He started counting aloud. Meanwhile, knowing this was setting the gunman on edge, I slowly crept back to the broken-up door. I risked one eye and still couldn't make out anything; the light had been switched off. Suddenly, there was a sound and a shape came rushing at the door, crashing through with a roar. I started to move sideways, finger at the ready. The door gave up under the weight of the push and I just about managed to get out of the way. The man was stocky, furious, almost naked and charging like a wounded bear. The automatic machine he was holding was empty because when he got back his footing and saw me, he lifted it with both hands like a club to smash me on the head.

'Yuh bloodclaaaaaat!!!!' I heard him shout.

Calmly, I raised the shotgun and hit him square in the middle of the chest with the hardwood butt. He let out a scream and folded up, his weapon hitting the tiled floor with a metallic 'clang'. He wasn't unconscious, just wheezing and coughing, eyes wild and rolling side to side. Then he threw up.

'Suspect down,' I called out to Rico.

He came down to where I was, his gun still drawn, the unlit cigarillo between his teeth to look down at the man lying bare-chested on the floor in his shorts.

'You're under arrest,' Rico told him.

The man mumbled something indistinct. He looked quite young, with just the shadow of a moustache and a brown complexion. I had never seen him before. Rico was looking down at him, like he was trying to recall who he might be. He said, 'Cuff him and bring him down. The locals must be on their way.'

When I got downstairs with him, the oversized living room impressed me. Wide screen TV, a couple of video recorders, music systems, leather furniture, chandeliers hanging from the ceiling. This was a real palace. I had counted four bedrooms upstairs, two downstairs and other rooms which branched out from the main corridor.

I hooked up the stony face youth to the front door grille. He seemed to be recovering and started cursing so I backhanded him across the mouth, warned him to be quiet or else, and started looking around. The coffee table in the front room offered evidence of drug abuse, an unfinished crack pipe laying amidst several vials, half a bottle of whisky and a small bag of ganja. We had interrupted a real party. The body of the slim man, probably Fitz's cousin, lay across the couch, one hand inches away from an automatic machine gun. In the far corner, eyes wide with fear, the two girls stood huddled against the bar.

Rico came down. He had retrieved his SLR and was carrying a brown leather attaché case.

'That's why our friend went upstairs, instead of running through the back door.'

He dropped the case on the couch, totally oblivious to the corpse spread out there, flicked it open. Cash in US dollars, a few thousands dollars it seemed, and a very neat plastic-wrapped parcel which contained a white powdery substance. This was unlikely to be washing powder, but Rico checked it, just in case . . .

'So, let's see who we have here,' he said, sifting through a bunch of letters and bills he had picked up from a folder. I saw him frown, then shake his head. From the table, he picked up a lighter, ignoring the rest of the illegal substances spread there, and carefully lit his cigarillo.

'Let's move out, Carly. The party's over.'

'Come!' I told the girls. I got the prisoner and went outside. On the front yard, Fitz was lying on his back, eyes wide open on the dark skies. I pushed the captive firmly inside the van, got the girls in. One of them had started crying. Rico climbed in with his attaché case and I kicked up the van's engine. The whole operation, since we had first entered the house, had lasted less than fifteen minutes. Two police vehicles were just about getting to the gate when we made out. They came to an abrupt halt and officers started jumping out, weapons drawn and aiming at the van. So Rico came out, his hands up in the air, holding out his badge, calling out loud:

'Detective Inspector Glenford. Hold your fire!'

I watched him step up to the officer in charge and confer with him. Rico wasn't into too much talking, especially when he had just been into action. He came back to the van, climbed in. The cigarillo was getting shorter, the strong smell floating around the cabin.

'Let's go, they'll take care of the cleaning up,' he told me.

I geared up and drove out, ignoring the curious looks of uniformed police standing around their vehicles. The area was not known for the kind of Wild West scene they were about to find inside. The little crowd of bewildered residents gathered around the gates were wondering what had caused this invasion of uniforms in their usually quiet street. Down the hill, Rico got back his jeep and we drove to the headquarters to report on the impromptu intervention. It had turned out not to be the quiet evening I had planned.

CHAPTER TEN

Freeze!

When Rico was called to Superintendent Wilkins' office even before the morning briefing, I had no doubt what the topic was. We had found out, on reaching the headquarters, that our suspect had been released shortly after being brought in and, although Rico didn't say anything to me, I could tell he was less than pleased. Over time, I had developed a real skill for listening to conversations taking place in the Super's office from my desk strategically placed next to the wall in the adjoining room. Pretending to be typing an overdue report, I listened to the storm next door.

'US currency in excess of twenty thousand dollars, over one kilo of high grade cocaine plus an array of brand new imported weapons. If this is not enough evidence for a prosecution then, we're going to have to release quite a lot of suspects!' Rico sounded very unhappy.

'Okay, but this is a specific situation. That young man is not with any organized gang. We are dealing with an individual who's taken a wrong turn, not with a criminal.' The Super had not been shot at by the 'young man' the previous night, he could afford to be broad minded.

'No? Well, what do you call a man who's importing guns and dealing drugs? And you're right to say he's not with a gang: my understanding is that he's setting up to run his own operation. That kid has got ambition!'

'You did interview him, I understand.'

'Yes, and he more or less laughed in my face and told me he wouldn't go to jail. He was right.'

'According to his lawyer, he didn't know you were police officers. He thought he was being attacked by gangsters.'

'We identified ourselves, he knew very well who we were, but that didn't stop him from shooting at us.'

Wilkins paused, cleared his throat. 'Let's put this into perspective, Inspector. We are talking about Mr Walter's son, as in Walter & Brown Inc. A man like him cannot afford to have his name mixed up in a crime story all over the *Gleaner*.'

'Right, and I guess Mr Walter is going to take care of the problem himself, because that kid is bad news and isn't going to get any better now that he knows he can get away with anything.'

'He's only a misguided young man. He recently returned from the States where he's been studying. Apparently he's had a few problems settling down there.'

'He's been deported for drugs offences. I checked.'

'He made a mistake, due to bad influences, moving with the wrong crowd, from what his father said.'

'Yeah, and he's graduated since that. One of the dead guys at the house used to be an enforcer for a Rockfort outfit, and the other one was sent back from the States three month ago after serving time for a murder charge in Philadelphia. Young Walters is a bona fide criminal, sir.'

Wilkins knew that the picture Rico was drawing was not exaggerated. On the other hand, some pressure had come down from on high, that was obvious. 'Look, Glenford, this is the kind of situation that requires some discretion. We need to do what we can so that Mr Walter doesn't suffer any embarrassment.'

'You are asking me to take part in a cover-up, sir. No disrespect but this unit was set up precisely because the locals could not be trusted to be independent from partisan politics.

'I am quite aware of the reason this unit was set up, Inspector Glenford.' Wilkins said very dryly, trying to regain some form of control in the debate. 'But pulling rank doesn't make wrong right.' The Superintendent paused. 'Look, I don't like this kind of thing any more than you do, but as you are aware, Mr Walter is an MP, a very influential man, with very strong political connections.'

'Then what was the point of setting up a special structure to investigate corruption in the Force if even our unit is under the control of the politician?' Rico sounded disgusted.

'I don't think it is quite like that, but this is a special case ... The matter is dropped.'

'Dropped?'

'Yes. You are not to pursue any further investigations concerning Mr Walter's son. This is an order.'

There was a tense silence. I could imagine the eye contact taking place on the other side of the wall.

'Whatever you say. Don't you think we should at least try to find out his connections?'

'Certainly.'

'Right, but how are we supposed to conduct our enquiries when you've just released the main suspect?'

'I can't help you with this.'

'And you really think this is the last time you're going to hear about Mr Walter junior, sir?!'

'Time will tell.'

The sound of a chair being vacated, then the office door opened and closed. Rico walked down the corridor and jumped in his jeep. I didn't see him until later that afternoon when he called me and two more unit members to go and investigate reports of a shoot-out in the Waterhouse area. By then he was back to his usual impassive self. But his last question to Superintendent Wilkins proved to be prophetic.

*   *   *

Tracing the illegal importation of the weapons found in the van wasn't going to be easy. All the same, it had to be easier than trying to trace back the trail of the cocaine! Where to start? Fitz was just a driver and couldn't have helped us, even if he was alive. The two gangsters we met at the house were dead, and Maxi, the only one who knew the deal, was out of bounds.

What we did have was the weapons' serial numbers and these could be checked with the relevant firearms licensing bureau in the States. That's what we did first thing that Monday morning. It took a little time to get through to the right department on the phone but it worked. All the same, that only gave us the date and place of purchase and the name of the person licensed to do the transaction. More than likely, the licence had been stolen and doctored. A call to the ATF bureau confirmed this. It was a safe bet that posse members in Miami were behind the scheme.

We didn't have much to go on, so our next line of enquiry was the shipping of the package. Rico set out two things as a basis for our research: the package must have arrived at the docks from Miami only a couple of days, at the most, before Fitz was sent to pick it up. This type of merchandise was never left unattended for long. And it must have been part of a larger shipment of legally imported goods. On checking, we found that only two ships from Miami had reached Kingston in the week before the bust. This still left us with a lot of cargo manifests to go through, not to mention hundreds of potential suspects to be interviewed. It was a daunting task.

So early the next morning, we took a drive to the docks to find out who had been on duty on the night Fitz drove out there for the pick-up. We were relying on the assumption that it all happened on the same day. We got to talk to the customs supervisor, a large greying man who was very helpful, especially so because he happened to remember Rico from the days they both lived in the Crossroads area. He checked his staff rotation chart and gave us a name. We then went down to the customs control office and introduced ourselves.

Oliver Mannings had been in the post as a customs officer for eight years. In his early thirties, he had a short beard and a ready smile, wore his uniform well-pressed and was busy tucking in a sizeable sandwich when we walked in. Mannings excused himself, explaining that he had been covering for a colleague the previous night and just about managed to go home and change before taking up his shift. No time for breakfast. We exchanged pleasantries for a while, then Rico explained the aim of our visit. The customs man thought about it before confirming that he was indeed on duty on the night in question. Rico asked whether he could recall a white van coming to collect a parcel that night. Mannings paused then said he didn't recollect such a vehicle but that, in any case, the pick-up couldn't have happened at night. The customs clearance office for imported merchandise closed every weekday at 3 p.m. Rico and I were thinking alike: supposing that Fitz had come for the package that day, he must have gone somewhere between his trip to the docks and his fateful stop in Spanish Town around nightfall that evening.

'Were you on duty during the day?' Rico asked.

Mannings shook his head. 'I started my shift at six o'clock, until four in the morning.'

'Can you tell us who was on duty that morning?'

The customs officer asked: 'This is about an importation of illegal substances?'

'Is there anything you can tell us?' Rico asked him in return.

Mannings shrugged. 'We had a big bust a couple of months ago, you heard about it I'm sure. Nothing since that.'

He was referring to half a ton of cocaine packed in frozen meat boxes, seized by the customs earlier that year. The Crime Squad had led the investigation and eventually arrested a well-known Chinese trader. Rumours of collusion on the part of some senior customs officers had surfaced for a while, but no one was actually named.

'So, who could we ask about that van? It could have been another day last week, but we think it was that same Thursday.'

'One of my colleagues was on duty Thursday morning, but she's off today.' Rico said we couldn't wait for the said customs officer to be back, so Mannings gave us a name and an address, then we thanked him and left him to his interrupted breakfast.

The modest house in a busy part of Papine was surrounded by a painted wall planted on top with broken bottle bits. The owner wasn't taking chances. The gate was closed and only opened after we rang the bell three or four times. A teenage girl informed us that her auntie Beryl wasn't well but Rico flashed his badge and told her we needed to talk to her about an important matter so we eventually were led into a bright living room. Comfortable in my bamboo chair, I admired the good taste of the decorating. Potted plants climbed around the furniture and the large bay windows leading to the back garden revealed a water pool and patio. The teenage girl had disappeared inside the house. From the street, the heckling of children came through.

Mrs Beryl Johnson finally entered the room, dressed in a housecoat and her hair tied up hastily. Her eyes peered at us behind wide glasses. She came to us, one hand over the left side of her face and we got up to greet her.

'You'll have to excuse me; I just had a tooth out this morning and I don't feel very well.'

Rico introduced us. 'We're very sorry to disturb you at such a bad time. We're not going to take much of your time.'

'I'll be alright tomorrow,' Mrs Johnson said confidently. 'What can I do for you?'

'Well, we just come from your office,' Rico explained. 'We talked with Mr Mannings and he gave us your address. Once again, we apologize for disturbing you but maybe you could help us with our investigation.' Quietly, I always admired Rico's way with words.

'What is it about?'

'You were on duty last Thursday?' It wasn't really a question.

'Last Thursday? Yes, I was. I did early shifts all week.'

'Good. Would you by any chance recall a white van coming through to collect a package. We think it was Thursday.'

The customs officer reflected on that, fighting the pain and the effects of the painkillers.

'A white van? Yes, I think so.'

'With a red stripe all around,' Rico said, then added. 'I know you see quite a lot of vehicles every day but if you could remember, it would be very helpful.'

'I think so, yes, a white van with red stripe,' the woman repeated.

'Is there any way you can retrace what type of goods this van took out?'

'Yes, certainly.' I watched the eyes go from Rico to me and back. 'What did you say you're investigating?'

'Well, to tell you the truth, there's been a little mix-up with some goods that a friend of mine imported,' Rico started. 'The reason he asked me to help him with it is that he's a little embarrassed.'

'Embarrassed?'

'Yes, the goods have ... well ... disappeared.'

'Disappeared?!' Very concerned, she sounded, Mrs Johnson.

Rico nodded soberly. 'Yes, very mysteriously. And as you must understand, my friend would rather this doesn't get out. He can't be seen looking for the criminals himself, so he asked us to sort it out for him. He's very upset.'

Rico was looking at me, so I just said, 'Yes, madam, very upset, but we will get back his property, have no doubt about this.'

The woman shifted from Rico to me, licked her lips and adjusted her glasses. 'But, he didn't tell me anything about it!'

'If you were a man in his position, would you like it to be known that you've been robbed?!' Rico asked very judiciously.

'You know how people love to disrespect the law in this country.'
A glance from the master storyteller.

'So, Mrs Johnson, could you tell us who was driving this van, last Thursday?' I asked.

'The van, well it was a man, a little man, very dark, with a hat on. I didn't see him for long.'

'Do you recall what it was he took away? How many boxes?'

'One, a big box, a crate. A fridge-freezer.'

'A fridge-freezer?' I repeated, very interested.

'Yes,' Mrs Johnson said.

The woman had responded perfectly to our psychological approach, and I felt we had also had a little luck but then again Rico had manoeuvred too well for her.

'What colour?' Rico asked.

'What?'

'The fridge-freezer, what colour was it?'

She stopped, confused. 'I . . . I don't know.'

'You didn't see it?'

'No . . .'

'Oh, you didn't open the crate, that's right?'

'No, I mean, yes.'

'You opened it?'

'No, I didn't open the crate,' The voice was dry, almost inimical. Mrs Johnson wasn't stupid, she was a customs officer, just one step below Special Squad officers like us in terms of interrogating people, but Detective Inspector Rico Glenford was a master tactician when it came to mentally outwitting suspects. I had been watching him for years. He spread out his hands in a would-be appeasing gesture. 'Mrs Johnson, let me explain something to you. Our concern here is to find our friend's property before whoever stole it disposes of it. I am asking you these questions to find out exactly what happened that day. I need to know if you saw what was in the crate. You didn't, so that's all I wanted to know.'

I had caught his glance and knew which way to swing. 'Mrs Johnson, are you supposed to open every box before clearing them out?' I asked.

'They always inspect them in the warehouse, but sometimes we ask for certain items to be rechecked at the gate.'

'I'm just curious,' I said, glancing at Rico, very calm in his bamboo chair. 'I mean, what attracts your attention, what makes you want to open certain boxes and not others? Is it to do with the type of person who comes to pick them up?'

'Hmm, yes, I suppose, yes.'

'Okay, so, this little dark man with the van ...' I pushed on, '... he didn't look suspicious. I mean, that's why you didn't ask him to open the crate, right?'

Mrs Johnson didn't answer. Hands on her knees, she left me to scrutinize Rico's face from behind her glasses. We waited, and it must have felt very uncomfortable for her, these few seconds. Finally: 'Look, officers, the documents said it was a fridge-freezer from Miami in the crate. I don't know nothing else. I was asked to try and make the documents go through quickly, instead of waiting a week or more. I just did it as a favour for a friend, it's nothing illegal, we all do it sometimes to help family. I don't want no problems.'

There it was, the fridge-freezer in the white van breezing through the customs gate.

'You won't have any problems, Mrs Johnson,' Rico's smoothest voice assured the worried woman. 'You are helping us to retrace our friend's property, we are very grateful to you.'

She was looking at Rico like she couldn't decide whether he was man or beast. 'What was in the crate?' she asked him eventually.

'A fridge-freezer,' he answered, very naturally.

This time, Mrs Johnson's eyes reflected total blankness. A dose of Rico's mind-twisting, combined with action of the toothache and painkillers; she'd be in shock for a few more days.

'One more question, Mrs Johnson,' he said, picking on what was still missing. 'Are you sure you delivered the fridge-freezer to the right man? Maybe that's what happened.'

The question seemed to give Mrs Johnson a little boost of energy. 'No, that's not what happened. It was the right man who took away the crate!'

'How can you be sure?' I probed further.

'He called me and described the man, and he had the card.'

'Well, if he had the card, then, no mistake. It was the right man.'

Mrs Johnson didn't catch the quick eye contact between Rico and me. I thought I read satisfaction at my performance from the master.

'Could you show us this card, Mrs Johnson?'

The woman looked at Rico in silence, then said: 'I think I should call first to make sure.'

Rico shrugged. 'Call him if you want.' He looked at his watch. 'He should still be at the office.'

He let the woman get up and go to her telephone, sat amidst climber plants on varnished bamboo shelves. She dialled a number, asked Rico: 'I'm sorry, what did you say your name was?'

'Glenford, Detective Inspector Glenford. Tell him I am taking you to the headquarters to sign your statement, he can meet us there. We'll have lunch.'

I watched the woman's finger press down on the receiver's switch. 'To the headquarters, but why?'

'This is a favour for a friend, just like you, but we also have other cases, you see. If you come with us now, a sergeant can take down your statement while I go over a list of suspects with our colleague. That way, we won't waste any more time.'

'Look Inspector.' Mrs Johnson stood by her pretty shelf, the colourful garden at her back wafted sweet fragrances into the room. 'I would rather this affair doesn't involve me in any way.'

'But you are a witness, madam, maybe not right now but if this goes to court . . .'

'To court? I can't go to court!' I watched her put down the telephone receiver. All this must have wreaked hell on her already frayed nerves. Mrs Johnson came back to her couch and sat, both hands holding her gathered knees, always a sure sign of confession in a woman, I had learned.

'You must understand something here, Inspector Glenford. I would appreciate if you could keep my name out of this unfortunate incident. I wouldn't like my husband to hear about it.'

'But you didn't do anything wrong, just a favour. I'm sure he would understand.' Rico sounded genuinely sincere. Mrs Johnson adjusted her glasses, pushed back a lock of hair from her forehead.

'No, he wouldn't, believe me.' Her voice lowered somewhat. 'I don't want him to find out I did a favour for that particular man. He knows we used to be friends, you see, before I got married, and he is a little funny about it, you know how it is . . .'

Rico knew. He inhaled slowly, like he was weighing out circumstances, assessing what he could do. 'Alright, Mrs Johnson, I understand, and you're right; it's best to, what do they say, let sleeping dogs lie.' He smiled, as though satisfied by the proverb's timely quote. 'This is what we're going to do.'

There was hope again on Mrs Johnson's eyes.

'We'll go back to the station, work with our friend on what we already have. He doesn't need to know we spoke to you, it's up to you whether you wish to tell him or not. The main thing is, the man he sent to you took the fridge-freezer out. We will find this man, don't worry.'

Rico got up, so did I. 'And don't worry about your husband, he doesn't need to be bothered with little things like that.' Rico advanced an indulgent smile, kindness itself. 'We'll leave you now. I hope your toothache goes away soon.'

'Goodbye Mrs Johnson, and thank you,' I said, following Rico towards the door.

'Ah, I almost forgot.' He turned and said, one hand to his forgetful head. 'Could I have this card?' It was like Mrs Johnson was suspended in mid-air for a quick second, very still, then she must have had a fleeting thought for her hard-working husband because she spun around and left the room.

Back on the traffic filled Hope Road, Rico looked at my expression, smiled and said, 'No feel nuh way, you know.'

'Fe wha?'

'I know yuh well want to read the name on the card.'

I shrugged. 'Dat alright; but I got her to talk about the card, right?'

Rico blew his horn and gestured to an offending driver who'd forgotten to signal before edging right to turn off the main road. 'I didn't need the card.'

'Eeh? So how you was gonna know who the man was?'

He didn't answer right away, took time to switch over the cassette in the machine.

'I did know before we even walk in the woman house.'

'What?'

Rico made a suitable pause to enjoy my surprise. 'A policeman's job is to know everything that happens in his town, especially knowing which man deal with which woman. That often helps to solve crimes.'

I thought about this.

'So what; how yuh find out who that woman was dealing with years ago?'

'Years ago?' Rico smirked, taking his eyes off the road to look at me. He let out a dry laugh: 'I sorry for the poor hard-working husband!'

A shocked little angel flew past us, hands clasped on his innocent ears. I could now understand that Mrs Johnson would be so kind as to do a favour for an 'old friend'.

'You feel seh she know what was in the crate?'

Rico shook his head slowly. 'I could be wrong, the woman could be involved from the start, but I think she's being used by the man to get the drugs through discreetly.'

'In the fridge-freezer ...' I said, my mind connecting the bits of information together.

'Yeah, and I feel it's not the first time. But now he's made a mistake and after she calls him, he's gonna know I'm onto him.' Rico turned right into the street leading to the headquarters. 'He's just starting to realize he's out in the open, and someone is going to pay the price.'

'How yuh know that?' I asked, unconvinced.

'Because he was having a long discussion about it with Maxi last night.'

Who called who, I never found out, but the day after our visit to Mrs Johnson, Rico called me aside just before lunch and gave me a meeting-point and a time. At 1 p.m., I was parked in front of the Flying Duck, on Constant Spring mall, watching a table inside the busy oriental restaurant. Of the two men seated there, one ate heartily, the other just sipped from a glass in between exchanges. Even from where I sat, you could tell the conversation was less than relaxed. Eventually, Rico put down his fork. He wiped the corners of his mouth carefully with a paper napkin, shook his head and opened up his palms upwards, a gesture I often observed which meant 'there's nothing I can do'. Shortly after that, the other man got up and left the restaurant. His light grey suit was well cut, made to measure I guessed, wine-coloured tie on a white shirt, clean-shaven and with the unhurried pace of a court judge.

He could have passed for a judge, but the slender man

opening the door of the dark blue BMW was in fact a senior member of the famed Crime Squad, JCF's leading investigative unit. Inspector William Bailey drove off just as Rico emerged from the restaurant. Rico hadn't showed me the card, neither had he revealed the name of his lunch guest, so I was a little surprised. The man wasn't on the little guess-list I had been toying with since the previous day. Although I had never worked under him, I had seen him quite a few times on crime scenes, usually after we had 'cleaned up'. By all accounts, Bailey was a very thorough and intelligent policeman, someone whose progress in his profession was the reward of hard work and studies. He was said to be one year short of his qualification as a lawyer. Although the bad-minded and envious whispered that being the nephew of the ex-Minister of Justice had smoothed his way up the ladder, there was no evidence that Bailey's rise resulted from overt political powerplays. The grapevine had him as a strong contender for the much coveted post of Assistant Commissioner in time to come.

Rico got into the passenger seat. The jeep was squeezed between two cars across the road. At this hour traffic blocked access to the mall. The good and the great of Kingston had made the select restaurant their usual lunch-time meeting place. All kinds of businesses took place over the neat lacquered tables.

'Bailey?' I said, frowning, still a little shocked at what was happening.

Rico nodded. I thought he seemed a little sad.

'Who can you trust?' I asked.

Rico seemed lost in thoughts of his own for a moment. Around us, the midday rush hour was beating its rhythm. A higgler I knew, large gold earrings and golden smile, waved at me from a passing car.

'We started in the Force the same year, me and him.' I heard Rico say. 'Wilkins had to send one of us to the States for training. I went, Bailey became the star of the Crime Unit.'

'What him say?'

'What him say?' Rico and I looked at each other. 'Him say him asked Fitz to pick up the freezer for him and that's all. What Fitz do after that is nothing to do with him.'

I started to wonder whether Rico was right after all. 'You ask him about Maxi?'

Rico shook his head slowly. He was staring far ahead through the windscreen. 'I don't need to. He knows that I know.'

'So, what we do now?'

Rico breathed in and out, deeply, like something was weighing down his chest. 'We have to talk to Maxi.'

'Wilkins' not going to like that.'

'Wilkins' not going to know.' Rico turned to face me. His face was hard, very still, set like a mask. 'Bailey is smart, Carly, very smart. I don't really know how it all started but I think he's been operating safely for a while. He made only one mistake, and now he's in danger. The boy is the only one who can hurt him. That means he's a marked man.'

I thought about where Rico was at.

'But he can't touch Maxi, his father ...' Rico's glance stopped me.

'What would you do, if you was Bailey?'

CHAPTER ELEVEN

Signposts

London, England

Mimi had come especially from Jamaica to celebrate her brother's wedding and now she was about to go back, having buried him. Though she wasn't Miss Ruby's child, Rico and her had grown up in the same neighbourhood and the fact that her mother had once been Miss Ruby's love rival didn't affect the way Rico's mother treated her. Mimi was beloved of everyone who knew her. Short and plump, round of face, with an easy smile, she was all heart but brave as any man. She worked as a primary school teacher. Her own two children spent a lot of time at Miss Ruby's house, their own grandmother having died early from 'sugar'. Mimi and I got along great; she often said that she was sorry she didn't catch me before her husband married her, which I took as a compliment, given that the man in question was also a very nice person.

Rico loved Mimi, had kept in contact with her by phone since leaving Jamaica and so I reflected she might know something that would help me understand what had happened. He had called me but twice, yet I knew it wasn't by neglect or anything like that. I understood Rico needed to break away from his life as a policeman, mentally, and I was too close to that life for him to talk to me about anything else. Her suitcase already packed for the following day, Mimi sat watching the street from the bedroom window. On her face, grief had drawn lines that told the story of tears shed for her dead brother. Hands in her lap, she turned as I knocked on her open door.

'Come in, Carly.'

I took a chair. On the bed lay one of the pictures taken in front of the town hall, moments before the fatal shot that felled Rico. I sat, picked up the photograph. We were all there, well dressed, smiling, Rico and Nicola looking beautiful.

I replaced the picture. 'I still can't work it out, Mimi,' I said.

The usually talkative Mimi seemed subdued.

'I tried to find out who could have wanted to hurt Rico, I talked to a couple of people who knew him, worked with him, but nobody knows.'

'It doesn't matter any more,' Mimi told me. I could see she felt the same way as Miss Ruby. Rico was dead and that's where it stopped.

'Mimi,' I said, 'back home, Rico could have got killed years ago, any day and by anyone. But to die like that on his wedding day, in England, you cyan tell me it don't matter. Somebody killed him and some people know who, and why. And I not going to stop until I find out.'

'Mimi looked at me, pain alive deep in her tired eyes. 'And when yuh find out, Carly, what yuh gwan do?'

I kept silent for a few seconds, seeing what she meant. 'I will do the same t'ing Rico woulda done if it had been me on this picture and he was the one left alive.' I could see Mimi knew I was right; Rico would never have left my murderers go unpunished, not the Rico I knew.

'Mimi, I know you kept contact with him since he came over . . .'

'He called sometimes, almost every month.'

'Right, is there anything he might have said, anything you might have picked up that could help me? Did he sound like he was having problems or anything?'

Mimi shrugged. 'Him never said much, just asked about the children.'

'Him sent money over, I found the transfer tickets.'

'Yes, he used to send me money to help me out, plus some to put aside for a project.'

'A project?'

'Oh, yuh never knew,' Mimi remarked. 'Him ask me to open an account for him, in my name, for the school.'

'What school?'

Mimi sighed, took her time to explain, patiently, the way she would to one of the children she taught back home.

'Rico called me about six months ago, one evening. He said he wanted to set up something which would help people back home, a school for kids to get training, something like a technical training centre. He wasn't sure exactly about that, but he said he could get money to finance it and he asked me to open an account for the money he was going to send.'

I was surprised. I realized Rico must have done a lot of thinking since leaving Jamaica. Still, I could relate to such an idea; Rico had always talked about the lack of direction and opportunities for young people back home. To him, much of the crime problem we faced stemmed from this situation. So, Rico wanted to set up a school.

'Him tell yuh how him was going to finance the project?' I asked Mimi.

She shook her head. 'No, him just say him would get the money.'

'How much money him was talking about?'

'Him ask me to check about it, about the legal aspect of the project, what was needed, to contact the Ministry of Education and find out how to do it. I told him, after doing some research, the project would take maybe a couple of million pounds.'

'Wha him say?'

'Him say him would get some of the money and then contact

the banks to get the rest. I also checked about some funding from the authorities.'

That whole thing sounded serious. Rico must have really considered all aspects of the project before talking about it, that's the way he was.

'Mimi, tell me now; how much money him send over to put in the account.'

I watched Mimi stretch to get hold of her bag near the bedhead. 'I have the book here with me,' she said 'I bring him to show him I did like him tell me fe do.' The idea that Rico wouldn't trust Mimi was unthinkable, but she had wanted to show her brother proof all the same. I took the Jamaica National book Mimi was handing me.

'There's about one hundred and forty thousand pounds' worth in there,' I said, looking at Mimi.

'One hundred and thirty-seven thousand,' she corrected.

That was a lot of money. From the entries' dates, Rico had started sending money around six months before, between twenty-five and thirty thousands pounds a time. I gave Mimi back the book.

'Yuh ask him where him was getting the money from?'

Mimi almost smiled, for the first time. 'Yuh know how Rico stay; him only tell yuh what yuh need to know. Him was always like that.'

That was absolutely true. I reflected on these new elements, all the while getting back to the same question: where was he getting the money and how did he expect to get enough to finance his project?

'There's something else, Carly.' Mimi's voice brought me out of my reflections. 'A couple of days before the wedding, Rico ask me to memorize a number. Him say him would tell me what it was later. But, him never get time to.'

'A number?' I repeated.

Mimi nodded. 'Yes, him say I shouldn't write it down, just keep it in my head.'

'Yuh 'member it?' I asked.

She nodded again, then said, '303 04 37.'

'303 04 37,' I repeated after her. 'Yuh sure?'

'Yes man, him make me repeat it three times and ask me it later the same day, just to check. Ah dat. 303 04 37.'

'Him never say what kind of number, if it's a phone number or what?'

Mimi shook her head. 'No, him was going to tell me later.'

I sighed, wondering why would Rico do that, why not tell Mimi right out what the number meant. It looked like a phone number, but whose? With the one on his mobile, that was now two numbers left by Rico. I would have to try calling this one.

'That's all? Not'ing else yuh 'member?'

'That's all, Carly. I can't really make sense of it either.'

That was a lot more than I knew before. 'What time is your flight tomorrow?'

'In the afternoon, I have to get to Heathrow by three o'clock.'

'Yuh arrange for a taxi or yuh want me do it?'

'It's alright, Babsy taking me down there.' Babsy was Mimi's long-time friend who'd been living in England for years.

'Alright, Mimi. I have to make some moves now. I see yuh later, seen?' I got up and started out. I was reaching the door when she called out.

'Carly.' I turned around.

'Yuh be careful.'

I smiled. 'Yeah man, nuh worry.'

I left Mimi to her thoughts, went downstairs then out of the house.

Zafirah was more than happy to let me go through the books. She said Ruffneck Security was incorporated, its taxes paid and all employees declared; everything was above board. I spent some time checking the figures, the income from the bookings over the previous year, the salaries paid and it confirmed what I already suspected: there was no way Rico could have transferred an average of twenty-five grand a month to Jamaica out of what he made with his business. So where in the world was he getting this money from? Furthermore, for him to commit himself to raising even half a million pounds, he had to be assured of a serious cashflow over a reasonable period of time. What was he into that I couldn't find traces of?

I asked Zafirah more questions, probing like a policeman knows how to, not giving much information about what I had found out. She didn't seem to know anything else about Rico's life. She said a promoter had called that morning, wanting to know whether the firm could cover security for several dates booked for some of his soul artists around the country. He didn't seem to know anything about Rico's demise. She said she had the staff and could do the job, like I suggested she did. She also told the man, called Larry Boldon, I would call him to close the deal. So I did, and Zafirah took care of the details after that. I left her there, promising to call her the next day so she could take me out to dinner.

Next, I took a cab to Brixton. I had got from Zafirah's files the address of Milk & Honey Records, the label/production/promotion company of Bungee, one of the firm's first and most regular customers. Bungee and Rico knew each other from back home, I knew that. I had decided against calling Bungee himself. I knew he had been away in the States but had called the office the previous week, having learned of what had happened to Rico. Zafirah said he sounded well upset on the phone.

'Do you have an appointment?' The brown sister behind the black designer desk fitted the profile of the secretary every black businessman wishes to have. I smiled.

'No, but if you tell him his old friend Carlton from Jamaica is here to see him, I'm sure he'll find a little time for me.'

The young woman seemed to weigh my words for a while. Somehow, she must have felt I wouldn't take no for an answer.

'Mr Pearson is in a meeting right now. If you'd like to wait.' I thanked her and dropped into the plush leather chair near the glass door. I didn't try to make conversation with Bungee's secretary; she probably had every visitor hitting on her and it wouldn't do to be just another guy. She didn't look very busy though, leisurely typing something on her desk computer. I caught her glancing my way once or twice. Music magazines covered the low table in front of me so I picked one up and got into a Mary J. Blige interview. It took a good half hour before two white men, thirty-something, trendy musical executives types emerged from the office. They went out, and the secretary called her boss on the intercom phone and announced me. Soon after, Bungee appeared. I got up.

'Wha' yuh ah say, Bungee?' I could feel the secretary's curious gaze on me. Did I really know her boss?

'Carly, come in man, come in. Bwoy, long time.' Bungee led the way inside his office. He had a very good memory; the last time we met, I had driven Rico to the morgue to view the body of a youngster shot to death by robbers the previous night. He was Bungee's nephew and we met him there, holding up the grieving mother. We never really talked socially aside from that tragic morning but he recalled my face and even my name. People back home tend to do so very easily about policemen anyway.

'Sit down, man. Yuh want a drink?'

I said I'd have a Coke. We sat either side of Bungee's desk, piles of papers, CDs and pictures on top of it. In the far corner, an impressive music system, more CDs lined up above it on three shelves.

'So when yuh come over?'

'The day before the wedding. I was the best man.'

Bungee was looking straight in my face. He knew how close

Rico and I were. 'I was away in Miami, I found out through some friends when I got back. I cyan believe . . .'

I sighed. 'It don't make no sense to me, Bungee. I been trying to understand what happened, but so far I don't get nowhere.'

'Bwoy, I used to check Rico from time to time, yuh know. Like how him set up the security firm, I give him some work and t'ings. Me and him was brethren from time, yuh know that.'

'Me know, man. That's why I come to look for yuh. Maybe him tell yuh somet'ing.'

Bungee was sitting back in his chair, an unlit cigarette in his mouth. He seemed a little rounder than when I knew him back home, his face somewhat fatter, with the same thick eyebrows. The scar descending from behind his left ear disappeared behind his shirt collar.

'Last time I sight him was for the Luciano tour. I give him two tickets and him come to the Birmingham show with him woman.'

'When was that?' I asked.

'About . . . three months ago.'

I nodded. Bungee added. 'Him did look alright to me, not like someone who have problems or anything. Fe him business was working alright, getting bigger.'

'Tell me about this, Bungee, yuh feel seh him coulda make some enemies? Him ever have any dispute with anybody, about money or anyt'ing?'

Bungee made a face, shook his head. 'I never hear not'ing like that. Yuh know, in the music business, everybody know each other, so I woulda know if Rico have problems with a man.'

I exhaled deeply, not feeling any closer to understanding what had happened. 'But somebody shot him, and it look to me like it's a hit. That means Rico made some serious enemies, somewhere.'

Bungee was pulling on the cigarette now, blowing smoke, his face showing concentration. I was wondering whether I should tell him about Rico's project.

'Yuh know somet'ing, Carly, yuh right. It has to be somebody big to call that kind of hit.' Bungee paused, looked at me straight, before going on: 'And it's only two kind of business I know whe man coulda take out a contract pon somebody.'

We kept the eye contact for a few seconds through the smoke.

'So wha yuh ah seh, Bungee?'

'Yuh is the police, I just tell yuh what I t'ink. I could be wrong.'

'Me ah police, true, but yuh deh yah long time now. Yuh know how t'ings run.'

Bungee stubbed out the roach in the big Marlboro ashtray, raised his eyebrows like he often did. 'Like I said; aside from the security business, I don't know not'ing about Rico's runnings. But if is a contract killing, the way me see it, it's only arms or drugs.'

I let this sink in. It made sense that anyone who'd buy a contract, and it seemed to be what happened, had to be in the big league. But I still was finding it hard to connect Rico with that type of activity. The thought of the school project surfaced.

'Yuh really feel seh Rico coulda got involved with them type of runnings? After everyt'ing we go through ah Yard to fight against that?'

Bungee shrugged. 'I don't know, Carly. Rico was a real police, straight, and that nearly get him killed back home, so it's hard for me to believe anyt'ing like that.'

I sat back in the chair, watching the descending sun through the window blinds of Bungee's office. The only facts I had pointed in one direction, but I couldn't reconcile this with the man I knew. Maybe it was me, maybe I was simply refusing to accept the truth.

'It's hard for me too, Bungee. That man saved my life, him teach me right from wrong, him show me reality.'

'People can change . . .'

'Yeah.'

'Still, maybe it's not that, maybe Rico come up against something we cyan figure out. 'Nuff t'ings can happen in this country, yuh know.' Bungee's word rang like he was trying to make up for suggesting Rico could have turned bad.

''Nuff t'ings can happen, yes . . .'

'So, what happen to Merleene, sah?' Maybe Bungee meant to take my mind off the bad vibes by asking me this, but it couldn't make me feel any better.

'Merleene is old story. Me and her couldn't work it out.'

'Ah so it go sometimes. Yuh know seh Barbara left me?!' I shook my head.

'Yeah man, I bring her over lickle after I get here, set her up, treat her really nice. Yuh know how she ever want to come to England. Well, me dear sah, the girl nuh pick up with one bwoy from up yah, diss me and gone. One time me try fe go and reason with her and the bwoy get bright pon me, so me kuff him. The dyamm bitch nuh call the police pon me?! Bwoy, me ah tell yuh, Carly: yuh cyan trust woman at all.'

Bungee and I talked about old times until the office got dark. Then he decided we should have dinner together, so we went to some place he knew in West London in his BMW. The Jamaican restaurant was nice, the food great and everyone treated Bungee like he was a visiting dignitary. We ate, drank some beer, talked some more, about the way things used to be. Then Bungee dropped me all the way home. He told me I should keep operating the security firm, said he would get us some work. I got home and slept like a log.

CHAPTER TWELVE

Helping Hands

'You a hard man to get hold of, Tips.'

He looked up from his steaming coffee cup, smiled but I somehow felt he wasn't overjoyed to see me. I had come to the little restaurant, guessing that Tips would be there rather than at the cab office.

'T'ings kinda rough for me right now, the cab office don't bring in enough, so I have try and get organized.'

I sat in one of the vacant plastic chairs. At this early hour, only a few weary-looking white workers were there, busy having their breakfast and chatting about the night shift they had just finished. A sleepy looking waitress, not the one who loved Tips so much, dragged herself to the table from the counter.

'What you having, dear?'

'Coffee, please.' Tips was downing toast, eggs and meat, something pink and unsavoury-looking.

'So, how it go, Carly?' he asked between mouthfuls.

'Checking around, but I still don't get nowhere. Yuh get anyt'ing?'

Tips put down his fork and sipped from his coffee cup, sat back in the chair. 'Boy, me ah tell yuh, the truth, Carly: this whole business around Rico kinda sensitive. Nobody want to talk 'bout it, and you can't ask too much questions neither. Coming like someone big deh behind this t'ing and everybody frightened.'

'What about you, Tips; you frightened too?'

Blank stare. 'I don't fear no man, you know that. But in this country, we don't run t'ings, so you must tread carefully. We don't have no cover, no topnotch to help we out if we slip, you know what I mean?'

I drank some of the coffee, hot and strong but good enough to fight off the cold rain. 'Yeah, I know what yuh mean. I did want ask yuh somet'ing; what could Rico do for somebody buy a contract on him?'

Tips frowned. 'Who tell yuh seh is a contract?'

I paused, our eyes locked for a moment. 'Before I come here this morning, I go back to the town hall. The shot was fired from across the road, from a car it look like. That's about seventy yards, with two-way traffic, twelve o'clock hour, 'nuff cars. Whoever can put a bullet dead centre in a man chest in these conditions got to be a marksman. This was no drive-by, Tips.'

Tips said nothing. The conversation seemed to have cut down his appetite. 'Yuh right, yuh know. But who could have buy a hit like that, and fe what?'

'Ah dat I want find out. I go to Brixton go check Bungee yesterday. Yuh 'member Bungee?'

'Yeah . . .'

'Him tell me seh is only arms or drugs dealers, big-time people, coulda buy a hit like this. What yuh t'ink about that?'

'Bungee supposed to know about drugs dealers,' Tips smirked.

'Why yuh say that?'

'Dat fucker get busted for importing and supplying, twice. Him get'way first time, do eighteen month after that. How yuh t'ink him get the money fe start him record business?'

'So, how dem never deport him?'

'Him get married to a white woman when him first get here, to get him papers.' Tips added with an unkind grin, 'Ah dat mek him wife lef' him when she come over from back home.'

So much for the sad story . . . Tips seemed to have something against Bungee. I couldn't tell whether it was something from back home. There was something I needed to ask Tips. I went for my wallet.

'Tell me if you recognize this number.' I pulled out a folded paper. Tips took it, read it. Nothing registered on his face. He shook his head.

'Where you get this from?'

'From Rico's mobile phone. Him dial it on the morning of the wedding.'

'Yuh try it?'

'Yeah, I keep getting the same message, a woman's voice . . .'

'A woman?'

I nodded. 'Yeah, talk about "not here right now, call back later."'

'Black woman?'

'Maybe. It's hard to tell with the accent, how you call it: "cockney"?'

Tips picked up his radio and answered a call from Loretta. 'So it look like Rico did keep a girl pon the side,' he commented wryly when he had finished.

'I don't think it's that, man. Would you call your girl on your wedding day, on your mobile, and leave the number recorded too?'

Tips shrugged. 'Maybe dem did have some problems, maybe she find out about the wedding . . .'

'No, I don't feel so. To me, if him call that woman, it must have been important. It was a business call, but what business him have with her, I don't know.'

Tips was still holding the piece of paper. I said: 'Tell me something; can I find out the address fe this number?'

'It can be done, if yuh ask the right people.'

'Yuh can help me on this?'

Silence; Tips breathed in. More people, wet from the rain, were coming in, ordering breakfast. The smell from the grill behind the counter was getting stronger.

'I will try get it for you. Call me tomorrow.'

I looked at Tips. 'This is important, I need it fast.'

Tips sighed, I picked up my baseball cap from the table. 'Alright, call me later.' Tips was ready to leave too, so we went out and I walked with him in the rain to the cab office. I told him I'd call around four and left him.

'Have you decided? The waiter, smiling and smart in his waistcoat, had left us enough time to go through the menu. Zafirah waited for me to answer so I picked something from the entrees, plus a curry chicken. She asked for her order and the waiter disappeared. Outside the drizzle continued, unabated. Since I had let Zafirah down twice on her dinner invitation, and I had nothing pressing except to call Tips back later, I decided it was time to make good. She had taken me in her Fiat Uno to a little Indian restaurant not too far from the office and inside it was pleasant, cool and quiet. The Asian music in the background was soothing and just loud enough so you couldn't hear the conversations from the few other customers. And neither could they hear ours, which was just as well . . .

'Rico's friend told you he was into arms dealing?!' Zafirah continued where she had left off before the waiter had interrupted us.

'He just said arms or drugs dealers were the kind of people to buy a contract on someone.'

Zafirah's frown reflected her concentration. She had asked me how far I got with my enquiries. 'What do you think?'

I sighed. 'To tell you the truth; I don't really know what to think any more.'

'You think Rico was into crime?!'

I took a little time before answering her. 'Rico was a policeman; that's how I knew him, that's all I know. But someone killed him, and it looks like it was for something serious. So far, I have no idea what happened but I start to think I need to keep my mind open, because Rico might have got involved in things I don't know about.'

I could feel Zafirah's eyes into mine, probing, wanting to find out what was on my mind. I was starting to realize she had really liked Rico, more than just how an employee appreciates a good boss.

'Tell me what happened in Jamaica.'

'What?'

'I mean; why did Rico leave the police? Why did he come over here?'

'Didn't you ask him?'

'I did.'

'What did he say?'

'He just said he was tired of it, he wanted to live a quieter life.'

I couldn't suppress a smile. 'Yeah?'

'Why d'you smile?' Zafirah asked.

I shrugged. 'I feel like that sometimes too, I'd love a quieter life.'

Two dark eyes were scrutinizing my face.

'You don't want to tell me the real reason ...'

'Why d'you want to know?'

'Because I think the reason he left got something to do with the reason he was killed.'

I wasn't smiling any more. Something in what Zafirah had just said reached me. 'You could be right.'

'So? ...' She was a determined woman.

'Well, it's a long story ... but let's just say that Rico came to a point where he couldn't do his job without getting in the way of certain people, big people. You understand?'

Zafirah asked: 'What kind of people? Politicians?'

The woman was sharp. 'Politics back home is a heavy game.'

'We're talking about corruption here, right?'

I nodded. 'Yeah.'

She waited for the waiter to place the trays of food in front of us. It all looked pretty and smelled spicy. 'So Rico left the Force because he wouldn't play along, look the other way?'

'Yeah, that's what happened.'

'He must have made some enemies . . .' With her pertinent questions, Zafirah was leading me in a direction I had not really explored.

'You mean that some people Rico had upset back then in Jamaica could be behind his murder?'

'I don't know. What do you think?'

I picked up my glass of Coke, in a way to avoid answering directly: simply because I didn't know what I thought. Faces flashed in my mind, ghosts from my past, from Rico's past.

We finished the meal. Zafirah had work on for the afternoon: Bungee had called and asked for some arrangements for some tour he was organizing. He was true to his word of getting us some business. The rain had eased up but the grey skies didn't promise anything better for the rest of the day.

'Can I drop you anywhere?' Zafirah asked on the way down.

'No, it's okay. I have a couple of moves to make but I'll get a cab. Thanks.'

'Can I ask you a question?' I saw her glance my way.

'Sure.'

She took a little time. 'You said Rico left because he wouldn't play along with the big boys, right?'

I nodded.

'So, what about you? Why did you stay?' I could hear the real question, and I think she knew I would.

'I was less exposed than him . . .' I waited a little, turned her way. 'But I never sold out either, never.'

A little sly smile appeared on Zafirah's delicate features. 'I know you didn't.'

Our eyes met for a short second, then she crossed the road towards her car.

Four forty-five . . . The Heineken in front of me was on its last legs. Joy had said she wouldn't be late, she finished work at four today she said. I had called her just the once since our evening together at the Alley Cat. And then I had promised but failed to call her back the following day. Despite that, she sounded happy enough to hear my voice when I called earlier to say I was in the area. She told me to go to the same pub and wait for her – she wouldn't be long.

I had too much on my mind to worry about women but I knew there was always a lot to learn from talking to them when following an investigation. It was all the more true in a town I didn't know and where I couldn't really go out and operate like I would have on my own turf.

'I'm sorry; my boss asked for a favour and it took a little longer than I thought. You're alright?'

'Yeah. How you doing?'

'Fine.' Joy dropped her bag, took off her jacket. The dark blue dress hugged a form I had only guessed at the first time. With her silky hair tied up in a bun and her dark Indian eyes, she was a hard sight to ignore.

'What you having?'

Joy sat across from me, hands crossed over the table. 'No, no. I'm buying.'

'The next one if you want. This one is mine, to apologize for not calling you.'

'In that case, I accept. Is it too early for a brandy and Coke you think?'

I smiled. 'It's just the right time.'

'You're so right. I had a terrible day!'

I went to the bar and got Joy her drink, plus a fresh Heineken for myself. 'So, Carlton?' she asked after we both had sipped some. 'You like London?'

'It's new to me.'

Joy smiled. 'I was planning on taking you around, showing you the sights. But you forgot about me so . . .'

'Don't say that. I didn't forget.'

'Well, you probably found another guide.' I caught her hint, shook my head like Al Pacino in *Scarface* saying to his Colombian host, 'No, not in the car.'

'No, no other guide.'

Her squint made me feel like she intended to be that guide.

'So, what have you been up to?' Joy's voice, I realized, could be soft or sharp, but her eyes always seemed to have a voice of their own, the way they probed and questioned.

'To tell you the truth, I've been trying to find out what happened to my friend.'

She waited a little, then asked: 'Did the police find out anything? Did they arrest anybody?'

I shook my head. 'No, nobody knows anything.'

'Somebody must know,' she said, and she was right, of course.

'Some people know and I will find them. But I don't know the scene and I have no leads so far.'

Joy's index finger was circling the top of her glass, she seemed to be concentrating on that. She said: 'You know . . . my sister's boyfriend got shot dead too, a couple of months ago. He was Jamaican. The police didn't find out who did it. They said it was drugs-related, score-settling between Jamaicans. I think they don't really care anyway.'

'Was he into drugs?' I asked.

Joy sighed. 'I don't know, to be honest. My sister says he wasn't at first but then he started mixing with the wrong crowd, and then he got shot, just like that.'

The pub wasn't that busy this late afternoon, and no one could have noticed our two stern faces in the far corner near the unattended pool tables but the temperature had dropped a couple of degrees. I told Joy: 'Better we leave all this death business alone, miss, otherwise you'll go home feeling I made you sad.'

She smiled a little. 'No, it's not your fault.' There was a pause and I could feel she was about to say something else, but she must have changed her mind. After a sip from her drink, Joy shook her head: 'This town is getting rough, you know. You should see the cases I come across in my job!'

'Yeah? What do you do?' I asked.

'I'm a probation officer.' My surprise must have shown on my face.

'I don't look like one, right? So, what is a probation officer supposed to be like?'

'Hmm, I don't know. But I'm sure you're good at your job.'

Joy laughed. 'Why d'you say that?'

I smiled. 'Well, you must make people stay out of prison, fe real . . .'

She threw me that squint, the one she put on whenever I made her a compliment, picked up her glass and sipped. 'What about you, d'you work back home?'

I shook my head, serious. 'No, I rob people for a living.'

'What?'

She didn't quite know what to make of it, but it was getting me time to think. Once again, I could sidestep or come clean. 'Ah joke, man.'

'I didn't think you were serious. You wouldn't tell me anyway. So, are you gonna tell me, or is it confidential?'

'It is confidential,' I said, 'But I will tell you anyway, 'cause I trust you.' Joy waited, her eyes expectantly peering into mine, like she could read the answer there.

'I'm a policeman.'

She watched me, waited for me to say 'Joke', but I didn't, so she asked, 'Really?'

I just nodded.

'Well,' Joy was scrutinizing me now, assessing whether I

fitted the profile she had of me with what I'd just told her. 'I guess you could be . . .' She seemed to be thinking about something for a moment. Meanwhile, I wondered whether someone in her line of work could be of help to my investigation.

'Joy, I want to ask you a question.'

'Go ahead.'

'It's kind of professional, after all: we're in the same line of work.'

'I guess we are.'

'Okay, you deal with criminals, right, black or white, or both?'

'Both, but we see more black people than white.'

'Tell me; have you ever come across a case of contract killing?'

Joy frowned. 'Contract? You mean, like . . .'

'Like somebody wants somebody else dead, so they buy a contract on that person.'

She paused. 'I've never had that.' She was still thinking about my question, I could tell. 'I guess there must be cases, but I think it's more to do with the white gangsters.'

I asked again: 'Another question: have you ever had cases of black people involved in arms dealing?'

'Arms dealing? You mean selling guns?'

'Not just selling a couple of handguns, I mean big-scale dealing?'

'I don't think so.'

'Who sells the weapons?'

'Some black people sell guns, but they're just retailers, as far as I know. I believe they buy from white families, or the Irish connection. I'm just guessing here.'

I nodded, following my train of thought. 'What about drugs?'

Joy's eyes and mine locked for a few silent seconds. 'What about drugs?' she asked

'What's the situation?'

'You name it, it's happening . . . England caught up with the States rapidly. Importation, distribution, gang wars, robberies. We've got it all.' Joy paused. 'I'd say around sixty per cent of the cases I come across are drugs-related one way or the other. And I'm talking about youngsters, really young kids.'

'Yeah, I know what you mean. The police keeping busy, eh?'

'The police are often part of the problem. Some years ago, nobody would believe it, but now it's clear that some officers have "shares" in the business. They're only human, after all.' Joy's sarcastic tone stressed her point. Outside the window, darkness was descending early on the town.

'Can I use your phone?' Joy pushed her mobile lying on the table my way.

'Of course, go ahead.'

I was dialling the cab office number when she said, 'Got a date?'

I smiled at the inquisitive look on her face but didn't answer. Tips was on a job, Loretta said, so I tried his mobile, hoping the line was open. It was, the voice coming across after half a dozen rings.

'Tips . . . what happen? . . . – Yuh get t'rough? . . . Alright, yeah . . .'

I signalled to Joy, who was listening while sipping away the rest of her drink. 'You have a pen?' She dug in her handbag, handed me a pen and paper.

'Yeah . . . gwan.' I wrote down the address Tips was giving me. 'You have good connections, man! . . . Yeah man, me find it, nuh worry . . . When? . . . I feel seh I better check it out this evening . . . I gwan go down right now . . . yeah, I taking a taxi and go deh now . . . Yeah man, I call you when I get back . . . Seen . . . T'anks, y'hear? . . . Cool.'

I gave Joy back her phone. 'I have something to check, maybe I can get a lead.'

'You found someone who knows something?' she asked.

'I got to go check this address, maybe I can find out some answers down there.'

'It's in West London.' Joy had already read it upside down. 'Would you like me to take you there?'

'No, I have to go alone.'

'You sure?'

I thought about it before nodding, 'Yeah.'

'I thought we could have had dinner.' Joy's dark eyes shone like dinner was only one of the things she had planned for me but I was learning that she wasn't that easy to read. Dinner could have been enjoyable.

'I really have to check out this place first,' I said.

'Will you call me when you get back?'

'Alright.'

'Yeah, like last time. You're probably gonna disappear for another week!' There it was again: was she really interested or just toying with me?

I squinted at her, touched her hand over the table. 'Come on, Joy. You know I have certain important things to do, but we going to spend time together.'

'Promise?'

'Fe real, man. You go home and I call you when I done my move. Come.' We got up and left the pub. By then, a little crowd was in and the music had got louder. Joy drove fast but well, steering the Renault 5 through the evening traffic. She dropped me at a cab station, told me to be careful and to call her as soon as I got back. I said I would, on both counts. Before I stepped out of the car she gave me a little kiss, for the road.

CHAPTER THIRTEEN

Rat Trap

The cab driver found the road without problems, and parked in front of number eight, like I asked him to. I paid him and got out. The street was just off Ladbroke Grove, the main road, wide, with trees all along the length of it. The night felt cool, breezy but nice. I looked up at the two-storey house; one window was lit up right at the top. I pushed the iron gate open, walked up the few steps to the front door and rang the A bell. At last, I was about to find out who this mysterious woman was that Rico had called on his last day. Surely she had to hold some of the answers to the mystery. I could see no lights downstairs.

Whether the woman had been out or she simply didn't answer the phone, I couldn't know. But if I could see her, then she would have to talk to me. I rang the bell some more, but no answer. The street was quiet, residential. I thought about ringing the top bell, asking the neighbours about the woman I was looking for, but somehow I held back from doing that. So I left the front door and decided to check out the back of the house. Back down to the front yard, past the tall square plastic bins, I walked around the house until I got to the back where three steps led to a door. The garden looked unkempt in the semi-darkness, a thick edge throwing shadows under a weak moonglow at the far end.

I couldn't hear any noises from inside, not a sound coming

from behind the door. Through the glass upper portion, thick darkness in what I thought might be a kitchen. Maybe the woman had moved out, maybe she was on holidays. Yet her number was on Rico's phone, his last call in fact, so there had to be a reason why he called and I needed to find out that reason.

For a second, I thought that maybe Tips had made a mistake on the address. I took hold of the door handle, turned it: it clicked open. Unsure what to make of it, I pushed open the door, slowly, listening for any sounds from inside. Carefully I stepped inside. The moonlight just about allowed my eyes to make out the outline of a sink, a table and chairs, a cooker. I walked inside, tiptoeing. It just wouldn't do to get busted for burglary, but I had gone that far so I might as well explore the house.

I felt my way, following the wall, until I came to a room where the outdoor street lamps threw a distant light. This was a living room, I could tell, looking out on the front of the house. I hesitated to try on the light switch. No sounds from inside; the house seemed empty. Why would the owner leave the back door open? I stood by the living room entrance, my hand covering the light switch, pondering whether to press it or not. I did.

The room was spacious enough, decorated in thick, printed, velvet-like wallpaper. A wide leather couch took most of the space opposite the window, two tall standing lamps either side and several potted climbing plants spreading out their limbs. The wide screen TV and stereo system alone must have cost a few months salary, of mine anyway. Thick leather, oriental-looking cushions stood on the carpet-covered floor, matching the Chinese prints on the walls. I stepped up to the windows and closed the curtains. The place smelled like it had been empty for a while.

The phone sat on a varnished low table to the right hand of the couch, I lifted the receiver: the line was working. Without really thinking about it, I clicked opened the compartment of the answering machine and took up the cassette inside, slipped it in my pocket. A policeman's reflex I guess. I could see other rooms along the inside passage and was about to move on when I heard a sudden rush of noise coming from the kitchen side. I turned on my heels, and then they were there, three uniformed policemen at the door of the room, staring at me, one plain clothes white man behind them. I was too shocked to do anything, had no time and nowhere to run anyway.

'You're under arrest!' I heard the plain clothes man say.

My head totally empty, I stood there as the officers surrounded me, saw no use in resisting when they closed the handcuffs around my wrists.

'Bring him over!' the same man said.

The uniforms took me along the passage to another room, a bedroom. When they switched on the light, I found myself staring at a form spread out on the bed, a large rug-covered bed. The woman was white, in her twenties, clothed only in panties and a white vest. Her wide opened eyes seemed to contemplate something on the ceiling. I knew enough about wounds to know that the red stain on the left side of her chest concealed a stab wound straight to the heart.

'I'm arresting you for murder and attempted burglary. Anything you say might be used against you ...' I didn't even hear what the man was saying. My head was empty for now, like I wasn't really there but watching some kind of movie unfolding on a screen. The only thing I registered, by instinct, was that the bedroom seemed upside down, like it had been searched in a rush. Before I could get my thoughts together, I found myself in the back of a police Rover being driven out at speed to an unknown destination.

'So, why don't you tell us all about it?'

They had left me locked up in a cell for the night. I knew it was a technique and I didn't care how long they wanted to leave me there anyway. While inside, sitting on the hard bunk, I reflected that it had been a long time, a lifetime I felt, since I had been locked up. Still, this cubicle was much more comfortable than the one we were used to back home. In these hours I spent staring at the toilet bowl in that small cell, all my life since the first shot drilled through me that Kingston morning, on the bike, flashed past in my mind. I relived it all. Then fell asleep. The next thing I know, some fat white man in a white shirt was shaking me awake.

I looked at the policeman standing by the room window, his hands in the pockets of his pants and shrugged.

'Tell you what?'

I was finding it weird that I got arrested in West London and the policeman interrogating me was the one who had asked me all the questions back at Rico's house that day. McCallum, he said his name was when he came in. I couldn't recall the name of the red-haired young cop sitting across from me.

'Come on, Mr Nash. You appear on the scene, the next day your best friend gets murdered and shortly after, we find you at the scene of another murder. Either you walk around with a curse or you're not quite what you seem to be. So, why did you come to this country?'

I sighed. There was no use playing silent with these cops. 'I told you. My friend invited me over to be his best man.'

The inspector nodded, flattening his tie, his stomach straining the shirt. 'Right. And do you happen to have any idea who killed him?'

'That's what I've been trying to find out.'

'And?'

'I got nowhere so far.'

'Oh, I wouldn't say. You're already featuring in another murder case.'

'I didn't even know there was a dead person in this house.'

The man walked up to the table, rested his open palms

on top, looking at me. 'And what were you doing in this house then?'

'I found a phone number on my friend's mobile phone, that was the last number he called before he got shot. I was just following that lead.'

'Ah, I see,' the policeman said, looking at his young colleague. 'So you are conducting an investigation!'

'I'm a policeman,' I told him.

'Yes, we know that.' They had taken my JCF police ID from me on arriving at the station, along with the rest of my belongings.

'But you see, Mr Nash, in this country you're just a tourist. You must leave all the investigating to us.'

I looked up at him. 'Okay, and how far have you got?' I asked, looking straight at the man. 'Have you found out who killed my friend?'

The inspector walked back to the window, hands in his pockets, turned. 'We come across quite a few murders amongst members of the Jamaican community. In my experience, most of these are related to the drugs trade . . . so we are looking in that direction.'

'You're saying my friend was involved with drugs?' I asked.

'Nothing can be ruled out, we're looking into it.' He came back to the table, finally sat in the empty chair next to his silent colleague.

'Your friend was quite a big man in Jamaica from what we found out. Brilliant records, head of a special unit. Tell me, Mr Nash; why did he leave the Force?'

'You checked with his superior, I think. What did he tell you?' I was curious to know what Wilkins had told them, if they had managed to talk to him. It must have been a shock to him to learn of Rico's death.

'All we were told was that he resigned for personal reasons.' The inspector didn't believe that, I could tell from the way he was looking at me.

'That's what happened.'

'We also asked about you. Apparently you're highly thought of, a very good element, to use your commanding officer's phrase.' It was nice to hear it. So they did talk to Wilkins after all. The inspector added, somewhat ironically: 'Obviously, that was before the murder . . .'

I shrugged. 'I didn't kill that woman, and you know it.'

'Do we?'

'It's a set-up.' I had had time to reflect on that while locked up earlier on. Tips and I would have a few things to discuss when I got out of here, if I got out . . .

'How d'you figure that?'

'Look, I had this number, I wanted to talk to that person and find out what she knew about my friend. Someone got the address for me.'

'Who did?'

'A friend.'

'Right. And now, you're facing a murder charge and I wouldn't fancy your chances in court with a story like that!'

'It's the truth.' The inspector nodded. I noticed they hadn't brought any tape machine in for the interrogation. Maybe it was a good sign. The only thing on the table was a brown folder.

'So, you obtain an address from a friend. You show up at the house and find a body.'

'I didn't find the body. Your colleagues showed it to me.' Something struck me. I asked: 'Did you find out how long that woman had been dead? I was only there ten minutes, and the death must have happened sometime earlier, so I couldn't have done it. Unless you think I'm stupid enough to kill someone and hang around in their house!'

'We're expecting the results of the autopsy soon.'

'And then I walk in the house and all of a sudden, the police show up. Don't you think it's too much of a coincidence?' The two policemen were looking at each other. Maybe they were starting to realize I wasn't just a dumb black man after all. Just then there was a knock on the door and a blonde female officer pushed her head in.

'Excuse me, sir. The Super would like a word.' The inspector got up and followed her. I could feel the red-haired younger policeman looking at me. He hadn't said a word all along but I could feel him observing me from across the table. Just like I thought he would, he started asking me questions.

'Tell me, Mr Nash; what were you looking for in the house?'

'I was looking for someone, someone alive.' The man shifted in his chair, tapped his fingers on the wooden table a few times, like he was thinking.

'You see, we think your late friend was involved in something illegal and that the security firm was just a front.'

'Something illegal like what?'

The young policeman made a face. 'Like drugs running, money laundering . . .'

I didn't answer him. He said: 'Maybe you're telling the truth; maybe you don't know anything about it . . . or maybe you do.'

I told him straight. 'My friend was a policeman, one of the best, and I don't believe a word of all this.'

'There's a lot of money on the other side of town, a lot of money. Policemen have weaknesses too.'

I really didn't like his tone, didn't like what he was hinting at. I said: 'Yeah, that applies to you too, isn't it?' He didn't like that, I saw it in his greenish eyes. But I didn't care what he liked or not and before I let him accuse Rico of anything, he'd better have some kind of solid evidence. The door opened and Inspector McCallum came back in. He dropped the file he was carrying on the table, sat looking at me. 'We've just received the autopsy report from the lab, Mr Nash.'

I waited.

'And it seems you were right. The woman died around four-thirty in the afternoon.'

A couple of hours before I got there. I nodded. 'That means you have nothing on me. Can I go now?'

McCallum let show a little smile, not very warm. 'We're releasing you. But before we do, I'd like you to do something for me.'

He motioned to his colleague who pushed the folder his way.

'Take a look at these, tell me if you recognize any.'

He opened the folder in front of me. Inside were half a dozen photos, of various sizes, and a few sheets of typed paper. I glanced at the policeman, then started going through the shots. The first one showed a small size picture of a man's face, bearded and barechest. It had been taken as the man laid on the floor, eyes open, dead. I didn't know him. I went through the others, casually, not stopping on any one in particular. The second and third were taken from a distance with a telephoto lens, on the street. I didn't know either of the two men. The fourth one I knew, a face from back in the old days. He had left the island not long after I became a policeman. I almost stopped on the fifth photograph. I could guess it had been sent over from Jamaica because the background showed trees in the backyard of a house. The face was smiling at me, dark features over the battledress with the marks of a sergeant on it. I passed it over like I had the others, picked up the last one but this one I didn't know and never would: he was dead, a full-length body lying on the concrete floor of a car park. There were three impact of bullets visible on the chest, another had taken away the left side of the face. I couldn't recognize anyone there.

'So, Mr Nash, any familiar faces amongst these?' McCallum asked.

I made a face, shook my head. 'I never had to go after any of these men back in Jamaica.'

I knew he didn't believe I hadn't recognized any of the photos but McCallum probably guessed I wouldn't admit to knowing anyone. 'Well, all these are part of a drug connection we've been following for a couple of years.' He added, after a little silence: 'They are all dead now, unfortunately.'

I showed no reaction.

'I'll tell you something for free, Mr Nash, just in case you are as innocent as you say you are. We found a number of ex-members of the Jamaican police and armed forces are involved in drugs-related activities. You understand now our interest in you.'

'And I'm telling you something else. I am an active member of the Jamaican police, and I'm not involved in the . . . activities you're talking about,' I said. 'Am I free to leave?'

'You are.' Then he asked, without the hint of a smile, although it surely was meant as a joke: 'Would you like a lift back to East London?' I got up, looked at the two policemen in turn, then made for the door without another word. McCallum followed me out to the foyer where I got back my belongings. Outside the police station, a rising sun made all things to shine. Maybe it was going to be a better day after all.

CHAPTER FOURTEEN

In Too Deep

Jamaica

Looking back on the events that followed, I realized later that Rico knew all along which way Bailey was going to play it out. Why he didn't go and tell Wilkins all he knew, I never asked him. I guess somehow, the friendship Bailey and him once had prevented him from doing what could be considered his duty. I believe he thought about it but couldn't do it. In the days following the meeting with Bailey, Rico was very quiet, keeping things inside. Rico had always been open with me, like a big brother, sharing thoughts and aspects of his character screened from other colleagues. True, I was his brother-in-law, but that never is a guarantee of trust. Rico trusted me and I never betrayed that trust. Yet that one time, he kept silent about all the things spinning in his head. I am convinced Rico and Bailey talked it out openly during that Chinese lunch. By the time it was over, both knew it would end in a showdown. I think Rico knew Bailey had only one possible move and that made him sad.

That same evening, Rico went to Maxi's house, alone, to try and warn the boy about what he thought was going to happen. When I eventually got to mention this the next day, he simply muttered 'That boy is a damned maniac'. Maxi couldn't be protected against his will, Wilkins couldn't be called upon without naming Bailey; what could Rico do? We didn't have to wait long . . .

Two days later, a call came through to the radio room at the headquarters that interrupted the little Friday evening gathering we were having. I had just opened my second chilled Red Stripe when I saw Chappie, the operator, motion to me from the door of the foyer.

'We have a situation in Harbour View, shootings, hostages, the locals have the place surrounded.'

Three vehicles rushed to the scene, thirteen Special Squad men in all. Rico's jeep was leading the pack, me at the wheel, him beside me, Booker and Mulligan at the back. Rico had pulled a long cigarillo from the wooden box in his glove box, slipped it between his lips. We found half a dozen police cars spread out at the end of a road called Southern Cross Drive, armed officers covering a house. Shattered windows and dark impact marks in the white walls testified to the battle already engaged. All lights in the house were off. Groups of residents huddled at a safe distance, debating. The officer in charge, large and greying, with a thick moustache, recognized Rico, saluted him.

'Three men, Inspector, maybe four. They got here about an hour ago. The neighbours called us when they heard three shots inside the house.'

'How many people inside?'

'Two men, one woman, for sure. And a baby . . .'

'A baby?!'

'Yes, about three months old. We asked them to release the hostages and come out but, as you see . . .' The officer motioned with his hand to the broken glass from two of his vehicles and the bullet holes in the bonnets and doors, '. . . it didn't work out.'

'How many weapons? What type?'

'Automatics, one AK, one Uzi, plus another, Mach 10 maybe.'

Rico nodded, the cigarillo hanging from his mouth corner.

'Okay, we'll take over from here.' Rico gave orders and we took position behind the vehicles, in the yards on both sides of the adjoining houses, and at the back. We all wore bullet-proof vests, but for Rico in his Levi denim shirt. Two men with scope rifles took position on the roofs across the road. I watched Rico's gaze stop on a grey Landcruiser parked a little way from the surrounded house in front of a shop.

'Did you see the men?' he asked an officer.

'No sir.'

He turned to me, 'Carly, go and ask these people what they saw.' I went, knowing already what Rico knew. This was one of the vehicles we had seen at Maxi's house that night. The shopkeeper, a small-sized chatty woman with a lisp, was more than happy to be asked questions by a policeman.

'Yes, officer, three a dem, one big one, brown skin, and two more, black and ugly. One of dem did carry a long bag. I know right away dem did up to no good. Soon as them get in, dem start shout and make noise. Den me hear some shots, dem must ah kill somebody because I hear the woman scream. She have one young baby, y'know! A long time me ah watch dem, officer. 'Nuff people ah run through this house, and a pure criminals. Ah drugs bizness, me ah tell yuh! . . .'

I got back to Rico and told him one man did answer to Maxi's profile. Rico looked unusually quiet, deep in thought. He gave radio instructions for the snipers to await his signal. The local officer in charge brought us a loudhailer. Rico took the cigarillo out of his mouth.

'Maxi, Maxi, this is Inspector Glenford, can you hear me?'

No answer.

'Maxi, we have to talk, let's work this out.' Rico waited a little, but the house was strangely quiet. The watching residents had fallen silent in the descending darkness.

'Maxi, you and your boys have to come out. Release the people dem. Let the woman and the baby go free, me and you work out this thing, okay?'

A voice came shouting from the first floor, from inside, Maxi's voice.

'I want my car. I'll release the woman, . . . and the baby.'

'Maxi, come out, man; me and you talk. Nobody will hurt you, you have my word.'

'I don't trust no police.'

'Look Maxi; I know you've been set up, and I know who did it. Just come out and talk to me, you're safe, you have my word, man to man.'

There was silence from inside, which is always a good sign. If there were three men in there, that meant three ways of looking at the situation. At least one had to see the hopelessness of the situation. This could work either way. Unless, of course, the three of them were drugged up to their eyeballs!

'Gimme a car and I give you the woman and the youth.'

All eyes were on Rico. He paused, his eyes were squinting against the floodlights from the roofs of our vehicles. 'Let the woman and her child go, then we make a deal. But you have to gimme something first.'

Incongruous, crazy-sounding, a burst of deep laughter sounded out of the first floor, filling the warm night air. 'You want something first?! Okay, I'll give you something.' Some shuffling went on inside and suddenly, a shape appeared on the window still in the glare of the powerful lamps, the upper body of a man, limp, lifeless it seemed. It hovered for a second on the edge then, jerked out from behind, it toppled over, head first, the legs following the rest on the downdrop. The body hit the front yard with a dull thud. Women in the watching crowd gasped, one screamed; a short, gut-deep cry of horror.

Maxi's voice came out, clear, steady. 'Now, you gimme a car, man, or I execute somebody else.'

The look on Rico's face was like stone, his mouth tight, the loudhailer in one hand, the cigarillo in the other. Our eyes met, his squinting to a slit. Yet, when he spoke, the voice was neutral, detached from the anger welling inside.

'Ok, Maxi, I guess you know what you're doing. I'll get you a car, but I must see the woman and the baby first. Show me that they are safe.'

We all waited, hoping, until the face of a young woman, eyes wide with fear, appeared at the first floor. Cradled in her arms was a small child, a girl. Behind the woman I could make out a larger silhouette, keeping away from the opening. Then they all disappeared from view.

'You seen dem now, so bring up my car in front of the house, see the keys here!' Something flew out of the window, landed just outside the fence. One of our men went to pick it up, carefully.

'Ok, Maxi; you got a deal,' Rico said simply. I watched him put back the cigarillo in his mouth, slowly, his eyes narrow and still. He asked Booker to bring the Landcruiser in front of the house, leaving the engine running.

Where could Maxi and his boys go? Did he really expect to make it out of Town with his hostages? There was no way Rico was going to let this happen; in fact they wouldn't even reach the bottom of the road. My guess was that Maxi was so high he probably thought he was acting out a movie. Surely the years he had spent running around with the posses over in the States had made him lose touch with the Jamaican realities. Back here, a gunman had only one place to go. A gunman with a hostage was going to get there even faster. Right now, there was already a corpse laid out in the front yard. Time had run out for Maxi ...

Rico motioned me to come closer. 'I want one of them alive. Pass the word.' Our eyes met, I nodded. The instructions went on the radio to all our men, right up to the snipers on top of the roofs.

Rico meant that whoever was less threatening to the hostages, whoever would have the good fortune of offering a clear shot would be wounded and spared from instant death. Maxi wouldn't be that man, no doubt about that. Whoever his father was didn't matter any more, I could see it clearly on Rico's face. I had a thought for Wilkins, wondering whether he was already on his way down to try and save the renegade son of his politician friend.

'Maxi, can you hear me?' Rico called out.

'Yeah, I hear you.'

'Your car's ready.'

'I want all police move out of the way,' Maxi said from the first floor. 'And don't forget your boys on the roof.'

'Everybody moves out, come on!' Rico called out on the loudhailer; this way Maxi could hear the order being given.

'If I see one police, the woman dead. And turn off dem fucking lights, or I kill everybody!' Sounded edgy, Maxi . . .

'Ok, you got it. Just don't get nervous, everything's gonna be alright,' Rico reassured him.

On the radio, instructions circulated to pull out of sight. The local police had already retreated to the outside; they got all the anxious watchers to get inside their homes. Our men moved the vehicles, but kept them ready to drive out in pursuit, engines running. We knew Maxi could see everything from his upstairs window so all of us found vantage points within and around the back of the surrounding residences, some behind the garden edges of the last houses down the street. The snipers disappeared from the roof, but only to relocate discreetly inside the facing houses.

Going around the back, I had crawled my way back to reach behind the low boundary wall of the house next door to the opposite one. M16 by my side, the radio on very low volume in my hand, I lay on the grass, covering the gate where Maxi was going to appear from behind a thick edge of shrubs.

Within a couple of minutes, the road was empty of all police presence, except for Rico. Cigarillo hanging from his mouth, he was leaning easy against the gate of the opposite house, apparently as relaxed as a man on a date.

'Okay Maxi, the way is clear now,' he called out.

We waited. Nothing happened for a while. Maybe, the men with the guns were getting shaky. Once they were outside, all was going to hinge upon the steadiness of their nerves. The street was quiet, the kind of eerie calm that always announces an imminent storm. Then, something moved inside. We waited.

Indistinct at first in the semi darkness, silhouettes appeared at the door of the house. They moved slowly, all huddled together in a compact mass and it was only when the glow of the street lamps fell on them that I managed to work out who was who. Up front was the young woman clutching her infant. I could see her eyes, wide and still. To her right, AK covering any eventual moves, one of Maxi's men. I thought I recognized him but with a hat leaning low on his face and the distance, I couldn't be sure.

Maxi stood right behind the woman, holding on to her it seemed. His right arm was right around her, his hand pressing a Uzi, at least it looked like one, against the side of her neck. He wasn't taking no chance. To the left of Maxi, the other gangster was back to the road, his arm around the neck of a short and thin man dressed only in shorts and a white vest. The man was dragging him backwards, his head turning from left to right, his free hand holding a handgun. They all moved forward slowly, Maxi and his men scanning the surroundings suspiciously.

'I did what you asked Maxi, see the car here,' Rico said to the leader.

'What the fuck you doing here? I said no police or I start shooting!' The little group had stopped just halfway to the gate. The dead body lay behind them, to the right, against the wall.

'I'm just here to make sure nobody interfere. Relax, man, everything is gonna be alright.'

'Let me see your hands, your hands, raise your hands!' Maxi sounded nervous.

Rico obliged, got off the pillar, raised both hands, the left one holding the cigarillo.

'Turn around, now. Turn around.' Maxi suspected a gun

tucked at the back. He must have known who he was facing and the reputation alone made him edgy. To reassure him, Rico spun around on the spot, slowly.

'Okay? Now Maxi, leave the baby, man. You don't need her.'

'Everybody's coming with me. I don't trust no bloodclaat police!'

'I know that, but you have two people already. Just gimme the baby and move on.'

Maxi looked left and right, the muzzle of his Uzi pushed into the woman's neck. She must have been very afraid, but she made no noise or moves. Her eyes were staring at the man standing across the road, the man trying to save her baby.

'I ain't giving you nobody. You have ten seconds to move from here before I start shooting. One, two . . .' Maxi started counting.

I knew Rico had manoeuvred to get the men and their hostages right where he wanted them: out under the lights, where we had a chance to exploit any opening. Smartly, Booker had parked the Landcruiser a little to the right of the gate. Right in front, it would have provided cover for the gangsters. Fortunately, crazy as he was, Maxi hadn't picked up on this.

'Maxi, man, I try to help you out of this situation, I set things up the way you want. All I'm asking you is to let the little girl go.' Rico stood across the road from the angry armed man, arms akimbo, insisting that Maxi had to do something for him. I knew Rico sincerely wanted to take the baby away from the group; none of us was comfortable with it. At the same time, the most important thing was to prevent the men getting to the car. Once they were inside, controlling the situation would be much more difficult and any armed action at this stage would endanger the hostages' lives. So Rico had to keep Maxi busy until we could get a clean break on the men. Moreover, they all had to be taken down at the same time, that was vital.

'Five, six . . .' Maxi was still counting, getting angrier now.

His men looked highly nervous, sensing the invisible stare of a dozen pairs of eyes on them behind their guns sights. A most uncomfortable feeling, no doubt.

A light crackle on my radio, I brought it up to my ear.

'Carly ... Carly ...' Peter Green, one of the snipers crouching laying in wait on the first floor above me.

'Yeah, I'm here.'

'We have the brown one and the one on the right.'

I was watching the scene from behind the shrubs, keeping low. I knew Rico was playing for time to give us a chance to take the three men down but I could feel the increasing frustration in Maxi's voice.

'I'll take the one with the AK. But wait for my signal. Over.'

'Okay ... over.'

My finger was bent around the steel trigger of my rifle, I licked my dry lips, tensing to spring into action. Rico's .45 was with me but there he was, toying with this crazed Maxi, wide open and holding his cigarillo, apparently as relaxed as could be. Unless the cigarillo was a gadget I didn't know about, Rico was pushing his luck a little too far.

'Maxi, let's get in the car, man.' The man with the AK seemed to grasp the danger of standing up, exposed as they were. But Maxi was either too high or too careless, or both, to see this. Some men can't stand provocation, and he was one of these.

'Shut up!' he shouted to his accomplice. 'I'm gonna kill that cop.'

'Come on, Maxi, there's one dead body already, that's enough for the day. Just gimme the little girl and go.'

'I'm tired of fucking around with you. You asked for it.' Maxi's Uzi left the woman's neck and levelled on Rico, fifty yards away on the other side of the fence. I had wondered earlier on how the woman had managed to keep her little girl from crying for so long. In any case, suddenly, her tiny voice rose, catching everybody unaware. It was as if Maxi's threat had upset her. She started crying, her trembling mother doing her best to hush her up. I could feel time was up. Maxi's time was up, he was at the end of his tether and Rico was much too far up the rope without a net. But he said: 'Look Maxi, I know you been set up, and I know who did it too.' The Uzi was lined up on Rico's chest. He went on. 'It's your police friend who called you here today, isn't it?'

High and crazy as he was, that last line registered with Maxi. He would have liked to listen some more but he could feel time was against him.

'Come on, man; just gimme the little girl. Can't you see she's afraid? Come on, let her go.' Rico took one step forward, right hand out, open.

'Don't move!' Maxi shouted.

I heard Rico kiss his teeth. 'You know something, Maxi, I thought you was a bad boy. But bad boy don't hide behind a woman and pickney!' What was Rico trying to do? He had managed to draw Maxi's gun from the woman onto him, that was enough for us to act. I could tell from where I was that Maxi was about to crack up. And it's never good news for a man to have a nervous breakdown while holding a Uzi! I brought the radio up to my mouth, pressed the call button.

'Cho man; yuh just a pussy!'

'Now, Peter now!' I called out. I knew Maxi was going to shoot now. To call a paranoid, cracked-out armed man a 'pussy', you had to be ready for the gunplay. And Rico was not! I came up from behind the wall, raised myself on one knee just as the Uzi barked five rapid fire shots. An icy claw gripped my bowels as I watched Rico shake under the slugs. He raised both arms, his back hit the concrete pillar behind him. Then he slowly slumped to the ground.

My brain now empty, I levelled the M16 on the right-hand man, my finger pressed on the trigger, from the ground upwards. Leg, side and shoulder hits: the man dropped his AK and screamed in pain. I didn't hear the cracking sound of the sniper's rifle but I saw the left-hand man drop to the ground without a sound. At exactly the same time, Maxi's head jerked sideways, the left side of his skull bored right through by the high-velocity bullet. No more than ten seconds had ticked between Maxi's first shot and the moment he dropped dead to the ground. I remember the woman, very still, holding the whimpering little girl, the short skinny man in his shorts and vest, dropping to his knees, his face frozen.

Our men were all coming out now, running towards the hostages. I jumped the wall and rushed to the spot where Rico sat, legs spread out, his chin resting on his chest. I knelt beside him. Booker had run down there too, Peter Greene, also the officer from the local police unit; we all were there. The bent cigarillo lay in the dust. Five neat holes formed a diagonal on the designer denim shirt. But there was no blood.

Then Booker reached out and opened it out, the thick grey material of a flak jacket appeared. I shook my head in disbelief. Booker smiled at me and shrugged. Rico heaved and stirred, so we lifted him up to his feet. The raising of Lazarus . . .

Some people say a man's life is preset, already planned from on high before he's born. They say there are roads you have to travel, doors you must open, because this is the way it is ordained, and no matter how long it takes you, no matter what else you do, you will pass through these hoops. Some call it destiny.

Rico brought back the three dead bodies, two gangsters and one hostage, to Wilkins. He told him that this was the result of releasing Maxi and there were some pretty sharp words between them. Wilkins himself interrogated the wounded gunman whose life we had spared. My M16 slugs had torn up his flesh but he would live, although his hip wouldn't allow him to bogle any more. What he said confirmed Rico's feeling: Maxi had been called by someone who informed him the people he had entrusted to sell some of his drugs were holding back on him, and cutting the product to make money on the side. When pressed, the gunman told us Maxi's caller was a policeman. He said he didn't know his name. Rico didn't tell Wilkins he knew who the man was. He was going to deal with the problem his own way.

He didn't talk to me about it, but I sensed he went to see Bailey, because that was how he was. Giving up his former comrade wasn't his style, but Bailey knew things were up. Whatever was said between them, I never found out. One week after that bloody evening in Harbour View, two unidentified men opened fire on Rico's jeep not far from Riverton. He was alone at the time, off-duty. I saw the car parked in front of the headquarters the next morning: forty-three impacts in the body alone, not counting the bullets that wrecked the windscreen and windows. But Rico survived. Only three bullets hit him, one in the hand, one in the shoulder, and one that grazed his forehead so close to the left eye that he must have seen it fly by.

The Riverton ambush had Bailey's signature on it. Maybe Rico gave Bailey a chance to run, maybe Bailey had no place to go or maybe he was too arrogant to recognize the favour he was being granted. In any case, the gunmen missed, and Rico, his left arm bandaged, went home to rest. That's what he told me anyway. Two days later, a patrol picked up a body not far from the Caymanas race track. Bailey had a single bullet through the throat. His gun was beside him, three bullets missing from his magazine. No one asked any questions, no one was ever arrested for the killing of the inspector. I never asked Rico about it. I didn't need to.

Mr Walter wanted someone to blame for the death of his son. Maybe no one told him about Bailey, or maybe he wanted someone else to pay for it; who knows. The Bailey incident, though never officially explained, caused many waves within the Force. The Commissioner's anti-corruption drive was in full swing and heads, big ones, had started rolling. Some were running to their political friends, but even these didn't seem to be able to help much any more. It was every man for his skin. Our unit was untouched so I guess we were corruption-free, but on the whole, the big sweep-up scooped up quite a few names previously thought untouchable.

Then, one night, a couple of months after the Bailey affair, Rico came up to see me and said he was quitting. I didn't believe him at first. He had been quieter than usual these last weeks, like something was on his mind. Rico said he had decided to leave the Force and emigrate.

I tried to talk it over with him but he seemed determined. The fact that Lucy and him had finally separated, this time for good it looked like, certainly played a part in his decision. I knew he loved her and I guess she did love him, in her own way. Later on, I wondered whether the death of Jingles just before the birth of Aisha had changed her for good. She took too much of a shock too young, she never managed to recover enough to really love again. Rico tried to understand her, but he was a man living a tough life. What he needed was a woman more solidly grounded than Lucy was. That's what I think happened anyway.

So Rico resigned, to the regret of Wilkins. He packed, sorted out his business, and one bright morning I took him and Miss Ruby to the airport. I watched the London-bound plane take off, taking away my only true friend. Then I went to pick up my two girls and drove them to the ice cream parlour.

CHAPTER FIFTEEN

A Friend in Need ...

London

After a long shower and breakfast, I sat in the living room, meditating on the events of the last twenty-four hours. Miss Ruby and Nicola weren't in, probably out shopping, taking advantage of the sunny weather. The doctor said walking would be good for Nicola. I had time to unwind and think it all over on the train ride back home. It was looking as if I was on the right track, the way I got set up at the dead woman's house. And the surest thing about it was that Tips was part of the set-up, if not behind it himself, which meant that he'd been playing me for a fool all along. One thing I have never liked was being played for a fool. I had never trusted Tips, never had to anyway because we had no dealings together and were never friends. If he had anything to do with Rico's death, he was history, that was for sure. In any case, he knew something and he was going to talk to me now.

My conversation with the police had not been in vain either. I was starting to look at this whole story differently. So, they had discovered a drugs operation run by ex-police and soldiers from Yard. Nothing strange about that. It happened even back home, and not just with ex-members! The question was, was Rico really part of that connection? Whether I liked it or not,

I had to face the fact that he was doing something illegal to be able to move the kind of money he had sent to Mimi, and that something was more than likely drugs. Yet, I still couldn't see Rico dealing drugs. He was a leader, after all, and whatever route he'd taken on coming to England, he was likely to be in charge of the runnings. Could Rico really be the leader of this alleged ex-police and soldiers syndicate? Tips had a lot of talking to do . . .

On the table in front of me was the cassette I had taken out of the woman's answering machine. The police had given it back to me with the rest of my things. I got up and inserted it in the answerphone recorder. With a little luck, it would still carry messages back to the day of Rico's death, unless the woman had a lot of callers and was often absent from her house!

I rewound the cassette to the beginning and pressed PLAY. I sat and listened. Three messages from the same person, a white male from the sound of the voice. It seemed he'd been looking for the woman for a while. Her name was Tracy. A female voice then, laughing at some shared joke I couldn't catch. Two more messages from another man, sounding angry. I couldn't tell how old these calls were. The only way I was going to get any useful information was if these calls dated from more than two weeks ago and if the woman had been away for a while or not answering her phone since. I heard the same woman's voice again, saying she'd been looking for Tracy for a week. 'What's going on?' she asked. That's what I wanted to know. So Tracy, Rico's last contact, had been missing for over a week, but when? Another female voice followed, stern-sounding, saying she was surprised Tracy didn't get back to her about the job and to please call her if she was still interested.

Then, as I was getting pessimistic, it came on, not very clear, with some background noise but I couldn't miss it: Rico's voice. I sat up. 'Tracy, it's me. I've been calling you. Something's happening . . . Move everything, you understand, move it all and send it like I told you. It's urgent, send it. Try and get back to me as soon as possible. Take care.' That was it, that was Rico's last call. I rewound, frowning, turned up the volume and replayed it twice more, listening carefully. Then I switched it off.

I thanked God for the flash of inspiration that had made me pick up the cassette just before the cops got in. I had learned over the years that it was always wise to follow those kind of vibrations. But now I had listened to Rico's instructions to the woman, I still couldn't make sense of it all. There was something Rico had wanted moved. He said it was urgent, that something was happening. But what? He told the woman to send it: send what, and where?

I remained there for a good while, meditating on the clues, turning them over in my mind and trying to imagine what exactly Rico's instructions referred to. It could all fit with what I had learned so far. Was it drugs that the girl had, and Rico wanted moved? Were the police onto him? Why did Tracy go missing? I know she didn't get back to him, and that she ended up dead two weeks after him. Somewhere in the message, I sensed Rico's feeling of imminent danger. Of course, as always, he had been right . . .

I picked up the cassette, put it in my flight bag upstairs and left the house. It was not all clear to me, but I was getting hints that Rico had been running a scheme and somewhere, someone had messed up the runnings. Knowing the man and how careful he was, it could only have been from inside that the operation got sunk. And I knew someone who would enlighten me on that.

I had gone to the cab office straight out of the police station, but of course Tips wasn't there. Just as well; the way I felt, I would have reacted badly to any more bullshit. Loretta said he'd called her earlier on to say he was going to be busy today. His mobile was off, of course. My feeling was that he didn't feel safe after setting me up and he'd decided to keep away until later. He had probably found out by now I had been released.

But Loretta was nice to me, and I was charming to her, especially that morning, even though I was feeling smelly and

crushed up after a night in a cell. I told her I had been to Tips'
house only once, at night, that I couldn't quite find the place
again. The fat woman explained to me how to get there, drew
a plan on a sheet of paper. I told her I had a surprise for him,
not to let him know I was coming in case he called. I also told
Loretta I would get back to her later, whatever she took it to
mean . . .

Being lied to and locked up had stirred me up inside. The
way I felt now, I was going to go all out to find out the truth.
I knew the police were going to try to follow my moves, to
find out where I fitted in the scheme of things. The remarks
of the younger police officer stuck in my mind; maybe there
was something there that I would need to explore.

For now, following my plan of action, I found a call-box
and dialled Joy's work number. She started by saying how much
she had waited and how wicked I was to her, so I cut her and
said I was sorry but I had spent the night in a police cell. Joy
said 'Oh my God!' but I reassured her I was alright and that I
needed a favour. I told her I was coming to her, to explain to
me how to get to her workplace. I hung up and went there by
bus, to Stamford Hill. When I got there, Joy hugged me under
the inquisitive looks of her workmates, which was cool by me.
Then she introduced me to all of them. We went outside and
I told her I couldn't explain everything now, that I was onto a
lead but I needed to check a few places: could she lend me her
car for the day?

Joy raised her eyebrows. 'Carlton, I dearly love this little
car.'

'I just need it for the day. You don't have to worry about
it: it be safe with me.'

'Safe?! I just look at you and see danger.'

I made a face at her, she shook her head and smiled. Out of
her jeans pocket she took the keys. 'You call me on the mobile
as soon as you're finished with it, okay?'

'Yeah man, and thanks, I'll pay back the favour.'

'Yes, you will,' Joy said with a quizzical glance. Then she asked: 'You need any money?'

I took it as a joke and laughed. 'No man: I'm alright.'

Joy smiled and the dimples appeared. 'You be careful, and I'm not talking about the car.'

I nodded. That girl was a nice person, and the only friend I had, it seemed. I picked up the Renault and moved off.

Tips' homebase reminded me a little of the Tivoli Gardens housing scheme. Little kids, on school holidays, rode on their bicycles and roller skates, groups of smaller ones hung around the playground while their mothers chatted on the flats' landings, enjoying the sun, sipping drinks and smoking. I hadn't realized so many women smoked cigarettes in England, but it seemed a widespread habit.

Parked beside a big delivery van, I waited, leaning back in the bucket seat of Joy's car. I figured that it made no sense running around looking for Tips; he knew I wanted to see him and that's probably what he thought I'd do. I guessed that, since he thought I didn't know where he lived, he was bound to show up at some point. So I waited, sipping the malted drink I'd bought on the way, checking out 'The Voice'. Apparently, England wasn't the quiet place I always imagined it to be.

A couple of pretty girls passed by, dressed minimally; my eyes followed them for a minute. Then a bright yellow Audi came to park in front of Tips' flats, the sound of the engine completely drowned by a throbbing, hardcore hip-hop bass. The two black teenagers inside it were bobbing their heads wildly up and down, like drunken mules. One came out, jeans low on the hips, and long vest, his head tied with a red bandana, sunglasses atop his nose. Walking like he the boss of the whole block, he yelled something three or four times, looking at a window upstairs. The noise from the car alone would have woken up the dead so yelling was just unnecessary. Sure enough, a tall youth in shorts and extra-large T-shirt appeared at the flats' entrance door. The pair talked for a while with much arm-waving and gesturing. Eventually, the tall one went into his pockets and handed the other one something. They parted, the bandana man jumped back in the yellow car and it drove off in a roar of sounds. I smiled at the idea of making a spot check on the two youngsters, just to scare them a little. Then again, they could well be strapped, while I wasn't . . .

I must have dozed off for a little while, slipped into an easy half-conscious state, soothed by the sun's warmth and the voices of the children in the nearby playground. Timely, I opened my eyes to see Tips' car enter the parking bay opposite. I stayed as I was, leaning back as I watched him get out and walk towards the flats. I moved after he entered the main door. Loretta told me his flat was on the third floor. I could hear his steps above me. Keeping to the outside of the stairwell, I quietly waited until he was on his landing. Tips had his key in the lock when I appeared beside him. He tried to stay composed but I read surprise, and something else, in his narrow eyes.

'Me and you ha fe talk, sah.' Tips had unlocked his door but wasn't opening it.

'Wait, wha'ppen? Me deh pon a fast move right now, Carly . . .'

'Tips, I say me and you talk now! I getting tired of people fucking around with me, seen?!'

From my tone of voice and the obvious look of cold anger on my face, Tips must have realized I wasn't going to take any shit. He opened the door, motioned me to follow him inside.

'Alright . . . Come in.' I closed the door behind me, I walked into the flat, through to a living room.

'You want a drink?'

'No, me cool.' I let myself onto one of the printed fabric chairs, Tips sat across on a wide divan.

'So wha'ppen, Carly?' Tips eyes didn't stay still, avoiding mine. I sighed deeply.

'Wha'ppen? I spent the night in a cell, that's what happen?'

'Wha? You lie!' I really didn't want to spend too much time playing 'Give Us a Clue' with Tips.

'I went to the address you sent me to.'

'So, wha'ppen?' Tips looked interested, but I was getting irritated by his 'wha'ppen?'

'The woman dead, this is wha'ppen!'

'Yuh kill her?' That got me out.

'Look now sah; the woman already dead when I got there. And guess what: just after I got inside, who come and grab me? Nuh the police! Ah talk about dem arrest me fe murder!'

Tips shook his head in disbelief. 'Dem let yuh out still?'

'Yeah, dem ask me whole heap a question then them let me out. No charges, not'ing, dem just let me go. You don't find that funny?'

'Boy, dem must have found out ah nuh yuh do it?'

I let a few seconds pass. The way I felt, I wasn't about to waste any more time listening to Tips' pretences. I shifted position in my chair, placed my hands flat on the arms. My eyes got hold of Tips' shifty gaze.

'Tips, yuh ah hear me: I don't want yuh fe tell me any more foolishness. Before you say anything, mek I explain something to yuh. I know Rico did run a money scheme, I believe seh is drugs him did a deal with and I know seh yuh know about it. Now, we have two ways to deal with it: yuh tell me everyt'ing, and I deal with the matter. Or yuh try and fuck around with me again, and then it's yuh and me.'

He knew that I was dead serious, he could read it in my face, but Tips still tried to show off. 'Watcha now, sah; me nuh like a man come threaten me ina me house, yuh see me?'

I sat up, very coldly. I said: 'I not threatening yuh, friend,' I let the last word stand out a little. 'But anyhow I find out yuh have any part in Rico killing, yuh will never see your village again, you can trust me on this.' Then I just got up and started out of the room.

I heard Tips call out: 'Hol' on, hol' on, Carly . . .' I turned around, looked at him, sitting on the edge of his divan. I thought I could see the shadow of shame floating around his head like a bad halo.

'Sit down, man.' I walked back to the chair and sat. If ever guilt can be read on a man's face, then Tips' own was a living book.

'Yuh set me up last night,' I stated coldly.

'No, man, ah nuh so.' That was a weak denial, and I had heard quite a few in my time.

'Then how come police was ah wait for me down deh?'

Tips just shook his head. 'Dem must have been watching the house.'

I kissed my teeth in annoyance, sneered: 'Yeah, dem get there after the murder but them still leave the body inside and wait for me fe show up!' I paused to let Tips grasp the implications, then asked: 'Tell me the truth: how much yuh getting fe this?'

Tips looked at me straight for the first time. He swallowed hard. 'I don't sell my brethren dem.'

'No?' Then I asked, 'How you get the address?'

'I asked a friend who have a contact, a girl, who work in a police station. She can do him favours sometimes.'

'What about your friend? Who is him?'

Tips' face registered his reluctance to answer my question. 'Them t'ings confidential, you know. Why you ask me this?'

What I was starting to understand was that he was afraid, I could smell the fear on him. I said: 'I gwan tell yuh somet'ing, just so yuh know I understand wha' ah gwan. Yuh know how the woman die? One stab wound, left side of the chest. She had some cuts on her neck and face too; looked like somebody torture her before she dead, specialist work too.'

I waited to see Tips' reaction, but he just stared down, his large brow knitted in concentration. 'I seen enough dead bodies back home to know a Yardman work when I see it.' I added: 'I have some more t'ings to check, and when

222

I done checking, I comin' fe yuh and your brethren. So be ready.'

I got up but Tips' voice rose before I could take the first step out. 'Alright ... al'right, I gwan tell yuh what I know.'

'Talk, man, talk.' Tips seemed kind of embarrassed now. The deep groove in the middle of his left cheek was visible through the stubble of beard. He inhaled deep.

'This is all about money, 'nuff money ...'

I waited, because when several people die brutally one after the other, it is usually something to do with money.

'The woman you find, she supposed to be working for some big people. She was moving money around for them. Some of that money went missing.' Tips shrugged, his heavy shoulders bulging underneath the T-shirt. 'Dem must have got to her just before you.'

I was weighing out the info; something was still unclear to me. 'So, you telling me the woman was laundering cash, right?'

Tips nodded, glanced around although there was no one within earshot to spy on his revelations. 'Drugs money, big amounts.' I was linking things in my mind.

'So, why Rico call the woman for?' Tips didn't answer, he was letting me get there, and I didn't really want to get where he wanted me at.

'You mean to say Rico was involved with them runnings?' I thought about this, tried to make it fit with the man I knew.

'Rico took money from some guys, drugs money.' Tips could see I wasn't buying the story and a weighty silence prevailed for a while.

'So, you want me to believe that Rico, who almost lose him life fighting against drugs wouda come ah England to rob drugs money?! That is what you saying, right?'

No answer from the big man.

'Tell me something; you know dem guys, the drugs guys?' Tips made a face.

'It's not just any guys, Carly.'

'No?'

'No, this thing is big, too big to mess with.'

'You ah hear me, Tips; that don't matter to me, I have a job to do. All I need from you is names, I will take care of the rest.' He breathed heavily, shook his head. I thought I glimpsed a flicker of sadness in his squinting eyes. When he spoke, the words were strained, toneless.

'Even if you know for sure who the guys are, you can't deal with the matter like back home, you must remember that, Carly. This is a different scene, and here yuh is only a civilian.'

'Yeah, but this is not business, this is personal. And it's the same story; drugs, corruption and killing.'

Tips had sold me half of a story, something that he thought would get me off his case. Now he was stalling; that's how I knew he was hiding something and protecting someone. But why? So I dropped the bomb on him.

'What about Blackjack, Tips?' This time he froze, caught out, eyes wide open while his brain tried to cope with the unexpected question. Tips had been a tough man, someone hard to catch off guard, but lying and betrayal had eaten out his insides. I watched him cover his face with his hands, shake his head slowly.

'I tell yuh what I have, so yuh don't gimme any more stories: the police showed me pictures of several Yard man, all ex-police or soldiers, all dead. Dem say dem was part of a drugs operation. Blackjack was one of them.'

Blackjack, as he was known, was a soldier. Corporal Neville Hammond had been one of the elements picked up to serve in the ACID patrols about the same time as I started in the police. Of Indian descent, medium height, with dark, thin features he was fearless in action and loyal to his friends. Though we never served together, I had met him through Rico, who seemed to like and respect him. We had a beer together a couple of times. Blackjack was cool to hang out with. He had been tipped for promotion when drama cut short his career.

After one particularly bloody gun battle, one police unit had wounded and caught a wanted man from Hannah Town. He was the leader and only survivor of a gang that used to terrorize the area. Locked up, the man was due to appear in court to face charges for the murder of a couple of shopkeepers. The only witness to the case was a woman who lived not far from where the crime was committed. She testified and the criminal was sentenced. Three days later, the woman's house was doused with petrol and set on fire. She died, together with her cousin and baby girl. That woman and child had been visiting for the night. They were Blackjack's wife and daughter ...

After that, Blackjack went berserk. He traced the arsonists, friends of the jailed man, disposed of them one by one, killing them so viciously that even hardened members of the special units were shocked on seeing the corpses. Two of them he burned alive, another was bled to death like a sheep and the last one was castrated. Of course, his superiors couldn't handle him any more. He had to resign from the army and spent time in a psychiatric hospital before he eventually left the island, to settle in Canada. Tips had been part of the unit who had shot and caught the gang leader.

'I wanted to tell yuh, Carly, God knows, but so much bad t'ings happen, and Blackjack was my brethren ...' Tips' voice was a hoarse whisper, his eyes empty, staring at one of the wooden carvings on his living room unit.

'What about the drugs runnings? Blackjack was ina it?'

'He wasn't into drugs when I first come over. I buck him up while him was driving for some firm. When I started the cab office, I got him to come and work fe me. Him was alright, better than when him left Jamaica. He told me some doctors treated him back in Canada and him get over slowly. Blackjack was alright, man ...' I listened, watching Tips show some kind of emotion for the first time. Right now he seemed to relive it as he talked.

'So what happen?'

'When Rico get here, we used to work together, making a little money, just to turn over but it was alright. In the evenings, we used to get some drinks and talk about old times, drink and talk. It was alright, man. Then everyt'ing change.'

I waited, but it was as if Tips just wanted to stay on the good times. I asked: 'How Blackjack get killed?' Tips' face tightened like he felt anger at the thought of his dead comrade.

'One night, I was off work, at home, when Blackjack call me. Him tell me to meet him by him place, that somet'ing urgent was happening. So I drive down there and the man open the boot of the car and inside was a dead man. Him seh him do a fare for a man down South London, some guy he used to carry regular. Him seh the guy run back to the car bleeding, some guys try rob him. There was blood on the back seat everywhere. Blackjack say him try take the guy to hospital but him die on the way. So, him get back home and call me. Then him go inside the man coat and pull out a package. Some drugs, cocaine.'

I was listening intently. Tips looked at me then went on.

'We realized that anyhow we call the police, we was going to get problems. Them wasn't gonna believe a story like that, yuh understand. So we decided to keep the drugs and make a money offa it. Dem time deh we just ah struggle to make ends meet, two ki's ah cocaine we weigh out.'

'What about the body?' I enquired.

Tips shrugged. 'We carry it out ina the woods and bury it. Anyway, first t'ing we do, we call Rico and explain the situation to him. We tell him seh we want to turn over the drugs and make some money.'

'Wha Rico say?'

'Rico? Him say if we try deal with it, we bound to get police problems, like how the scene kinda new to we and ah pure informers deh 'bout. If we give it out to some dealers, dem bound fe try rob we and we couldn't get into no rough stuff and get deported. So Rico tell we seh him know somebody who can turn over the stuff fe we, no stress, no danger. We say alright and give him the two ki's.'

'That somebody ... that was the white girl, Tracy?' Tips nodded.

'Yeah ...'

'Then?'

'Then couple weeks later, we meet and Rico open up a bag and take out some wads, pure cash. We share it.' I was taking the story in, trying to figure out what went on in Rico's mind. Then again, I asked myself what I would have done if it had been me.

'What happen after?' I was curious, knowing that the taste of money is highly addictive. I was right.

'After? Bwoy; that money was easy to get! So after a while, we start t'ink now. We realize we coulda operate a scheme safely, all we had to do was take the stuff from the dealers and make Rico's contact turn it over.' Tips waited for my reaction but I just stared at him blankly. He went on.

'One time, I get a tip about a deal suppose to go down. Yuh get to hear 'nuff t'ings ina the cabbing business. So me hear 'bout it and call the man dem and make dem know. We decide to rob the deal, but we haffe do it neatly, army-style, tight and fast, no shooting.'

'Ouno get guns though?' I asked. Tips looked at me like I was naive.

'Then, yuh t'ink seh we coulda go pon a robbery without guns? I get couple of pieces, then we check out all the details and on the night of the deal, we mask up and drop pon the boy them. Dem never know what happen; we get in, rob the cash and the drugs and get out in less than five minutes. We get over five grand and two and half ki's that time. And nobody find out who do it!'

I had to admire the move. 'What ouno do with the money?' Tips took a little time to answer to this.

'Rico seh we shoulda use some of the money to help people

back home. Him say if we gwan rob drugs dealers, then we haffe do somet'ing intelligent with the money. Him tell we about some project him have back home, about setting up some school fe de area yout's dem.' The way Tips was speaking, I could tell he hadn't been too hot on the idea. I was to remember this impression.

'So we decide fe go half-half; we split half ah the money and keep the rest in a safe place for the school project.' Now things were falling into place. There was still one piece of information missing.

'Who did keep the money? The project money?' I was discovering that Tips' face revealed much more than his words.

He said: 'Rico did set up a safe deposit box. Him used to drop off the drugs to the girl, then she turn it over and put the money in the box fe collection. Rico was picking up the cash himself and bring it in for the split. Everyt'ing was working good.' Any operation organized by Rico always did.

'What went wrong?' Tips paused, licked his lips, eyes still for a few seconds.

'Blackjack decide to set up a robbery fe himself . . .'

'Why?' Tips shrugged.

'Him wanted more money, and him was getting hooked on drugs.' I waited for Tips to explain. He did.

'Him get with the girl, she started him using drugs.'

'What girl?'

'The white girl.'

'Rico's contact?' Tips simply nodded, his gaze away through the open living-room window. That was crazy. Now I was getting to understand how Rico's safe set-up had got busted.

'That's how Blackjack died?'

'Yeah. He got fucked up and went out on his own. The dealer shot him dead.' I shook my head, feeling bad that a once-brilliant soldier could end up shot down like a junkie dog.

'A Yard man him rob?' Tips nodded, looking stern at the mention of his friend's death.

228

I sat back, piecing it all together, making it fit like a puzzle. And yet, not everything was clear.

'So, what about Rico?'

Tips sighed. 'The last robbery we do, before Blackjack get killed, we hit some Turkish runners. We got away with eight ki's of stuff, heroin this time! We never know so much was there, it was just a tip. Yuh can imagine how much money dem man deh lose!' I could well imagine. Now for the really important question.

'Ouno get back the money?' A frown seized Tips' features. I saw him shake his head.

'Since so much stuff had to be moved, and it was a different market, Rico said the money would take a little longer to get back. We was supposed to get it at the end of this month.' There was genuine bitterness in Tips' voice. Rico got shot on the 25th, just short of the big payday!

'What about the box?' Tips fixed me for a while, he said simply, 'Not'n nuh in deh.'

I nodded, leaned back in the chair. The room was quiet except for the voices of the children at play outside filtering through. Both of us kept quiet. Tips seemed to brood over the mention of the money; that's what it looked like to me anyway. I was chilling out now. No more questions, as prosecuting attorneys say. In Tips' last answer was the key to the whole drama, the reason why he'd been lying to me all this time. I don't think he realized it at the time but Tips had just sold himself. I was now certain he had something to do with Rico's fate. And that spelt his death sentence.

CHAPTER SIXTEEN

Jack of All Trades

The windows down, I waited for the light to change. The track playing was cool and laid back, bumping just enough to make the traffic jam bearable. I was in no hurry anyway. Six-thirty on Holloway Road, a setting sun and a mind longing for the bliss of emptiness. I couldn't get away from the string of thoughts playing hide-and-seek in my head. The conversation with Tips had left me with a bad taste, like bile coming up to the mouth, stinging and bitter. Money is the root of all evil, they say, the love of it ...

Tips knew the box was empty because he had checked it, therefore he had to have the key. Yet he had told me that Rico himself did the money pick-ups, and I knew the man well enough to be sure he wouldn't trust anyone else with that. There were two possible ways Tips could have obtained the key: either Rico had given it him before he died, which I seriously doubted, or he'd got the double from the only other person who'd have one, Tracy. I had seen her dead body and I knew how much pain a knife can cause in an experienced hand. Whether that hand belonged to Tips or to his mysterious friend, I would have to find out. Yet, the bitter irony was that Tracy had cheated her killer. She had surrendered the key but knew he wouldn't get the money. Now the message on the cassette made sense: somehow, Tracy had received and executed Rico's last instructions and moved the money somewhere else! 'Send it out', Rico had told her. But send it where?

I had called Joy earlier. She sounded happy, whether because her beloved vehicle was safe or just to hear me, I couldn't tell. In any case, she gave me her address and told me she was waiting for me. It sounded good to me that she'd invite me home but I was unsure what her real feelings about me were. I could feel she kinda liked me but there were those strange looks and colder vibes that she sent at times, and I didn't know what to make of it. Not that it bothered me: I was on a mission and Joy was the only one who was willing to do what she could to help. That was all that really mattered. I had looked up her road on the map from the glove box; I was getting there.

I missed it at first because it was a small, dead-end street but eventually I came to park right in front of number twenty-seven. She was probably watching out for me because I was hardly out of the car when Joy appeared at the gate, smiling in her track pants and T-shirt.

'You was afraid for your car, right?' I said. She shrugged, taking my arm like I was her husband returning from work.

'You're a policeman; it's in safe hands.'

I smiled, followed her inside the house. The room was spacious, wood-panelled, with a central staircase that spiralled up. Climbing plants covered the railing. Low cushions, a large Japanese screen dividing the dining and sitting areas and tall potted plants surrounding it all. The place smelled of incense and fruits. Through the large windows, I could see a garden with wild shrubs, a swing and an old wooden shed at the far end. Joy sat me down, zoomed into the adjoining kitchen and brought back a can of Coke which she poured out in a tall glass. She sat beside me. I felt welcome.

'How you feeling?' she asked. The chill of the cold drink was seeping inside me. I inhaled deeply, let the air out. After the vile atmosphere of earlier on, Joy's house and smile were bringing me back to the living.

'Much better now,' I told her.

'You got what you wanted?' I made a face.

'Yeah ...'

'What? What's wrong?' she asked. I didn't really feel like talking about what I had learned, not now anyway.

'Not'ing wrong; I'm just ... weary, you know.'

'Well, relax yourself. You're safe here.' She got up and went to select some CDs on the stereo, came back to sit by my side. Outside, slowly, the sky was turning dark purple. The smooth tones of Keith Sweat rose across the room.

'Have you eaten?' I had all but forgotten about that. I shook my head.

'Me neither, what d'you fancy?'

'Food,' I said. Joy smiled, that little girl smile she had.

'Okay, but what kind?'

'Wha'. You gonna cook?'

'You saying that like you think I can't cook!' she said.

'No man, but it's too late to go shopping.'

'I have some salt fish here ...'

'Alright, if you feel like cooking.'

'You just chill out, it won't take long,' Joy said. Before she got to the kitchen she asked: 'You want anything stronger than that?'

'You trying to get me drunk?' I joked. Joy raised her eyebrows at me, she had a very peculiar way of doing that whenever she didn't want to answer a question.

'Anyhow, the bar's over there.' She was pointing to the far corner, left of the couch. Then she disappeared inside the kitchen. I checked her bar and added a little Johnnie Walker to my Coke, sipped some of that while Keith Sweat purred to a lady, offering to freak her.

For me the day was over. I had to cope with the unpalatable facts I had learned today, then push on and find out all the details Tips had left out in trying to get himself off the hook. From the kitchen, Joy's voice sang along with the track, high and

233

melodious like a church alto. I sank further into the couch, closed my eyes and let the tension slip away from my body . . .

'Carlton . . . Carlton.' For a few short hazy seconds, I wondered who that voice belonged to. I could hear it but didn't want to leave my dream. I opened my eyes and saw Joy's face over me, scanned around and remembered where I was.

'You slept so well, I wasn't sure if I should wake you up!' Joy smiled. I stretched. Even a short sleep could get me back in shape; years of soldier life do that to you.

'My cell wasn't too comfortable last night,' I said. Joy laughed.

'Where's your bathroom?' I asked. She directed me upstairs. When I came down, the smell from the dinner table caught my hungry stomach and we sat together and got down to business. Joy was a fine cook. She asked if it was alright, and I said she had nothing to worry about. She had even made dessert; some ice-cream and apple crumble, and I went through it in the same way. After that, I felt new. We sat on the couch and watched the evening news. Joy mixed two whisky cocas and came to sit right beside me.

'I'm not much of a drinker . . .' I said.

'That's not strong. Anyway, it looks like you had a hard day. That's to help you relax.' I threw her a quizzical glance and took a sip. We started to talk, just chatting. Joy told me about her trip to Jamaica with two girlfriends a couple of years before. She had a great time and she mentioned a lot of places she went to I knew, but she hardly spent any time in Kingston. She asked me about my life, and I told her about my background, the early years, the story of how I joined the Force. She seemed to find this fascinating. The phone rang. When she hung up, she said the call came from the local police station: they had stopped a youngster she had worked with, nothing too serious, but she needed to go there and speak for him so they'd let him go. Joy insisted that she wouldn't be long, that I should wait for her. What could I say? I told her I'd chill out and wait.

Once Joy had gone, I went through the TV channels but couldn't find anything interesting. So I decided to check out the CD collection lined up on the shelves above the music centre and was pleasantly surprised to find an extensive selection of reggae music, some revivals, some roots and up-to-date ragga sounds. I picked three and loaded them up on the CD trays, programmed the tracks at random and went back to the couch to relax. The whisky-coca had me mellow, soothing my head after the trying day I had. My eye caught two thick photo albums on the lower shelf of the coffee table. You can learn a lot about someone's personality from checking out their albums, and I didn't think Joy would mind, anyway. Leafing through, I found childhood pictures, holiday snaps, a few college group pictures. Joy's face hadn't changed a bit from when she was a child, I could tell. I browsed through a few pages of family shots, girls group picture on a beach, Disneyworld holiday photos . . .

Turning a page, my eyes stopped on a couple, arm-in-arm, in front of a night club. The woman was Joy, again. I kept staring at that picture, just couldn't get my eyes off it. The hair was longer than it used to, and the short beard made him look slightly older but it was him no doubt. The conversation with Tips earlier on came rushing to my mind. The shot the police had shown me had probably been sent from back home but this was the first time I had seen a recent picture of him.

Blackjack looked happy, well dressed, with a pretty girl on his arm. He always had good taste when it came to women, and most women seemed to find it hard to resist to his charm. Friends of his he moved with used to joke that he used some 'coolie-magic' on girls and would beg him to give them some of it!

So Joy knew Blackjack. My guess was he had been her man rather than just a friend: I could tell that much from the photo. It was becoming obvious to me that the girl had something on her mind in looking me up. Now I needed to find out how much she knew about him and his activities in London. Sure, a man like Blackjack would run schemes and never let his woman know but Joy was a smart girl. She must have known Rico – in fact I was wondering now whether she really was Nicola's friend at all. The more I thought about it, the more I was becoming convinced there was a lot Joy knew which I needed to know. When the door opened I was watching a series on TV and the albums were back in their place.

'Sorry, it took a little longer than I thought,' Joy said, dropping her handbag. She came to sit beside me.

'Did you get him off?' I asked.

'Oh, they didn't have much on him but you know how the police can get awkward at times.' She smiled.

'Yeah, I know all about that.'

'I see you found some music you like,' Joy remarked.

Something hit me right then. I nodded and said casually, 'Blackjack used to love music ... how come you never told me about him?' I saw the change on her face.

'What?' I picked up the album from the table shelf, found the right page.

'You two make a nice couple, fe real!' I waited. Joy was sitting straight, staring at the picture, her hands flat in her lap. Then, without warning two tears come bursting out of her slanted eyes. I could sense the tension from her body.

'Sorry, I didn't mean to search your things,' I lied.

She took time to dry her eyes, sighed and said: 'It's okay. That's why I asked you to come.' So she did have a plan all along ...

'The man who got killed, your sister's boyfriend you told me, it was him.' It wasn't a question. I stood her dark gaze. She nodded.

'How long did you know him?' I asked. Joy picked up my glass, got up and went to the bar. She came back with two fresh whisky and Cokes.

'Neville and I lived together for fourteen months, in this

house.' Neville . . . Blackjack must have trusted her to a point to give his right name.

'Joy, I know it must be hard for you to talk about it, but I have a lot of questions in my mind and you must have the answers.'

Two steely eyes held mine for a few seconds then drifted away to stare at the ancient Egyptian motifs of the printed curtains behind the TV.

'There's a lot I don't understand . . .' I paused, the girl was still looking away but I knew she was listening.

'I need help,' I told her. Joy's eyes turned back to me, intense. Then I heard her ask: 'You're gonna take care of the man who killed him?' The question took me by surprise. I had been right: she was a tough woman.

I stood her gaze and said, 'I'll take care of anyone who hurt my brethren dem. Just tell me what you know.'

In her expression I could read not sorrow but the determination that is born from pain. Joy was a survivor, that was clear. She asked me: 'You know how he died?'

'I heard one version of the story; he was shot during a robbery.' Joy really had a beautiful face, maybe more so with the expression of deep hurt that tensed her features now. She inhaled and sat back in the couch. Her voice was steady as she started.

'I met Neville a couple of months after he got here. A friend of mine had a party and he came over with a couple of other Jamaican guys. I could tell he wanted to talk to me but I wasn't really interested . . . I was just out of a bad relationship and the last thing I wanted was to get involved with a Yardman . . .' She looked at me.

'I don't mean to stereotype but most of those I knew were into crime, drugs, pimping, that kind of thing.' I nodded.

'Anyway, I was doing my thing and suddenly he came to me and said . . .' Joy was back there, recalling the exact words. '. . . he told me he realized I didn't want to dance with him, or even talk with him but he thought I was really beautiful. That's what he said. He told me he would have loved a chance to have a discussion with me, even if only for five minutes, because he knew I thought he was just like any other Jamaican in England, but he wasn't. Anyway, he said, he would have loved to drop me home but if I refused, he'd still like to meet me some other time, to have dinner maybe. He told me I should keep an open mind and hear him out.'

Joy stopped, and I smiled in spite of the tragic situation, smiled at Blackjack's smoothness of words, remembering his soft voice and penetrating dark eyes. I knew Blackjack was a man who always meant every word he said as he said it; he was like that. He must have really been impressed with Joy.

'So I let him drop me home, and by the time we got there, that man had totally changed my opinion of him, the way I figured he was. We talked, talked in his car until early morning. He didn't even ask to come up, he just seemed to be happy to talk to me. I was still a little cautious of him. I know how convincing Jamaican men can be. But he took me out a couple of times. Eventually, I fell in love with him.' The look on her face was pure tenderness as she recalled the beginning of her love story.

'When you met Neville, was he driving taxi?' I asked Joy.

'Yeah, his friend was running a cab office, so he got a job working there for.'

'You met his friend?'

'Neville introduced us once.' I thought I could hear something in the way Joy answered, so I pushed on.

'What was he like?' There was a pause, a significant silence.

'I didn't like the way he looked at me. There was something about that man, something false, you know what I mean? I couldn't tell what it was, but my spirit didn't take to him. I told Neville, but he was very trusting with his friends, too trusting.'

I decided to ask it straight. 'Tell me something, Joy: did you ever suspect Neville to be involved with drugs?'

She didn't hold back. 'You mean if he was dealing or anything like that? To be honest, I didn't think so at the time. But after a while, I noticed he was going out a little more, and he had more money to spend as well. When I asked him about it, he said cabbing wasn't earning him enough money and he was investing in some business with some friends, that's all he said. He was buying me presents. I didn't think nothing of it at the time. But the last few months before he died, I know something had changed in him.' Joy paused before adding, her voice a little more strained, 'That's what killed him.'

'What happened?' I saw Joy shake her head, and her eyes came to meet mine.

'You know what happened to him back in Jamaica? About his wife and child? Neville never quite recovered from that. He told me how he spent some time going through therapy in Canada before coming here, but deep down inside, his spirit never healed. Many nights, he used to wake up shouting, covered in sweat, shaking. He really tried to overcome it, but there was just too much pain inside of him.'

'You think that's what drove him to drugs?' I asked.

For what seemed like a long time, the buzzing of the television turned down low filled the silence between us. Joy inhaled deeply before answering.

'Some of the things I know now, I only figured out after he died. But I believe Neville was used. I think he was set up. Because he was still fighting with his demons, he was vulnerable to bad influences. That's why I said he was too trusting ...'

'Tell me what you think, even what you can't prove. I trust your intuition.'

'I know Neville started using drugs around three months before he died. I noticed some changes in him; he became very moody at times. Also, he was seeing somebody, a woman ... I never found out who it was but I'm sure of it. When I asked him what was going on, he just told me he was gonna get some money, a lot of it. He didn't want to answer my questions, that's how I know he was doing something wrong, because he used to confide in me before. I told him I knew he was on drugs and I could help him maybe, but he had become just like the rest of the macho guys on the street. I couldn't talk to him any more. But I stayed with him, hoping he would turn back again. I cared for him, I really did.'

There is something even the most insensitive of policemen should respect, and it's the tears of a grieving woman, because we all came from a woman. And I wasn't on a case here; I was a man trying to find out why his friends died. So I gave Joy the time to cry, silently, watched the tears slide slowly down her amber cheeks, feeling almost embarrassed to witness her sorrow. I was the cause of it.

'I feel bad to bring back all dem bad vibes, Sis, fe real. I know it's hard for you still.'

'It's alright. Someone has to find out the truth. I owe it to Neville.'

'Can you tell me about the robbery?'

'I don't know much. Only, I went home about six that Monday. Neville was there, on the phone to someone. He hung up shortly after I came in. He seemed agitated, restless. I prepared dinner, but he wouldn't eat anything. He stayed with me until about nine, we watched TV, but I could feel his mind was somewhere else. He was in one of his silent moods. Then he got up and said he had to go out, on business he said. I was on the phone with my sister Mel, I remember. He went out.'

I waited, waited for Joy to trip back to that fateful night. Her eyes had narrowed to slits.

'Around twelve, just after twelve, I had already gone to bed, the phone woke me up. It was Neville. He sounded out of breath. He said he had been shot, he was wounded. I got scared, I asked where he was, he said down by Clapton Park, in Hackney. I told him I was on my way. I could hear his breathing, hard, painful on the line. He told me, he said ... he said "it's a set-up ... they knew ..." He called my name, then the line went dead.'

Joy didn't say another word for a full minute. When she spoke, I felt the drama in her voice, though she tried hard to maintain a normal tone.

'When I got there, I found several police vehicles and an ambulance just leaving. I followed it to the hospital but the doctors said Neville was already dead. He had died on the street, by the phone box.'

I didn't feel like asking anything else. Pain is something that's best left buried. But I knew what she wanted, and also I was starting to read the whole story from a different angle.

'Who shot Neville?' I asked. Joy was staring at the curtains, hands clasped in her lap.

'Roddy,' she said simply.

CHAPTER SEVENTEEN

Deep Sea Fishing

Sitting at the kitchen table with my cup of hot chocolate, I was finding it hard to clear my mind. There was no getting away from the bits of conversation that kept surfacing, going round and round in my head, Joy's voice, haunting, telling the story of her dead man. A plate of salt fish and fried dumplings lay untouched in front of me. I had hardly slept, my subconscious working overtime at connecting the story together, linking all the pieces of the puzzle into a coherent whole. The scribbled-up bits of writing paper on the table didn't amount to much.

I had got up at six, showered and come down to try and work out my next move. Somewhere in there was the clue to Rico's death, and the hand behind it. So absorbed in my inner thoughts was I, I didn't notice Miss Ruby coming in the kitchen until she stood there by my side.

'How yuh feeling, me son?'

'Not too bad, madda.'

'Yuh look tired; yuh must take some rest. I have somet'ing for yuh.' Miss Ruby lifted the briefcase she was carrying and placed it on the other side of the table.

'Wha' dis?' I asked.

'Rico give me this to keep about a week before the wedding. I don't know not'ing about it, but it's best yuh should have it.' I looked at the case, frowning, then at Miss Ruby.

'I know yuh not going to go back home until your heart satisfied, but yuh must look after yourself. Finish your breakfast first, yuh hear?'

The old lady left me there, perplexed. I did what she said, finishing the food she had prepared for me, all the while eyeing the brown leather case. It had two four-figure combination locks and metal corners. When I lifted it up, it weighed but nothing moved inside when I shook it up. What could this be? Rico had given this to his mother to keep, so it had to be important.

Now I had to figure out how to open it, to find out what was inside. I wasn't prepared to try out numbers. I had no time for that. Rico had meant to get back the case later, so himself alone had the combination, unless he had entrusted someone else with it. If he had given the case to his mother, he wouldn't have given his wife the opening code, it wouldn't make any sense. Who else . . .

Something hit me, an idea which I just had to try. Out of my wallet I pulled the piece of paper where I had jotted down the telephone number I'd got from Mimi. Maybe it wasn't a telephone number after all. I had tried it the next day, using both area codes but got a dead line both times. I rewrote the sequence on my sheet of paper.

303 04 37

I looked at it for a moment, wrote it down again, spacing it out. The locks needed four figures; which one should I use and which one should I leave out? I tried the first four, then the last four; nothing worked. I then left out the threes, left out the zeros plus one three; still no luck.

At that point, something came up. While we were in training, Rico had taught us a little of what he had learnt at police college in the States. Cyphers and codes, he called it. Although it wasn't of much use for police work in Jamaica, it was good to know all the same. I started by the simplest of the coding systems he had shown us, digging deep into my memory. First, I took the original order of the figures, adding together the ones with a zero. That gave me: 6-4-3-7.

I tried it on the locks, without success. I was certain the sequence was coded, I could feel it. Then I changed that new sequence over: 7-3-4-6, and tried it on the locks; still no luck. Thinking back, I did my best to recall the coding skills I had never used. I put the figures in chronological order; both ways; 7-6-4-3 and 3-4-6-7. I tested the locks with both of these.

At the second try, the left one clicked; I nodded with satisfaction. So it was coded! But the second one responded to another sequence: just like Rico. Years later, from beyond the grave, the man was testing me to see whether his lesson had been remembered! I toyed with the sequence on the right-hand lock, changing the figures over, but nothing worked. It had to be a mix of the coding systems we'd been given.

I wrote the left lock sequence separately on the reverse of the sheet of paper; 3-4-6-7. The fourth system, as far as I could recall, meant using the last figure and subtracting the others from it, using the result as a new element in their place. I thought it might work Because 7 was the highest one and it came last. I took 3 out of 7, then 4, then 6, then 7 and got a new sequence; 4-3-1-0. I tried this but it still didn't open the lock.

By now I was getting frustrated, shaking my head sombrely as I was running out of ideas. Then it came to me that maybe 0 wasn't a playing figure, I thought I could recall something about that. So I replaced 0 by the original figure, 7. 4-3-1-7. This time I told myself, if it doesn't work, I'll blast the damn thing open; but of course I knew I wouldn't do it. Rico expected me to solve the problem so I must be able to do it. More doubtful than Thomas the Apostle, I tried the lock, it clicked open and that little metallic noise was the sweetest thing to me. Smiling broadly, I lifted up the lid. My smile disappeared in a flash and my eyes opened wide; I understood right away why the case didn't make any noise when shaken. It was filled to the top with brand new US dollar bills.

I must have remained like that, both hands on the lid, mouth open, for quite a few seconds. Being an honest, hard-working, lowly-paid policeman, I had never seen so much money. I guess anyone faced with that kind of sight, especially on his kitchen table, feels his brain stop working for a while. Once I had recovered, I counted the notes in one stack; ten times a hundred: one thousand dollars per stack. Then I counted the stacks: thirty-seven.

Thirty-seven thousand US dollars were in that little case and that case was in my hands! I reflected that it might have caused the death of three persons already and explained why those still alive and in the know might be so eager to find it. Yet, if that part of Tips' story was true, it was small change compared to the amount expected from the eight kilos of drugs Rico and his men had taken from the Turkish gang. From what I could work out, that deal was worth over two hundred thousand English pounds! A lot of people would kill without blinking for that kind of money. I closed the case, locked it in my travel bag upstairs, having jotted down and memorized the sequences. Then I left the house.

I needed to walk to clear my mind and think over my next move. The sun was out, people enjoying the morning, normal people doing normal things, unaware of the sinister thoughts in my head. I thought about going back to visit Tips but I quickly realized that I had no desire to see his lying face. By now I was certain he was guilty as hell, maybe not of killing Rico, for he didn't have the guts or the brain for that, but he knew more than he had told me. One thing I had worked out from Joy's story was that he had something to do with Blackjack's death.

'They knew . . .' the mortally wounded soldier had told his woman on the line before collapsing. The robbery was a set-up, and who would have more of a reason to want his friend and partner dead than Tips? This way, there would be more to share and he didn't need Blackjack because only Rico knew where the money was. It wasn't hard to guess that Tips was the one who had told Roddy about the robbery to take place, and I was ready to bet my right hand that he himself had organized that fake robbery.

Something else had been bugging me, something that fitted with the other elements of the drama. Blackjack had tried to flee on foot, and that made no sense. No one ever goes on a robbery without a getaway car, and very few people go on a job of this kind alone. Blackjack would have had partners, I was sure of it, and he trusted very few people. My gut feeling was that Tips had set up the robbery, gone along to make sure Blackjack did as expected and then driven away the vehicle before the arrival of the police. A cold-hearted son of a bitch, he was!

I hopped on a bus going down to Whitechapel. The way things had been happening those last few days, I hadn't had time to call Zafirah. I thought it would be good to talk to her; the woman had a very sharp mind, could maybe see something I had missed. I found her in conversation with two big guys, one of them wearing dark glasses and a white vest that revealed muscles puffed up by hours spent on the workbench. His friend was shorter and leaner, sporting a tracksuit and a towel around his neck. Chewing gum, he was letting his friend do the talking.

'I need my money now; I have some problems to sort out, I'm telling you,' the muscle man was saying. His voice was rather high-pitched for a big man, with a strong London accent.

'And I'm telling you pay day is on the fifteen, you know that. So you come back next week and you'll get your money.' Sitting on the sofa, I listened while browsing through a copy of *New Nation* picked up from the magazine table.

'I can't wait till next week, I have debts to pay.'

'I'm sorry but there's nothing I can do. We have procedures. The best I could do is give you a cheque but you still couldn't cash it in until the fifteen.'

'These people don't take cheques, I need cash and I need it now.' The big guy sounded nervous; I could guess he owed some serious people, the way he seemed anxious to pay them. Zafirah was showing much patience, remaining polite but firm.

'You got to have some cash you can advance me. Do me a favour, alright?'

'There's nothing I can do, sorry.' The man was restless, shifting from one foot to the next, visibly frustrated. The other one just stood there, hands in his pockets, chewing on his gum.

'Listen, you owe me fucking money and I want it now. What the fuck is wrong with you? I ain't leaving here till I get my cash, you understand?'

Now the guy was getting out of order. Quietly from my corner, I said: 'Friend, I think the lady had been patient with you. Maybe you should just apologize and leave now.' The two men had glanced at me when I went in. Now they both turned to look at me, still turning the pages of my newspaper. I knew the big guy wasn't going to like my remark.

'You wha'?' He was staring down at me from behind his shades. He looked so edgy, I was starting to think he was on something. Maybe steroids, maybe something else. I looked up at him.

'I'll say it again slowly, so you hear me good: apologize and go home.' I wasn't sounding threatening, I didn't think so anyway. Zafirah was watching, the other man too.

The muscle man seemed surprised I could talk to him like that, he just stood there for a couple of seconds, looking at me. Then he said: 'This is none of your fucking business, so keep out of it, alright?!' I put down the paper slowly, shaking my head. I got up, although I really didn't feel like it.

'This is my business, and now you just made a mistake. I don't like people swearing at me. But I'm gonna give you a chance, because I know you have money problems. Leave now.' Either out of stupidity or shame of backing down, the man insisted on being nasty.

'Or fucking what?' he asked me, his chest out, feet apart

like he was ready to stand his ground. I took two steps forward around the table. We were now a yard apart, looking at each other. I was a little taller than him but fifty pounds lighter. I smiled and that puzzled the man.

'Or I'm gonna help you to leave.'

'Go on then!' he growled.

'Alright.' I spread out my right hand towards the big guy, as if to grab him by the front of his vest, slowly enough for him to react. He took the bait and swung my way, sending out a right hook that could have dropped me had it connected with my face.

He was a heavy puncher but slow. Sidestepping swiftly, not even bothering to parry, I sent out my right forearm and hit him on the Adam's apple, not hard enough to kill. I heard a choking sound and the man's glasses flew off. Then I doubled with a hook low in his floating ribs. There was a dull sound and he cried out in pain, bending over and dropping to his knees. That was enough. My eyes locked onto the other man but clearly, he wanted no part of this fight. He had even stopped chewing. Behind her desk, Zafirah hadn't moved. I said to the gasping man:

'I'm the new boss and you're fired. Come for your money on the fifteenth. And take my advice; stay off the drugs.'

I turned to his friend: 'Get him out of here!' The man did as I said, lifting up the big guy, holding him up to walk him out of the door. I got back to my seat.

'You'll have to replace him,' I told Zafirah.

'I've never liked that guy,' she said with a little smile, then: 'Did you get my message?'

'What message?'

'I called the house, they told me you'd just left. We have two more bookings, one from some white man who's having a techno gig. Both were sent to us by Bungee.' So Bungee had kept his promise to get us more jobs . . .

'Can you handle it?'

Zafirah nodded. 'No problem . . . Would you like a drink?'

'Okay.' She got up and got me a Coke, poured herself some mineral water and came to sit beside me.

'So, what have you been up to, chasing girls?'

'No, chasing killers.' I summed up the events of the previous three days for Zafirah. After listening intently, she asked: 'Do you think your friend Tips works for the police?'

I hadn't come to that conclusion yet but it would explain a lot of things. I sipped a little Coke.

'Either him or somebody he knows . . .'

'He got the address of the girl for you, someone killed her before you got there. Probably the same man who killed your other friend, the soldier.' She had to be right, I wasn't buying the story about the Turkish guys or the laundering syndicate.

'Tips has run out of time. My next move is to talk to his friend, Roddy. And I'm sure some other guy is working with him too . . .'

Zafirah shook her head. 'I never suspected Rico of being involved in that kind of things.'

I shrugged. 'Me neither, you know. He had a vision of doing something for the youths back home, he decided to do it his own way . . .' We kept quiet for a while, the traffic noise from outside reaching in.

'So what about the robbery money?'

'I don't know what the girl did with it, but some people want it bad. I have an idea how to bring them out.'

'You've got to be careful, Carly. These people are dangerous.'

I nodded. 'I know.'

Zafirah's eyes were searching mine. 'What are you planning to do next? You said you had an idea . . .'

I had an idea but it wasn't that thought out. Finding a way to bring out the shadow man, the one behind Roddy, was my priority. Once I knew him, I was sure I would be closer to the solution to my problem: finding out Rico's killer. But that man was after one thing, the money, so my main card was to get him to believe I had found it.

Another aspect of things was the police. Zafirah got me thinking about that; what was their role in the whole affair? Tips or Roddy might be working for them. It was certain that the police worked with informants to penetrate the drugs business but it was equally certain that some policemen were getting paid in the process.

The more I thought about it, the more I was becoming convinced there was a police informant in this business. I couldn't imagine how a bounty of several thousand pounds wouldn't attract the interest of one or two unscrupulous police officers. I recalled the remark of the red-haired policeman about being human and having weaknesses. For me, the money wasn't a priority, although I'd rather find it myself and try to spend it the way Rico wanted to than leave it to a couple of greedy drugs dealers or corrupt cops. My mission was to find out and eliminate Rico's killer and to do that, I now had to go all out.

I hadn't seen Joy since the other night. To make the move I was planning, I was going to need a vehicle and she was the only person likely to lend me one. Nicola had proposed I use Rico's jeep but it was too big and conspicuous and, to tell the truth, I wouldn't have felt comfortable driving it. Joy wasn't at work when I called; she had a day off. I called her mobile but it was engaged. I left the house and went to look for a barber. At dinner the previous night, Zarifah had told me I looked better with more hair but that wasn't my opinion. Back home I'd visit my barber at Smoochies every week religiously, keeping up my 'marines' look but since arriving in England I had neglected this. I ended up in Clapton, not far from the place Joy had said Blackjack died. Might as well check on something while I was in the area, so I left the barber for later and pushed down the road.

Walking down, I came across a little group of youths hanging out in the square in front of the shops, smoking ganja more or less openly with a beatbox pumping out some dancehall tracks. The sun was out again, had been almost every day for three weeks now, high and hot. English people were becoming all red, walking around in beach clothes and talking about the drought.

I passed the youths, went down and around the block then came back up, stopped by the smokers.

'Wha'ppen. I looking for Roddy. Ouno nuh see him?' The youth I addressed wore a bandana, Tupac-style, glasses and no shirt. He looked me up and down, shook his head.

'No,' he said. I shifted from one foot to the next, scratched my stubble of beard, asked again.

'Him tell me two thirty. Dat man deh always late!' I must have looked the part because another youth, slim with short, thick locks asked: 'What you looking for? We can set you up ...'

I said: 'Cool, man. Is only Roddy I dealing with.' The youth shrugged.

'He's never around till evening.' I kissed my teeth, shook my head.

'Bwoy! Alright, I gwan call him. Cool.'

I left them and headed straight for the phone box and called Joy's mobile. This time it rang. I explained to her I needed to borrow her car later, if it was alright with her. She said 'no problem' but only if I let her take me to dinner. We arranged to meet in Dalston around six. I hung up and walked back up to find the black barber I had spotted earlier in the week.

Though I was in two minds about letting Joy come along, I decided against it. I was out to find Roddy and, I hoped, his partner but I had no idea how things could turn out if I succeeded. I would have to play it by ear. So I dropped Joy home after dinner, spent a little time watching TV with her then, around ten, I moved out. I decided to start with the Alley

Cat, since this seemed to be the hot spot for the early evening. I had a hard time finding a parking space. The pavement in front of the pub was packed with people, and still cars kept arriving. It took me time and effort to get a Heineken, then I settled behind a group of people a little distance from the entrance. I had a feeling that Roddy was going to show up at some point.

The crowd was bustling, noisy and colourful, lots of women, some very appetizing in their finery, the men posturing and posing to attract their attention. The DJ sounded well in the mood too, switching between reggae and soul with skill, the speakers booming loud enough to keep neighbours awake in a mile radius. It would have been nice to have a real vacation in London, have a mind free to appreciate the good times and really unwind. But I knew before the end of that mission I would have to kill or be killed, there was no two ways about it.

The Heineken was almost empty when the long red car appeared around the corner. Roddy was driving, his usual dapper self, a striped black-and-white shirt opened on his vest, gold shining from his neck. In the passenger seat, another man. He got out when the car stopped and crossed to get inside the pub. I had a fairly good look at him: a youth wearing a brand name two-piece suit, medium height, slender. A Yard man from the way he strutted, but unknown to me.

Roddy moved on and double-parked a little way down the road. Slowly, I walked towards my car, careful to keep covered by the crowd. I still couldn't recall from where, but I knew Roddy from Jamaica, I was sure of it by now. That meant that he probably knew me too. I passed level with Roddy's car, walked on till I got to my vehicle and started the engine, waiting. In my mirror, I watched the youth come back to Roddy and get in the car. Just like I thought, the pub was used as a retailing point by Roddy for his product. He had just sent the youth to do a pick-up. They drove off and I waited till they went around the bend out of sight to follow them. The traffic was rather dense so I managed to keep track of the Saab unnoticed.

Like I thought, Roddy and his friend were heading for another hotspot. It looked like collection day. Once again, Roddy stayed in while his partner went inside the club. The Bluebird was a club Joy had mentioned to me; it seemed a nice enough place, the entrance full of neon lights of various colours, the walls painted white and pink. Two burly men in suits, one white, one black, manned the door. The girls went in free but the men were required to pay. Yet I observed that the youth in the suit simply greeted the two bouncers and walked in. Special status . . .

I was parked a few cars down from the Saab, watching the movements in and out. Roddy's head was bobbing up and down like he was enjoying the music in his expensive car. Two girls, young but trying to look older, stopped by his window and talked with him for a while. Then the youth came back to the car and they got in the queue to enter the club. The red car moved off and I followed, still careful to keep discreet.

Driving down, I was hoping Roddy wasn't the main supplier for the whole of North London, otherwise I was in for a long night. I had no plan though, just to find out where he was going to, wishing hard that he would, at some point, lead me to his hidden partner. My feeling was that the youth with him in the car was just a runner he was using to make his collections.

We stopped at another after-hours black pub in Finsbury Park, then drove to a quiet street in Islington. I was thinking that maybe Roddy had spotted the tail and they were going to try to block me. Since I had no gun and Roddy was likely to be packing, I had better be sharp. This time it was Roddy who left the car and walked up to a house. I saw him ring the bell and go inside. The youth was listening to music, I could hear the bass from where I was parked, fifty yards down on the corner of the street, all lights out. I waited a good twenty minutes. It was getting to twelve now.

The lights on the ground floor went out and soon Roddy appeared, followed by a tall, slim young woman in a short skirt and top, high heels that clicked on the concrete in the silent street. They got in the car and drove out. I waited, letting the Saab get ahead a little before moving after them. From Islington, we ran through Shoreditch and straight onto Tower Bridge. Their raving spot seemed to be somewhere in South London. Weaving through the steady flow of vehicles, I was keeping up with the red car, leaving three cars between me and my target. As a Yard man and drugsman, Roddy had to be pretty sharp; he could spot a tail if it was too obvious. I had been following him for a couple of hours now and I must have been doing a good job. My car had a small but nervous engine, able to pick up speed if required.

We got to Peckham High Street where much activity was happening around a club. 'Lullabies' was shining in big lit-up letters above the door. That was where Roddy was going, for he circled back to find a suitable space for his big car. I had less problem parking and decided to go and wait near a busy food trailer, from where I could monitor the entrance of the club. A little crowd hung around the door, newly arrived, still fresh in their pretty clothes, and others who had already experienced the heat inside and were cooling off.

Quite a few Yard crews were there. I recognized some, men who I hadn't seen for years, one or two from my old area. I was keeping to the shadows, just in case, although in England, police or not, your status depended on whether you could hold your own or not. I probably had a few enemies in that friendly crowd. All the same, I was out to identify one man and he was likely to know me, so it was best for me to see him first. I had had a haircut earlier on but kept the low beard I had grown, even bought a flat cap that I wore low down, all part of my undercover profile. Roddy, his youth and his girl got to the door. A couple of friends greeted him, he dropped some money at the gate, then led the way inside. They were out to rave, I might be in for a long wait. Apparently, the venue was featuring a well-known visiting sound from Jamaica. As always, such occasions warranted a gathering of all Yard elements of the London scene. The man I wanted had to be in there tonight, I was sure of it.

Making up my mind, I stepped out of my observation and crossed the road. I dropped a note to the gateman who glanced at my face, gave me my change and turned to the next guest. The corridor was busy, filled with ravers, some going out, some turning left towards the bar, some pushing ahead to the darker main room. Walking in was like entering a sauna. Fortunately my size allowed me to catch some air from above but I felt sorry for short people! The smell was strong, drifting on the wafts of smoke floating around.

I found a small space just by the door and started checking around. Fortunately for me, I soon saw Roddy's young soldier coming in from the bar with drinks, so I locked onto him, and he led me to where Roddy had stopped, all the way down to the back wall, to the right of the control tower. A little group was around, him being a major player on the scene; friends and colleagues, all birds of a feather congregated together to enjoy the occasion and deal with business topics. Their girls huddled slightly to the left of the men, nearer the wall, protected from unsuspecting hunters and within reach. I made myself some space a few yards to the right of the group. The crowd was already thick and more people kept arriving. It was still early.

Pacific was a good sound, versatile and appreciated by all. Johnny Deuce, the owner, was a man I used to see in our area quite often as a youth, when he came to visit Jingles. They had been friends, relatives even from what Jingles had told me, their fathers originating from the same parish. The man had been involved in the music scene from the early days, one-time musician, then producer and promoter. He had survived a serious shooting incident following a dispute with some people from Waterhouse. The difference was supposed to be about money but at the time, it had been rumoured that his vocal support of one of the political parties had upset a local gang leader. As a result, a war party was sent to wreck one of his dances. One of the operators was shot dead and Johnny Deuce received three bullets. He survived though and his little problem was sorted out by a meeting between all concerned local parties, the way it's usually done. Sound systems are deemed neutral, it was decided, and as long as their owners keep out of politics, their safety is more or less guaranteed. All the same, Johnny had many powerful friends and a couple of month later, the local leader responsible for the attack got shot dead in a gunfight, officially over a girl ...

Tonight, Pacific had its audience well in hand. The selections unfolded smoothly, the men whistled and shouted, made gunshots sounds, the girls cooed for their favourites and the liquor flowed. Sweating, I rocked along, one eye on Roddy and his group, the other on one fit young lady who kept smiling at me. When it came time to rub, I hardly lifted a finger in her direction and she swiftly came to hug me. We synchronized our hips and started swaying together. After all, I told myself, this was part of my undercover profile! The girl was a good dancer. We went through a few tunes, didn't say much to each other but action speaks louder than words. Once the selector switched to rougher music, I sent my dancing partner to get us some drinks. We talked a little, the huge sound out of the speakers not allowing much conversation. More people had been gathering around Roddy's group, some faces I knew, some not. Much smoking and drinking was going on, these men spending freely since their income was obviously from independent means.

A couple of hours went by without much else happening than dancing on and off. By now, the atmosphere was hot in all senses of the word. I knew that if I went out for fresh air, it would be hell to get back in so I had to hold on, keep track of Roddy until he was ready. I still had no idea who was his main man, so large was his crew by now. Eventually, I noticed his girl and him talking and, shortly after, they started out. I quickly took leave of my girl, taking the number as she slipped it to me. Roddy's soldier was staying behind. I followed the couple through to the door, emerging in the cool night air behind them. I moved to get back to the spot where I had stopped earlier, long enough to watch Roddy. He stopped to talked to someone in a black Mercedes parked opposite the club, then him and his girl moved on.

I got to my car, kicked up the engine and drove off slowly, leaving time for the Saab to start out. Roddy drove slowly and I was trying to leave space between him and me. I saw him turn around at the gas station and as he did so, I had the bad feeling he looked in my direction. I couldn't tell whether he had noticed me or not. I turned and followed on though, this time letting a couple of cars get between us.

Then I saw the Saab stop a hundred yards or so up the road by a lit-up cab station, and the girl got out. Roddy drove on. This didn't seem right. I geared up to keep up speed with the red car which now was moving away fast. It didn't take a left at the light to get back the way we had come in, though. Roddy was doing around eighty miles an hour on the long open road leading further into South London. I hung on, keeping track, but something inside me was telling me to be aware. Yet what could I do; if I left his tail, it would all have been in vain and nothing gained. Stubbornly, I got to one hundred miles on the clock. The Saab had a couple of hundred yards on me. I could make out Roddy's head; he seemed to be on the phone. There wasn't much traffic so it was getting harder to be discreet but I drove on.

Two things happened at the same time, ringing my inner alarm bell: Roddy slowed down progressively, right back down to fifty miles an hour, and in my rearview mirror, two headlights were getting closer. There was plenty of space to overtake but the headlights kept flashing me.

Dazzled by the powerful headlights, it was hard to make out the car behind, now getting very close. Then, between two flashes, I saw it: the distinctive Benz sign atop the bonnet. It all connected in my mind and I understood what was happening:

Roddy had made me out and called his friend. They were going to block me and finish me off. Sure enough, the Saab had slowed down to ten miles an hour, crawling in front of me while the Mercedes was almost to my back bumper. Once the two cars had me stuck, I would have no way out. I was about to get shot on the spot, no doubt.

There wasn't much time left, and not many options; since both vehicles were much heavier than mine, I couldn't hope to push either one away to make space. I only had a couple of seconds to make my move and stay alive. I did it. Roddy braked, stopped. The Mercedes was a couple of yards away now, ready to hit me. My head empty, I dropped back in first gear, gassed up to the floor and pulled the wheel to the right, full. With enough power, I would have to hit the corner of the Saab bumper to have a chance of escaping the trap.

My timing had to be right, and it was. I felt the bumper of the Benz hit me from behind just as mine impacted with the red car. There was a sound, loud and dry, and I felt the little car surge forward, and come free. I hadn't really had time to think about it but I wasn't surprised when it came.

Two cracks appeared in the left side of my windscreen, two dry cracks from a gun, blasting away my back window. Just about the spot where my head had been a second earlier. Had I waited just a fraction longer to roll the car to the right, I'd have been good for it! Second and third gear – I got some lead on my enemies.

I had an open road ahead now but I quickly realized that, chased by two powerful cars and without even a gun, I didn't have the ghost of a chance of making it. I could already see the headlights of the two cars getting closer. So I geared down, pressed hard on the brake and depressed the clutch: emergency spin just like I had learned all those years ago. The Saab was coming in fast, the Benz right behind. Cold inside, I pressed on the gas and geared up. It was my nerves against theirs, their brain speed to match mine. Their mistake was that the Mercedes took a little too long to catch up and come level with the Saab. I put on my full headlights and put my foot down, zoomed past the black car just as it caught up the other one. One quick stirring to the left to avoid it and I passed.

After that I didn't look back: full speed ahead until I got to the light to turn left, back the way I had come. I still wasn't home free but God must have been watching for just as I got into the right lane. I heard the wailing of a siren and a police van's blue flashlight appeared at the junction I had just left. They might have seen me but by now the two big cars were arriving their way and that's where the van stopped. Speeding on the wrong side of a one way road; it was going to be expensive. As for the gun they might find on them, well ... Muttering a quick thank-you prayer, I drove on.

CHAPTER EIGHTEEN

The Wages of Sin

'Don't worry about the windows, I'll deal with that.'

'I don't care about the windows: you could have got killed!' In her extra large T-shirt, Joy had just slipped out of slumber into shock. I had summed up the story of my night and it had totally freaked her out. I had been right not to take her along. The kettle clicked in the kitchen; she got up and came back with two mugs of tea.

'Did you see the other guy?'

I shook my head. 'The Merc had tinted windows. I got him out but now he knows me and I don't know him.'

Stretching on the sofa, my body releasing the tension, I was feeling totally empty-headed. In a sense, my move hadn't been in vain; although it could have cost me my life had I not been sharp enough. Both Roddy and his partner had seen me, while I hadn't managed to identify the latter. They both knew I was after them. I smiled, thinking how it would have turned if Roddy had noticed me earlier on in the dance . . .

'You find it funny?!' Joy asked, frowning.

'I think I'm gonna have to bullet-proof your car.' She had to smile and shake her head.

'You Jamaicans really are crazy!' It was going on six, dawn had broken and it looked like it was going to be another sunny day.

I must have dozed off. Something was ringing in my dream, in fact ringing in my ears. The room was bright; lying on my back on the sofa, I descended back to reality's plane. Nine-forty; I'd only slept a couple of hours. Rubbing my face with both hands, I got up to put a stop to that brain-drilling bell. Where the hell was Joy?

'Hello.'

'Wha'ppen, sah?' I don't know what surprised me the most; that it was a Yardman's voice or that anyone could call me at Joy's.

'Who dis?'

'Then yuh forget me already?! Nuh yuh was ah follow my car last night? Listen good, man: we have yuh girlfriend. Have the money ready fe tonight, else the girl gwan come back to yuh, piece by piece. Yuh over? I call yuh at seven.' The line went 'click' in my ear. That was it. Amazing how a few words can clear a sleepy head. Putting the receiver back down, the words replayed in my mind automatically, like an answerphone. Money. At seven. We have yuh girlfriend. They had Joy. I quickly ran through the few rooms, still hoping somehow I had misunderstood, checked outside for the car, but I knew. They had Joy!

I sat back on the couch. What was happening? Was it Roddy or his partner on the phone? Did it matter? I didn't know how they got Joy's address; I knew they couldn't have followed me. Still, they had got Tracy's address too. My brain was trying to think straight, coming back to that main fact; two killers had kidnapped Joy. Collateral to that was the demand for money. I didn't even think: 'what money?' They thought I had Rico's money!

Getting up back, I headed for the bathroom. No way to think straight without a cold shower. I opened up the tap, took off my clothes and stepped into the spray. The water ran all over me, loosened my knotted muscles, beat its rhythm on my skull. I had to get my head clear, analyse the situation fast, weigh the odds, check what cards I had left to win. For there was no other way out but to win; I knew what kind of people I was coming up against and knew better than to underestimate them. Not to mention the fact that they were on their turf; I was just a little better than a tourist! The water ran over me, washed my body and cleared my mind By the time I dried up, I knew what cards I had in hands. Before I left the house, I made one phone call; I didn't get who I wanted but the message I left would do the job. Outside, I stepped out in the early sun with my mind made up.

'He's gone on a job to Tottenham. He said to wait for him.' Loretta gave me one of those suggestive smiles she always flashed at me whenever I came to the cab office. They say big women are vicious, and that one for sure looked like she was. This morning however, I wasn't even in the mood to joke.

I sat and waited, hearing but not listening to the small talk of the morning drivers, some just starting their day, a few having worked the whole night and wanting to last through to the afternoon to earn some marketday fares. Tips showed up just as I was getting impatient. Though he was wearing glasses, I could tell he wasn't overjoyed to see me. The message I had left had been clear enough to get his attention though ...

'Wha'ppen Carly?' I got up and walked up to him.

'T'ings ah gwan, sah; we haffe talk.'

'I have work to do, yuh know ...' I didn't even let him finish.

'Don't fuck around with me, Tips; I know yuh set up Blackjack so don't talk to me about your raasclaat work!' Tips glanced around; obviously he didn't want his drivers to hear certain things.

'Come, man: mek we talk outside.' I followed him out, anger seething inside, I didn't have to act it. Outside on the pavement, I turned to him, stony-faced, pointed my finger to his face.

'Yuh sell out your brethren for blood money; yuh is a dead man.'

A passing white woman on her way to the market turned, looked at us curiously.

'We cyan talk here, come to the car,' Tips said. His voice didn't sound that firm any longer. We got to the side street where he usually left his car. He unlocked it and we got in. I turned to him right away.

'You ah fucking dog, Tips. I tell yuh to your face.'

'Wha yuh ah deal with?'

'I have a good mind to kill yuh raasclaat, ah dat me ah deal with!' He knew I was serious about it, but Tips still made the mistake of playing hard.

'Hey, mind how yuh chat to me!' My left hand reached behind my back, under my shirt, for the sharpened paper cutter I had taken from Joy's house. Tips didn't catch my move on time. I switched hands. The next thing he knew, the sharp point was digging into the side of his stomach through his ganzee. He gasped.

'Carly . . . cool man!' I pushed the blade further in, feeling it penetrate the soft flesh under the floating ribs.

'Cool?! I gwan dig out yuh kidney, make yuh bleed to death in this car.' Tips still had his glasses on; I grabbed them with my left hand, tossed them on the back seat.

'I want yuh to look in my eyes while I kill yuh.'

'Carly, I beg yuh, make we talk.' Tips could feel the blade going deeper the more he was trying to get away from it. The door was preventing him from escaping any further. The street was not that busy, nobody was going to interfere.

'Talking time done. Yuh gimme too much lies. I know what happened now. I don't need yuh no more.' Sweat was wetting Tips' large brow. In his eyes was the fear of death all cowards experience at some point. I twisted my wrist a little, Tips cried out.

'Yuh bawl like a girl, fat bwoy. Yuh sell out Blackjack and Rico; this is payback time.' Another twist of the wrist: the blade was in a full inch now, opening a hole in his flesh. Tips was scared, no more fronting.

'I never sell out Rico . . .'

'Wrong answer.' I twisted some more. At that point, I didn't really care whether Tips bled to death all over the seat of his car, and I think he realized that.

'It's the police!'

'Seh wha'' The big man was breathing hard and fast.

'The police, it's them. Them set up the whole t'ing.'

'Yuh want me to believe the police kill Rico? Yuh still take me fe fool, eeeh?!' The pain was starting to show on Tips' face, his eyes wide open in terror.

'I begging yuh, Carly, just hol' on. Gimme a chance fe tell yuh the truth.'

'Yuh don't know truth from lies no more. Yuh sell out yuh soul, Tips.'

'I swear, gimme a chance, brethren.' I stared into his eyes and there was death, its shadow veiling that man's gaze. Whether I killed him or not, Tips wouldn't make it alive; the dead were calling him.

'Hear this; me and yuh is not brethren, yuh understand . . . I gwan give yuh a chance, but only one, Tips. Yuh know why? Because one innocent girl might be dead before tonight, and maybe yuh can help her out.' Tips saw hope, he grabbed for it.

'I do anyt'ing fe help yuh, Carly. Just let me go and fix this, I bleeding.'

'The next place I stick yuh is your bloodclaat throat, don't fuck me around, yuh hear?'

'I help yuh, I swear.' Tips winced in pain as I pulled out the blade, fast. His ganzee was stained all over the side and back.

'Drive, we going to your house,' I told him coldly. My cutter was still pointing at him, half of the blade dark and wet.

Tips started out his engine and drove off. His forehead and face was bathed in sweat, his breath sharp. I really didn't care about the man's pain; I was quite ready to cause him more should he try and fool around with me. The traffic wasn't busy yet. Kingsland Road was bright and open as Tips, teeth clenched, pushed seventy. He was in a hurry to get home, anxious to tend to his wound. We parked in front of his block. In my right hand, the stiletto was open, covered by the newspaper I had picked up from the back seat of the car. Up the stairs and down the landing, I kept close to the big man, just in case he came up with any crazy idea.

'You're home already?' A woman, black, slender and looking older than her thirty or so years, pulled her bathrobe around her as she noticed Tips was not alone.

'Oh, hi! Excuse me,' she said, disappearing down the corridor.

'Go shopping. I have business to deal with,' Tips growled without looking at her. I followed him in the living room, closed the door behind us. Tips painfully pulled his stained ganzee above his head, took it off. His lower left side was wet with blood, but the excess fat around his stomach provided a buffer, protecting the vital organs. It looked worse than it was. I saw Tips wince as he dabbed away the red sticky liquid with the ruined ganzee. Standing between him and the door, the rolled newspaper in my hand, I could have finished him off if I focused on the way this man had sold out his friends, my friends, but I still needed him. From the corridor, we heard: 'See you later,' then the front door slammed shut.

'I want to fix this; it could get infected.' Tips was looking at me, he didn't see any sympathy on my face. I motioned towards the door with my head, eyes very still staring at him. I followed him to the bathroom, all the time watching his movements carefully, the way a hunter watches out for a final attack from his wounded prey. I even checked the medicine cabinet, just in case ... Soap and water, then alcohol that made Tips' face contract under its sting. Leaning against the bathroom door, I watched him press cotton wool on the hole and stick it up with a large plaster.

'Whe' yuh piece?' Tips turned to look at me like he didn't know what I was asking?

'I gwan ask yuh only one more time; which part yuh keep yuh gun?' Tips closed the door of the cabinet.

'We cyan keep gun on yah like ah Yard, yuh know, police well strict . . .' All I did was drop the newspaper to the floor, exposing the shiny blade in my hand. That must have jogged Tips' memory.

'Alright, next door . . .' I let him pass and followed him to the toilet. Under the carpet, the tiles had been loosened and the concrete dug out to allow for a square hole just big enough for a cigar box. I held out my hand, Tips handed it over. Covered in plastic, it contained a silvery gun with short barrel: a .38 snub nose, the kind of toy that made a lot of noise and enough damage to drop a body with one shot. Very efficient at close range.

Tips and I got back to the living room. Seated bare-chested on the couch, his stomach protruding over the belt of his trousers, he seemed much less confident than usual. I was across from him, inspecting the weapon. I had cleaned his blood off the knife and it was now back at my waist.

'Alright, time to talk. I ask yuh questions, yuh answer straight. No long talk . . . else I could get nervous and make some more holes ina yuh,' I told Tips coldly. He was just looking at me, knowing I didn't care whether he lived or not.

'Roddy work for the police?' Tips met my eyes and nodded slowly.

'Me nuh hear yuh,' I said, the short barrel of the gun casually directed his way.

'Yeah . . .'

'Yuh work fe dem too?'

'Dem have me on a charge. I do certain t'ings, when dem ask me.'

'What kind ah t'ings?' Tips' voice had gone down low,

almost confidential, as if he feared his house was bugged or something. 'Robberies, dem set me up pon a job and I do it. Dem get a cut.'

I kept silent for a moment. So that was the way it worked!

'So, the robberies ouno do with Rico and Blackjack, it's police set that up?' I saw Tips nod, he knew exactly what I was asking him. Then he added: 'Except the Turkish one, ah me find out that one.'

I could almost hear pride in Tips' tone of voice. That explained why the police, those handling this sideshow, were so anxious to get their hands on that money. It was the biggest deal and they had been kept out of it by Tips.

'Rico and Blackjack never knew about yuh and the police?' Tips' eyes were down as he shook his head. I didn't care about or believe in his remorse.

'Which police is it?' There was a slight hesitation, as if Tips still had scruples about giving up his 'handler'. But the crooked cop was far, while the .38 was near, very near.

'Mitchell, detective sergeant.'

'Wha him look like?' I asked.

'Young, red-haired bwoy, local officer.' This time I nodded. It all made sense now. I knew this one was after the money.

'Him one?'

Tips looked at me. 'Is only him I know . . . but him ah work for somebody else, another cop.' Tips had to be right; there was someone manipulating the show. The young cop was the one to handle the street side of things but another was calling the shots and reaping the profits.

I thought about the police officer who had interrogated me but something was telling me he wasn't in the scheme. I asked: 'What dem have pon yuh?'

A deep sigh rose out of Tips' broad chest. I was waiting, so he said: 'Yuh know wha me tell yuh about the dead man in the car, whe we get the drugs first time?' I nodded, recalling the story.

'Ah me drive that man and find the drugs.' So much for the lie about Blackjack ...

'So wha'ppen?' Tips' sorrowful look didn't interest me, he could see that.

'A lickle after that, that red-hair police bwoy pull me up one day and take me in. Him seh dem want me for some other t'ing. But him never take me to the station, him carry me to one place near some docks and pull one a gun on me. I never know what ah gwan, but him say I kill one ah him friend and now him goin'to kill me ... After a while, I get to understand him talking about the dead man in my car, but I tell him I don't know not'ing whe him ah talk. Him tell me him don't really care about the man, or whether I kill him or not but him lose money because the man was working fe him, so I must take fe him place. I tell him I is not no informer, I even tell him I was a police back home. Him say him know all about me and him just want me to rob dealers and pay him a cut, that way I can make my money easy. Him say I can deal with the drugs and pay him a percentage ... or else him will get me deported. Him gimme three days to think about it.'

Somehow, I didn't think that story was a lie. It wasn't that I trusted Tips any, but that explained a lot of things. Even a man of low character needs a motivation, whatever it is, to do what he does. For Tips, that deal was saving him from the crooked police's threat but also giving him an easy means to make lots of money. And he was good at lying, which surely helped in selling Rico the scheme.

'But yuh set up Blackjack to die ...' Tips moved on the couch as he noticed the little gun in my hand pointing towards his belly.

'It wasn't like that, Carly. I never know!'

'Yuh was with him, and yuh left him ...' I sounded like an executioner, and I was, because it wouldn't take much for me to spill Tips' guts all over his nice carpet when I thought about my dead comrade. He knew death was hooking her long finger his way.

'I was there, true. Me and him go pon the job but I never know about the set-up then, I swear!'

'It's fear make yuh swear, Tips. Blackjack die alone, on the street.'

'Hear me out, Carly! I beg yuh just hear me out first.' Tips must have seen how tight my trigger finger was.

'Talk.'

'That police bwoy, him call me and gimme an address, like usually, tell me to do it that same night. So me and Blackjack decide to pull it.'

'Why ouno never tell Rico?'

There was a pause before Tips said: 'Rico did want to keep most of the money we got for this school business back home.'

I nodded, Tips didn't need to explain any more about that.

'So, we go down there. I never know who we was gonna hit, ah so it used to work. When we get there, we bust in and stick up the man, him take out the drugs and give we. Then as we get back down, on the way out, we get shot at but we couldn't see who it is. Now the other guy was coming down behind us, shooting also. We try to shoot it out and run. Blackjack get shot and drop the drugs, then him try to run but them shoot him again. I made it to the car and drive off.' Tips stopped, looking shaken by the story of that fateful night. He shook his head.

'I find out after that Roddy, the dealer, also work for the same police but them feel seh him was holding out on them, so them get we to rob him. I never know, Carly, yuh haffe believe me.'

'Who is Roddy's brethren?'

'I don't know, I never see him.' There was a silent stare between us, then I asked:

'What about Roddy, yuh work with him now.'

He couldn't deny that, and he knew it, so he said: 'Roddy find out I was the other man that night, him stick me up one night. Is him tell me the police set him up.'

'How come him never kill yuh?' Tips sighed again.

'How come?' I repeated.

'I tell him we have some money coming in, 'nuff money, and him can have some of it.'

'But yuh tell him about Rico?'

'No, sah; I never tell him nothing about Rico, believe me!'

'Yuh lie!' The short muzzle rose up once more, scanning for a target, a fat one.

'I tell yuh I never tell him not'ing about Rico!' Tips' voice had risen like he wanted to be believed, or didn't want to die now.

I left it at that. After reflecting on all this for a moment, I briefly explained to Tips about the events of the previous night, and Joy's kidnapping.

'But yuh don't have the money . . .' he said. The way he said that, I knew Tips was rotten to the core; even in his position, he still thought about that big bag of cash and where it could be!

'Them man don't know that, else the girl done dead long time . . .' I looked at the fat treacherous man.

'And that's whe yuh gwan help me. Me and dem have a meeting tonight.'

'Anyhow dem see me with yuh, me dead!' Tips declared

'That don't matter to me, but ah nuh dat I want yuh do.' Tips seemed relieved for a moment that I didn't want him with me. Might as well carry a snake in my pocket anyway.

'Gimme your money.' At first he frowned and looked like he didn't quite hear me, so I said again, 'Your money, Tips. I gwan use your money to free up that girl.'

'What money?' he asked.

'The money Rico paid you in advance.'

'Wha?'

I sighed, kissed my teeth to show I wasn't in the mood for games. Though I was fishing, I was almost sure I was right. It was just that Tips couldn't understand how I would know about it.

'Just once more; yuh get about fifty thousands couple days

before the wedding. I want it, and I want it right now. Take your time before yuh answer.' He knew what that meant, to take time before he answered. Tips must have used that sentence a few times when he was still a policeman back home. A wrong answer given too quickly and that was your last. It took him less than twenty seconds.

'Alright.' Tips got up, I did too. In the bedroom, he went inside the wardrobe and dug under a pile of boxes and bags. All the time, I was keeping the gun loose by my side, just in case. You can do a lot of things to a man, but to take away his money is sometimes too much for him to bear. Tips had done too much wrong for the sake of money for me to trust him now. He brought out an old-looking travel bag, placed it on the bed, looking at me.

'Wha'ppen, open it!' Reluctantly, Tips unzipped the bag, left it open. I could see piles of fifty-pound notes inside.

'How much in deh?' I asked.

'Forty,' he said in a low voice. I looked at Tips, bare-chested, his big belly sticky out with the plaster and cotton wool red from his blood. I looked him straight in the eyes.

'Yuh fucked up, Tips.' He stood there with his arms to his side. He said:

'So wha; yuh gwan kill me now?' I took a little time before answering.

'It's all yuh a worry about, saving your worthless life?' I said. 'No, I not gwan kill yuh, I leave that to somebody else.' I walked slowly to the side of the bed, zipped the bag shut.

'Yuh shoulda stay with Rico; you woulda get enough money to retire to your village.'

Bag in hand, I started out of the bedroom. I heard Tips say: 'Dem man deh not gwan let yuh live, yuh know that.'

I turned and faced him, squinted and asked: 'Yuh ever wonder why some man die with them eyes open and some with them eyes closed?' I walked away, closed back the front door behind me. Tips had a lot of talking to do with his ghosts.

CHAPTER NINETEEN

Bad Cards

I was going all out because that was the only way both Joy and I were going to survive the night. So far, my plan was working. I went home. Nicola was just about to go out when I got in. She didn't ask me where I had spent the night but just threw me a quizzical glance. Of course, Miss Ruby mentioned nothing about it either. She simply asked whether I had had breakfast. I think she knew I was hungry, so she insisted on making me some lunch and sat me in the kitchen while she cooked, talking about back home, the good old days.

I felt strange hearing about all that, especially with the predicament I was in. She kept going back in time, telling me stories about Rico as a youth, his schooldays, how he used to get into trouble and have to hide from bigger boys. Probably, once the immediate shock and sorrow of the loss was overcome, she was starting to miss her son so she hung on to the memories, reliving the happy days in her mind.

I sipped my tea and listened, all the while spinning the elements of my plan in my head. It wasn't exactly a plan, to be precise, more like a 'double or quits' scheme that aimed first and foremost at getting Joy out of Roddy's murderous hands. After that, it was all about playing it by ear.

Miss Ruby and I ate together. Nicola had gone to spend the afternoon with her best friend down in West London. I was in no hurry, I had all day, until seven, to go and wait for my call. Yet there was one more card I needed. I knew it was a little crazy but I had nothing to lose. I had a short nap after lunch, showered and changed. Checking myself in the mirror, it occurred to me how weird it was that I should worry about my appearance when I was going out on a desperate mission like this one.

Once I was satisfied I looked sharp enough, I slipped the snub nose .38 under my shirt, put on my shades and picked up the case from under my bed. I had taken the money out of it and replaced it with the cash I had taken from Tips. Forty thousands were in the bag, just like he said. He must have wondered how I knew he had that money. Rico would always make sure he never held back on people, that was how he was. And I was smart enough to know a man like that would keep his share of the money close to him. I left the house.

Outside, the setting sun glowed above the roofs, the heat lingering all over the busy street. Buses full with people heading home after their working day, children racing bicycles on the pavements, and mothers struggling to drag yelling youngsters out of the sweetie shops; scenes of a tranquil end of day. I picked up a cab and got lost in the drive-time music show from a local radio station. I got to Joy's house. The first thing I did was make a call. It took me a little time to get to the person I wanted but eventually I got through. After setting up what I wanted, I put down the phone and relaxed, watching TV.

Almost seven-twenty before the phone rang. I picked it up after the third time.

'Yaow ... wha'ppen? ...' The same voice, deep, cocky.

'Cool.'

'So wha; yuh get the money?'

'Yeah, it deh yah.'

A little pause on the other side, probably a word with someone else ...

'Alright, mek we meet, so yuh can get back your girlfriend.'

I heard sarcasm in the tone of voice but it didn't matter to me. I asked 'Which part?'

'Yuh know Homerton? Come to the centre next to the flats in Kingsmead estate.'

'Near by whe yuh live?' I sneered. 'Dem place deh coming like graveyard! I don't like that, star, I want a spot where people deh 'bout, so I can feel safe.'

I wanted Roddy to think I was nervous. It worked. I heard him say: 'Nuh fret, man, we just swap: the girl fe the money, not'ing more.'

'Alright. Me set the meeting place: yuh know the big supermarket on the way to Stamford Hill, next to a big car dealer. Yuh know whe me ah talk?' A pause.

'Me know it, but too much people down deh.'

'That cool, man. We just meet down there, make the swap and done. Wha yuh ah say?'

There was a pause, Roddy was checking with his friend, I guessed. I couldn't expect to have the advantage, but my priority was for Joy to have an easy exit, somewhere next to a busy street. Finally, Roddy's voice came back on.

'Alright, we meet down deh fe eight-thirty.' Long enough to set up an ambush . . .

'Eight-thirty. I'll be there,' I said.

'I bring the girl, yuh bring the money, just me and you.'

Roddy was being smart now. I told him: 'Don't worry, man. I don't have nobody over here, yuh know that.'

'Alright. Later.' The line went dead. So there it was, the meeting was set. Apparently, Roddy and his friend's main concern was to get their hands on the big bag of cash; they didn't worry that much about me, it seemed. Which didn't mean they might not want to empty a clip in my skin, just to make their point! The play was going to be tight. What would their reaction be on opening the case and finding out there was much less there than they expected?

I dialled the mobile number I had obtained earlier on,

got through and set up the meeting for eight-fifteen. Another number: I gave some instructions about time and place. It was all set and I had forty-five minutes to go, so I switched off the television and the light and laid down in the dark. Eyes closed, I concentrated on my breathing, in and out, in and out, deeply until I could empty my mind . . .

'So, what is this all about, Mr Nash.'

Detective Sergeant Mitchell was fixing his blue eyes on me in the near darkness of the car. I had driven up in a taxi to meet him right on the other side of the town hall in a side street. My phone call earlier had got his attention but he still didn't know what I wanted from him.

'Well, I have a problem and you might be able to help me.'

'We all have problems, Mr Nash, but mine is that you interrupted an important outing with my wife. This better be worth it.'

I smiled. 'I am asking for your help, from one police officer to another. After all, we both swore to protect and serve.' He didn't find that funny, I could tell.

'Alright, let's have it.'

'Okay; You know a man called Roddy, one of my country-men?' The policeman didn't react, he just sat there staring at me with those eyes.

'Right, that man is a drug dealer, a criminal. He has kidnapped a young woman I know and threatens to kill her unless I give him some money, a large amount of money.' I could tell, no matter how much Detective Sergeant Mitchell was trying to hide it, that I had him interested. I went on.

'Without getting into too many details, this is all to do with some drugs robbery money he's been trying to get his hands on . . . and he thinks I have that money.'

'Do you?' the white man asked quietly. There and then, he had betrayed himself, but he didn't know how much I knew.

'No, I don't, but I don't want that girl to die for that.'

'Your girlfriend, is she?'

'No, but he thinks she is. She's got nothing to do with this business.'

I watched the police officer stretched back in the seat of his car, sigh heavily. Then he asked: 'I suppose you found out what happened to your dead friend?'

I shook my head. 'Not yet, but I'm getting there.'

'Hmm ..., but you know he was involved in something illegal, right?' The man was looking at me. I shrugged.

'I guess he found out being a policeman didn't pay enough.' I held his gaze for a few seconds, to get the message across.

'Alright, so what do you want from me?' Here it was; I had to put this tactfully.

'Well, I know this guy is going to try to kill me and the girl once he's got the money ...'

'I thought you said you didn't have the money?'

'I said I didn't have that money. But I managed to borrow some, to save the girl's life.'

Detective Sergeant Mitchell's eyes drifted down to the case between my feet, then back to me. He asked: 'And you think they might take that and let you, and the girl, off the hook?' I shook my head slowly, smiling.

'These are my people, I know them well: these guys don't let anyone off the hook when it comes to money. And they don't leave no witnesses either.' Mitchell made a face, meaning he believed me.

'So what are you planning to do then?' I gave it to him straight.

'What I would like is for you to give me a hand in freeing that girl and get paid for the favour.' Silence in the car as the policeman weighed out my offer. I added: 'That way you protect an innocent woman and serve your best interests.'

And Mitchell could get his crooked hands on the money he thought Roddy had been holding back from him. It was a simple plan, one that had occurred to me out of need, and would, if it worked, achieve at least some results. And he still didn't suspect I knew the truth about him and Roddy.

'Out of curiosity, Mr Nash, how much have you got in this briefcase?' He was going for it; greed makes the fool blind.

'Only forty grand.' I said modestly.

The policeman raised his eyebrows. 'That's all?'

I made a sorry face. 'Not enough for that greedy fucker Roddy,' I said, baiting my man.

'Some people are like that,' Detective Sergeant Mitchell commented wryly.

'So, you gonna help me?'

I paid the cab and got out, my briefcase in my hand. The supermarket had closed and the place was deserted but for a few cleaning women talking loudly as they were leaving their evening shift. I had covered my back as much as I could, now it was going to be down to brains and guts. I knew Roddy was planning to outsmart me, and the meeting place was surely not to his taste, but that wouldn't stop him and his friend trying something.

Slowly, I walked down towards the far side of the parking. There weren't many vehicles left. Leaning against the side of a car, out of sight from the road, I waited. My watch said eight-forty and still no sign of Roddy, but I knew he would come. I guessed he had sent someone to check out the place before coming himself but that didn't worry me. Probably he preferred not to involve too many people in the operation; in his kind of circle, the less eyes see you collect a lump sum, the better ...

Another couple of minutes passed by before two beams stopped at the entrance of the parking lot. I recognized the car and stood up, took a few steps into the open, where I could be seen. The car manoeuvred and parked along the road, ready to move off again. The engine was switched off and I watched a silhouette step out. Bare-headed, the man was in a suit. He walked my way, all the time I was watching the car. He stopped and we faced each other.

'Wha'ppen sah, show me the money nuh!'

I placed the case on top of the car bonnet. 'Show me the girl first.'

Roddy smiled, a smile that spelled nothing good. 'I don't have time to play, show me the money or I go back and work pon your girl.'

'You want the cash too much to do that, bring out the girl. Mek me see her, then I open the case.' Roddy probably knew a little about me. He shook his head, picked up his phone in his jacket pocket and dialled.

'Bring out the girl,' he said.

I watched the car; the back door opened and Joy stepped out, looking around. She spotted us but didn't move. I was wondering how many men Roddy had brought as back-up. Roddy was watching me, his phone still in hand. Slowly, I unlocked the case and opened it.

'See money yah!' I said. Roddy took one step closer, looked but didn't touch the money.

'How much in deh?' he asked.

'How much yuh expect?'

'Is three hundred grand your brethren get from the big job.'

'How yuh know that?'

Roddy wasn't going to tell me. He said, 'Watcha now; I want all the money or I keep the girl.'

'Hear me nuh; I never know not'ing about this whole business. Is just that I get, I don't know what happened to the rest of the money.'

'So, which part yuh get this?' Roddy asked.

'Ah my business dat.' Roddy shook his head.

'Yuh take me fe fool? Bring me the rest of the money.'

I stared at him. 'You shoulda ask the white girl whe she

put it before you kill her.' For a couple of seconds, it looked as if Roddy was wondering whether to believe me or not. I said: 'Better yuh take this and gimme the girl.' I paused and very neatly pulled out the small .38 from under my shirt. 'Or we go all out and settle t'ings right now.'

Roddy's eyes shifted from me to the gun, then he said, 'Your girl be the first one to dead.' I shook my head.

'She not my girl, but if she don't make it, you nah make it neither. Make up your mind, I can't stay here all night.'

I had my gun on him. Roddy was probably strapped too, but he wasn't going to get a chance to pull on me. He knew I wasn't bluffing, so why not take the money and go; he wasn't losing anything. Carefully, he put one hand out and closed back the case lid.

'The girl's life not worth that much to me,' he said. I let him take up the case. He pressed the redial on his phone.

'Yaow . . .' he started.

'Make me talk to her.' I asked. Roddy hesitated then, 'Put the girl on the phone.' I stretched out my hand, he handed me his mobile.

'Joy,' I said. 'Yeah. Take it easy, everyt'ing alright. Listen: just walk down towards the station . . . yeah, walk down right now, don't stop . . . do what I tell you. I see yuh later.'

I gave back Roddy his phone. 'Let her go,' he told his man in the car.

'Me and yuh wait here till the girl gone. I don't want her to have any accident,' I said.

We both watched Joy walk away from the car nervously, looking very stiff. But she did what I said and moved down the road as fast as she could. I made a silent wish that Zafirah got my instructions right.

Roddy was ready to move out. I was still keeping an eye on his free right hand. I could see he didn't like to be held in check. Still, he had made something out of the deal. Our eyes locked for a few seconds.

'Best yuh go back home, officer. Ah we run this town.' I shrugged.

'Maybe I stay over and do like yuh; business look good on yah.' Roddy nodded.

'Me see yuh, man.' He turned and started out, back towards his car. I didn't move, watched him leave.

'Stop right there.' I didn't really expect it, coming out from my right. Out of the shadows appeared Detective Sergeant Mitchell, a sly smile on his face and something dark and long sticking out of his right hand.

'What have we here then?' he said. 'Hi Roddy, how is it going?' Roddy's eyes tracked from the white man to me. 'Yuh bloodclaat . . .' he muttered.

'I'm a police officer, yuh forget?' I said.

'Not here, you ain't. Drop your weapon, Mr Nash, slowly.' Mitchell's gun was pointing my way. I did what he said.

'Now, let's see what you got here, Roddy.' Standing there with the case in his hand, Roddy didn't look like he wanted to let go of it. I knew he would have loved to draw on the policeman but the other one knew it too, so he kept his gun trained on him. The way Mitchell was in shadow, and couldn't be seen from the car, Roddy's friend must have been wondering what was happening.

'Come on, I'll take this.' Mitchell told Roddy, pointing at the case with his gun. That's when I noticed the extension on the muzzle of what looked like a semi-automatic 9 mm.

'This is my money; not'ing to do with yuh,' Roddy said stubbornly. Mitchell stood at a safe distance, nothing to be tried. I saw him smile in the dark.

'You been holding back on us, son. I believe this is the back-pay you owe. Come on, put the case down. I might be nice and let you go.'

Slowly, Roddy bent down to stand the case on the floor. 'Yuh fucking t'ief,' he said. I saw his move before he started it; I knew he would try it. I would have like to tell him not to, not out of love for him but just because he didn't stand a chance of succeeding.

The case left the floor, swung in the air towards the white detective. At the same time, Roddy reached under his jacket for his piece. He almost made it. Mitchell probably knew Roddy wouldn't let him take away the cash without a fight, so he was ready. He calmly sidestepped out of the way of the flying case. I didn't hear more than two muffled sounds as the slugs left Mitchell's gun. Roddy was fast, but not fast enough. He managed to pull out his gun but not to aim. His arms flew back under the impact as two bullets entered his chest, then he dropped down on the floor and remained there, very still, very dead. I hadn't moved a muscle. One thought entered my mind right as I turned and met Mitchell's blue eyes: I'm next!

'The love of money . . .' Mitchell smirked, shaking his head disapprovingly. He seemed quite content, stepped to the case and picked it up. I glanced towards the red car, on the other side, across the parking lot, expecting it to drive off but nothing happened. Roddy's soldier had probably fled on foot after witnessing the incident . . .

'So, your girlfriend is free and your mate here won't bother you no more. I guessed I've earned my wages, eh?!' Mitchell was a cool son of a bitch. He was still holding his gun nonchalantly, muzzle towards the ground. I nodded.

'That was overtime work.' The white man smiled, not a very warm smile, but it gave me a little hope. I reasoned that if he had wanted me dead, he could have shot me already. Unless he was a sadistic type of man and wanted to play around first.

'Roddy asked you about the rest of the money . . .' There we were! I shrugged.

'I don't know anything about it, believe it or not.'

Mitchell seemed to be thinking about something. Then he said, 'Your dead friend left a lot of loot hidden somewhere, and no one has been able to find it so far. I was hoping he might have left you a note or something.' It was a question.

'He didn't,' I said. 'I don't think he knew he was going to die so soon. You found out anything yet?' I might as well turn it around.

'Nothing, I'm afraid. Whoever did it didn't care about getting the money first,' Mitchell said. Right there, something came to my mind, something which I didn't think Mitchell should hear; I wasn't going to give him any reason to kill me. I was now sure he was involved somehow.

'I guess I'll never know,' I told him. 'So, what now?'

'Now? I'm very late, so I'd better have a good story for my wife.' He laughed, a less than merry laugh. 'As for you, well; it would be best you go back home. England can be a very unhealthy place for some of you people.'

So he was leaving me alive. Mitchell walked to where I had dropped my gun, picked it up and slipped it in his jacket pocket. 'I won't even arrest you for this, as a favour to a fellow officer.' He grinned.

I nodded. 'Thank you,' I said.

'And thank you too.' He motioned, his hand holding the case. Then he walked away, leaving me standing. I hadn't moved from the spot where Roddy had found me on arriving. On the ground lay Roddy in his expensive suit, both arms spread, one leg folded under him. Live by the gun, as they say.

I was watching Mitchell's silhouette walking down, now almost out of the shadow zone along the supermarket. It happened so fast that I almost missed it. Mitchell was level with the corner of the building when he seemed to stop, like he was going to turn to look my way but he didn't. Instead, he bent over, reached out with his hand in the air, then I watched him slump to the ground, slowly, his back sliding against the wall. I was about a hundred yards away from where he now sat, motionless. I started running towards him.

There was a large dark stain, wet, spreading all over the front of the detective's shirt. His head was leaning on his chest; he was already dead. The briefcase was missing. The slamming of a door made me turn, just in time to catch the roar of the engine and the screeching of the tyres of the Saab. I watched it speed away down the road. On the ground, Mitchell's body looked like a big red-haired puppet. Kneeling down, I quickly searched his pocket, got back my gun. His own, with the silencer, was missing. I couldn't believe what had just happened but this wasn't the time or the place to meditate about it. No one seemed to have witnessed the incident. I drew back in the shadows, ran alongside the supermarket wall, around it and onto the street. I slowed down, walking normally but without looking back. The first turn right led me into a little street going I didn't know where. It didn't matter; there was going to be a manhunt when they found the policeman's body and I sure didn't want to be anywhere around.

I didn't go home that night. After walking for a while through back streets I found myself near a place called Newington Green. It was getting to ten o'clock. From a phone box, I dialled Zafirah's cell phone. I had hesitated to get her involved in the rescue operation but there was no one else I could trust. In fact she had seemed excited by the whole thing! She sounded relieved to hear from me. Joy was in the background, asking if I was alright. I gave Zafirah my position and both women came to pick me up soon after. On the way to Zafirah's house, I told them how I had left two dead bodies on the scene, one of them a police officer. The women listened to the details in shocked silence.

We got to the house and sat in the living room. Joy was tired from the ordeal but alright. She said Roddy was waiting by her car when she left me in her house that morning. She had been blindfolded and didn't know where she was taken. She had heard Roddy and another man talking in the car, but she didn't know who he was. They had left her in a bedroom somewhere; a young woman had brought her food but didn't talk to her. She wasn't mistreated but was glad when she saw me in the parking lot. Zafirah had followed my instructions to the letter and picked her up right on spot when they had let her go. Somehow, I got the impression Joy was glad to hear Roddy was dead. I sat there with the two women, trying to relax and gather my thoughts.

It had been a busy day. The more I dug into the story behind Rico's killing, the more people were dying. Right where I was, I still hadn't found out who was responsible for my friend's demise. Everything pointed to the elusive killer who had taken out the white policeman right under my eyes, yet he didn't quite fit the profile. Mitchell's killing was the work of a Yardman, I was sure of it, probably the same who had murdered Tracy, the white girl. But Rico's shooting was a clean, contract-type job, and to my mind, this was in a different league altogether. Maybe Tips had told me one truth; maybe the Turkish syndicate had traced back the robbery to Rico and hit him. But then, why kill him without first getting paid back? It was precisely that remark from Mitchell, the greedy cop which led me to believe he wasn't behind the hit, though he seemed to know something about it. But he had died with that secret.

Someone must be watching over me. Zafirah went to bed, leaving Joy and me to talk a little, music playing while we watched a late movie. Joy fell asleep first, right in the chair. It had been a stressful day for her. I woke her up and sent her upstairs to Zafirah's spare bed. I stayed up for a while, trying to make sense of the whole thing. Then I finally dropped off.

As usual, I woke up around six. It was a clear Sunday morning. First thing I did was call home to reassure Nicola and Miss Ruby. 'T'ank God, yuh safe, me son!' was the first thing the old lady said. Then she told me how three armed policemen had woken them up at two in the morning; they wanted to talk to me in connection with two murders, one of the victims was one of their colleagues!

Joy came down before Zafirah. I was wondering whether I should let her know that I was now a wanted man. I did. The first question she asked was the very same that had been bugging me since I had put down the phone: how was I gonna prove I didn't kill Sergeant Mitchell? The police would never believe my story and there were no witnesses to back it up. For Roddy, it must have looked to them like a gang killing.

One thing I couldn't quite figure out, though, was how the police got the idea that I had killed the crooked cop? I didn't think Mitchell would have talked about our joint mission to anyone; he was working 'freelance' that night. Unless ... yes; unless he had reported to his colleague, the one handling the whole drugs and robbery scam, about the swap in the car park. It had to be that.

So now a corrupt policeman I didn't know had me set up for a murder I didn't commit. I sat, sipping on a cup of tea Joy had made, the fact that I was now a wanted man slowly sinking in. It was a sensible precaution for me and Joy to hide in Zafirah's home but we couldn't stay here. Somewhere in this town was the policeman's real murderer and I wanted him now more than ever. But how to flush him out now that I was being sought by every cop in London?

'I could go to the police and tell them I was kidnapped ...'

'They wouldn't believe you,' I answered Joy's suggestion.

A white cop had been killed by a black man, it wouldn't matter to them which black man. The fact that I was a policeman in Jamaica wouldn't weigh much in my favour, especially because someone knew the whole story and would make sure I went down for it. To Mitchell's crooked partner, I was becoming a dangerous witness. Though I didn't know who he was, I was sure he existed and that could be enough to warrant an unexplained death in a cell. The only thing this mystery police officer might want from me was the information about the missing money. As long as he thought I knew where the big stash was, he would want to keep me alive. Roddy's partner had exactly the same problem. That made two greedy individuals wanting something from me; I had become a very popular man ...

'Maybe you could just call your boss in Jamaica and explain

to him what happened. He could sort it out with the English police for you,' Joy said.

I could see she was really worried about my situation. It sure would make Wilkins' day to learn I was wanted for the murder of a white policeman! Even if he could get me off the hook, I would surely get deported under some kind of pretence and would never get to find out the truth about Rico's death. I wasn't quite ready to go yet, so I needed to work out a solution on my own.

'It could work,' I said, just to reassure her. My mind was working on something else, checking all angles of the problem. There had to be a way out, one last card to play. I didn't hear what Joy was saying at first, lost as I was in my thoughts. She was looking at me.

'Come again,' I said.

'It's easy to get one if you have the right connections.'

'To get what?'

'A passport.' I held her gaze for a few seconds, still thinking but now registering what Joy had just said.

'A passport . . .' I repeated. Yes, a passport: that was exactly what I needed!

'What do you find so funny? You have to get out otherwise the police will find you, sooner or later!' Joy pointed out, a worried expression across her face. I must have been grinning. Although she didn't realize it, Joy had just put me on the right track. A passport; there was my last card!

'You right, you know; I have to get a passport.'

'A friend's husband knows people. I could ask her,' Joy said.

'It's alright; I know somebody who will help me,' I told her.

Tips' wife didn't seem to be in a good mood. She said he had been working all night and was asleep. I told her to shake him up, it was very important for him. The man sounded like a famished bear when he came on. I told him to listen carefully because I was on the run and had very little time to waste. Roddy was dead, Mitchell the crooked cop too. The police were after me for both murders. I wanted him to do two things for me: get me a passport and set up Roddy's partner for me. I had some of Rico's money. I explained that I had got it from his mother, who had it all the time, and I would pay him twenty thousand pounds if he managed to get me a passport within forty-eight hours. I would also give him an extra five thousand pounds for giving up Roddy's partner. After that, there would be no more bad blood between us for his part in Blackjack's death. I needed him to decide right now ... By the time I put down the phone, I could feel Joy's stunned gaze set on me.

'You're crazy!' she said simply, shaking her head in bewilderment.

Tips had gone for my deal: I knew he would. I told him Roddy's mysterious partner had taken his money and that was a way for him to make some back. He didn't ask me for any more cash from Rico's money; he knew I could still kill him for Blackjack. What he was going to do for me was a way to atone for his betrayal. Tips understood this very well. I knew he wasn't going back to bed for now! All I had to do was to arrange for Miss Ruby to bring some of my money some place where Joy could pick it up. I knew the police must be watching the place, waiting for me to show up. I had told Tips half now, half when the job was done. I could call one of his drivers to drop the money to him though. I'd rather he didn't see Joy.

When I asked Tips to give up Roddy's friend, he didn't tell me he didn't know him, like he did before. He was now faced with the choice of betraying him to me or me to him. The only thing that would influence his choice was that he thought I could pay him more! That's how I knew I could trust Tips.

I called Miss Ruby. She understood I needed help and told me she would get the money out for me. I arranged for Joy to meet her and called the cab office to order a driver to drop off the money to Tips. I gave Joy a photo for the passport. The play was set. Then I just sat back and watched some TV. The bait was in the water, there was nothing to do but wait for the shark to take it.

Time goes slow when you're holed up somewhere waiting. I thanked God for Zafirah's patience. In fact, she seemed really worried about what was going to happen to me and wanted to help in whatever way she could. For the best of three days, I watched a lot of television, read papers and magazines, played music, just like a man on vacation. Zafirah refused to let me out. She pointed out that the British police were very efficient, especially when it came to something as serious as the killing of a policeman: I would be arrested within hours if I set foot outside.

So she did everything to make me comfortable. Like a man waiting to go into battle, I didn't feel that hungry, but I ate some of what either of the two women cooked for me, knowing I had to keep up my energy levels. I exercised a little, slept and did my best to empty my mind. I knew this was the last play of the intricate story I had discovered, step by step, since arriving in the country and for me, it was going to be double or quit.

One thing I had learned early in life was never to understimate my enemies. I had seen first hand just how dangerous the man I was going against was. I would need to be at least as good as him to survive. This would be the final test, and it was for Rico.

Monday evening, I checked on Tips. Though the line was supposedly safe, I kept the conversation brief. The passport would be ready the following day. On the other topic, Tips said he was trying something that would put me onto the man I wanted. I told Tips I needed a straight set-up, me and the man alone. Tips assured me he would make it work. I said I would call at 6 p.m. the next day and hung up.

Joy came around with a bag of Chinese food, more than we could eat. I could sense her watching me discreetly while I ate, glancing at me with an undefinable look. After the food we had a drink, watched some videos Joy had picked up from the store. Sitting on the couch, a woman by my side, I felt strangely detached from the situation, like I wasn't really deep in trouble and about to throw my life on the line.

Joy had also bought some clothes, since I didn't have access to my suitcase. I had given her some money and insisted she used it instead of her own, as she wanted to. Two pants, one ganzee, one shirt and a tracksuit and trainers she brought me, all the right size. She explained that I would look less conspicuous in a tracksuit and baseball hat on the street, as Jamaicans tended to dress a little flashy and thus get noticed. She said she had learned all this in her job, where she worked in conjunction with the police.

I could sense a closeness developing between me and Joy, the way she behaved 'normally', a little too normally. This wasn't a normal situation. After I had found the picture of her and Blackjack, I understood how she had planned everything from the start. Joy had been deeply hurt by her lover's death and revenge was for her not an act of hate, but of love, a duty to her murdered man. I could relate to that. Yet the experiences of the last few days, the danger and the search for the truth behind the two deaths we were set to avenge, one each, all this had made us partners. The nature of this partnership I couldn't quite define though.

But whatever, it didn't really matter to me right then. I felt like a contender before a title bout: I needed to feel the surge of raw energy, fuelled by cold fury, race in my veins. The love of a woman would have softened me, taken off the edge I was riding on. I was on a mission, one which required me to be bad, merciless and raw. I was grateful we were in another woman's home, the presence of Zafirah ensuring we maintained proprieties.

Tuesday morning was grey, windy and the rain didn't seem far away. The day was winding on slowly, I was getting tired of waiting. I called Zafirah at work. She asked what I was going to do, but I couldn't tell her everything. I tried to reassure her that my boss in Jamaica would sort it out with the British police; there was nothing to worry about. It wasn't hard to tell she didn't quite believe me. She told me to be careful. She was going to be out late that night but she left me her mobile number and I promised to call her if there was any news, good or bad.

The rain started around four, thick fat clouds darkening the skies. The night would descend early today. Joy called around five, saying she was on her way and asking whether I wanted anything. She arrived soon after and started cooking. Just past six o'clock, I called Tips. He wasn't at the office, nor at home. Loretta said she'd give him my message. I called the office again at seven; Tips was on the road, he'd be back soon.

We ate. I could understand what Blackjack had seen in Joy, a man who had lost his family and been through so much. It felt like his spirit was still wandering around the house, watching me, waiting for me to be his instrument of revenge.

I got Tips on the line just before ten. He sounded weary. Everything was alright, he said. I could pick up the book at his house. The thought came to my mind that he might be setting me up, but I would just have to take that chance. It was less risky than meeting on the street. Before I hung up he said he had my 'fish' on the line; he would tell me when I got there. I could feel Joy's gaze on me as I put down the receiver. I got up and went to get changed, came back to the living room in my new tracksuit.

'It suits you,' Joy commented, smiling.

'You have good taste,' I said. She seemed tense. I didn't want to do too much talking, so I just said I wouldn't be long, I would just pick up the passport and come back. Joy wanted me to use her car but I thought it was safer for me to take a cab. Besides, I'd rather leave her on standby, just in case I needed a pick-up.

'You're my getaway driver,' I smiled at her.

But Joy wasn't smiling tonight. She slipped her mobile phone in my tracksuit top pocket. Before I got to the door, she asked: 'That guy, Tips, he gave up Neville, didn't he?' She was standing by the couch, arms crossed on her chest. I adjusted the hat on my head.

'He's giving me the killing hand,' I said. I knew what she was asking. I told her, 'Don't worry about anyt'ing. I soon come.'

Joy walked up to me, opened her arms and hugged me like I was going on a faraway trip.

The good weather had gone for good, it seemed. The rain had stopped earlier on but had started again, light but insistent, making the road shine under the street lights. The driver, a talkative middle-aged Indian or Pakistani, chatted all the way down. I didn't mind that, especially since he didn't require me to say very much, his conversation switching from the state of the country to the latest cricket test and onwards to the mean disposition of nowadays women. I got off at the entrance of Tips' estate, wanting to circle around first and get a feel of the place, just in case, before going up to the flat.

Drops of rain tip-tapping on the peak of my baseball cap, I walked all the way around the first block of flats. The place was quiet, though some windows were still lit up, with here and there the sound of a television filtering out. My watch read ten forty-nine in the glare of the lamp above the entrance of Tips' flats. Quietly I climbed up, leaving the stairlight off. No noise on the landing. I approached the flat door and stuck my ear against it: the murmur of a television but nothing else. Knocking twice, I eased up the .38 from my waist, stuck it in my pants' right pocket, my hand on it. There was the shuffling of feet, someone was peering through the peephole.

'Who is it?' I recognized Tips' wife voice, almost whispering in alarm.

'It's Carlton ... Tips is expecting me.' The door was unlocked from inside and the woman's face appeared.

'He's just gone out, someone came for him.' I frowned. 'Who?'

'Some friend of his, I don't know his name.' That sounded strange. Tips knew I was coming for my book, how could he go out?!

'How long was that?' I asked, fixing the puzzled woman. She was probably on the early side of thirty, her eyes wide and tired-looking under the low lighting of the landing.

'Oh, only about ten minutes ago. Someone phoned and he went out. He said he would only be a minute.' Deep inside me, an alarm bell was ringing.

'Would you like to wait for him?' the woman offered. I shook my head, my mind trying to analyse the situation.

'No, thank you. I'll call back.' I turned and walked down the landing. Something was wrong here, I could feel it. Downstairs, the drizzle greeted me, gusts of wind now blowing water on my face. Tips usually parked around the back at night. I walked around the block; the car was there, parked with the others. Where could he have gone? I was getting that tingling in the pit of my stomach, just like back home on night missions, when danger was imminent and bullets might come flying at you any time.

Scanning the silence around me, I walked to the car, circling around to approach it from the back. My hand was still on the stubby gun in my pocket, my finger loose around the trigger. Through the back windscreen, I could make out a shape in the driving seat.

Cautiously, I got to the passenger window. Tips was there alright, slumped forward in the seat, his head resting on the steering wheel, his open eyes fixing me through the glass. You didn't have to be a coroner to know he was dead. My mind recorded it but my senses froze for a moment. In the semi-darkness, two empty eyes were staring at me. I backed away from the car, slowly started spinning around, suddenly conscious of being exposed. The gun was already out of my pocket.

Whether the words hit me before the poke in the small of my back or vice versa; I wasn't sure.

'Let it go! Easy.'

Through the tracksuit top, something hard and round-shaped was pushing against my spine. I stood still, released my grip on the gun, all the time thinking one thing: 'This time I'm dead.' A gloved hand took the .38 from me. I heard the deep voice again.

'Hands on yuh head. Move, man!' The poking in my back was insistent, probing me forward, so I obeyed. And still the rain dropped, thin and intense. It was while passing around the back of Tips' car that I noticed it, the length of rag jutting out from the petrol tank of the car, down to the ground.

I walked on, my brain working furiously to catch up, think it through. Tips' dead eyes were printed on my mind. The iron stick in my back kept pushing in. Three cars down was a dark Mercedes. Somehow, I had been careless, fatally so. I had been caught out ... Now what?

It seemed clear I didn't stand much of a chance of surviving the night unless I reacted fast. My mind was still on the petrol-soaked car with the dead man inside. We were getting to the Mercedes. Better to go down trying ... I could feel the man behind me. I waited for the gun barrel to poke me once more. Swiftly, I spun to the right, sending my arm out but he must have been expecting it.

The gun butt hit me across the left side of the face, hard. I felt a firm hand grab me by the collar, push me against the car. Pain in my cheekbone, blood dripping from the cut flesh but that didn't matter right then. I was expecting a shot.

'Yuh not fast enough for me.'

The deep voice was cold but casual, no anger. For the first time, I was facing him, beyond the long tube of the silencer pointing at my forehead. My heart must have missed a beat but it wasn't for fear of the gun.

'Lookman?' I gasped, totally shocked.

'So yuh still 'member me . . .'

My brain was totally empty for several seconds, just staring at the man in the dark as the rain danced around us, adding to the feel of eeriness. For a couple of seconds, shocked surprise had me dumb. Incredulous, I was staring at the face.

'Ah yuh!?'

'We have t'ings to talk about, Carly. If I get what I want, maybe I give yuh a chance.' He grinned, that same malevolent old-time grin.

'Yuh better drive . . . I don't want to shoot yuh before we talk.' Lookman backed out, motioned with the gun for me to move. I opened the door of the Benz, got in the driving seat.

'Don't try anyt'ing,' he said, as he quickly got to the other side. From under the flat leather cap, the eyes which had haunted the nights spent recovering from my bullet wounds years ago were looking at me. The man had an older look about him, deep lines etched under his eyes and his face looking wider, fatter, but with the same squarish jaw. A padded dark anorak added to the impression of bulkiness. Years of living abroad had given Lookman bulge . . .

'Long time, man.' He didn't really sound jovial although, somehow, Lookman seemed satisfied to see me, especially since he had trapped me well and good. This was no time for it, but my mind was racing through all the unanswered questions I had been wrestling with. And now sat right before me the man behind it all, not a stranger at all but my worst long-time enemy, a ghost from my turbulent past.

'Yeah, long time . . .' I said.

Lookman had pulled out a pack of cigarettes from his inside pocket and was lighting one, all the time keeping me covered with the long gun, Mitchell's gun. Closing the metal lighter cover, he said, 'Tips' lighter . . . Him don't need it no more.' He was staring at me.

'Drive,' he said. The key was already in the ignition. I kicked the engine alive; it purred like the snoring of a big cat. Switching on the wipers, I got out of the parking lot. Lookman threw me a sideways glance.

'Yuh cyan trust nobody nowadays,' he said. Then, all in one movement, he pressed on his window's electric switch to lower it down, flicked on the lighter and casually flung it out towards Tips' car as we were passing it by. Lookman must have spilled gas on the ground before I got there, because immediately there was a rush of brightness in the dark.

'Drive, man!' The silencer tube hit me in the ribs and I pressed on the gas. I knew what was going to happen. We had barely turned around the block before an almighty explosion resounded behind us. Cold as a dead fish, Lookman told me: 'Don't worry, Carly. I make sure I save your passport.' Out of his pocket, he was waving the book at me with a satisfied grin. He put it back.

'Yuh never have to burn him up,' I said. There was a silence in the car, broken only by the samba of the raindrops outside.

'Tips draw some bad cards,' Lookman said simply.

Tips had hurt me more than he had hurt him, but I still couldn't have done what he just did. Right at the end, Tips had tried to redeem himself, maybe remembering at last who he once was.

'Whe we goin'?' I asked. To the right, the road led back into Hackney, left was the way out through Shoreditch.

'Take Tower Bridge,' Lookman said.

I drove on. The initial surprise over, my mind was now analysing the situation. I had found the man I had been looking for, only he had caught me instead of me catching him. I knew Lookman well enough to realize he wasn't going to give me a chance. It was going to be him or me, and so far it looked like it was going to be me.

'Yuh know seh I wasn't surprised to see yuh ina England?' Lookman seemed to be enjoying his controlling position. Pulling on his cigarette, he was looking at me like a fox who's got his paws on a fat chicken.

'I just come for Rico's wedding.'

'The wedding? Nuh the money yuh come fe pick up?' We were right over Tower Bridge, the lights from the quays reflecting across the dark waters beneath. I shook my head, knowing he wasn't going to believe me anyway.

'I never know not'ing about no money runnings, believe it or not.'

Lookman kept quiet for a moment, then he asked, 'But yuh get it though?' I had to think fast. If I said I didn't have Rico's money, the money he had killed for so readily, Lookman had no reason to let me live. We had a score to settle, and he knew I wouldn't hesitate to take him out. Yet I didn't have what he wanted.

'If a police hide somet'ing, only a police can find it,' I said cryptically.

Lookman smirked. 'Yeah man. I hear seeh yuh good at your job.' I nodded quietly, turned to look him in the eye.

'Better than any criminal,' I told him coldly. We were driving on, right into South London. I didn't know where Lookman was taking me but I had no intention of going there. All the time, I was assessing my chances to outplay him. He wanted money, so that's what I had to play. Old Kent Road was clear, shining with rain.

'So, yuh want all ah Rico's money, right?' I waited for the answer for a few seconds. Lookman was thinking.

'There was three shares, but all de man dem dead ... Somebody have to inherit the wealth, nuh true?' Good sound criminal logic, it was. 'And is yuh the next of kin?'

I didn't feel like joking but there was something so perverse in Lookman's vision of things ... I turned to look at him and met his alert gaze.

'So what; yuh want some too?'

'Some? The question is; why should I give yuh anyt'ing at all. Yuh kill my brethren dem ...'

Lookman's tone grew harsher as he told me, 'Watcha now:

it don't matter who kill who. Is the man who hold the gun who win ev'ryt'ing. Yuh understand?' That wasn't the way I saw it. I shrugged.

'Right now, is yuh have the gun but me have the money. Understand this!'

'Alright, hear this: me and yuh can make a deal then. Say we split it fifty-fifty.'

'I have a better idea . . .' I said. 'Say we split it seventy-thirty, my way?'

'Don't fuck with me, Carly. Me will shot yuh raas.'

I took my eyes off the road, faced Lookman square in the eyes. 'Yeah? Shoot me nuh!'

Right away, I put my foot down on the gas, all the way down. The big car lurched forward, the speedometer needle climbing up, steadily up as I pushed on. In and out the outside lane, overtaking vehicles, we were soon speeding into Deptford.

'Slow it down,' Lookman growled, sticking the silencer hard into my ribs.

'Shoot me nuh! Shoot, man, if yuh bad.'

I had the Merc doing one-twenty, zooming past cars, beams flashing to warn others to get out of the way. The rain had eased up at last. Lookman had raised his gun and stuck the silencer barrel to my left temple.

'Stop the car, now!'

I laughed. 'Fuck yuh! Shoot me, me nuh care again. Me and yuh will die together tonight.' Lookman must have started to realize I might not be bluffing after all. He took the gun off my head.

'Alright, alright . . . Make me and yuh talk.'

'Talk? Talk 'bout wha?' I took a red light and heard tyres screeching, cars braking to avoid crashing into us. The meter read one thirty-five. I had no idea where I was heading.

'Cool, nuh Carly! Me and yuh make a deal. Stop the car man!'

'Drop the gun.' I turned and saw him frowning. 'T'row the

gun on the back seat, and t'row mine too.' Ahead was the blue light of a police station, a few hundred yards away. At that speed, we would be there within seconds.

'T'row the guns at the back, or I drive right into the police station.' Lookman had seen it too. He wasted five more seconds wondering just how serious I was.

'Me is a police, Yuh is a criminal . . . Yuh wan' try your luck with dem?' I looked his way and he must have seen something in my eyes that convinced him.

'Yuh ah mad bloodclaat!' he swore. Then he flung his gun on the back seat, pulled the .38 out of his anorak pocket and threw it down there too. Barely one hundred yards was left before we reached the station. I eased up on the gas, braked and dropped back into third. The tyres screamed as I steered hard to the left, down in second gear, skidding on the wet tarmac into a narrow road. Lookman was backed up in his seat, tensing up for the crash. The back of the Merc slid to the right, the tyre hit the pavement.

I released the brakes and gassed up hard. The tyres wizzed furiously before the car leapt forward. We just about made it without scraping into the boundary garden wall of the first house. Now I had to be fast . . .

Running the car at seventy-five down the side street, I was swinging the power-steered wheel left and right, the car dancing like a ship in a storm. Another side street was cutting across. I ran through the stop at eighty, Lookman holding on to the top handle, his feet apart and bracing himself.

'Stop the fucking car!' I heard him shout.

'Yuh kill people but yuh fraid fe dead, yuh fucker yuh!' I sneered.

Down into second gear, I swung into the third back street we met, spinning the wheel left with one hand. The car hit a wire fence sideways, the tyres biting the pavement. Back into third, pushing on the gas, I was making the most of the engine. To the right ran a train line, a steep bushy rise leading up to it. Fifty yards down, I saw what I was looking for, a row of old warehouses with an empty courtyard. Piles of empty pallets were stacked up in front of the iron shutters of the stores.

I didn't even slow down: down into second, one swing of the wheel to the right and down on the gas, the big car roared into the gate, crashing right through it and kept going, plugging into a pile of pallets. I had prepared myself for the hit: the car hadn't even stopped yet and I had opened my door and bailed out, just in time to avoid the stack dropping onto the windscreen. I landed on my side, a little roughly, scraping my right hand on the rough ground but I was out of the way.

Getting up quickly, I ran around the back of the car. The windscreen had splintered under the impact of the falling pallets but didn't shatter. Access to the front was blocked so I pulled open the back door and got in to grab the discarded weapons before Lookman. I did well: he had dived under the dashboard for cover but was already recovering and making a grab for the guns. The .38 had slipped to the floor but the long gun was lying openly on the back seat. I was the fastest; it was Lookman's turn to face the open end of the silencer.

'Get out, man!' I ordered him.

I watched Lookman climb over to the back and out of the car. The yard was badly lit, with a mound of empty cardboard boxes against a raised concrete loading bay. With the 9 mm in my hand, things were looking definitely better for me. Lookman was standing by the back of the car. He had lost his cap in the crash and was fixing me with a venomous stare.

'Yuh shoulda never let me drive; yuh forget that was my speciality,' I told him with a wry smile. 'Come over this way, man.'

I backed out towards the far end of the yard, still covering him. We stood five yards apart at the bottom of the concrete steps leading up to the loading bay. The area was quiet, no habitations around and no traffic. Across the road, beyond a wooden board fence, rose the dark outline of an unfinished building.

'Yuh did want to talk, nuh true?'

Lookman stood there with his arms to his sides in his big anorak. 'Yuh can keep the money.' That was the first thing he said.

I shook my head at him. 'I don't have the money, Lookman; yuh ah fool . . .' I saw his furious expression grow even darker.

'So what yuh want from me?'

'It's payback time, Lookman; yuh run from me years ago but I got yuh now.'

'Then kill me and done . . .'

'Not yet, man; I want to know the truth first.'

'Me nah have not'ing fe tell yuh, so yuh better shoot me now.'

'Yuh have 'nuff fe tell me, so if yuh don't start talk, I will take one leg first, then the other, and go on till yuh ready.' Lookman knew very well this was no bluff. He was cruel by taste, but I was wicked by circumstance. He was aware I would do just what I said. To the hardest of men, death is easier to face than pain. I asked:

'So, how yuh wan' do this?' He kissed his teeth, more upset to have been outplayed than fearful of his imminent demise.

'What yuh wan' know?'

'Who kill Rico?'

'Yuh really t'ink seh ah me?' I didn't, to be honest.

'That wasn't your style, but I know yuh know who do it.'

There was a pause. Lookman said: 'I want a smoke . . .' A reasonable last request. I nodded.

'Just be careful.'

I watched him take out his cigarettes from his pocket, then his lighter. Even at that distance, Lookman could be dangerous. We had grown up in the same neighbourhood; I knew exactly what he could do. He pulled on the cigarette, the tip glowing red, blew out some smoke.

'Talk, man,' I said.

Lookman eyed me curiously and said, 'Rico was robbing dealers, him and him brethren dem, yuh know that?'

'I nodded, waiting.

'What yuh don't know is that Mitchell was getting fe him information from me. That fucker wanted money, always more money. Me and him did do business long before Rico come on the scene. When Tips kill the dealer, Mitchell decide to use him for the robberies.'

I asked: 'Is Tips give up Rico?'

Lookman answered with another question. 'Tips tell yuh it's the Turkish man dem rob whe hit Rico?'

'That's what he said, but I don't buy that.'

'Ah lie that. Most of dem people whe dead ina this business, is Tips give them up.'

Lookman was right on that, even if he himself had been the killer. He went on: 'Rico was no fool; him soon find out Tips was working for the police, and which police was handling him. Yuh know how him find out?'

'No, I don't know that.'

'Because Rico was on the same case, that was his job.'

I didn't understand right away what Lookman was talking about. He shook his head. 'Yuh don't even know!'

'Tell me nuh!' Lookman was enjoying this, I could tell. He had the same malevolent grin as before, with eyes that missed nothing and gave nothing away.

'Rico was supposed to identify the man dem who bring in the most drugs. The English police t'ink seh it's Jamaicans import the biggest shipments, dem ask the police back home fe help. That was Rico's mission on yah.' I could feel the weight of Lookman's eyes on me.

'How yuh know this?' I asked. Lookman let out a hollow laugh.

'Yuh t'ink it's every police whe want to die poor like yuh?'

Beyond the intended insult, Lookman was just reminding me of the reason Rico had left Jamaica in the first place. So, some crooked police officer back home had found out what Rico was doing in England and passed the news onto the British-based dealers. I could understand that. But there was yet one thing I needed to hear.

'So which one ah ouno do it?' Lookman blew out some smoke, more relaxed now. He said:

'Yah so nuh different from Yard, Carly. Whether black or white, a police is just a man. Fe him badge not going to make him rich. So much money ina this drugs t'ing that some ah dem cyan resist it.' That wasn't answering my question. I lined up the gunsight on Lookman's head.

'I asked yuh one question. Which one ha ouno, yuh or your brethren?' Lookman paused and faced me.

'Yuh nuh hear wha me ah say, man. Yuh really t'ink seh drugs coulda run on yah without police involved at a higher level?' He let the question hang in the air, then added in a lower tone of voice, like he was explaining something complicated to a child, 'Rico was good, yuh know that better than me. Him find out something him shouldn't know. That's why dem kill him.'

My ears let the words sink in but somewhere my brain was stalling to accept the fact. Lookman could be blaming Rico's death on a crooked white policeman to save himself. But then he knew I wasn't going to let him off the hook anyway, so why would he lie about that? I had learned that, quite often, your enemy has less interest in deceiving you than your own friend.

'Yuh don't believe me?' Lookman was fixing me from behind the smoke, his piercing little eyes drilling into me.

I nodded. 'Yuh don't have no reason to lie to me.'

He pulled on the cigarette, looked straight at me for a few long seconds, then I heard him say: 'I never lie about your sister neither, back then ...' Our eyes locked, hard, heavy with the weight of old enmity. Lookman said: 'I know me and yuh never really get on, but I never need to make up a story if I did want to deal with yuh.'

'Some man don't like a woman to refuse them,' I said coldly.

I saw Lookman's sneer. "Nuff woman deh bout, Carly. Only a fool take dem t'ings to heart.' Although this was the hour of truth, that was one I wasn't quite ready to swallow.

'Like I said; in this life, we all react to t'ings the way we feel is right,' he said, flicking away the cigarette butt.

There was but one last question. 'So Rico find out which police was running the show over here, and the man get him killed to protect himself. But tell me one more t'ing, Lookman: who tell the man about Rico?'

'Nuh Tips?!' Lookman answered casually. Had Tips been alive, he would have surely blamed Lookman for this, I felt. Somehow it seemed to me Lookman was closer to the crooked police than Tips. He knew more and had more to lose from seeing his set-up being wrecked by Rico.

'Tips was a coward,' I said. 'Him was a greedy dog, but him did owe Rico. I don't feel seh him woulda go that far on the wrong side.' After all, Tips had tried to turn back, right at the end. Lookman was shaking his head with a grin.

'Yuh know somet'ing, Carly; yuh still nuh understand how this works.' Something seemed amusing to him. He said: 'There is no right side and wrong side, no good man or bad man. Every man just react to t'ings the way him feel is right. It's all about making the right move at the right time.'

I let Lookman's words ring, waited a little.

'The right move . . .' I repeated, stone cold inside. 'Like how you did for Jingles?' Lookman looked at me in silence for a couple of seconds.

'Bwoy . . . Jingles now . . . Jingles didn't want to play ball. The big man dem wanted him out. When yuh in the top league, yuh have to play ball . . . or get out of the field.' Simple logic, dead cold and simple.

'How much dem pay yuh for that?'

'Believe it or not, money never involved. Jingles was dead the day him refuse to get into the drugs business. Too much profit was ina that, so de man dem wanted somebody who could run

304

t'ings properly.' I was just listening, taking in the justification of betrayal.

'Someone like yuh . . .' Lookman shrugged.

'It was not'ing personal, Carly. If I never do it, dem woulda kill me and give another man the job; ah so business run.'

'Yeah, business. Ah dat yuh call it? Yuh murder people fe money, yuh nuh have no honour.' Maybe something inside him reacted to this, because for a moment I saw him squint.

'Honour? Honour is for dead people. And make I tell yuh somet'ing: when I kill somebody, I don't hide behind a badge, yuh hear?' Lookman paused, pointed at me.

'Yuh t'ink seh yuh different from me? Me and yuh is just the same; we react to t'ings that happen to we.' He gestured with his free hand. 'Tell me somet'ing; yuh t'ink yuh would have turn police if dem man never try kill yuh?' I didn't answer that. Lookman was getting into the philosophy of life, an aspect of him I didn't know. He shook his head.

'Ah dat shooting whe make yuh change your life, or else yuh woulda become just like me.'

'I woulda never become like yuh, Lookman, no matter what happen to me.' Lookman laughed, like it sounded funny to him.

'Me is a survivor, Carly, a born survivor, 'cause I come from the ghetto. And yuh will do anyt'ing to survive too, because yuh come from the same place; don't forget this.'

I certainly felt no kinship with Lookman at that moment. In fact, had I let emotions overrun me, I probably would have emptied a clip into him to cut out his wise words. I told him: 'I don't forget anyt'ing. Tonight is your judgement.'

Lookman's eyes were on me, very still, as I raised the gun, pointing at his head. I heard him say quietly: 'If it was yuh, yuh woulda done the same t'ing.'

My finger was already on the trigger. With the silencer, no one would hear the shots. I had personal reasons for executing Lookman. Of course, I realized that to get me off the hook for Mitchell's murder, he would have had to confess to the police, but I knew he would never do that. I guess I had been a policeman for too long, for I still felt I had to give him that option.

'I gwan give yuh a chance, Lookman,' I told him, 'One chance.' He was looking at me with the predator mask that seemed permanently set on his features, his true face.

'I take yuh in and yuh tell the police about Mitchell's killing, or I deal with yuh right now. Take your time before yuh answer.'

Lookman had already been tensing for the shot. I saw him squint and then he remarked, 'Mitchell was dirty but him was still a policeman. Me is a black man, if I do that, them will keep me in jail here for years. I'll never see Jamaica again.'

'Yuh will get life for that. Twenty years, maybe less, before them deport yuh. It's your choice.'

The silence between us lasted almost a full minute, Lookman staring at something beyond me, considering my offer. Finally he looked at me and said; 'I cyan do it, Carly. Growing old in a cage is not for me.'

I knew he wouldn't go for it, and I could relate to that. Nodding, I told him, 'Yuh had your chance.' I raised the gun again. Lookman put out his two hands.

'Hol' on, Carly, hol' on!'

I waited; I didn't expect a man like him, a cold-blooded killer, to start begging. I lowered the gun, curious. The weariness and lack of emotions inside me seemed strange even to me. Lookman waited a couple of seconds, then he asked. 'Yuh nuh want your passport?'

Slowly, he was going for his inside pocket, his left hand up to show me he wasn't trying anything. The book came out. For maybe less than three seconds, I glanced at the passport Lookman was handing to me. The silencer was still levelled on him. I've faced dangerous men all my life, had close calls with maybe three or four vicious killers, but Lookman was in a category of his own. Instinctively, I pressed the trigger at the same time as the passport hit me in the face. Lookman had already leapt to the left, avoiding the shot. I caught a glimpse of something shining in front of my face and immediately drew back. There was a sharp bolt of pain in my right forearm. I winced and dropped the gun. Aware of Lookman's closing in, I kicked up, straight, felt the tip of my right trainer sink into his lower stomach.

I could feel my arm hurting where the blade had penetrated into it, slicing through the tracksuit sleeve, but one thing concerned me more: the gun. The weapon was lying on the ground between me and him. Lookman was onto it too. Quickly, as he lunged forward to cut, I dodged and kicked him again, hitting only his knee this time. I heard him cry out and he drew backwards, just long enough for me to reach down and whip out the stiletto I had strapped to my right leg with a thick elastic band. Though I could feel blood sticking my sleeve to my arm, I had the sharp knife well in hand. Feet apart, left arm level, I automatically started stepping sideways, eyes alert to Lookman's every move. I saw a faint smile on his face.

'Yuh fast, man!' he said.

We were standing face to face, blade against blade, after all these years and maybe that was the way it had been meant to be. No matter how much he had deserved it, no matter how many good reasons I had to drill a bullet into Lookman's head, I might still have felt bad about killing him in cold blood. But now, it was altogether different; I was taking on the man at his own game. I could see in his eyes that he felt he had me where he wanted me. Inside his head, Lookman had the fight already won. That was why he was smiling.

The gun was still within reach of both of us, yet I knew it didn't matter to either of us any more. I glanced at Lookman's knife, a pearl-handled ratchet with a five-inch blade, pretty, glimmering under the faint glow of the street lights reaching us. As the tallest of the two, I had the longest reach but not necessarily the advantage. It was all down to speed and reflexes, foot moves, cunning, skills acquired through practice at the hard school of street survival. Lookman had lived by the knife. Back then, very few men I knew of could have faced him with a blade and lived to talk about it. If anything, he had to be even better at his craft now.

'Yuh shoulda shoot me first time, Carly!'

'This is your last fight, Lookman, so show me your best moves,' I taunted him.

He let out a scornful laugh. The time for talking was over so I sprang forward and sliced at his face. Lookman jumped back, swinging at my arm; he missed. He came back, very fast, linking his moves so I couldn't hit back; head stab, feint, body cut, shuffle and chest slice with return cut. I blanked out the pain in my arm, concentrating only on the fight. I attacked, using my reach to needle my adversary. He was dodging well but one of my downward cuts caught his knife hand, not too deep but enough to gnaw at his pride. I saw his eyes get even narrower, so I smiled at him. It worked; Lookman jumped up and started coming at me hard, cutting and stabbing with frenzy.

The essential and basic asset of a knife fighter is to keep a cool head at all times, but tonight Lookman seemed to have lost that. I could see he was in a hurry to finish with me now, hurt in his pride that I could get to him so easily. His breath was coming in and out harder now, his movements still fluid but his mind too focused on me; he was taking it too personal. Shuffling sideways, I moved out of range from a vicious chest stab then slid back in with a downwards slice. Lookman drew back from my blade, sent in a deep thrust towards my arm but I pulled out in time; his blade whizzed past, missing by less than an inch.

A knife fight may be the tensest contest between two men; the slightest mistake, a fraction of second when the focus slips, and it's all over. Co-ordination between eyes and hands has to be perfect, as well as the balance to guarantee optimum reaction to your adversary's movements within the shortest delay. It is nothing but a ballet, a deadly, merciless dance which only one of the partners will survive. Tonight I intended to be the one who would go home, so I had to make the most of what I had. Lookman might have been more skilful and experienced than me with a knife but I felt I had the mental edge on him. We were circling each other in the deserted yard, breathing, watching each other, waiting for the opening in the other's guard. I said: 'Wha'ppen sah; yuh getting tired?'

Lookman didn't reply but I knew he didn't like me talking. So I added with a sneer, 'Yuh bad when it comes to using knife on woman. Come cut me nuh!'

He wanted to, swore under his breath and sprang forward, slicing in and out at my chest. He was still very fast and the return cut a small piece out of my new tracksuit at the shoulder. I shook my head.

'Missed. Try again, man.' I was getting him mad now. It was getting down to a battle of nerves. I knew Lookman wanted the fight to finish quickly. The longer it lasted, the more his self-confidence was suffering. I was losing blood from my arm but it didn't weaken me so far because of the surge of adrenaline; I had waited years for that moment.

I saw Lookman's move before he started it, which was a sign he was getting slower. But that didn't mean he was less accurate; his feint to the body and upwards thrust to the throat came much too close to target for comfort. I drew back sharply, so Lookman moved in again, stabbing straight for the heart: he was out for the kill. I had the time to edge sideways so he missed but I didn't expect the same move twice and this time the tip of his blade touched me on the right side, just where I had dropped Joy's small cell phone in the tracksuit top pocket. I felt the impact of the blade on the phone as it pushed back against my right pectoral. I sliced at Lookman, he jumped back and his eyes met mine; he had expected his thrust to go in.

'Nice try,' I told him.

That unnerved him some more. I knew I had to end it very

309

soon. The longer I waited, the weaker I would get. Then it would be to Lookman's advantage, as he had more experience than I had of that type of situation. There was one move I was now thinking of, something which I had seen done years before but had never tried myself. I said, 'It look like this is not your night, man. Give it up, I just take yuh in and done.'

That was an insult he couldn't take; to suggest he surrendered and I arrested him was getting him really upset, I could see it in his face. He growled: 'Yuh dead now!'

Balancing on the balls of my feet, I waited for his move, eyes alert, thumb and forefinger firm on the handle of my knife. Lookman's blade was dancing before my face now, exploring the space in front of me, taunting, drawing figures in the air to break my concentration. By now I knew he usually feinted face-high cuts then stabbed low at the chest and stomach. I would only have one shot at what I wanted to try, so it had to be perfect.

It must have seemed to him as if my guard was too open, my hands too far apart, for Lookman suddenly rushed forward, his right arm fully extended, his knife going straight for my stomach. I had no time to think, my timing had to be perfect. And it was ...

As Lookman's knife rushed towards my belly, I switched hands, picking up the stiletto in my left hand. Meanwhile, I placed all my weight onto my left foot and pivoted, right foot circling towards the rear, thus sending my body into a profile position. My right hand grabbed Lookman's wrist, closing around it like a vice and pulling hard. Following his own momentum, he couldn't steady up himself fast enough to counter me. I stabbed through the anorak and shirt and heard his breath as the steel sank into his flesh. Quickly, I pulled out my blade and stepped back.

Lookman turned to face me, an expression between surprise and fury painted across his face. He stood there, put one hand on his wound and brought it to his face to look at it. Then he looked at me again. The knife was still in his hand, useless now. We stayed like that for what seemed like a long time until Lookman winced and bent over. He tried to hide it but I could see he was starting to feel pain. Sweat was pearling on his brow. He said: 'Yuh bad . . .'

He took a few steps and went to where the pile of empty cardboard boxes stood, slowly let himself down to the ground. I walked to where he sat, his back against the boxes, a dark wet patch spoiling the side of the pretty white shirt. The knife was still in his hand but I knew he couldn't use it any more. His breath sounded harsh, painful.

I knelt down, sank my wet blade into the ground and made to take the knife from Lookman's hand but he was holding on tight.

'Leave it with me, man.'

Our eyes met and I read that this was his last wish; he wanted to die with his tool. I drew back my hand. Maybe for the first time, I saw him smile faintly, a grin veiled with pain and a kind of proud sadness.

'Yuh good, Carly. Trust me,' he said.

'Yuh shoulda let me take yuh in.'

Lookman swallowed hard, he was sweating more now. 'It better like that.'

'I can take yuh to the hospital, still . . .' The blood on the shirt was dark and thick. The liver was touched, there was nothing that could help Lookman, he wouldn't last half an hour. He knew it too.

'No, man; make we just sit and talk.'

There I was, sitting on the ground in a deserted yard in England, side by side with the man I had wanted so badly all those years. I sat with Lookman, stayed there with him like a man would for an old comrade, unable to tend to his body but tending to his soul. There was no hate inside me, no anger, no satisfaction at all, nothing in fact, whether good or bad, just a weird feeling of timelessness and fatigue. We remained like that for a while, silent, close like we could never have been before.

Life had set us apart as enemies but death was binding us, the past didn't matter any more. I heard him say:

'I want yuh do somet'ing fe me, Carly.' Lookman's breath was deep, he wouldn't last too long. He was finding it painful to talk, but he forced himself.

'I have a youth,' he went on. 'She live ina Spring Village, yuh know whe it deh. Her mother name Belinda. I never see the little girl . . . she born after I left Yard. Her birthday coming up next month, try and give her somet'ing for me, Carly. I beg yuh do me this favour, alright?'

'I do it, man. Don't worry.' The man's breath was strained, I could see his chest heaving in the quiet night. He said:

'Carly, yuh ah hear me; me is a killer, true dat, but I'm not nuh liar. Yuh sista did know Rico before I cut her.'

I turned and stared into Lookman's eyes, those that were watching their last night sky. He swallowed and said: 'Him couldn't tell yuh either. I just want yuh to know this.'

There was nothing I could answer. Lookman didn't expect any answer anyway. He was quiet for a while, his eyes closed, beads of sweat running slowly down his weathered face. I thought he was sinking already but then I heard him say in a low voice.

'One t'ing yuh fe do for me, Carly.'

'Wha dat?' I asked.

'Make sure everybody know Lookman die like a man.'

'Yeah man, everybody will know that.' That was Lookman's last request. We sat there in silence for a few more minutes then I heard him gasp and his body tensed up. He opened his eyes one last time, staring at the dark yard in front of him, then the breath left him.

After a while, I took Lookman's knife from his hand, folded it and slipped it in my pocket. I picked up Mitchell's gun, and my passport. I didn't want to drive the Benz no more. I retrieved the .38 from the car and walked out of the yard. Joy's phone was still working, so I called and fixed a meeting point. I kept walking, not really certain of how I truly felt. I walked. Joy was there real fast. She could see I didn't feel like answering questions, so she didn't ask any.

CHAPTER TWENTY

Many Rivers

'The doctor say Nicola will probably have the baby early but she will be alright.' Miss Ruby switched off the gas under the pan and came to sit at the table. I noticed she was moving slow, painfully almost.

'Yuh alright, madda,' I asked.

She smiled. 'I'm alright, it's just a little cold I catch in my back. It hurts more at night but it's not too bad.'

As long as I had known her, I had never heard Miss Ruby complain. She was tougher than many but you could tell the weight of years was starting to take its toll on her. I had asked her before but I thought I might change her mind.

'Yuh sure yuh don't want to come home? Cold weather nuh good for yuh . . .' She shook her head.

'I'll be alright, me son. I have to be here to take care of Nicola, and the baby when it comes.'

I knew there was no use insisting; Miss Ruby had set herself that mission and I could understand that. Nicola's baby was her sole interest now, the main reason for her to go on and she wasn't going anywhere. Looking at her across the table, I realized how much love I felt for the old lady. She had always been there for me, and leaving her wasn't going to be that easy now.

Three days had gone since that bloody night in South London. The first thing I did on reaching home was to call

Wilkins. The time difference made it early evening in Jamaica but the Super was still in his office. He didn't sound that surprised to hear from me. I summed up briefly the course of events that had happened to me, Wilkins listened and when I was done, he simply said, 'You didn't have much of a vacation, Nash.'

We didn't say much on the phone. Wilkins just confirmed that Rico had been asked, unofficially, to conduct an investigation into the Jamaica-UK drugs connection and had passed some information onto him which would be acted upon. That was his way of telling me he knew the identity of the crooked senior police officer who ran the drugs scam in London. He told me not to worry, he was calling up and sorting out my problems right away. Cryptically, Wilkins told me I should not answer any questions from the British police but simply refer them to my commanding officer, which meant himself.

Before hanging up, he said: 'Nash, I had the visit of a young woman, a British woman, last week. She said her sister had asked her to leave a package for you, a present. Anyway, I have it here for you when you return.' I thanked him, puzzled, then he added after a little silence. 'Inspector Glenford was right about you.' That's all he said.

Next I called Inspector McCallum at the police station. He wasn't there so I relayed the information about Lookman's body to the desk sergeant and told him to pass it on. I hung up. Joy kept worrying about my arm, talking about infection; so I let her tend to it but when she started cleaning it, she said I needed stitches. She wouldn't stop until I finally got up and let her take me to the casualty department. We waited a while before I got to see a nurse; there seemed to have been quite a few accidents that night, some much worse than mine. When I finally put my head down, I slept for nine hours straight.

Early the following morning, I went to the police station. Wilkins had been right; it was all cleared up and I was free to go within an hour. Inspector McCallum didn't even ask me about the dead bodies I had left behind. He was treating me just like a foreign colleague who had helped with a case, which I was. I guess somewhere, some kind of inside shake-up was going to happen at some point. Yet again, it might not. I could sense McCallum and the other policeman present with me in the room were looking at me curiously: maybe they were wondering whether I knew the name of their 'renegade'. I left the station and called Zafirah. She picked me up and took me to lunch.

I had three days before my flight. My first visit to England had been an intense experience, I had lost a lot and learned a lot. It would take a little time for me to draw all the lessons there were to be taken from that episode of my life. In a few weeks time, back to the routine of my daily life on the island, it might all seem like a distant dream.

'I always knew yuh would be alright, Carly,' Miss Ruby said. 'I prayed for yuh, God was on your side.' The old lady was getting up. She picked up two mugs and poured out some hot chocolate from the pan.

'Yuh right . . . I want to ask yuh somet'ing, madda.'

Miss Ruby placed a mug in front of me and sat back with the other. 'Yes, me son. Ask me anyt'ing.' I looked at her and paused. I just had to know. 'Tell me: Rico did know Lucy before I got shot? Try and remember.'

The glint I caught in Miss Ruby's eye told me she had no need to try. She remembered perfectly. Despite the heat, she dipped her lip in the mug and sipped a little of the sweet-smelling chocolate. Then she looked at me.

'Rico meet your sister couple weeks before that, but he only bring her home to me when you was in hospital.' Our eyes met, and I could see she knew why I had asked. She took another sip then wiped her lips slowly, the way elders do.

'Life follows its own course, me son,' she told me. 'Sometimes it's no use even looking back.'

Many rivers . . .

It's been a long time since my last book. It's been even longer that I felt good about writing something. What you have in your hands took almost two years to write but more importantly, before I put down the first line, it took another two years of pondering and wondering, trying to decide whether I should really bother to get back into writing at all.

Doubt has got to be man's worst enemy. Not that I ever doubted whether I could write. What is important to me is not to be dubbed the greatest author that ever lived, but to know that a few hundred readers had a good time while reading my stories. As a writer, if your book got people thinking, started some of them on a journey, then you done good. My problem was to decide whether my writing meant anything at all, beside entertainment.

Doubt crept on me unawares after the publishing of *Yush!*. I felt comfortable with the style of the writing itself but the question I was asking myself was 'Is there any purpose to it?' Over the years, I had many discussions with my former publishers, The X Press, and could never agree on that point. I could understand their way of looking at things: write three 'Yardie' novels a year, get paid and don't worry about the rest!

Well, I couldn't help but worry about the rest. Maybe I'm a hopeless idealist but I know I would never feel good writing just for money. Sure, it's better to make a living doing something you like but a story you lay down simply for the cash don't have no soul. With me it wouldn't anyway.

By the end of 1995, I was also going through some kind of personal crisis and found myself physically weakened and mentally exhausted. Too much pressure from many different angles had me feeling like I was about to blow up. So I moved out. They say a change is as good as a rest. For me it was. I first travelled to West Africa with a friend who had asked me to research and write for a film project. We spent a few months doing that but, as so often happens on the old continent, things didn't turn out as planned. My friend had to fly back. I found that I was in no hurry to leave.

By the time I had recovered my health and got my mind straight, I was already on an inner trip which I couldn't let go of. Africa is like that; it sets fire to your hopes, illusions and fears, then stands you up naked in front of your true nature. You either accept it or insanity swallows you up. I moved on. I went south to Central Africa. By then I was almost broke but I called on some people I had met in Cameroon and got me a job offshore, working on oil rigs. For months, I got on some military-like life; hard work, tight security, discipline. Some of that stuff was downright risky but one good thing with danger, it clears your mind up. Eventually I got off that trip and found other ways to make a living. But that high seas stint got me back focused.

That's when I started thinking about a story I had stored in my mind. It sounded exciting, so I began scribbling. When I finally got my hands on a computer, working from my notes, the story took shape rapidly. I had the bare bones within a couple of months. After that, it was getting down to the real work of style, flavour and taste. To make sure it could flow, I used the attitude I learned writing *Yush!*: forget everyone and write for yourself, have some fun. And I did.

I had to beg or borrow computer time (I didn't steal 'cause I don't do that). I sneaked into the office of a friend at all kind of funny hours, bribing the nightshift guards with change for a couple of beers ... And I got it done. The result is the first made-in-Africa Victor Headley novel. I feel it's the best thing

I've ever written. I know it is because it helped me regain my self-confidence as a writer.

Some of you will think it's a gangster story, others will read it as a police story ... and y'all are right. Let's define something here: a gangster is someone who feels he has to break society's rules to make it in life, a police officer is someone who believes his job is to enforce society's rules. A crooked policeman is someone who uses his badge to act like a ganster. This is what that story is about.

But it's also about truth and trust. Most people will tell you part of the truth, the part they think you should know. Whether it's to fool you or to protect you, very few people will tell you the whole truth and nothing but the truth. Check it out.

Trust now ... trust is a matter of percentage, to me anyway. How much do you trust your brother, your best friend, your next best friend, your wife, your neighbour? Sometimes you can trust your enemy much more than your friend. Bob Marley said it better than I could.

The story you have read is not unique in any way. Though it's background is Jamaica, its characters could have been nationals from a number of developing countries of Central or Latin America or Asia. They are just people trying to escape the hopelessness of their day-to-day existence. By any means necessary. Skin tone's got nothing to do with it, nothing at all.

Off Duty touches on the problem of corruption of law-enforcement officers. Back in 1992, when *Yardie* came out, the police in Britain got uptight because I had suggested that some police officers were paid by a shebeen operator. It was only one sentence of the novel, but the way the media blew up the story, using an interview with a senior officer who blamed me for being irresponsible, you'd have thought I had written the whole book around that single allegation. I went low-profile then, because I heard that the police wanted to 'talk' to me, and you know what that might mean.

Six months later, when the story of the drug-handling officers blew up in Stoke Newington, it wasn't possible to pretend it only happens in the USA any more. Let's be clear; whether in London, New York or Bogotá, some police are involved in the trade, as are some customs officials and some politicians. Some will talk about 'a few rotten apples', yet back home people often say: 'One rotten apple spoils the barrel'.

There's just too much money in drugs not to have some law-enforcement agents fall into temptation. To see a man spend in a week what you hardly earn in a year is a gut-wrenching feeling, imagine . . .

Some years back, I got stopped by a couple of officers in a Panda in Clapton. Once I had shown them the papers for the BMW, the older policeman was cool but the younger one with him was bugging about how he couldn't afford a car like this on his salary. I told him to get one on HP . . . It's all about envy. We're all too human when it comes to material things and the consumer culture we grow up in makes drugs the fastest rags-to-riches road.

Within our communities, we can see the impact of the trade everyday. As well as the depravation and violence it breeds, we also notice the increased cash flow it generates, how it permeates even sections of the population who play no direct role in it. Dealers and players buy clothes, jewellery and motorcars. But they also buy gasoline, pay rents and feed families, and they spend cash on a lot of other goods and services. Travel agents, hair and beauty salons, record stores, even schools and universities are part of the drugs-money spending circuit. There is hardly any section of the economy which is not fuelled, no matter how remotely, by money earned from the narcotics trade. There ain't no such thing as 'clean' money.

On another level, *Off Duty* is a story about life and its cycles. Down here in Africa, they often say that 'each man is another man's crossroad'. It sounds true to me. Looking back, we all find that, at some point in our lives, someone caused us to make a change, take a different direction than the one we were set on. And that's the role we play in others' destinies, no matter how unaware we are of it. But it can go both ways: One word, one moment spent with someone can just as well sink you as save you. Sometimes I think it's all run in advance, pre-set: that's what some people call 'karma'.

I'll stop being wise now. I just want to thank my new publishers Hodder and Stoughton, and especially my new editor Nicholas Blincoe for believing in the new story and bringing it out. Also a special request to my agent Cicely Dayes for her tireless efforts in working with me, even though I am sometimes difficult to reach. Finally, I hope and pray this story will inspire many of you to write your own and pour water into the universal well of the living Word.

May God's peace dwell within you.

Love.

Victor Headley.

The Congo, 2000

Peter May

THE KILLING ROOM

Eighteen women, murdered by a skilled surgical hand, are found in a mass grave in Shanghai. The deaths are disturbingly similar to an unsolved case in Beijing – it appears that autopsies have been carried out while the victims were still alive.

Beijing detective Li Yan travels to the capital of China's economic revolution to investigate, and finds the most horrifying catalogue of killings ever uncovered in the Middle Kingdom. American pathologist Margaret Campbell arrives to conduct the autopsies, only to discover her relationship with Li threatened by the policewoman leading the investigation.

But each of them is faced with their own personal nightmare when the investigation uncovers a ruthless killer of inhuman capacity.

The Killing Room is Peter May's third novel featuring Margaret Campbell and Li Yan: *The Firemaker* ('Intense and fascinating' *Good Book Guide*) and *The Fourth Sacrifice* are both Coronet paperbacks. Have you read them both?

A NEW ENGLISH LIBRARY PAPERBACK

Pat O'Keefe

THERMAL IMAGE

London's Burning Without the Acting
Thermal Image is the searing first novel from London fireman
Pat O'Keefe, bringing to life the thrilling and often brutal
reality of firefighting and crime in East London.

Steve Jay is a fireman on the edge. Crippling debts and
relationship problems are coming between him and the job he
loves. But his problems are only just beginning. A horrific fire
tests him and his watch to the limit and when an old friend
offers him serious money to investigate an infamous case from
the past, it sounds like the answer to his prayers. But the
decision to meet the challenge quickly plunges Jay into a
nightmare of arson and murder.

Pat O'Keefe is an Operational Station Officer in the London
Fire Brigade. He is also the holder of a fifth degree black belt
in Karate and fought twenty-eight times as a kick-boxer,
including bouts against three world champions including Nigel
Benn. A kick-boxing commentator on Sky Sports, he has also
written a book on the subject. THERMAL IMAGE is his first
novel.

A NEW ENGLISH LIBRARY PAPERBACK

A selection of bestsellers from Hodder & Stoughton

Fruitful Bodies	Morag Joss	0 340 76804 5	£5.99	☐
The Killing Room	Peter May	0 340 76865 7	£5.99	☐
Thermal Image	Pat O'Keefe	0 340 82016 0	£6.99	☐

All Hodder & Stoughton books are available at your local bookshop or newsagent, or can be ordered direct from the publisher. Just tick the titles you want and fill in the form below. Prices and availability subject to change without notice.

Hodder & Stoughton Books, Cash Sales Department, Bookpoint, 39 Milton Park, Abingdon, OXON, OX14 4TD, UK. E-mail address: orders@bookpoint.co.uk. If you have a credit card you may order by telephone – (01235) 400414.

Please enclose a cheque or postal order made payable to Bookpoint Ltd to the value of the cover price and allow the following for postage and packing:
UK & BFPO: £1.00 for the first book, 50p for the second book and 30p for each additional book ordered up to a maximum charge of £3.00.
OVERSEAS & EIRE: £2.00 for the first book, £1.00 for the second book and 50p for each additional book.

Name ....

Address ....

....

....

If you would prefer to pay by credit card, please complete:
Please debit my Visa / Access / Diner's Club / American Express (delete as applicable) card no:

Signature ....

Expiry Date ....

If you would NOT like to receive further information on our products please tick the box. ☐